The Little French Girl

By Anne Douglas Sedgwick

NATAL PUBLISHING LLC
ARS LONGA, VITA BREVIS

PART I

CHAPTER I

A clock struck eight, a loud yet distant clock. The strokes, Alix thought, seemed to glide downwards rather than to fall through the fog and tumult of the station, and, counting them as they emerged, they were so slow and heavy that they made her think of tawny drones pushing their way forth from among the thickets of hot thyme in the jardin potager at Montarel. Sitting straightly in her corner of the Victoria waiting-room, the little French girl fixed her mind upon the picture thus evoked so that she should not feel too sharply the alarming meaning of the hour, and seemed again to watch the blunt, sagacious faces of the drones as they paused in sulky deliberation on the tip of a spray before launching themselves into the sunlight. What could be more unlike Montarel than this cold and paltry scene? What more unlike that air, tranced with sunlight and silence, than this dense atmosphere? Yet the heavy, gliding notes brought back the drones so vividly that she found herself again in the high-terraced garden under the sun-baked old château. The magnolia-trees ate into the crumbling walls and opened lemon-scented cups beneath her as she leaned her arms on the hot stone and looked across the visionary plains to the Alps on the horizon, blue, impalpable, less substantial to the sight than the clouds that sailed in grandiose snowy fleets above them. Alix had always felt that it was like taking great breaths to see the plains and like spreading immense wings to see the mountains, and something of invulnerable dignity, of inaccessible remoteness in her demeanour as she sat there might well have been derived from generations who had lived and died in the presence of natural sublimities. Her brows were contemplative, her lips proud. She was evidently a foreigner, a creature nurtured in climes golden yet austere and springing from an aromatic, rocky soil. The pallor of her extreme fatigue could not efface the sunny tones of her skin; her hair was the blacker for its bronzed lights, and if her eyes were blue, it was not the English blue of a water-side forget-me-not, but the dense, impalpable blue of the Alps seen across great distances.

Two women, pausing on their way out to look at her, drew her mind back from Montarel. She knew that she might look younger than her years. Her bobbed hair was cut straight across her forehead and her skirt displayed a childish length of leg. It was no wonder that, seeing her there, alone, they should speak of her with curiosity, perhaps with solicitude; for there was kindness in their eyes. But she did not like pity, and, drawing herself up more straightly, wrapping her arms in the scarf that muffled her shoulders, she fixed her eyes blankly above their heads until they had passed on. They were kind women; but very ugly. Like jugs. All the people that she had seen since landing on this day of grey and purple flesh-tones had made her think of the earthenware jugs that old Marthe used to range along her upper shelves in the little dark shop that stood on the turn of the road leading down from the château to the village. Their eyes were joyless yet untragic. Their clothes expressed no enterprise. She did not think that they could feel ecstasy, ever, or despair. Yet they were the people of Captain Owen, and she could not be really forgotten, for Captain Owen's family were to come for her. It was only some mistake; but more than the strokes of the clock the women's eyes had made her feel how late it was, how young she was, and how hungry.

Maman's déjeuner, the long buttered petits pains with ham in them, she had eaten on the boat; and, far away, seen across the leaden waters of the November channel, was the bright petit déjeuner, in Paris that morning, and Maman before the wood fire, her beauty still clouded by sleep, sweet, sombre, and gay as only she could be, her russet locks tossed back and her white arms bare in the white woollen peignoir. "They will, I know, be good to my darling," Maman had said, buttering her roll while Albertine brought in the coffee, "and keep her warm and well-fed through this hard winter." Firmness and resource breathed from Maman. She knew what she was doing and Alix saw herself powerless in her hands. Yet she could read her, too. Even though she could not always interpret the words, she could always read Maman, and the meaning, as it were, of the sentence would come to her in a feeling rather than in an idea. She had felt that morning that Maman's heart was not at ease. It was true that the Armistice had been signed but the other day, that the war was hardly over, and that everything would be more expensive than ever. It was true that she was going to friends, though to unknown friends; to the family of their dear Captain Owen, killed in battle only nine months ago. He had so often said that they must know his family, and it had been his mother who had written so kindly to say that Giles would meet her. But if all this were so natural, why had she felt that touch of artifice in Maman's manner, that resource in her so many reasons? Perhaps they did not really want her. And perhaps there was some mistake and they did not expect her to-night. If no one came, what was she to do? She had only five shillings in her purse. The porter had placed her little box and her dressing-case on the seat beside her, and if no one came was she to sit on here all night, in the waiting-room, this horrid feeling, half hunger, half fear, gnawing at the pit of her stomach? "Dieu, que j'ai faim!" she thought; and as she now leaned back her head and closed her eyes, the sadness that flowed into her carried her far back to Montarel again and it was Grand-père that she saw, passing under the pollarded lime-trees with his dragging footsteps and looking down on the ground as he went, with no eyes for the climbing vineyards, no eyes for the plains, the river, the Alps; his short white beard and jutting nose giving him still the air of a commandant, high on his fortress; but so old, so ill, so poor and so despairing.

The dappled shadows of the limes lay brightly blue at his feet. His bleached hands were clasped behind him on his stick. He wore a black silk skull-cap and a white silk handkerchief was knotted around his neck. It had always frightened her a little to see Grand-père, and it frightened her now to remember him, the commandant, defeated, broken; yet still with that sombre fire smouldering in his eyes. "Tout-à-fait une tête de Port-Royal," she had heard someone say of him once; and so a devout noble of the time of Louis Quatorze might have looked. Only she did not see Grand-père as appeased, withdrawn from the world and its illusions; he brooded, rather, in bitterness upon them. He minded everything so terribly.

She remembered as if it were yesterday the dreadful summer afternoon when the bell had clanged hoarsely in the courtyard, and Mélanie, wiping her steaming arms on her apron, had come clapping in her savates across the paving-stones to let in the opulent gentleman who had arrived in his motor to take away the Clouets. That was the day that had revealed to her what Grand-père's poverty must be. He had sold the Clouets at last; after selling so many things. The great gaunt salles, the little panelled salons, the rows of incommodious bedrooms, looking, from high up, over the plains, all were empty; and the Clouets now were to go.

With a child's awed heart, half comprehending, Alix had followed Mélanie and the stranger, up the winding staircase in the turret—Mélanie took him by that circuitous route so that Grand-père should catch no glimpse of him; along the chill stone passages, to the little room where she and Grand-père sat and read in the evenings. The lit de repos stood there, draped in its tattered brocades, dignified and irrelevant, for no one ever thought of lying down on it; and Grand-père's old bergère, and her tabouret drawn up to the table before her histories. And there, upon the sea-green panelled walls, the silvery Clouets hung, Mouverays among them; frigidly smiling in their ruffs.

Mélanie, mute, grim, inscrutable, helped the gentleman from Paris to take them down, one by one, and wrap them up and carry them across the courtyard to the waiting car: and Alix had watched it all, knowing that a final disaster had fallen upon her house.

But poverty had not been the only reason for Grand-père's bitterness. Even when he sat to watch her and Marie-Jeanne, his hands folded on his stick, quiet and at peace in the evening air as it might have seemed, she was aware of the bitterness brooding there, unappeased, at the bottom of the deep, considering look bent upon them. There had been no time to think about it while she played with Marie-Jeanne. Marie-Jeanne was the blacksmith's daughter and there had been many happy days with her at Montarel. Marie-Jeanne had black eyes and her pig-tails were tied together with red tape and plaited so tightly that they surrounded her shrewd little face with a wiry circle. They brought up a family of dolls in a corner of the jardin potager; Alix was the father, for she had never cared fosteringly for dolls, and Marie-Jeanne the mother. They whipped their tops in the courtyard where the tall blue lilies stood in the damp about the well. The Renaissance wrought-iron windlass was all rusted and broken; and the lilies had thrust their cord-like roots through the cracked earthenware of their great pots. Looking out of the door in the courtyard, one might see the cheerful matelassière sitting in the shade of the enormous horse-chestnut-tree on the wayside grass. The heaped wool seemed to curdle and foam about her like a turbulent yet cosy sea. She combed it out on her loom and smiled and nodded at Alix. "Bonjour, la jolie petite demoiselle," she would say. Mélanie grumbled at the matelassière and said she was a thief; but she gave Alix a bowl of café au lait to carry out to her when she remade their mattresses, and Alix felt a pleasing sense of complicity in lawlessness when the matelassière, bending her lips to the steaming coffee, would close one eye at her in a long wink. She seemed a very happy person.

The road led down to the village, stony, steep, and golden with the vineyards on either hand. The little houses were washed with pink and fawn and cream and their roofs were the colour of the underside of an old mushroom. Strings of onions hung from their eaves, and milk cheeses in flat wicker baskets. After the village came the river and the old stone bridge that led across to the forest, tall and dark, marching up the mountain and haunted by legends of ghosts and knights and fairies. Mélanie, when she was in a good humour, would tell of these, seated in the evening on her own particular little terrace where she kept the fowls and picked over the herbs that were to be dried for tisane. But old Mère Gavrault was the best story-teller, and Alix was sometimes allowed to go to the forest with her and find cêpes and help her to gather faggots for her winter store. Mère Gavrault told stories of goblins and headless riders. They would have been blood-curdling stories, had she not told them with such an unmoved, smiling face. It was difficult to think that Mère Gavrault would find anything blood-curdling. She had lost so many children and grandchildren and her husband had been drowned in the river. She had lived through everything, and only wanted faggots to keep her warm in winter. Her face in its close, clean cap of coarse linen was hard and brown and wrinkled. Yet she was only sixty-five years old; the age of madame Gérardin, one of Maman's friends in Paris, whom Alix did not like. Clean, clean, old Mère Gavrault, and she had lived through everything and only wanted faggots; while madame Gérardin wanted innumerable things—cigarettes all day, for one of them; and if one were to wash her bright countenance, what strange colours would stain the water, what thick, pale sediments sink! Almost passionately Alix felt her preference for Mère Gavrault, who smelt of dew and smoke and who was as clean as a stone or an apple. Madame Gérardin was as much Paris as Mère Gavrault was Montarel. Yet Maman was Paris, too, and there was nothing in the world Alix loved as she did her mother. She had always loved her, and longed for her, through all those mysterious yearly separations that took her away from her to set her down at distant Montarel. And Grand-père must have known that she longed for her. Was it not here that the deepest reason for the bitterness lay? He had never spoken to her of her mother. Never; never. Not once through all the years that she had gone to him. They had not been unhappy, those days of childhood with Marie-Jeanne at Montarel; even without Maman they had known a childish gladness. But it was as if, from the earliest age, she had had, as it were, to be happy round the corner. One's heart was there, aching, if one looked at it; and one tiptoed away cautiously and, at a safe distance, raced off to join Marie-Jeanne. But at night, when she could no longer hide from her heart, all the sadness of Grand-père's eyes would flow into her and she would lie, for hours, awake, thinking of him and of Maman.

It was because of Maman that his footsteps had dragged and his eyes had fixed themselves so obstinately on the ground; perhaps it was because of her that the Clouets had been sold;—Maman who was his daughter-in-law and who did not bear his name. "La belle madame Vervier; divorcée, vous savez."—The phrase came back to her, with its knife-like cut, as she had first heard it whispered. It conjured up a vision of harsh, cruel repudiation, of Maman driven forth from Montarel, running out at the courtyard door, down the steep road, like one of the hapless princesses in the fairy-tales;—crying, flying, stumbling on the stones. Grand-père and her father had driven her out. So it must have been. Because of some fault; some disastrous fault. Yet they had been cruel. Her father's portrait hung in the dining-room at Montarel. He was in uniform; young, though grey-haired; with stern lips and cold blue eyes; like Grand-père's; like her own. She was a Mouveray in every tint and feature; yet how unlike them. For though, by chance currents, such other aspects of the story as a child may apprehend came drifting to her, the first picture of harsh repudiation made a background to the later knowledge, and she saw Maman as a delicate flower or fruit crushed and broken between stony hands. Passionately she was Maman's child; passionately she repelled their harshness. Yet her heart ached for Grand-père, and his sadness flowed into her as she sat with closed eyes thinking of him, of Marie-Jeanne, of Mère Gavrault and Montarel; Grand-père dead and the château sold; the solitary, sunny old château on the hill that she would never see again.

CHAPTER II

Alix opened her eyes. Someone was standing still before her. Of all the footsteps that came and went, these had stopped. For a moment, so deeply was she sunk in the vision of the past, she stared bewildered at the young man in khaki, forgetting where she was and how she had come there. Then a jostling, irrelevant crowd of recent memories pressed forward:—"They will be glad to see my darling"; the grey Channel; the faces like earthenware jugs. And, even before she had identified him as monsieur Giles, a suffocating relief rose in her at the sight of him, while, strangely, one more memory seemed, on the threshold of the new life, to offer itself with a special significance, a special interpretation of what she was to find;—the memory of Maman, herself, and Captain Owen standing together in the Place de la Concorde and of Maman's voice saying to him, as they looked at the spot where the guillotine had been, at Strasbourg, still in her crêpe, and up the Champs Élysées, while splendid clouds sailed in the blue above them:—"We are not like you, mon ami. Tocsins, tumbrils, trumpets are in our blood;—Saint Bartholomew; the Revolution; Napoleon. Your history knows no rivers of blood and no arcs of triumph."

It was monsieur Giles, of course, and he was like Captain Owen, only en laid. He was tall and young and grave with round, solemn eyes, staring at her, and a big mouth. And he was very good; she saw that at once; and then she saw that he was deeply troubled. "I'm so horribly sorry," was what he said. But it was more than embarrassment at the miscarriage of their meeting and dismay at her plight, though the echo of her own distressful state came to her from his face. She, who from the earliest age seemed to have been fashioned by life to read the signs of discomfort and restraint in the faces of those about her, knew now unerringly that this good young man, who had no tocsins or tumbrils or trumpets in his blood, was deeply troubled at seeing her. "I'm so horribly sorry," he repeated, and he seized her dressing-case, Maman's old discarded one with the tarnished monogram "H. de M.," from which the crest had fallen away. "You've been here for hours," he said. "Your mother's letter did not give the day. Her wire only came this afternoon, late. We are a good way from London and trains are bad." He was not trying to throw the blame on anybody. His voice accepted it all for himself; but she knew that the mistake had been Maman's, Maman so forceful, so practical, yet so careless, too. Maman had taken it for granted that they lived quite near London; she had taken it for granted that the wire would arrive in good time.

"Have you had anything to eat?" monsieur Giles almost shouted at her. "Where's your box? Is this all? I'm so horribly sorry."

"Yes, this is all. It has not been so long, really. I have not eaten. I was afraid to go to the restaurant lest I should miss you."

Her English was so good that she saw him at once a little reassured. He had shouted like that partly from embarrassment and partly because he thought she might only understand if he talked loud. His face, as he seized her box in his other hand, echoed her smile as it had echoed her distress. It was a kind face. It echoed people's feelings easily.

"Let me take the bag; you cannot carry all," said Alix.

But he shoved himself sideways through the door and then held it open while she passed out, commenting as he did so, "But, I say, you're not a child!"

"A year makes a great difference," said Alix. "And I was not really so young; already fifteen, when Captain Owen first saw me, last October, in Cannes."

Monsieur Giles said nothing to this, and she wondered what Captain Owen had written of her and Maman after that first meeting.

Now they were sitting opposite each other at a little table that seemed to have a great many cruets and salt-cellars upon it. It was a very bright and very ugly room, and through the doors, opening and shutting incessantly, came the muffled roar of incoming trains; but after the waiting-room it was homelike. She was safe with monsieur Giles. He was a person who made you feel safe. Soup was put before them, all substance and no savour, but she ate it eagerly, and said that, yes, please, she would like fish.

"And then the beef," said Giles to the waiter, who had a pallid face and looked, Alix thought, detached and meditative as he was, like a littérateur.

"I don't advise the beef, Sir," he said in a low, impassive voice. "It's specially tough to-day, Sir. You'd do better with the mutton."

"Mutton, then, by all means!" said Giles, laughing. "Rather nice, that, what?" he asked, smiling at Alix across the table when the waiter was gone.

He showed beautiful white teeth when he smiled. They were his only beauty; though she liked his golden-green eyes, fig-coloured. His face was vehement, almost violent in structure with a prominent nose and so high a top to his head that it seemed to be boiling over. Though he looked so kind, he looked also as if he could get angry rather easily, with a steady, reasonable anger, and the more she observed him the less she found him like his brother. Captain Owen's lips, though broad, had been delicately curved, and his nut-shaped eyes had always seemed to smile a little lazily. Sweetness rather than strength had been in his face and an air of taking everything lightly. She had always felt of him that he would fight just as if he were playing tennis; whereas when Giles fought, she felt sure, he would clench his teeth and look fierce and sick. And though he was younger than Captain Owen, he was far more worn, strangely worn for one so young; and he was not at all homme du monde.

Captain Owen had always struck them as homme du monde. But even Maman could not have been sure about that, since she had so emphatically impressed upon Alix that she was to define for her with exactitude the social status of the Bradleys. Maman was sure that they were not noblesse; but Alix was to tell her whether they were petite noblesse or haute bourgeoisie, or, tout simplement, commerçants.

"Not that, I think," said Maman thoughtfully; "but with another race it is difficult to tell."

"And since Captain Owen was so much our friend, what interest can it have for us?" Alix had inquired, with the dryness she could sometimes show towards Maman.

Maman had replied that it made no difference at all as far as an individual, at large, as it were, unattached and irresponsible in a foreign country, was concerned; but that it did make a difference, all the difference, when it came to the family itself and its milieu. "At all events, they are rich, I am sure of that," said Maman; but Alix, as she ate her fish and looked across at monsieur Giles, was not so sure. He was rather shabby; even for an old uniform.

"You know," he said, "I'm not going to take you to Sussex to-night. It's too late and you're too tired. Don't try to eat that nasty sauce; scrape it off and leave it. I apologize for our sauces, Mademoiselle.—I'm going to take you to my aunt's. She'll be able to put us up and I'll telephone to her now. Don't run away in disgust with us and our sauces, while I'm gone."

There was no danger of that. Even when he was not there, Alix felt herself safe in the hands of monsieur Giles, and the waiter when he brought the mutton helped her very considerately, as though he recognized her as young and tired and a foreigner, and placed before her, almost with a paternal air, a dish half of which was devoted to pommes de terre à l'eau and half to a slab of dark green cabbage strangely struck into squares.

"I've wired to Mummy, too," said Giles, when he came back, "and told her we'll turn up to-morrow morning; so that's all right." And now he asked her questions. What did she read? Did she care for pictures and music? How had she learned to speak such admirable English?

Alix told him that she and Maman had often spoken English together and that she had had English governesses. "I always liked your books, too. That made it easier. 'Alice' and the rabbit and 'Pride and Prejudice' and 'Dombey and Son.' Have you read those?"

He said he had. "There are no books in France for girls to read as far as I can make out," he added; and Alix, suspecting a hint of detraction, replied: "Our chefs d'œuvre are for later in life. Perhaps great books cannot be written for girls."

"I question that!" said Giles, smiling at her. "Great books should be written for everybody."

"We can read Racine and Corneille and Lamartine," said Alix.

"And Bossuet," said Giles, grinning, "and 'Les Pensées de Pascal.' Awfully jolly, isn't it! Unfortunate child;—or, rather, fortunate, since you can read us."

Alix reflected, a little vexed.

"Here's another kind of sauce," said Giles, as a portion of apricot tart was placed before each of them surrounded by a yellow glutinous substance. "I'll grant you your cooking if you'll grant me the best books for everybody.—Anyhow, I see you're too tired to argue. We'll fight it out some other time."

"But how did you come to appreciate our cooking so well?" Alix asked. "It is made with flour, this sauce, not properly cooked;—that is the trouble."

"The trouble is that it's the same sauce as the one that went with the fish, only coloured to look different.—I travelled in France when I was a boy, you see. And I'm just back from nine months there. I was in the East before that, for the first years of the war."

"In France for nine months? Why did you not come to see us?" Alix asked. She asked it without stopping to think, for it was so strange that they should not have seen Captain Owen's brother.

"I was at the front, and wanted all my leaves at home," said Giles, and he smiled very brightly at her. He did not look at all embarrassed now; yet she had a surmise. He stopped himself from showing embarrassment. Surely he could have come? Had he not wanted to come? And he was going on talking, while he paid the bill, as if he felt she might be asking herself that question: "My aunt lives in a part of London called Chelsea. At the time 'Pride and Prejudice' was written, it was all gardens there; it's mostly flats now. We've changed very much, in all sorts of ways from the England of 'Pride and Prejudice'; just as you have from the France of Lamartine."

Everything was dimmed with fog as they drove through the streets and she was suddenly very sleepy, yet she kept on thinking, as she looked out, of those nine months that monsieur Giles had been in France. He must have been there, then, when Captain Owen was killed. How strange that he had never come, and that Captain Owen had never spoken of him. She was too sleepy, however, to think of it very carefully and, when they stopped at the brightly lighted door of a large building, she stumbled in alighting so that Giles, with a steadying "Hello, hello," put a hand under her elbow and guided her into a lift; and, still so sustained, she was presented a moment later to a stout, rosy lady with pince-nez and smooth grey hair who herself opened the door of a white and green appartement and said: "Poor child, she must be put to bed at once."

From Giles she passed to Aunt Bella, who smelt of toilet vinegar and had a seal ring on her small glazed-looking hand.

After that Alix was only drowsily aware of a little pink bedroom where a row of pink, blue and green water-colours framed in gilt hung upon the walls. Her head sank into a pillow and all the troubled thoughts into sleep; but, just before she was quite oblivious, a little tap came to the door; it opened softly and a tall head, silhouetted on the lighted hall, looked in, and Giles said, "Good-night, Alix."

It was treating her as a child and it made her feel very safe.

CHAPTER III

For many hours the little French girl slept on dreamlessly, and when she woke it was as if an abyss of space and time lay between her and yesterday morning. As she gazed up at the dim ceiling, only the most recent memories wove themselves softly into her returning sense of identity: the yellow sauce that Giles had told her to scrape off; his faded khaki necktie; Aunt Bella's small, glazed hands. Kindness, security, lay behind these appearances, and an apprehension of pain seemed at first substanceless and irrational. Then, with a gathering effort, it shaped itself: France; Maman; what was she doing and was she happy?—She had not been really happy yesterday morning. Why had monsieur Giles been so troubled when they met? And why had he never come to see them in all the nine months he had been in France?

There was a tap at the door and an elderly maid came in, neatly capped, bearing a brass hot-water-can, which she stood in the basin. Then she drew the curtains and turned up the electric light and placed by the bedside a very amusing little tea-set on a tray. It was Alix's initiation into early-morning tea, and for a moment, as she gazed at it, she feared it was to be all her breakfast until the maid, withdrawing, said, very distinctly, as though she might be deaf: "Breakfast at nine, Miss; and the bathroom is opposite."

That was all right, then. Alix lifted the lid of the little pot and sniffed at the tea and decided that the afternoon was the only time at which she felt drawn to it. And as for the two slices of bread and butter, they were very thin, but she would rather save her appetite. Meanwhile there was a real brouillard de Londres pressing close against the window, so close that one could see nothing—Alix had jumped up to look—except the spectral top of a tree below the window and, below the tree, a blurred street-lamp. It was interesting, exciting, to get up like this as if it were after dinner instead of before breakfast, for there were lights in the hall and bathroom and one's morning face had such a curious look as one combed one's hair under an electric bulb. She forgot her waking apprehensions as she dressed, and when she went into the dining-room and found Giles there, the day seemed to have started really well.

Giles was reading a newspaper, standing under the light. The room was small and he looked very large in it; so did a pink, frilled ham on the sideboard and an engraving hanging over the mantelpiece of an old, erect gentleman, en favoris, his hands on a book and with a very high collar.

When Aunt Bella came in a moment later, they all seemed quite crowded between the fog outside and the steam from the shining kettle on the table, and it was rather, Alix thought, as though they were floating in a little boat on a misty sea or suspended—this was a more exciting comparison—high in the air in an aeroplane.

She was seated opposite the mantelpiece, Giles under it, and, following her eyes, Aunt Bella said: "That is our great Mr. Gladstone, Alix. You've heard of Mr. Gladstone."

Alix had to confess that she had not.

"Well, you'll have heard of George Washington, then," said Aunt Bella. "There he is, behind you." And Alix turned round to look up at the austere face in powdered hair.

"He was an American, was he not, and your enemy?" she inquired.

"He was the enemy of one of our foolish kings," said Aunt Bella, "but an Englishman, and one we are all proud of. And that's Cobden." She completed her educational round with the third large engraving that hung near the window.

"And now, perhaps," said Giles, "you'll like to hear what they all did and why Aunt Bella has them hanging here. By the time you do that you'll have quite a good idea of modern English history."

Alix for a moment was afraid that Aunt Bella might really be going to instruct her, and she had not the least wish to know anything about any of the respectable gentlemen who presided over the breakfast-table.

But Giles was going on, with his bantering smile. "If you go to Aunt Bella, you'll get a one-sided impression, perhaps. She's a great Liberal. We are all Liberals in my family. What you'd call Republicans.—Aunt Bella, you're not asking this helpless French child to drink tea for her breakfast!"

"Doesn't she have tea?" Aunt Bella asked, and though Alix insisted that she did not mind it at all, there was much concerned conversation, and the elderly maid was summoned and told to ask cook to make some cocoa for the young lady.

"You hate tea, I suppose," said Giles, and Alix replied that she liked it very much at five o'clock, and Giles went on: "Whereas Aunt Bella likes it at all hours of the day and night; and Indian tea, I'm grieved to say; it's the only rift within our lute, Aunt Bella's Indian tea;—since we do agree about Gladstone. Now you're a Royalist, I suppose, Alix?"

"But surely no rational person in France is a Royalist any longer," said Aunt Bella.

"Grand-père did not love the Republic," said Alix, "but Maman admires Napoleon and the Revolution."

"I sometimes think we shall get both a revolution and a Napoleon in this country," said Aunt Bella, "at the rate things seem to be going."

"There'll never be a revolution in England," said Giles. "People who drink Indian tea could never make a revolution, could they, Alix?"

"I do not think so," Alix smiled. "Nor in a country with such fogs."

"That's a good idea! Eh, Aunt Bella? People must see each other clearly in order to hate each other sufficiently.—What?"

"That is just it," Alix nodded, laughing. "And you are all so kind. Kinder, I am sure, than we are."

She and Giles understood each other. He treated her like a child, yet they understood each other, really, better than he and Aunt Bella, for she looked a little cautious when Giles embarked on his sallies, as if she did not quite know in what admission he might not involve her unless she were careful. She took things au pied de la lettre, Aunt Bella, as, after all, an elderly lady would do who sat down to breakfast every morning with such cold comfort on her walls as Messieurs Gladstone, Cobden, and Washington. A row of smiling Watteau engravings hung round Maman's little dining-room in the rue de Penthièvre. Alix did not think that Gladstone, Cobden, or Washington would look with an eye of approval at Le Départ pour Cythère or the Assemblée Galante. Though Washington might. She liked him far the best of the three.

"And does your grandfather really expect to get the Bourbons back?" Aunt Bella inquired. "You are a Roman, I suppose, my dear child."

"A Roman?" Alix, for all her English, was perplexed. "I have no Italian blood."

"She means your church," said Giles. "And Catholics, in France, do really all want back a king, don't they?"

"I am a Catholic," said Alix, "and so, of course, was Grand-père, and he certainly did not like the Republic. We had a very unscrupulous, intriguing mayor at Montarel and perhaps that was one reason. But I do not think that Grand-père expected anything any more or thought at all about kings."

"A very strange people, the French," Aunt Bella remarked, as if the fact were so patent that one of them, being present, could not object to its statement. "A very strange people, indeed. And where do you say your grandfather lives, my dear?"

"He is dead," said Alix. "It was at Montarel he lived; near the Alps."

"You may have noticed the water-colours of Avignon that I did some years ago, hanging in your bedroom," said Aunt Bella. "Parts of France are very picturesque. But I prefer our scenery."

"And now," said Giles, looking at his watch, "we must be thinking about our train. Are you packed up, Alix?"

"Tell your mother," said Aunt Bella, "that I expect her on Thursday for the two committees. She'll spend the night, of course." And when Alix's box and bag had been brought and a taxi summoned, Aunt Bella said to her very kindly, as they stood for farewells in the hall: "You must come again and see me, my dear, when you are in London. I could take you to the National Gallery and Westminster Abbey, and, if you care about Social Work, you might be interested in my Infant Welfare Centre and Working Girls' Gymnasium."

"Is she an official, your aunt?" Alix inquired as she and Giles drove off to the station.

"An unofficial official," Giles explained. "She runs more things than most officials. She sits on councils and governs hospitals and makes speeches. There can't be a busier woman in London and she's a splendid old girl;—though I do enjoy pulling her leg." And then, since Alix was startled by this expression, also new to her, he had again to explain.

CHAPTER IV

The third-class carriage was not foul and wooden as it would have been in France, and they had it to themselves; but the cushions smelt of fog, and Alix thought she had never seen anything so ugly as the view from the window. It had been too dark to see the suburbs of London the night before, on the way up from Newhaven; but they lay all mean and low and toad-coloured this morning, wet under the lifted fog, and for as far as the eye could follow there was nothing to be seen but squatting roofs and gaunt factory chimneys.

"Bad, isn't it?" said Giles. He sat opposite her, looking out with his face so young and so worn. She liked him so much and felt so safe with him, and yet it frightened her a little to look at him, just—strange association—as it had frightened her to look at Grand-père. Only Giles was kinder, far, than Grand-père. "But worse, do you think," he went on, "than the suburbs of Paris?"

Alix did not quite like to say how much worse she thought it; it did not seem polite. "There, at least, one has the sky to look at," she suggested. "It is happier, I think."

"We're not always in a fog, you know," said Giles. "And Aunt Bella is very keen on Smoke Abatement. Perhaps we'll look happier some day."

"I am very glad your family does not live in London," said Alix. She felt more shy of Giles this morning, shut up with him in the intimacy of the chill, smoky carriage, than she had last night in the station dining-room. And it was as if she felt him more shy, too. They were making talk a little.

"Wouldn't you have come, if we'd lived in London?" he inquired.

"Maman would have sent me just the same, I think," said Alix. "She wanted me to know England. And your family, specially, of course. Captain Owen always said I must know his family."

"Oh, yes. Of course," said Giles. He got up then and looked at the heat regulator and said it was cold, did she mind? There seemed no heat. Then he sat down again and fell into a silence, his arms folded, his long legs stretched as best they could, before him, and they both, again, looked out of the window.

On it went, the dreadful city; but at last furtive squares and triangles of green were stealing into it and sparsely placed trees edged streets that adventured forth, at random, it seemed, to end, almost with a stare of forlorn astonishment, in fields ravaged of every trace of beauty. But the green spread and widened like a kindly tide, and though the brick and slate was encrusted at intervals, like an eruption, upon the land, there were copses and rises of meditative meadow and the white sky was melting here and there to a timid blue above little hamlets that seemed to have a heart and to be breathing with a life of their own. Beside a brook a girl was strolling with scarf and stick, two joyous dogs racing ahead of her; a cock-pheasant ran, startled, through a wood sprinkled with gold and russet, and presently there was a deeper echo of the blue overhead in the blue of quiet hills on the horizon.

"This is better, isn't it?" said Giles, bringing his eyes to her at last. "Don't you call this pretty?"

"Very pretty," said Alix. And it was pretty, though to her eyes it was also insignificant and confused, its lack of design or purpose teasing her mind with its contradiction of the instinct for order and shapeliness that dwelt there. "Is it because of the season and your mistiness that everything seems very near one? The horizon is so near, and even the sky comes quite close down."

"Like nice, kind arms, I always think," said Giles. "No, even in the Lake Country, even in Scotland, we don't get your splendid distances; or very rarely."

"But it is very pretty," Alix repeated. "I like the woods. Did you see the girl and the dogs a little while ago? I imagine that your sisters look like that."

"Our dogs look like that. Ruth and Rosemary aren't quite so grown up. We have three dogs. Are you fond of them?"

"Oh, very fond; though I have never had a dog of my own. Maman thinks them too much trouble for a little appartement in Paris. But I had a cat at Montarel. A yellow cat with blue eyes. Have you ever seen one like that? He was so affectionate and intelligent and remembered me perfectly from year to year. He used to put his paws on my breast and rub against my face. The thought of seeing him again made it easier to bear leaving Maman when my half-year at Montarel came round."

"Your half-year at Montarel?" Giles asked the question, but she saw that it was after a hesitation. She wondered how much Captain Owen had told them. She felt suddenly that she wanted to tell Giles everything there was to tell.

"I spent half the year with Grand-père at Montarel and half with Maman in Paris. Did you not know?" she said, looking him in the eyes. "My father and mother were parted. They were divorced. But it could not have been more Maman's error since the judge allowed her to have me for half the time. It is arranged like that, you know, as fairer. And since my father died when I was hardly more than a baby, it was Grand-père who had me for that side of the family.—I tell it to you as I imagine it to have been, for Maman has never spoken to me of it."

Giles was making it easy. He was looking at her with no sign of discomfort, looking, indeed, as if he knew it already. "Oh, yes," he said. And then he added: "And when your grandfather died? Was there no one else on his side of the family? Don't you go to Montarel any more?"

"No one at all," said Alix, shaking her head. "I am the last of the Mouverays. That was why the château was sold and why Maman has me now entirely. But though it was sad to lose my grandfather, I love my mother best of course."

"I hope you won't miss her too much," said Giles after a moment and in a kind voice. "We'll try to give you a happy life, you know."

"I am sure you will. But one must always miss one's mother and one's country. And then I always wonder if she is happy. Though I am only a child, she depends on me."

"You have the comfort of knowing that Paris is only a few hours away," said Giles, smiling.

"Ah, but Cannes isn't. She is to be at Cannes this winter."

"Oh, yes, I remember. She spends the winters at Cannes."

"She enjoys her life there. She plays tennis beautifully and has so many friends, as perhaps Captain Owen told you. But I know that she misses me. I have always been with her there before. I was with her, you know, when Captain Owen met us."

"I should rather say I did know," said Giles. "We heard all about your kindness to him, you may be sure. You may be sure we are a very grateful family." Giles spoke with heartiness, and though she felt something a little forced in it there was nothing forced in his evident kindness towards herself. They were talking happily. As they had talked last night at dinner.

"And you may be sure we heard all about you," said Alix, smiling across at him. "All about Ruth and Rosemary and Francis and Jack. What a large family you are. It must be very happy being so many."

"I say!" laughed Giles, "you have a good memory! To get us in our order, too."

"But how could I forget when he told us so much! We saw all your photographs so often. Only one does not get so clear an idea from photographs. I would not have known you from yours. And there was

Toppie. After your mother, he talked most of all about Toppie. I shall see her, too, shall I not?"

It was as if she had struck him. The violent red that mounted to his face was echoed in Alix's cheeks. It was as if, with her innocent words, she had struck him, and in the silence that followed them, while he gazed at her, and she, helplessly, gazed back, she saw that what had underlain the confusion of yesterday had simply been suffering. She had laid it bare. She was looking at it now.

He tried to master it; to conceal it; in a moment he stammered: "Oh, he talked most about Toppie, did he?"

"Was she not his betrothed?" asked Alix in a feeble voice. She felt exhausted. He had struck her, too.

"Of course she was," said Giles, and his eyes now lifted from her face and fixed themselves over her head on Maman's dressing-case.

"And—is she not still living?"

"Toppie? Living?" His eyes came back to her. "I should rather say so. You see," he went on at once, though Alix could not see the relevance, "she was so horribly cut up by his death."

"Of course," Alix murmured. "I am so sorry. I should not have spoken of him at all, when you have lost him. I did not mean to be stupid; unfeeling."

"But, good Heavens! you're not stupid! Not a bit unfeeling!" cried Giles, and seeing her distress, his eyes actually filled with tears. "It's not Owen at all. We often speak of him. It's Toppie. And it's I who am such a dunderhead. You see, she's all that's left of him. I mean, all that's loveliest; most sacred. She cared for him so much. She's like something in a shrine, to us all."

"Yes. Yes. I see. I understand," said Alix; though, still, she could not see. "I spoke lightly. I do not forgive myself."

"But it's nothing to do with you," Giles almost shouted as he had shouted at her last night. "I always get like that when she's talked about, with him. You poor, dear child, it's nothing on earth to do with you. It's absolutely my stupidity," Giles assured her, their suffusion giving his eyes a strange heaviness.

It must be left at that. There was nothing for her to say. He was suffering and he tried to conceal from her how much; but she had seen it too plainly. All unwittingly she had blundered, blundered horribly, in speaking of Captain Owen and his betrothed, and a sense of depression, dark, like the London fog, penetrating and bitter like the London smoke, settled upon her.

"Here's the station! There's Mummy!" cried Giles. They had sat silent, and now he sprang up as if with great gaiety. He was doing his best. He was trying to make her forget; it was a little stupid of him if he thought he could succeed, Alix felt; but she summoned a responsive smile with which to greet Giles's mother.

She recognized her at once as the train slid into the little station. She stood there, tall and slender, wistful and intent, with her spare grey skirt and black hat and scarf, and hair straying about her ears, as shy, as gentle as a girl. In her photograph, seen at Cannes, it had seemed incredible that she should be Captain Owen's mother, and though her face showed as faded and worn in the morning light, it was even more incredibly young. She must be fifty, yet Maman, unflawed and radiant in her thirty-seven summers, had a greater maturity of aspect. "She is so innocent," thought Alix; not clearly seeing, yet deeply feeling the meaning of the word.

She was walking beside the train, smiling up at them, her hand laid on the window of their carriage, and Giles did not wait for it to stop before he sprang out beside her and kissed her, doffing his cap. There was no confusion, no trouble, in the eyes of Giles's mother; they had nothing to hide; this was the next thought that came to Alix; they were only shy and sweet and sad. She did not speak at first. She took Alix by the hand and stood so holding her while Giles got out the dressing-case, and then led her along beside them, glancing down at her as they went; and Alix saw that with all the memories her own presence recalled, words were too difficult.

Giles was telling of the Victoria disaster. "I missed that first train, Mummy. I didn't get to Victoria till nearly two hours after hers had come in. But she's forgiven us. She's a most forgiving disposition," said Giles, "I've discovered that. She won't resent any of the wrongs we put upon her."

"Two hours! How dreadful! Oh, how dreadful!" Mrs. Bradley was exclaiming, "What must you have thought of us, Alix!"

"But it wasn't your wrong, at all," said Alix; "it was Maman's mistake. I think telegrams take very long now from France to England."

"There always are mistakes about meetings," said Mrs. Bradley. "Dreadful things always do seem to happen.—Shall I drive, Giles, dear? or sit behind with Alix so that we can talk? That will be best, I think."

They drove over commons and along woodland roads. The air was white and chill yet dimly transfused with sunlight, and there was a smell of wet pine-trees and wet withered heather. Alix's spirits lifted a little with the scent and swiftness, and they lifted still further, seeming, like the sky, to show a rift of blue, when in her gentle, slightly hoarse voice, Mrs. Bradley said: "Is your mother well, dear? How did you leave her?" This was the first inquiry about Maman she had heard, the first interest she had seen displayed. Giles, she remembered it now, had volunteered not a remark or question.

"She wrote so kindly," said Mrs. Bradley. "She understood, I know, how much we hoped to see you here, how much pleasure it would give us. I wish she could have come, too. Owen so often wrote about you both, from Cannes. He said you made him think of Jeanne d'Arc, and your mother of Madame Récamier.—I'm glad you still do your hair like that," said Mrs. Bradley, smiling shyly, and Alix saw that she had forgotten nothing and that all the links that Giles had ignored were cherished by her.

There were links, however, that she would not see. That must be, Alix reflected, what she had felt as her innocence. The pleasure that her coming might give to the Bradleys had never been part of Maman's motive. She had taken it for granted, but it had not counted. Maman had sent her because she had conceived of the winter in England as an advantage for her child and because—Alix saw further into these motives than Maman intended her to do—it had not been convenient to take her to Cannes. But there were few of Maman's motives, Alix felt, as she listened to the gentle, hesitating voice, that Mrs. Bradley would divine. Perhaps it was that that made Maman seem so much the older. Yet Maman, too, might have blindnesses. She would have been blind, for instance, in saying of Mrs. Bradley—and Alix could hear her saying it: "Un peu bê-bête, n'est-ce pas, ma chérie?" Mrs. Bradley was simple, very simple; but she was not bête. Alix felt that she understood Mrs. Bradley as Maman would not understand her, and it was perhaps because of this that Mrs. Bradley spoke presently about her dead son, for to any one who did not understand her she could not have spoken. She would never be bête about things like that. She was longing to speak about him, Alix saw; to ask questions, to reënforce her store of precious memories by such fragments as the little French girl could offer her. Alix told her of their walks above the sea at Cannes, of the concerts he had so loved, and of how much he had had to tell and teach them of flowers and birds.

"Oh, yes, the birds; he loved them," said Mrs. Bradley, turning away her eyes that were full of tears. She was like this November day, with its suffused sunlight, and fresh, sad fragrance; there were no tocsins or trumpets in her blood, either; yet all the same she knew what suffering was as well as Maman. The hoarseness of her voice had come, perhaps, in part from crying; something scared, that one caught in her glance at moments, had not been there, Alix felt sure, before the war; before the news of her son's death had been brought to her. And as Alix thought of Captain Owen's death and of what his mother must have felt, there rose in her memory a picture of a Spring morning in Paris, the wild, wet day, with shafts of sunlight slanting through the rain and striking great spaces on the pavements to azure. She had been standing at the window of their salon, looking at the rain and sunlight, and at the flower-woman on the corner opposite, her basket heaped with pink and white tulips, and she had heard Maman, suddenly, behind her, saying, as if she had forgotten that Alix was there: "Dieu!—Dieu!—Dieu!" And, looking round she had seen her with the letter in her lap and had read the catastrophe in her white face and horror-filled eyes. So many of their friends had fallen in the war, but for none of them had Maman mourned as she had for Captain Owen.

The car turned, now, with careful swiftness, into an entrance gate which opened against a well-clipped hedge. A curve among the trees brought them to the front of a large house, red brick below, gables above, with beams and plaster. A great many gables, a great many creepers, large windows open to the air. A kind, capacious house, promising comfort; but how ugly, thought Alix, as they alighted; "Combien peu intéressante." It was difficult to believe that from its cosy portals Captain Owen and Giles had gone forth to tragedy.

Two girls, at the sound of the car, had burst out upon the steps, and three dogs; an Irish terrier, a fox terrier, and a West Highland terrier;—"I like him best"—thought Alix of the last;—and they bounded in the air while the girls shouted:

"I say, Giles, you did serve us a turn last night! Your wire never got here until this morning! We sat up till eleven!"

They wore knitted jumpers and had corn-coloured hair and pink faces. They were delighted to see their brother back after his misadventures; the dogs were delighted to see him; only the dogs did not shout, which was an advantage. Alix had never heard such a noise.

"And here is Alix," said Mrs. Bradley, who had stopped to take the appealing fox terrier in her arms; the fox terrier was a lady, no longer young, and the uproar affected her too much; Mrs. Bradley soothed and reassured her.

Ruth and Rosemary, as though aware for the first time of Alix's presence, turned their attention to her and cried "Hello" heartily, while they shook her by the hand. They were like Aunt Bella in their rosiness, robustness, their air of doing things all the time with absorption and energy; and like Aunt Bella and the house they were "peu intéressantes."

"Did you have a good crossing? Are you a good sailor?" asked Rosemary; while Ruth said: "Let me carry up her bag.—Do you play hockey?—Jouissez-vous le hockey?"

"She speaks English better than you do," said Giles, pulling his sister's rope of hair; "and your French is a disgrace to your family."

They all went into a hall that had wide windows in unexpected places and an important oak staircase winding up from it, also in an unexpected place. Alix was dimly aware of earnest, cheerful attempts at originality in its design; but the originality did not go beyond the windows and staircases, the high wainscotting and oaken pillars. Everything else, from the brasses of the big chimney-place to the florid crétonnes on the window-seats, followed a bright household formula. The brightness would have been a little oppressive had it not lapsed to a benign shabbiness, and the two good-tempered maids who followed with Alix's box belonged to it all, ornamental in their crisp pink print dresses, yet a little dishevelled; their caps perched far back on large protuberances of hair and fashionable whiskers of curl coming forward on their cheeks.

Alix felt all sorts of things about the hall and about the crétonnes and about the maids as Ruth and Rosemary and the dogs hustled her along. What it amounted to she did not clearly know, except that Giles did not really go with the hall, while his sisters did, and that Mrs. Bradley did not like the caps and the whiskers, but that she would always sacrifice her own tastes—hardly aware that she had them—to other people's cheerfulness.

"Oh, well, of course you play tennis," Ruth was saying. "Everybody plays tennis. But you must learn hockey at once. It's the great game at our school and you're nowhere unless you play it.—Down Bobby, down! He's made friends with you already.—The mud will come off all right.—One can't mind mud if one has dogs, can one? Down, you silly duffer!"

"Never mind. Let him jump. I am fond of dogs," said Alix, patting the ardent head of the Irish terrier. "What is the name of the little, low, white one? He is quieter, but I think he likes me too."

"His name is Jock, and Mummy's fox terrier is Amy. Oh, they'll all like you, all right; they're as friendly as possible—though Amy can be a bit peevish at moments; Mummy spoils her.—Here's your room," said

Rosemary, ushering her in. "It's a jolly room, isn't it? Mummy thought you'd like the one with the view best. The other spare-room looks over the kitchen-garden. It's a jolly view, isn't it? One doesn't often get a view like that. Put the box here, Edie.—Oh, the bathroom is on the landing, that door, you see. We have our baths in the morning and the water doesn't run very hot for more than two. So will you have yours at night? Mummy does. Ruth and I like it best in the morning, and Giles doesn't mind if his is cold.—French people don't care about baths, anyway, do they?—Lunch will be ready in twenty minutes. Can you find your way down?" Rosemary added rapidly, her eye on the staircase where Giles was descending, "I want to speak to Giles."

"No, you don't! It's my place to tell him first!" screamed Ruth.

"It's about the football, Giles!"

"Oh, shut up!" shouted Giles affectionately. "What a frightful row you're making!"

And Alix at last heard them all hurtling down the stairs together.

Jock, who was old and a little melancholy, remained with her, seating himself on the hearth rug and surveying her with kindly but disenchanted eyes.

"Dieu! Quel bruit!" Alix addressed him. She felt that Jock agreed with her about the noise and in finding Ruth and Rosemary, as well as Bobby, too turbulent. She listened at the door to be sure that they were safely gone. Then she tiptoed softly down and peeped in at the bathroom. It was large and untidy. She, too, preferred her bath hot and in the morning. Ruth and Rosemary were kind, but your preferences would never stand in the way of theirs. No, never would she find them interesting. But they did not ask it of you, Alix reflected, going back to her room. All they asked of you was to let them bathe at the time that best pleased them, play hockey with them, and admire their view. She went to look at the view. A pleasant, heathery common dipping at its further edge to a birch-wood. That was all. And another gabled roof rose among pines on a near hillside. All comfort; no beauty, thought Alix, and the sky came so closely down that it made her feel suffocated. And as she leaned looking out she thought of the roll of the mighty Juras, and the plain, and the river shining across it. How tame this was, a piping, perching little bird beside an eagle of great flights and soarings. Why had Maman sent her here? She could never be happy; never, never, under this low sky, among these noisy girls. And wave after wave there mounted in her an old, well-remembered homesickness for Maman and a new homesickness for France.

CHAPTER V

She was not to escape Ruth and Rosemary for long. Already, at lunch, she felt that Giles, talking gravely with his mother of treaties and leagues and such dull matters, seemed to have relegated her to their category. Over the dining-room mantelpiece hung a portrait of the late Mr. Bradley; she knew it must be he from his likeness to Aunt Bella and Ruth and Rosemary, and Alix felt sure, as she looked up at his pink and yellow, his tweeds and watch-chain and good, shrewd eyes, that Mrs. Bradley's sons must always have interested her more than their father. But she would never have known this, just as she did not know, nor did they, that she was fonder of her boys than of Ruth and Rosemary. "But I believe that in this country everybody is fonder of sons," thought Alix, marvelling at the reappearance of the strange cabbage cut into squares and recalling impressions of English literature where, despite romantic surfaces, it was apparent to the discerning eye that men always counted for more than women.

Mrs. Bradley carved. It was a well-roasted leg of mutton, that made Alix think of the mutton in "Alice." The potatoes, too, were roasted and the entremets a bread-and-butter pudding. Mr. Bradley had been nourished on such meals. They would produce Mr. Bradleys.

"Now we will show you everything," said Ruth when luncheon was over. The implication seemed to be that a specially fortunate experience was in store for her. A fond complacency breathed from both girls. "And it is natural that one should love one's home," thought Alix, the tolerance of her comprehension giving her childish face a maturity beyond its years.

So she was led from the lawn to the shrubberies; shown the summer-house where in summer they had tea and the herbaceous border, neatly disposed for its winter sleep. The kitchen-garden was displayed, and at its far end they passed through a door to a little path, bordered by gorse-bushes, that ran beneath the garden-wall and then turned aside over the common. It was a sheltered, solitary little path, the branches of the garden fruit-trees hanging over it, and Alix felt that it might often be a refuge for her. It was a pretty path and had a character of its own. To Ruth and Rosemary its meaning lay in leading somewhere else, and they crossed the common and rambled in the birch-wood, inciting each other to long jumps over a sluggish little stream, half ditch, half brook, that flowed through it, and encouraging the dogs with loud cries to chase the scurrying rabbits on the further hillside.

"There's the jolliest walk along the top," said Ruth, "among the junipers. But perhaps you are tired. French girls aren't much good at walking, are they?"

"I walk a good deal in the country," said Alix, "but I think I will unpack my box now."

"Edie will have unpacked it for you," said Ruth, "so we'll go on; only say if you are tired. You wear sensible shoes, I must say. I thought all French girls pinched their toes."

So they continued to walk, talking as they went, asking her for none of her information, only imparting theirs, as if it must, self-evidently, have superior value. Alix heard them with interest when they told of Giles and of his scholastic feats at Oxford, feats interrupted by his departure for the war, but now to be resumed. Philosophy was Giles's special branch, and they told her that he was going to teach philosophy, at Oxford probably, and write it some day.

"Tiens!" said Alix, relapsing, as was her wont when surprised, into French. She knew nothing of philosophers and the word only conjured up a picture of someone aged and bearded who drank hemlock.

"Yes," said Ruth, accepting the ejaculation as a tribute, "he'll be a great man, all right, Giles."

And Alix also learned that Ruth and Rosemary both intended following professional careers and that their father had come from the north and had built Heathside and that their mother was a Londoner and that her father had been the editor of an important London paper. "What! Never heard of 'The Liberal'!" Ruth exclaimed. Ruth, as eldest, did most of the talking, subjected to frequent interruptions from Rosemary. "I should have thought even French people would have heard of 'The Liberal.' Oh, yes, he was a great swell, our grandfather."

Alix did not think she would have found him so. France, she saw, mainly existed for Ruth and Rosemary as a place where one's brothers had gone to fight and one's friends to nurse.

"And what is the pleasant house?" she inquired of them, when, after their walk along the hilltop, they had crossed the wood and emerged again upon the common.

It stood, with an air of serenity and detachment, half a mile away, a tall house of pale, eighteenth-century brick with a white door and white window-sills, a formal garden before it and a neat hedge dividing it from the road. One felt that the woods had grown up around it and that it preserved a tranquil personality of its own, unmoved by the haphazard accretions of a century.

"Oh, that's the Rectory; where Toppie lives," said Ruth. "You can see the church spire just above the trees to the right. Pleasant, do you call it? I think it's rather dismal; so bare and square. It needs lots of creepers and shrubberies to make it cheerful; but old Mr. Westmacott doesn't like them."

"Creepers would not be in the character of that house, I feel," said Alix; "and they would hide the pretty colour of the brick. There are a few roses, too, are there not?"

"Yes; a few. Toppie would have her roses. I hate a house without creepers."

"Shall I soon see Toppie, do you think?"

"Oh, you'll see her soon, all right," said Ruth. "She'll be coming in to tea to-day, probably."

"I know she's coming," said Rosemary. "She asked me yesterday if Alix would be here, and when I told her we'd had the wire, she said she'd come. I think she's rather keen on seeing you, Alix. Owen wrote a lot about you, you see."

They spoke without any emotion of Toppie. They took her for granted. She was not, to them, a shrine. But even before the scene in the train with Giles, Alix had had a special feeling about Toppie herself, and as she walked on with the chattering girls her mind went back to the day at Cannes when Captain Owen had first showed her and Maman Toppie's photograph. He carried the little leather case in his breast-pocket, his mother's picture on one side and hers on the other, and Maman had said, as she took the case from him and looked: "Elle est tout-à-fait ravissante."

"You don't see very much of her in that," said Captain Owen, wagging his foot a little, and Alix guessed that he was moved in speaking of his fiancée. "But it does show something. Lovely the shape of her face, isn't it? She's not exactly beautiful."

"Oh! 'exactly'! Who would care to be 'exactly' beautiful!" said Maman.

He had told them that Miss Westmacott—Toppie's real name was Enid Westmacott—had come with her father to live near them when she was only fifteen. Mr. Westmacott was the Rector of their parish and he had to explain to them—for Maman said that with all her English she could never get it quite clear—what rectors were and how they came to have daughters; and when Maman said, as though rectors must make up for having daughters by having devout ones, "Elle est très dévote?" Captain Owen, with his charming smile, rejoined, "Oh, much better than that!"

Later on, when they were alone, Maman had remarked to her: "She is pretty; but nothing more. Elle est nulle, cette Toppie; très, très nulle." But Alix had not agreed. Often she did not agree with Maman. The little photograph had not said much, but it had said something definite. "She is like someone in a tower." So she tried to fix her feeling.

"Even in a tower one may oneself be insignificant," said Maman, and to this Alix had replied: "Not if one is the tower oneself."

Toppie was there when they got in. A fire had been lighted for tea in the drawing-room, a long room with roses on the chairs and sofas and a high wainscotting of dark woodwork, and above that blue paper with old-fashioned crayon portraits and large photographs from famous pictures. A tall grey figure stood at the further end, and Alix knew at once that it was Toppie who turned her head to look at her like that. She was helping Mrs. Bradley arrange flowers, Michaelmas daisies, oak leaves, and sprays of golden larch. She held a large bronze vase and wore a grey tweed skirt and a grey woollen jumper and grey shoes strapping across the instep with a buckle. Her hair was as fair as primroses and was ruffled up a little above the black ribbon that bound it.

"This is Alix, Toppie, dear," said Mrs. Bradley in a gentle voice, and she came forward and passed her arm in Toppie's as if she knew that it must mean something very special to her to see the little French girl.

"I'm so glad," said Toppie. She gazed at Alix for a long moment, as though forgetting that she held the vase; then, looking round her, vague in her absorption, she set it down on a table and held out her hand.

The water from the vase had spilled over it, and as it closed on Alix's it made her think of the hand of a dryad, a naiad, or some chill, unearthly creature. "Yes; in towers," she thought, as Toppie's eyes dwelt on her. "And how much she loved him!"

She saw then that Giles was there. He was stretched out in a deep chair on one side of the fire, his hands clasped behind his head, and he was watching Toppie; her meeting with Toppie.

"And how much Giles loves her!" came the further thought, sharp with its sense of sudden elucidation. If he sat there, in that rather mannerless fashion, not helping with the water-cans, the baskets of flowers, the scissors, it was because he loved her and wanted to watch her.

Toppie, still with her absorption, had picked up the vase again and carried it to a far table.

"There; that's the best we can do with the garden just now," said Mrs. Bradley, smiling at her. "And without you, Toppie, I'd never have made the effort. Toppie thinks a room without flowers so sad. She made me come out with her and pick all these. It's astonishing, really, what one can still find in a November garden."

"They look awfully nice," said Giles.

"Well, to tell you the truth," said Ruth—Alix had already noted of her that, on all occasions, she gave her opinion without being asked—"they look to me rather dingy and frost-bitten. Rather a waste of time, I think, all this messing about to arrange flowers that don't exist!"—and Ruth laughed, pleased with her own good sense, and went to seat herself on the arm of Giles's chair.

"She bores him; but he would not like to say it," thought Alix, seeing Giles's kind but unwelcoming look. She had a feeling of excitement, yet of oppression. Toppie, she knew, was thinking of nothing but her.

The tea-table stood before the sofa on the other side of the fire from Giles, and Mrs. Bradley sat down to it and Toppie came beside her, and then, looking up at Alix, laying her hand on the place still vacant, said "Come here, Alix."

"There's room for me, too," cried Rosemary, plunging down between them. "My place is always near the cake!"

But Toppie looked at her quite coldly and said: "There's not room for you, Rosemary. Somewhere else, please. You make us all uncomfortable."

She was very fair, with a skin that would have been of a milky whiteness had it not been thickly freckled. Her lips were small and pale, her chin long and narrow; all her head, bound round with the black ribbon, was singularly narrow, and that, perhaps, was why her grey eyes seemed to look out from towers. "And how she has suffered!" thought Alix.

Nights; how many nights of sleepless suffering had not Toppie known. The tears had run down as she had lain in the long darknesses, remembering; always remembering, seeing his face before her always. Tears; vigils; remembrance;—all were in Toppie's eyes. "Oh, no, Maman; not nulle; anything but nulle," Alix thought, while, with a great wave of depression, the meaning of the war, of all its lonely suffering, swept over her. Was Captain Owen worth so much suffering? His personality lived most for Alix in the memory of his smile and his worth seemed to live in that, too. He had been charming; and there was worth in charm.

Tea was made and they were all talking of the things they did and the people they did them with. Alix heard of a Women's Institute, of Boy

Scouts and Girl Guides, and a village Choral Society that Mrs. Bradley conducted. Giles sang in it, and the girls and Jack and Francis when they were at home. "And you must sing with us, Alix," said Mrs. Bradley, and they asked her about her piano lessons and the singing at the Lycée, and she had to confess that she had never heard "The Messiah," at which there was a shout of good-natured protest from Ruth and Rosemary. "But you're not a musical nation, are you?" said Ruth; and disposed of France as a musical nation.

The talk made Alix think of the thick slices of bread-and-butter that Ruth and Rosemary and Giles were eating, it was so kindly and useful. Very different from the talk to which she was accustomed in Maman's salon; and Maman's salon itself was as different from this as the talk. It was small, yet it was stately. She and Maman had done their best for the "petit trou" of an appartement in the rue de Penthièvre, and Maman's russet head, as she sat with her cigarette at the tea-table, had melted and shone against the old tapestry, grey and green and citron, and her lovely face had seemed to belong to the Empire sconces and the carnations in their tall crystal vases that made light constellations on the mantelpiece. Maman's salon, though stately, was dense and rich and sweet, and the talk that passed, soft and shining, was like a beautiful, iridescent soap-bubble tossed so lightly from one to the other; from monsieur de Villanelle, with his pointed red beard and sad blue eyes and long Flemish nose like a Memling saint; to mademoiselle Blanche Fontaine; and from her to monsieur de Maubert, with his Jovian head; and from him to monsieur Jules, dark and gloomy, who sometimes let it drop in his abstraction, unless Maman gave it a little puff that carried it on to madame Gérardin, who received it with shrill little outcries, prettily playing with it—Alix had to own that she played prettily with talk—until it was safely back in Maman's hands again. And then another was blown. How Maman smiled; how she lifted gay yet sombre brows; how lovely they all thought her. And though one might see talk so light only as a soap-bubble, Alix dimly apprehended that it was fertile, creative; that it spread, like a sweet fragrance; that it floated like a winged seed on the breeze, out from Maman's salon to permeate, alter the world. It made a difference to the world what monsieur Villanelle thought about the last book and poem; what monsieur Jules thought about the last painter, mademoiselle Blanche about the last play, and monsieur de Maubert about the latest feat of Léon Daudet or Charles Maurras. And since, to all of them, it was in Maman's reception of their ideas that the final verdict lay, Maman, to the world at large, made the greatest difference of all.

"You'll see what a jolly life you'll have here, my dear kid," Rosemary remarked to her; Rosemary, undismayed by her rebuff, had worked through the bread-and-butter and was now eating quantities of cake. She was only six months older than Alix, but she assumed protecting airs towards her. "Girls in France have a beastly mewed-up time, haven't they?"

"Have you been much in France?" Alix asked her. She felt no call to combat Rosemary's conceptions. She was, indeed, completely indifferent to what they might be. She asked her question from mere politeness.

"Not much; but Ruth and I stayed with a French family once. My word! they were quaint! They thought the Bible improper reading for jeunes filles and picked their teeth at the table and I don't believe they ever took a bath. They almost had apoplexy when we said we had to have one every day; thought it would be sure to give us des rhumatismes."

"Many of us are quite clean," Alix remarked, and at this Giles laughed loudly.

"There's one for you, you young savage," he commented, whereupon Rosemary bounded at him and grappled with his hair.

"Help, Ruth! He's choking me!" she screamed, and Alix, with some astonishment, watched the uncouth game that followed, Giles throwing off his sisters alternately until they tumbled on the floor and sat, dishevelled and delighted, getting their breath and smoothing back their loosened hair.

"Not quite so much noise, dears," Mrs. Bradley remarked once or twice, but she continued calmly to converse with Toppie who glanced at the mêlée, Alix thought, with a remote, repudiating eye, while she said: "I find him a thoroughly bad boy. There's something fundamentally wrong with him."

"Oh, poor little fellow!" Mrs. Bradley sighed. "His home and heredity are great handicaps, aren't they?"

"I don't see why they should be," said Toppie. "Mrs. Brown is a patient hard-working woman and, though the father drinks, I don't think he is dishonest. Whereas Percy is a sneak and a liar. He does mean things and then is too much of a coward to confess them."

It was strange, thought Alix, listening, though not in the least interested in Percy Brown's heredity, that with a face so sweet Toppie should have so cold a voice. She would be sorry for Percy Brown, she felt sure, if she were to see him confronting Toppie.

"It's very difficult to confess when one has done a mean thing," Mrs. Bradley mused—and Alix almost had to laugh at hearing her, so impossible was it to imagine Mrs. Bradley involved in such a dilemma. "The cowardice and the meanness go together, don't they, and Percy is so young that they are not worse, really, than weakness and timidity. He may outgrow it."

"I don't think he will. I think he is fundamentally bad," said Toppie, but now with more sadness than severity, and, turning to Alix she said: "Will you come and have tea with me to-morrow? We could have a little walk first, and then you could come back to tea with me and my father."

"But she's going to school with us, Toppie! We have to teach her hockey!" cried Ruth.

"Not to-morrow. She need not begin till Monday, need you, Alix?" Alix thought not, and though Ruth declared, "You can't begin a day too soon for hockey," Alix and Toppie had decided the question between them.

CHAPTER VI

"Tell me everything; everything you remember," said Toppie. She was striding along over the heather, a grey woollen scarf tossed over her shoulder, a knitted cap drawn down closely over her ears, and she made Alix feel shy. She had seen that Toppie liked her and she had foreseen that she would question her. But as she felt the pressure of her longing she knew how little she could satisfy it.

"I think I remember him best of all as I first saw him," she said, searching her thoughts.

"Yes. As you first saw him. Tell me about it. How did you first see him? He wrote to me, often, from Cannes; so much about your mother; so much about you. He said you were the dearest little girl. I understand why he said it—if you don't mind my saying so.—But he couldn't tell me what I most wanted to know, could he? How he himself looked to you.—What he said to you.—How he seemed.—You understand, I know, though you are so young, how one longs for everything that remains on earth of anyone one loves. People's memories; they are precious. You understand that," said Toppie. And Alix felt that only by the pressure of her longing was she thus lifted above her natural reticence. The very words she used were not habitual to her; she would have been shy of using such words ordinarily.

"Yes; I understand," said Alix. "We saw him first on the great road that runs above the sea. Maman and I were going up and he was coming down, so that we saw him tall against the sky; limping a little as he came. He looked at us, and we looked at him;—it is almost as if one recognized the people who are destined to be our friends, is it not, Mademoiselle?—and when we had passed, I looked back at him and he was looking round at us. It had been a mutual impression. We talked of it afterwards. We saw him against the sky and he saw us against the sea; as if we had risen from it, like people in a fairy-tale, he told us; and Maman laughed and said that people didn't rise from the sea carrying parasols. I remember so well the expression of his eyes"—Alix felt still shyer, but she forced herself through the shyness—"gay and searching like a dog's; out-of-door eyes. He had field-glasses in his hand. And that very evening, at the Casino, a friend of Maman's brought him and introduced him to her. So it all began."

"Tall against the sky. Out-of-door eyes. Yes, I can see him.—Don't call me mademoiselle, Alix; call me Toppie.—And with his bird-glasses. He would have been watching birds. I see it all," said Toppie, her eyes before her. "And then?"

"Then he came to see us every day. It was of birds we talked on the first day that he and I and Maman went for a walk. I knew them a little; not their names; but their songs and their habits, from having been so much in the country; whereas Maman is so much the parisienne that she was very ignorant and she laughed at us and said they were all much alike; small, grey silhouettes in the leaves. And he used to say that I was like a black-cap and she like a nightingale; though we did not see those birds at Cannes."

"And then?" Toppie repeated as Alix paused.

"He was still very lame," said Alix, "so that he could not play tennis, but he used to come with us and watch Maman play; she is one of the finest players at Cannes; did he tell you? It is beautiful to watch her; she is perhaps at her best when playing tennis. And he used to write his letters in the garden of our little villa;—it was lent us, that Autumn, by friends; a charming little place; he will have told you of it. He must often have written you letters from the garden. And he and Maman sat there and read. He would read to her and she would correct his French, and she would read to him so that his ear might become accustomed to the correct accent. And sometimes it was I who read while he held, I remember, a skein of silk on his hands for Maman to wind to balls; lemon-coloured silk for a little jacket she was knitting me. She is so clever with her fingers."

"Oh, she was so good to him! I know!" Toppie exclaimed, her eyes still fixed on the distance. "I don't know what he would have done with himself if it hadn't been for her kindness. He had been so frightfully lonely there at Cannes. He found it such a dismal place until you came; perhaps because it is supposed to be so gay; and that, in war-time, must have been dreadful. No shade, I remember he said; only sun and shadows."

"Yes; I remember that he found so much sun depressing, and that seemed very strange to us, for we so love the sun. But there was real shade in our garden under the trees. The fuchsias, too, were in bloom everywhere, I remember, and I associate them so much with him; gay, delicate flowers."

"Fuchsias?" said Toppie. "But that's a soulless flower. How strange that he should have been associated with them in anyone's mind.— Fuchsias"—she seemed to be forcing herself to see them, too. "They grow so much in the Riviera, of course. But I always think of Owen with daffodils. Our woods are full of them here in Spring. Fuchsias. Yes? What else? You all laughed together? Your mother is so gay. He was happy?"

"Very happy, I think. We all laughed a great deal. Maman is not what one would call a gay person; but she can make gaiety. He teased me a great deal. I have never cared for dolls and he teased me about them. He said a girl must be made to care about dolls, and he bought dreadful little ones with small feet in painted boots and hid them in my napkin at dinner or even under my pillow, where I found them at night. I used to fling them at him—rush down to the salon where he and Maman sat, and fling them at him.—For I was already fifteen, and at that age one is not supposed to care about dolls, in any case. We had great games, it was a happy time, in spite of all the sadness. He was a happy person."

"Happy. Yes. A happy person," Toppie repeated. She turned her strange shining eyes on Alix. "He is happy now. He is here, you know. We are not parted. I feel him every day; always; near me. His happiness shines round me."

Alix was struck to dumbness. She felt afraid. Such thoughts were so alien to her that she even wondered if Toppie were quite sane.

Toppie went on. "You believe that, too, in your church, don't you?—that the dead are near us; not far away; not shut into a hard golden heaven we can't reach; but quite near and caring."

"We have purgatory. I do not understand all these doctrines. But I am not dévote," said Alix after a moment.

"Purgatory? That's only a name. That's only a symbol, like the golden heaven. And those who have died, giving their lives for us, will not have to pass through such an intermediary state.—You are too young. You have never lost anyone you loved."

"No one except my poor grandfather. I always pray for the repose of his soul. That is what we do in my church. Is it different in yours? And if they are reposing, how can they be near us?" Indeed, the thought of Grand-père as near, in his new, unimaginable state, was even more disquieting than Toppie herself.

Toppie seemed to feel that she had drawn her young companion beyond her depth. She was silent for a moment, gathering back her thoughts from their search for sympathy, and she asked, then: "Why do you say your poor grandfather? Was he unhappy?"

"I am afraid he was. Very unhappy."

"Oh, I am so sorry. You felt and shared it. I saw in your face at once, dear little Alix, that you had shared unhappiness.—You are so young; younger than your age in one way; yet in another you are so grown up; it is strange." Toppie's eyes mused on her for a moment. "Why was he unhappy?" she added gently. "Though, indeed, most people are."

"He was ruined. He had lost everything," said Alix. "Montarel, where the Mouverays have always lived, is sold now, and he knew before he died that it would be so. And he had lost everyone he loved, except me."

"Your mother is not his daughter, then?"

"No; my father was his son; his only child."

"But you and your mother were often with him?"

"Only I. He liked having me alone." Alix did not require consideration to find an answer. To Giles, in the train, frankness had been possible; but it was difficult to repeat such frankness. And Toppie, Alix felt, was so different from Giles. She would not understand Maman being divorced as he had. So she evaded her question.

They had reached the Rectory now, and she was glad not only that they had passed away from Grand-père and his causes for unhappiness, but from Captain Owen, too. She would have been sorry to have had to answer questions about the Paris days when so much of the brightness had dropped from him. Her memories of Captain Owen in Paris were all tinged with sadness; perhaps because the war was so much nearer in Paris and Captain Owen's return to it so imminent. It was as if, in seeing him there with them for his short leaves, they had seen death always beside him.

"I hope you will be here when our roses are out," said Toppie, in the Rectory garden. "Father and I are proud of our roses."

Alix counted on being back with Maman long before the time of roses, but she said that she hoped so, too, and as they passed a window she caught a glimpse of a tall, bleached man sitting at a writing-table, very erect, austere, and absorbed; like an old eighteenth-century print of d'Alembert, Diderot, or some such erudite wigged gentleman.

"Yes; it's my father," said Toppie. "You'll see him directly; at tea."

Alix stood still for a moment as they entered the drawing-room. It had everything of charm that the Bradleys' drawing-room lacked, except the charm of cheerfulness, for it was, though so serenely beautiful, perhaps a little sad. The eighteenth-century panelling was painted in dim green, and three tall windows at one side looked out at the garden while, at the other, was a beautiful fireplace. In the walls were deep niches filled with rows of old china, and sedate chairs with backs and seats embroidered in green and dove-colour were ranged along the wall.

"And look at my china roses," said Toppie, pleased, Alix saw, by her involuntary pause of pleasure. "Aren't they rather wonderful for November? Only smell how sweet." And Alix bent over the bowl filled with the little deep pink roses.

There was a sedate sofa to match the chairs, with the tea-table placed as at the Bradleys'; but how different was this tea. No thick bread-and-butter; no loaves of cake. Only a plate of little dry biscuits, that Alix liked, however, and another of bread-and-butter cut to a wafer-like thinness. And instead of the affectionate turmoil of Heathside was Toppie's sweet, chill voice and Mr. Westmacott's silence. He drank his tea, looking, with his crossed legs, which should have been in buckled knee-breeches, more than ever like d'Alembert; addressed a courteous question to Alix about her journey and her mother's health, and soon went away, back to his writing-table; but not, Alix felt, to do much of significance there. He had a tall head and a meditative eye; but there was something of the sheep in his appearance, too. If he had had the close curled wig, that went with his type he would, Alix thought, have looked very like a silent, dignified sheep that may, in the meadow, as it looks at you, emit once or twice a formal baa.

Toppie told her that her father was writing a book on the Stoics. "He has, fortunately, a great deal of time. It's a tiny parish; just right for a scholar like my father; more a scholar than a priest, I sometimes think. He is rather shy with people and his life here suits him perfectly."

"Are not Stoics the people who do not mind the things other people mind?" Alix inquired.

"They cared, perhaps, so much for some things that other things did not hurt," said Toppie, smiling. "I don't know much about them, myself, though; I'm not at all learned. I've never been to school."

"I am glad you are not learned. One may go to school and yet not be learned; as you can see from me," Alix smiled back. "But I can't imagine what those things can be that keep us from being hurt; can you?"

Toppie looked at her meditatively for a moment. "You said you were not dévote; but doesn't your religion tell you what things they are?" she asked.

"Le bon Dieu, do you mean?" Alix inquired doubtfully. "La Sainte Vierge? One's Guardian Angel?"

"Yes. When you go to church, to confession, aren't you told?"

"We are told a great deal; but I am afraid I have never paid much attention. I only go to confession once a year. Maman insists on it. I do not like it," said Alix. "Had the Stoics a bon Dieu and a Sainte Vierge to console them, then?"

"Oh, no! no!—you very ignorant child!" Toppie was perforce smiling again, though Alix saw that she was distressed. "They lived very nobly without our faith to help them.—In my church we do not have your beautiful Sainte Vierge to look to, you know."

"I know," said Alix. "And I do not understand why you should leave her out. I like her better than le bon Dieu, I must confess. But then rectors could not feel as we do about a Sainte Vierge, could they?"

"And why not?"

"Could one feel like that and be married?"

"Oh, you funny child!" Toppie was really laughing, and Alix, seeing how she amused her, laughed, too. This was so much better than talking about the dead.—"You mean a priest could not? We are quite different about that, too. But I see what you mean"—Toppie's eyes dwelt on her—"and sometimes I think that you are right. I think, perhaps"—Toppie was grave now—"that the best life could be lived if one were quite free; with no close human ties. One could live better for God, and for humanity, then. And we have nuns in our church, too, Alix."

"Oh, but it is dreadful to be a nun!" Alix exclaimed. "I had an old great-aunt who was a nun. Grand-père's sister. I was always taken to see her in her convent in Lyon. She came to a grille and blessed me through it. She was like a sad old fish in an aquarium. One felt that her flesh must be cold. It would be death to me, such a life. And you? Can you really imagine it?"

"Perhaps not an order like that, that shuts one quite away," said Toppie; "but there are nursing and teaching orders. Yes, I can imagine it. Not while I have my father; but if I were alone."

"No, no! Do not imagine it!" Alix exclaimed, and there rose before her the memory of Giles's face as he had watched Toppie yesterday evening. "Do not even imagine it. It is too dreadful. I am sorry that in your church you have nuns, too. That is foolish of you, I think, when you need not have them. It is different for priests. They have to administer the sacraments. But for a woman it is dreadful. Far, far better marry and be out in the world."

"Perhaps." Toppie was smiling sadly at her, seeing her, it was evident, as quite a child, yet touched by her feeling. "But if all question of marrying is over, the situation alters. You could not understand while you are so young.—See, Alix, I want you to look at this." She moved forward a fire-screen, a square of satin on a mahogany stand. "Are you interested in needlework? French girls do it so beautifully, I know. My mother embroidered this. She copied it from those old chairbacks. Do look at them. Her grandmother did those."

The screen, on a background of pearly satin, had two doves in a basket, entwined with laurel; and the chairs, in a softer, sadder key, repeated them.

"They are beautiful," said Alix. It seemed to her, as she looked at the gentle doves, that the dead, in Toppie's drawing-room, joined pale hands around her and whispered: "We are here." But it was so sad. The doves nestling side by side, so confident of love, made her think of all the partings of the world.

"My great-grandmother was married to a soldier," said Toppie, "and went out to India and died there when my grandfather was born. She did all those chairs while she was waiting for his birth. She was only twenty-one. I often think of her; so young; stitching her thoughts of home, her hopes for her baby—the past and the future—into the embroidery. And one feels how happy she must have been in her marriage to have chosen that design. My poor great-grandfather brought all her things back to England, with his little boy.—That funny little water-colour sketch is of him, in his frilled cap; with his ayah.—And he grew up to be a soldier, too, and was killed, out in India, fighting a frontier tribe. My mother was his only child. I was fourteen when she died. How happy you are to have your mother, Alix. She makes beautiful things, too. I shan't forget the little lemon silk jacket."

Alix's sense of sadness had deepened while Toppie spoke. So different Toppie's past; so different Toppie's mother, she felt sure: and the sense of sadness was in the difference. An abyss seemed to lie between her and Toppie, an abyss that Toppie did not see and could not, perhaps, even imagine. She could not place Toppie against any of the backgrounds familiar to her. She could not see her in Maman's salon, unless as one of those dim evasive figures, the "Misses" of her childhood, someone dressed differently, hovering diffidently and helping with the tea and cakes. She could see Toppie in Maman's salon as her governess, but in no other capacity. Toppie would not understand anything said there, or would not care to understand. She would draw away from the shining soap-bubble. She would look with cold dismay at madame Gérardin and mademoiselle Fontaine. It was sad to feel fond of someone and to feel them fond of you, and yet to see that only here, among her doves, could their worlds touch at all.

It was growing dark, and Toppie said that she would take her home, and, in the hall, lighted a little lantern for the walk across the common. They had gone halfway when they saw, in the distance, another lantern advancing towards them.

"It is Giles," said Toppie, pausing. "He has come for you. So I will go back. I have some letters to finish for the post."

"But come to meet him. He will, I am sure, be glad of a word with you," said Alix. She felt sure that it had been in the hope of a word with Toppie rather than to fetch herself that Giles had come.

"Oh, we have so many words; every day; all our lives long," said Toppie, and, though she continued to advance, Alix felt a slight constraint in her voice. "He is a dear, is he not, Giles?" she added, as if irrelevantly.

"Oh, a dear!" said Alix. "I felt him that at once. And so good; and so intelligent."—"More intelligent than Captain Owen; more good," was in her mind. But that made, she knew, no difference. People were not loved for their intelligence, or their goodness, either.

"A great dear, Giles," Toppie repeated, but with no intention, evidently, of being urged by her young companion's warmth beyond her own sense of due commendation. "Owen loved him devotedly. After his mother it was Giles he loved best of all his family."

"They were all three of the same pâte, were they not."

"Pâte?" Toppie questioned. Her French was not quite so good as Giles's.

"The paste, you know, of which earthenware or porcelain is made."

"I see. Yes. And Owen was porcelain; and Giles is earthenware; and dear Mrs. Bradley is both together." Toppie mused on the simile with satisfaction.

But it did not satisfy Alix. "Some earthenware is very rare and precious; tough and fine at once. And it wears and wears."

"But it never has the beauty," said Toppie.

Giles was now within speaking distance, and by the light of their lantern Alix saw that his eyes were fixed upon Toppie with an indefinable expression; not alarm; not inquiry; but a steady watchfulness that, to her perception, controlled these feelings.

"I was afraid you'd run away with our young guest and came out to look for you," he said. "It's six o'clock." While Alix, feeling a soft touch on her glove, looked down to see the earnest, illumined eyes of Jock.

"I didn't realize it was so late," said Toppie, and to Alix's ear the tone of her voice was altered. Toppie, for all her familiarity, would never, she felt, have talked with any of the Bradleys as she had with her this afternoon. "We've talked and talked; haven't we, Alix. I must fly!"

"Come in for a little. Mother's just back. She'd love to see you," said Giles.

"No, indeed, I can't. Give her my love. I'll drop in upon her to-morrow afternoon, after my class."

"Well, we'll go back with you, then. It's late for you to be out alone."

"For me! On the common! How absurd you are, Giles! Good-night."

"Good-night," said Giles. He showed no grievance; some shade, rather, seemed lifted from him, and in a moment, as he and she walked on together, Alix divined that his anxiety had been lest she had said anything to hurt Toppie or revived memories that cut too deep. It had not been so much to see Toppie as to watch over her that he had come.

The lantern made a soft round of light into which they advanced and the November air was pleasant. "And what have you talked and talked about?" Giles asked.

"All sorts of things," said Alix. She was glad to feel that she could give him fuller relief. "Her great-grandmother's embroideries and the Stoics and la Sainte Vierge."

"La Sainte Vierge!" said Giles, and he laughed. Yes, actually, he was speaking with her of the enshrined Toppie and she had made him laugh. "What did you have to say about la Sainte Vierge, pray?"

"Well," Alix paused. She saw that she had perhaps taken a wrong turn, but it was best to go on as though she did not think so. "It was of religion and le Paradis, you see; and whether the dead are with us here. Do you, too, think that they are, Giles?"

"The dead! With us here!—Oh. Yes, I see." Giles, after his exclamations of surprise, lapsed for a moment into silence. "She must like you very much, Alix, to talk to you about that," he said presently.

"I think she does like me. He liked me. It would always be that for Toppie, wouldn't it? And then I can give her more about him. We talked of that, too. Things she didn't know."

She felt Giles's eyes turn down towards her. He contemplated her as they walked forward. "What sort of things?"

"How we met him. How he looked. What we all did together. She loved hearing; but especially that he was happy. And it is that she feels. That he is with her now; and happy. Do you believe it, too?"

Giles walked on beside her in the darkness that was not yet quite dark, the light melted into it so softly and went so far. Alix could see Bobby racing on ahead. Jock went just before them, and Amy followed meekly, her nose at Giles's heels. It was easy to talk together in the melting darkness, and she must have given Giles a great deal to think about, for he said nothing for a long time. Then, as if he brought his thoughts back to her and her question with an effort, he said: "It doesn't follow, because we're dead, that we're happy."

"No; we are not happy in purgatory; and according to the church we must all go to purgatory, unless we have been great saints. She asked me about my religion. And we have purgatory, you see."

"I hope you didn't say anything about it that may have troubled her."

"Oh, I said nothing at all that troubled her," Alix assured him. "She did not take purgatory at all seriously."

"Do you?" Giles was smiling a little. How much relief she had given him!

"I am afraid not," Alix owned. "I am afraid I do not take heaven seriously either. But I did not tell her that. It might have grieved her. It always seems to me that we must go out like blown candles, when we are dead. I do not like to think it; but it seems so to me. Does it not to you?"

"No; it doesn't. You are a little pagan, Alix."

"A pagan! Not at all! I am a Catholic. I go to confession once a year."

Giles now laughed out. So much had she relieved him that her unspiritual state roused only mirth in him. "Doesn't your confessor give you any penances?"

"Yes. I have penances. I do them as I am told. The Chemin de la Croix—all round the church.—It is very tiring—dragging my prie dieu."

Giles went on laughing;—"Is it? By Jove! And your first communion? Weren't you prepared for that?"

"Yes. But that was five years ago. I was only a child then. I have altered my opinion of many things since then."

How much Giles found her still a child she heard in his laughter as he asked on: "But what right have you to say you aren't a pagan? What right have you to call yourself a Catholic?"

"I have been baptized," said Alix. "I have been confirmed. I go to confession, and to Mass, at least at Easter. Most certainly I am a Catholic. You might as well say I was not French because I did not believe in the Republic as to say I am not a Catholic because I don't believe in heaven. One is, or one is not. It is a question of being born so."

"I see. I see." Giles was looking down at her, so amused, yet also, she felt, touched by what she said. They entered the little door in the garden-wall. "There's something to be said for that way of looking at it," he owned. "It puts it neatly. It explains all sorts of things, in Catholicism and in France. You are a wonderful people, Alix."

CHAPTER VII

Of all her new experiences Alix most enjoyed "The Messiah."

The village choir was a feeble enough little affair, its energy concentrated in Giles's disciplined, sustaining baritone and the robust sopranos of Ruth, Rosemary, and the postmistress. The tenors were almost non-existent, and the altos, among whom Alix was placed at once, terribly weak. But the doctor's daughter, at the piano, accompanied so accurately, Mrs. Bradley, gentle and absorbed, with her wand, conducted so carefully, that it was a pleasure to sing, and the grave exultant music wove itself deeply into Alix's impressions of the new life. It made her think of Giles and of his mother, and of Toppie, too. It seemed to go with them; just as it seemed to go with the walk home by lantern-light, and even with the cheerful family supper afterwards where Giles boiled eggs over the fire, and Mrs. Bradley made cocoa on a spirit-lamp.

The High School, to which she and Ruth and Rosemary bicycled every day, was at once familiar and alien. It was like the Lycée, in shape, as it were; but not in texture. Hockey could not give it the flavour that it lacked. The girls, all of them, were too much like Ruth and Rosemary. They lived, she felt, in what they did, not in what they thought. They had a sense of fun, but no sense of irony, and with their sharp-cut edges, their hardy colour, they seemed to repel any suggestion of mystery, in life or in themselves. They accepted her at once. They seemed to like her, just as Ruth and Rosemary did. But she felt that anybody else who could hold a hockey stick and tell the truth would have done just as well.

With the Christmas holidays Jack and Francis came home from school. Heathside seethed with noise, pets and handicrafts. Giles, now demobilized, was preparing for his return to Oxford after Christmas. He went up and down to London a good deal and she had the sensation of having lost him; of being relegated by him to the family group. One day, however, he came into the dining-room while she was trying to write a letter on a corner of the table. It was only in the dining-room that a fire was lighted in the mornings, and Jack and Francis were carpentering at one end, while Ruth cut out blouses in the middle. It was difficult to try to tell Maman about "The Messiah" in such surroundings, and though she liked Jack and Francis so much she could not bring herself to like the white rat that ambled heavily about among the tools and crêpe de Chine.

"I say, that's not much of a place for letter-writing," Giles remarked. "Come to my study, Alix. I'm a favoured person and have a gas-fire going all morning."

"But she's going out with us directly, to see our ferrets!" shouted Jack and Francis. They were dear little boys; Francis brown, like Giles, and Jack fair like his sisters. Oddly, enough, with all their uproar, Alix felt them gentler, more respectful of one's identity, than Ruth and Rosemary.

"Do you want to see the ferrets, Alix?" Giles inquired. "Are you fond of ferrets?"

"I do not like what I hear of them," said Alix. "But cats, too, do dreadful things; and one loves cats."

"I'll defy anyone to love a ferret."

"We're not going to let her see the rabbiting. She says she doesn't want to, though she misses a lot. It's far kinder than traps. Bobby kills them in a minute."

"No; I do not want to see that. But will after lunch do for ferrets? I would rather finish my letters now," Alix owned. And though she was sorry to disappoint Jack and Francis, it was with a sense of escape that she followed Giles out of the dining-room.

The study was small, warm, and untidy. Under an ugly mantelpiece of carved oak was a bright little gas-fire, looking like incandescent dried apples, and on the mantelpiece were ranged pipes, family photographs, and quite a menagerie of small animal ornaments which Alix guessed to be family presents. There was a small metal bear on his hind legs holding spills in his arms, a horrible china cow, yellow with red spots and a place in her back for matches, and a foolish puppy in black velvet with a red flannel tongue and one ear that went up and one that went down. A very grubby and irrelevant statuette of Venus de Milo stood among them and Alix felt sorry for her.

"Behold my jewels!" said Giles with a grin. "Francis gave me that monster when he was three; that's from Jack and that from Rosemary. The Venus is an effort of Ruth's; brought to me from Paris. Everything you see there is either Christmas or birthdays."

"You are very faithful to your anniversaries," said Alix, smiling. "What a nice photograph of your mother."

"Isn't it?" said Giles, pleased. "You like my mother, don't you?"

"I like all your family," said Alix politely.

"Well, of course, in a way, you'd like them all," said Giles. "But I am afraid they rather wear you out. There are so many of them and they are so young and vigorous. You must take refuge here when they dash over you too much. I'll do my reading, and you can read or write or meditate, as you like. I shan't speak to you and you mustn't speak to me. I've noticed you are a kid who can keep still. We shall get on capitally."

So it was arranged, and as Alix took her place at the little writing-table he pulled forward for her, she noticed that there were many books along two sides of the room and along the other a row of large framed photographs of Greek and Sicilian temples that more than atoned for the mantelpiece. When she did not feel like reading or writing, she would look at those. They made her think, in the sense of space and tranquillity and splendour they gave her, of Montarel.

For the first mornings of her withdrawal there mingled with her sense of security an apprehension of the unsaid things that lay between her and Giles and that might still have to be said; but this grew less with every day. It became quite evident that Giles was going to say nothing. Perhaps, indeed, she had imagined something of the trouble and confusion she had felt in him at their first meeting. Perhaps in some odd, twisted way, it had all been because of Toppie; because the sight of her brought back so vividly the memory of the dead brother and of Toppie's loss. Whatever it had been, she did not think he would ever show it to her again.

She owed more than the peaceful mornings to him. He seemed to restore Maman to her. Now, at last, she could really tell Maman, with a mind composed, how surprised Mrs. Bradley had been at hearing that she wore a linen chemise next her skin and felt no need of wool; how like a dignified sheep was Toppie's father; how strange the sense of growing strength the choruses of "The Messiah" gave one, like a sort of calisthenic. And how Mrs. Bradley had taken her up to London to choose a delightful winter outfit; woollen jumpers, ribbed stockings, and a winter coat and hat. Alix told Maman all about this and about the fat, jovial old lady with short grey hair with whom they had had tea in Kensington, a friend of Mrs. Bradley's father and a public speaker. Some things, however, she did not tell her. She gave no account of Toppie's beliefs in regard to Captain Owen, and, a lesser matter, yet significant, she had never yet satisfied Maman as to the social status of her new friends.

Perhaps it was because Giles sat there, his pipe between his teeth, his feet propped up against the mantelpiece, his hand, as he perused the tome upon his knees, raised now and then to rub his hair on end, that it seemed so irrelevant to write about such things. After all what business was it of Maman's? She had had no further use for them than that they should warm and feed her child during a hard winter; what difference did their status make to her? It was true that she and Maman had always shared impressions to the last crumb of analysis, and it was with a slight sense of malice that she thus withheld from her the crumb for which she asked more than once. "Who are they? What are they, ma chérie?" Maman, from Cannes, inquired. "The train de vie you described seems that of the true confort anglais; but, apparently, there is no elegance. What are their relations? Do they go at all dans le monde? Is there a vie de château in the neighbourhood? I am interested in all you have to tell me of these excellent people." Naturally. But though Alix might not have felt it unmeet, a month ago, to tell Maman all this, she would have felt it unmeet now. How funny Giles would have thought it if he had known that she sat there informing Maman that his family did not go dans le monde at all, in the sense that Maman meant by le monde; and that they were decidedly of the bourgeoisie. It was not that Maman was wrong in wanting to know, or that Giles would have been right in thinking that le monde didn't matter. It was simply that she did not care to write in that way to Maman about him and his family.

Maman, meanwhile, was evidently enjoying many relations; dancing, dining, playing tennis, entertaining her friends. There were important names in her letters and Alix sometimes meditated a little over them. When she did not write or read, she meditated Giles's Greek temples and Maman's relations. The important names, in the world of art and letters— but that was not the world Maman meant in asking about the Bradleys— were male and female; in the world of fashion, male only. It was the marquis and the prince; but never the marquise and the princesse. Why? Alix wondered. Did Maman find the wives of fashion dull? But if one didn't know them, too, could one be said to be dans le vrai grand monde? She knew how Maman's gay, sombre eyes would meet the question (not that it was one that Alix would ever dream of putting to her): "Je suis du monde qui me plaît, ma chérie." But Alix was not quite sure that this was true. She was not sure that Maman's indifference was as securely grounded as Giles's. Perhaps real indifference only came from reading so much Plato and Aristotle. Yet she herself, who did not read Plato, was indifferent. It was only in regard to Maman that she was not indifferent, and perhaps it was true that it was only in regard to herself that Maman was not. Poor, beloved, beautiful Maman; and wronged; deeply wronged, Alix felt sure. Always, when she thought of her, her heart expanded in love and then contracted in anxiety. She saw her as a wild, lovely creature caught in a trap and only escaping maimed for life. She could not range as far and as freely as the unmaimed creatures; dimly Alix saw that, as the explanation of what was ambiguous in her position. She had lost the full liberty hers by birth and instinct. Yet, despite the limitations of her misfortune, she had every right to her own standards.

Judged by Maman's standards Alix could not conceal from herself that the Bradleys were very undistinguished. Maman would have hated the bounteous, graceless meals; Mrs. Bradley sitting at breakfast among the noise and porridge and kippers, heaped round with letters and circulars, reading an appeal for crippled babies while she poured out the tea and coffee and oftener than not slopping it into the saucer. "Oh, I'm so sorry, dear," she would exclaim; but Maman would have commented, dryly, that a woman so much occupied had better breakfast in bed and get through her correspondence out of sight. Maman could be terribly dry about disorder and gracelessness. Alix had never forgotten the terse and accurate reproofs that her own lapses in these respects had called down upon her in her childhood. As for the uproarious children, "Ces marmots-là ne sonts pas appétissants," was what Maman would have said of Ruth and Rosemary, taking their ease during the holidays and padding from sideboard to table in shabby bedroom slippers, while Jack and Francis had already got their hands dirty. Alix could not see Maman at that breakfast-table; but then there was no need to try to. She would never have come down at all to breakfast, and Alix could not really think of anything later in the day that she would have thought it worth while to come down to. A drive with Giles in the car, perhaps. She would have liked Giles. She would have liked him, perhaps, as much as she had liked Captain Owen. But as for the rest of the family, she would have found them only fit for the happy task of warming, feeding, and clothing her child. "Trop honorée," Maman might even remark, in the mood of mirthful impertinence she could display. Maman's impertinencies usually amused Alix; but she did not want to see them evoked, ever, by the Bradleys. It hurt her to think of it. Already she was too fond of them. Maman must never come to Heathside.

Christmas was now close upon them, and the house, like a mysterious boiling pot, bubbled with happy secrets. Francis came to lunch unaware of the strip of gold paper gummed to his nose; Ruth and Rosemary sat hunched in corners working surreptitiously at belated pieces of knitting. Giles went up to London with his mother for a day's shopping and came back in the evening with parcels hanging from every finger, and she and Toppie had a wonderful day there, for Mrs. Bradley had given her pocket-money to spend on presents and some had come from Maman, too, so that there was a real meaning for her in the long indecisions over crowded counters.

Alix usually went over to the Rectory to work at her presents with Toppie. She was making a tea-cloth for Mrs. Bradley and embroidering monograms, that elicited Toppie's admiration, on fine handkerchiefs for Ruth and Rosemary; and she had found the right books for the boys and a silver pencil for Giles. Toppie had a beautiful cushion for his chair at Oxford, and Toppie, too, had thought of Maman. Alix almost felt the tears rise to her eyes when she showed her the little frame of blue and silver she had embroidered enclosing a snapshot of Alix herself, standing at the edge of the wood with the dogs about her. She had not expected anyone to think of Maman. Maman, she knew, would not think of them. And then Christmas was different in France.

But Maman, all the same, remembered that it was specially kept in England. It was on Christmas Day itself, and not on the Nouvel An as Alix had expected, that the long parcel, brought over by a friend of Maman's, arrived for her from Cannes. Already she had had more presents than ever before in her life. A toilet-set from Mrs. Bradley; a writing-case from Giles; a scarf from Ruth, and a pair of stockings from Rosemary; from Jack a neat penknife, and from Francis a box of small brightly coloured handkerchiefs that were obviously what a little boy would admire. All the distributions took place at the breakfast-table, and Maman's parcel had not yet arrived when Alix unrolled from its tissue-paper Toppie's gift, and saw, in a tiny box of faded leather, the beautiful little old brooch, an emerald surrounded by pearls. It made her think at once of the doves and the laurel wreath and of Toppie's great-grandmother; of the past, brooded upon; never forgotten. She gazed at it in astonishment.

"I say!" Ruth exclaimed. They had all crowded round her to look. "She used to wear that. It belonged to some ancestress. She must be most awfully fond of you to give it to you, Alix."

Alix met Giles's eyes looking down at the brooch over their heads. She felt that she had gained in value for him from Toppie's fondness.

And it was after all this excitement that the post brought Maman's box and that the many wrappings of tissue-paper disclosed the most exquisite of evening dresses; white taffeta; crisp, supple, silvery; girdled with small white roses and their green leaves. The little card pinned to the breast said: "A ma chérie lointaine."

"I never saw anything so lovely!" said Rosemary, and Alix felt a wave of warmth for Rosemary go through her.

"It's too beautiful," said Mrs. Bradley.

"She made it herself, I am sure," said Alix. "It is wonderful how she makes these lovely things."

Giles was looking at her again. His look was different. It was as if her pride in Maman touched him as much as Toppie's brooch had done.

"It's so much too pretty for anything you do here, isn't it, dear," said Mrs. Bradley. "I think we must have a little dance when Giles comes home for the Easter holidays, so that you can wear it."

"Oh, Mummy!" cried Ruth and Rosemary. Rosemary had never yet been to a real dance.

"We'll have new dresses then, too," said Ruth. "Pink's my colour, and blue's Rosemary's."

"But can't I wear pink, too? Toppie wears blue in the evenings," Rosemary objected.

"Well, why shouldn't you both wear blue? I don't like to see sisters dressed alike. Besides, will Toppie come?" Ruth wondered.

"I believe she will, for Alix's sake," said Mrs. Bradley. "This will be Alix's dance."

"Blue will be much more becoming to you, really, Rosemary, with your golden hair," Alix assured her younger friend, who was looking a little sulky.

"And you must go and see if you can persuade Toppie to say she'll come, Alix," said Mrs. Bradley.

Alix saw how much Mrs. Bradley hoped that Toppie would consent, and Giles, his hands in his pockets, walked away to the window and looked out. "And how happy it would make Giles to see her in blue again," she thought.

They were all going for tea to the Rectory next day, but though it was stormy Alix put on her raincoat and made her way across the common that very afternoon. So familiar was that path now, so familiar the old gardener, in holiday attire to-day, touching his hat and wishing her a happy Christmas, and then Toppie's face of welcome at the door, for, seeing her from above, Toppie herself ran down to open to her.

"How sweet of you to come! There's just time to see you between services. Come in. Happy Christmas, dear child!" said Toppie.

"Oh, Toppie—the emerald! Never have I had so beautiful an ornament!" Alix exclaimed while Toppie helped her strip off the streaming coat.

"And never have I seen a little box as beautiful as yours," said Toppie, leading her into the drawing-room. Alix had made for Toppie a little satin box and had carefully copied the doves in the laurel-wreathed basket upon it. "It's too beautifully done," said Toppie. "How did you manage from memory?"

"I drew the doves one day, quickly, when you went out, and the colours are easy to carry in one's head. I am glad you like it. I am so fond of little boxes."

"So am I. I love them. I never can have too many of them."

The fire was lighted in the drawing-room, and in the soft obscurity Toppie with her high golden head looked like a tall white lighted cierge; a Christmas cierge in a votive chapel of a great cathedral; for though so sweet, so almost gay, the background to Toppie's gaiety was something dedicated and remote.

"Mine are not very exact. They are too big for the basket," said Alix, looking at the doves.

"I like them the more for that. I love the way they overflow," said Toppie. "Alix, can you guess what I have put in your box?"

They were sitting on the sofa, side by side, and Toppie's eyes, sweet, austere, were on her. "His letters from France. All the letters about you and your mother." Alix had not needed to be told. She had guessed from Toppie's look. "They just fit it," said Toppie. "As if it had been made for them." And, leaning forward, she kissed Alix lightly on the forehead. It felt a little to Alix as though the Virgin in the votive chapel had stooped down from her altar to kiss one. It was sweet; and it was also a little frightening. There was always something about Toppie that almost frightened her.

"Now, Toppie," she said presently. "I have come about something very important. I had from Maman this morning the very dress to go with your brooch; green and white; the loveliest dress. And Mrs. Bradley says they will have a dance at Easter so that I can wear it. And what we all hope is that you will be there. You will come, will you not, Toppie?"

Toppie was looking at her with her cold sweet look and it did not alter as she smiled and said: "Of course I'll come; and sit with Mrs. Bradley and look at you all."

"But you would dance, Toppie? And wear pale blue? It is your colour they say, and I have only seen you in grey. You must be very lovely in blue."

"Must I?" Toppie still smiled, and Alix had long since divined her to be invulnerable to praise. She wore her grey to-day; her Sunday grey; and her white neck and throat, unfreckled, were so fair that, imagining her in blue, Alix saw her as a birch-tree against the pale spring sky. But with the cold yet loving look she shook her head and said: "No; I won't dance."

"Oh, Toppie—No? Do you mean never?"

"Never," said Toppie.

"You can say that? When you are so young?"

"It doesn't need a promise, you know," said Toppie. "I don't have to take a pledge. Some things are for one time and some things for another. That time is past. But I'll come to the dance, of course, and love seeing you all; and grey, really, has always been my colour more than blue. I've always worn grey," said Toppie, smiling; and she went on, leaving that subject very definitely disposed of: "Tell me what you have all been doing since I saw you. Tying up parcels? Your box was so prettily tied."

"I like ribbons on étrennes. And green ribbon seems to go with Christmas and snow and fir-trees."

"Ruth and Rosemary had old knotted string round their parcels, poor dears, and brown paper," Toppie remarked. She always showed a certain kindly ruthlessness in her allusions to the Bradley sisters and Alix sometimes wondered what, if she had married their brother, their relations with their gentle but inflexible sister-in-law would have been. They admired Toppie; they feared her, a very little, for they were not of a nature to feel fear easily; but they did not love her. Already, strange though that was, they were far fonder of herself than of Toppie, and took her for granted as part of the family pack.

"It was a desperation at the end—for string! And all the shops shut," said Alix. "I bought my ribbon long ago. I had such nice presents from Ruth and Rosemary. Such patience it must take, to go down two whole stockings."

"Good girls," said Toppie. "And Giles gave you the writing-case." Her voice in speaking of Giles was so much kinder than when he was there— to be kept away. Alix always felt a little rise of indignation on Giles's account when she heard it. It was not as if Giles ever tried to draw near.

"Yes; a delightful writing-case. I keep finding new wonderful flaps and pockets in it. Everything is remembered. And a fountain pen, too. I have never had one before. It makes one's thoughts come so much more easily if one does not have to dip in the middle of them. I wrote to Maman with it this morning, when they were all at church. It is very happy for me, being there with Giles in his study."

"He told me that you were one of the very few people he could imagine having who wouldn't disturb him," said Toppie. "He said you were the most peaceful person."

"Did he? I am so glad. I like so very much being there— Toppie," she found herself saying quite suddenly, "Giles is the kindest person in the world."

Toppie looked at her. "Have you only just found that out?"

"No, I knew it the first time I saw him, I think. But he is more than that," said Alix, feeling the inadequacy of the word. "He is good. Because he understands. Some people are only good because they do not understand. You know what I mean?"

"Perfectly," Toppie nodded, grave and gentle. "You see things more clearly than most people, Alix. That is one of the reasons I am so fond of you."

"I don't see them as clearly as Giles does. Giles would see everything and never fail. It is his courage. The more there was to see, the more there was to bear, the more he would be standing there beside you." It was strange to her, as she spoke, to feel how deeply she knew all this about Giles, though she had never before formulated it to herself. And she added: "And never would he ask for anything for himself, Toppie."

Toppie considered her, arrested, it was evident; perhaps a little surprised. "Have you and Giles talked a great deal? Dear Giles. All that you say is true."

"No; we have talked very little."

Toppie continued to observe her. "You can't talk too much with him," she said after a little silence. "You can't see too much of him. He's a rock, Alix, and you can build on him."

"You, too, can build on him, Toppie," said Alix at this. Something changed in Toppie's look at that. It was withdrawal rather than reproof that Alix felt as Toppie said: "I have built on Giles for years. We have known each other for a very long time, you see, Alix."

CHAPTER VIII

It was only a few days after Christmas that a dreadful thing happened to Alix; the most dreadful thing that had ever happened to her.

They were all in the drawing-room after dinner—all except Francis and Jack who had gone to bed;—Ruth writing, Rosemary altering a blouse and Giles reading in his accustomed place. Alix sat beside Mrs. Bradley on the sofa, turned sideways while she held a skein of wool for her to wind, and she was never to forget the look of that heather-coloured wool.

"Alix," said Mrs. Bradley suddenly, "how was it that Owen didn't see you when he went to Paris on leave?—that one leave he had; in February last winter. You must have been away, I think, for he said nothing of you."

Alix sat there, holding up the wool, and, even as she faced Mrs. Bradley thus, steadying eyes and lips and hands, she was aware, though she could only see him as a blurred form, that Giles, suddenly, was watching her.

Captain Owen's leave! His one leave! He had come to Paris three times in that last winter, and the last had been in April only a fortnight before his death. And he had never told his family! Why had he not told them? Why! Why! The clamour of her thoughts seemed so to fill her ears that it was like sinking in the sea. She had the sensation of drowning, yet of keeping calm while she drowned, resourceful, even as she measured her calamity, and she heard her own voice speaking from far above her it seemed—while beneath Mrs. Bradley's eyes, beneath Giles's, her thoughts raced swiftly, swiftly;—"Yes; we should, of course, have seen him, but we were away; we were away in the country at that time."

"At Cannes, I suppose," said Mrs. Bradley. "What a pity for Owen. How lonely he must have been. He hadn't time to come home, you see; only the two days. And he knew nobody in Paris except the old professor's family, where Ruth and Rosemary stayed before the war."

"No; we were not at Cannes; we had gone to the sea in Normandy," said Alix. It was in her tradition, that an emergency should find one resourceful, yet, had she had time for the reflection, her own swiftness in resource might now have surprised herself. "Maman has a little house on the coast that we sometimes go to, but that she usually lets. We depend very much on letting it every summer. We went that time in February to put it in order for the spring. It could not be helped; tenants were coming early," said Alix.

"What a pity," Mrs. Bradley repeated sadly. "Or if only he could have managed to go to you there."

"You may be sure that we wired at once and suggested it; but the time was too short," said Alix.

Now she was able, since Mrs. Bradley said no more, to come to the surface, alive and apparently uninjured, but to her own consciousness floating like a helpless, battered object. Something dreadful had happened to her; she knew that; and to Maman; and to them all. But she could not see it clearly. Only by degrees, as Mrs. Bradley wound her last loops of wool and said, "Thank you, dear," and her hands could fold again in her lap, did it come to her that the dreadful thing was something that Captain Owen had done; and most of all to Maman.

He had been with them; staying with them; three times; the cherished friend; and he had never told his family. She sat there, very still, and tried to think why it could have been, and the picture that came to her was of Captain Owen sitting on one side of the fire in the little salon of the rue de Penthièvre; sitting as Giles now sat; looking across at Maman who, her finger in the pages of a half-closed book, returned his gaze with a strange sadness. And from this picture, lifting her eyes, she met Giles's fixed upon her and saw that Giles knew, too.

She looked back at him. All she could do was to look. To pretend not to see that he knew, to look away while she pretended, would only be to reveal more glaringly to him her sense of their mutual misfortune. Giles, too, knew that Captain Owen had been with them in Paris; he would not have looked at her like that if he had not known; with that dark and heavy look.

"Oh, I say!" groaned Rosemary, stretching herself out in her chair with a wide yawn of fatigue, "why was I such a fool as to take out this sleeve! It was well enough long, and I'll never get it in properly again."

"I told you to cut it kimono shape; you'd have had no trouble then," said Ruth. "Where's your house in Normandy, Alix? We were in Houlegate, years ago, when we were kids. I never thought of you in Normandy somehow. Only in Cannes, among the orange-trees you know, romantic child."

"It is at Vaudettes-sur-Mer," said Alix. "I like Normandy better than the Riviera."

"I never heard of Vaudettes-sur-Mer," said Ruth. "Is it pretty? Has it got a sandy beach?"

"No; it is galets, not sand; not until the tide is low; and Vaudettes is up on the cliff so that one has a long climb down to get to it. But the village is very pretty."

"Most French seaside villas are such hideous gimcrack things; worse than ours, I always think. Is your house an old one?"

"Yes; quite old; quite unspoiled. There are no modern villas yet at Vaudettes."

Giles got up.

"Are you going to bed, dear?" Mrs. Bradley asked.

"No; I'm going to read in my room."

"Do we make too much noise?"

"A little too much. Good-night everybody," said Giles.

"How tired Giles looks," said Mrs. Bradley.

"He's grinding too hard at his work," said Ruth.

Alix felt that it was not his work. Giles, too, had had a blow; and he was angry with her; darkly, heavily angry; why she could not tell. Only her heart swelled with a suffocating sense of resentment and of tears.

She did not go to the study next morning. She had thought and thought in the night, and she saw now that if Giles knew something that she knew, he also knew something she did not know. She was afraid of Giles and his knowledge; afraid of what they might have to say to each other. And she was angry with him, too, for making her afraid. Pain, dark and mysterious, pain that seemed to have come to her from his eyes, pressed upon her. And it made her think of the suffering that Grand-père's eyes had conveyed; and of Maman. What she feared was that he would speak to her of Maman.

She did not go; but Giles came to her. She was curled up in her scarf on the sofa in the cold drawing-room, and it made her think of the time that she had waited at Victoria and Giles had been so late. He was not late now; he was early; and he said at once, making no pretence about it: "Come, please, I want to talk to you."

She had felt herself angry with Giles, because of the injustice of his anger towards herself; but as she faced him in the study, the grey January morning outside the window, the gas-fire creaking in its dismal mirth in the grate, her anger went down. She felt pity for him. He, too, had not slept; he, too, had had a horrible night; and if he looked at her thus sternly it was, she saw, more because he was suffering than because he was angry. He stood before her, his hands thrust deeply in his pockets, and what he said was: "Look here, Alix, were you lying last night?"

Astonishment almost bereft her of breath. Lying? Could he have thought it possible that she was not lying? Could he have thought it possible—turning it over and over in his mind during the night—that she did not know about Captain Owen's leaves? It flashed across her that, if she could find another lie, now, for him, and say that she had not been lying, he might believe her. He would have no knowledge with which to contradict that lie. But, while she looked at him, feeling her face getting whiter and whiter, what strangely came to her was that she could not lie to Giles. It was better to share whatever pain there was to be shared with him than to be shut out, with her lie, in loneliness, if in safety. So, keeping her eyes on him, in a steady voice she said: "Yes. I was lying."

Giles at this contemplated her for a long time and it seemed to be with deep thoughtfulness rather than with any other feeling.

"Why?" he said at last.

"How could I not?" asked Alix.

"How could you not?—You can invent such a story, in every detail, and then come and ask me how not? What in Heaven's name do you mean?" said Giles. "Have you no sense of truth?"

"Your mother did not know. Captain Owen never told your mother." Alix's voice was trembling, for she heard the emotion in his. "Would you have had me say to her, after he had kept silence, that he had been with us three times in Paris?"

Giles's expression altered. "Three times?"

"Yes. Three. Not the once she thought. That time in February was the first. He came twice afterwards. You did not know?"

"No," said Giles, "I didn't know that. I thought it was only the once."

He stopped. He stopped for a long time after saying this and suddenly she saw the blood mounting to his face. He became, slowly, crimson. He did not know what to say. Oh, poor Giles, what was this horrible perplexity that so darkened his good face when all that he had to tell her, when it finally came, was so simple? "I wasn't in the same part of the front as he was. I didn't follow what he did. It was by chance that I saw him in Paris, that time in February. I had a leave, too. And I saw him there, walking in the Bois with your mother."

Giles had seen Maman! Alix felt herself grow dim with perplexity. She looked about her and sank down on a chair before her little writing-table. "Did you not speak to them?"

"No, I didn't speak to them." Giles stood there, in his helplessness, before her. "I thought they wanted to be alone."

"But Maman would so have wished to know you. I do not see why you did not speak. Yes. I remember that they went to the Bois. He was with us all the time, you see. He stayed with us," said Alix.

Poor Giles. How overwhelming was his plight! Could shame for his brother's inexplicable duplicity, shame for his own strange silence, that day in the Bois, account for such confusion? "Yes. I was afraid you were lying," was all he found to mutter.

"But you knew. You knew, and yet you kept it from your mother. It was for her sake that you kept it from her. It was for her sake I lied. What else could I do?" said Alix.

"Do you often lie like that? I mean—the house on the cliff;—the galet beach; the wire you sent him to come to you in Normandy;—were they all invented?" Giles ignored the question of his complicity.

"Some were invented and some not." Alix tried to steady her thoughts so that she might satisfy Giles as to this point—so irrelevant a point it seemed to her. "I do not think I could have invented it all so quickly. We have the little house at Vaudettes. We often go there. But of course we were not there then. I do not think I often lie. Only when it is necessary; like this."

Giles's eyes studied her. "And if you had spoken the truth last night— the whole truth—as you know it—what would you have said?"

"But what I have said to you, Giles. That he was with us three times. That all his leaves were with us;—the last a fortnight before he was killed. Was it not better that I should lie to her than that she should know her son had been disloyal to her—as well as to my mother?"

Giles, while she spoke, had put up his hand to rub in perplexity through his hair; now it paused. "To your mother?"

"Was it not a great wrong he did her, too?"

"How do you mean?" Giles's voice was short and sharp.

It came over her with a wave of old bitterness that this was an aspect of the question he had too much ignored. "Does my mother's dignity not count? It was as if he had something to hide in their friendship; as if he were ashamed. That was to do her a great wrong. He owed Maman so much. She had been home to him."

The memory of all that he owed Maman, the lonely young soldier; fireside talks; happy walks; plays, pictures, people; the lavishing of all she had to give;—the best, was it not, that life had to show?—struck too deeply at her, and suddenly she felt her eyes fill with tears. For Giles, too, made part of the wrong to Maman. His silence had had its complicity. It was as if he, too, tacitly, had helped Captain Owen to hide something of which he, too, was ashamed.

"I know, I know," Giles muttered. He saw her tears and he was dreadfully troubled. "Of course she was most awfully good to him.—I mean—I can't imagine why he said nothing—I can't imagine why."

But wasn't he lying now? He who had not spoken to his brother and to Maman in the Bois? The sharp tangle of her thoughts hurt her. She leaned her elbows on the table and her forehead on her hands. "I don't understand," she said, keeping herself from crying.

"Poor little kid! Poor little kid!" broke as if irresistibly from Giles. He was almost crying, too. He walked up and down behind her. She felt that he would have liked to kiss and comfort her as if she had been Ruth or Rosemary. But, turning away at last, he dropped into his chair before the fire and for a long time they were both silent.

"Look here, Alix," he said suddenly at last. He had, it was evident, been thinking things out to quite new conclusions. "I wasn't quite straight with you just now, and I want to be straight with you. I want you to be straight with me. Will you promise me to? Will you promise not to lie to me, ever?"

"Ever? How can I tell?" said Alix from between her hands. "It is sometimes necessary; if someone one loves is concerned."

"Well," Giles reflected on her proviso and, apparently, accepted it, "I can know you'll want to tell me the truth, can't I?"

"Yes. Oh, yes, Giles."

"Good. I believe you'll come to see it's always better. Even in a hateful puzzle like this, perhaps. Well, then, I'll begin. I wasn't straight just now. I can imagine why Owen didn't tell us about those Paris leaves. And I think it best you should be able to imagine it, too. It was because of Toppie."

"Toppie?" Alix echoed faintly.

Giles's back was turned to her as he sat before the fire. She could not see his face as he went on: "Yes, Toppie. They were engaged. They loved each other. You've seen what Toppie feels about him now. He is her past and he is her present; and her future, too. There's nobody in the world for her but him. Well. That's it. Can you imagine Toppie, while he was away in France, seeing as much of another man as Owen saw of your mother?"

Alix sat staring at the back of Giles's head. "She was not alone; in a strange country. Why should he not find a little peace and happiness with a friend?"

"Yes, I know. That seems all right. But why didn't he come home and see Toppie? He could have managed to get one leave for England, instead of three for Paris; almost certainly, if he'd wanted to. And put all that aside. The worst thing of all, the thing that would shatter Toppie's life if she could know it, is that he kept quiet about the last two leaves, and never wrote to any of us that he'd been with you and your mother for the first. What would Toppie feel if she could know that? I ask you."

"You mean," said Alix, pressing her forehead on her hands and staring, now, down at the table, "that he cared most for Maman?"

"Doesn't it look like it?"

She tried to think. "He would have come back to Toppie after the war. It was perhaps because of the war. He did not know, those times he came to us, that it was the end." The new, strange shapes of things Giles had set before her were mingling irrefutably with all her memories, and the memory of last night returned to her. Captain Owen and Maman on either side of the fire. Captain Owen's dwelling eyes. How much he had cared for Maman! Oh, how much! And, trying to answer her own thoughts, she went on: "Maman did not care most for him. I do not think so. She cared very much. His death was a great blow. But so many people care for Maman. He could have come back to Toppie; Maman would not have kept him."

When she had said this, it was as if the silence between her and Giles was altered in its quality. He said nothing for so long a time that the echoes of her own words began to sing in her head like brazen bells. They were true words. Yet they did not ring true. Long before Giles spoke, she wished she had not said them.

"And you think," he said, "that Toppie would have cared to marry a man who hadn't been kept from marrying her?" How dreadful was Giles's voice. Dark and heavy, as his eyes had been last night.

"No; no, Giles. I do not mean that. I am sorry. Not that. It was of Maman I was thinking. You think of Toppie and I think of Maman; the ones we love most. No; I see that she would not have married him."

"You do see, Alix. That's all I wanted. You see why he didn't tell us. And that's all we need say about it. He was my brother, and I was awfully fond of him. But he was very wrong. He did a great wrong. And you have lied for our sakes, and we've profited by it; if it is profit. All I pray is that you'll never feel you have to lie, for anyone's sake, again. There. That's over. We'll get to work. Have you everything you want?" Giles got up and took his pipe from the mantelpiece and his tobacco-pouch from his pocket. "And don't let me ever see you afraid to come in here in the morning. It made me feel quite queer to find you crouched away in the cold as if I'd been an ogre."

"I thought you were angry with me, Giles; and I thought I was angry with you. It makes me angry, always, at once, if I think people are displeased with me unfairly. I am like that."

"Jolly well it may have made you angry. Of course I was fairly sick about your lying; and the house on the cliff; and the wire to Owen; on the top of everything else."

"And even the house might have been a lie, you know," said Alix, looking up at him. "If it had needed to be invented, and if I could have invented it in time."

"I'm afraid it could. Yes; that's what I thought. And it made me feel sick. But you've promised me about lies, haven't you; and you must promise me, besides, that if you're ever angry you'll come and tell me so. To work, then," said Giles, and he dropped into his chair and took up Bergson.

Alix did not take up her pen. She sat above her paper, but she knew that the last thing she could think of doing that morning was to write to Maman. She might be able to read the book about birds, by Hudson, that Giles had given her, and she drew it towards her and opened it; but soon found she could not read. Her heart seemed to be trembling and her blood trembling. All her mind was shaken; and the picture that flashed, disappeared, and flashed again, was always that memory of Captain Owen's eyes as he gazed across at Maman from his place before the fire. It was not Maman's fault. How could she have averted, how could she have avoided such a devotion? A sense of intolerable grief broke down her silence.

"Giles," she said suddenly.

"What?" He put down his book at once. He, too, was not really reading. Perhaps his heart was trembling, too.

"May I say one thing more?"

"All right."

"It is Maman, Giles. It is what you think of her. Perhaps I am always angry with you, because of what you think of her. Let me say it now, then. He cared for her most. But if you knew her you would understand; you would not blame her; perhaps you would not blame him so much."

Giles had turned in his chair and was looking at her over his shoulder, in deep astonishment. "I've never said a word against your mother, Alix," he said in a low voice.

"It is worse than words, Giles. I am not so stupid. You put her out. You will not look at her. But if you could see her you would understand. Maman never asks for anything. Why should she? She only gives."

"I have seen her, you know," said Giles. In sudden, intense uneasiness, distress, even, he got up and walked away to the window and stood there, his back to her, looking out.

"Did that explain nothing?" said Alix.

"She is very beautiful," said Giles. "I never saw anyone so beautiful."

"Oh, more, much more than that. How could he help caring for her? How can one govern one's love for people? I do not mean that he was right. But he had always known Toppie, had he not? While Maman was something quite strange to him. And one thinks most, perhaps, of what is strange. Oh, I do not forget Toppie. But it would not have been to keep him true to Toppie, if she had sent him away."

"She is very beautiful," Giles repeated, almost dully; as if that were all he could find to say.

"Oh, Giles, if you could only know her!" said Alix. It was possible to speak like this to him now. And his back was turned to her and that made it easier. She leaned her forehead on her hands and looked down at the table while she went on: "Let me tell you what Maman makes me think of always. A mountain torrent. We have them in the mountains near Montarel. So swift, and dark, and clear, with such deep pools among the rocks; and such great leaps. Oh, more than beautiful! I saw an eagle once when I was kneeling by a pool. As I looked down into the water, it was as if I looked down into the sky and there was an eagle, wheeling in the blue—far, far below me. It gave me the strangest feeling; like Maman sometimes. And her lovely, small things; like the little pinks and campanulas that grow along the banks; so sweet and tiny; and little mésanges with bright blue heads, hanging upside down in the birches. There is no one like her. Everyone else is still and dull beside her. Who could help loving her? Toppie would love her, I am sure. You would love her, too, Giles, if you knew her."

He had turned, while she spoke, and was looking at her and, lifting her head, she met his eyes and saw how deeply she had touched him. Deeply touched, deeply troubled, Giles looked across at her; but she saw that he was thinking of her and not of Maman. It was as if he were so sorry for her, and so fond of her, that he hardly knew what to say. And what he did say at last was: "You are rather like a mountain torrent yourself; eagles and campanulas and all!"

"I? Oh, no." She was glad that Giles should think that of her, but it was of Maman she wanted him to think. "I am one of the still ones; one of the dull ones, beside Maman. And I never have great shattering leaps." She looked away from Giles as she saw further into her simile, saw things she wanted him—oh! so wanted him—to see and understand. "Let me tell you, Giles. When one loves her, that is what one fears for her—those great leaps down from the rocks. So splendid; so bright and splendid; but so dangerous. There is danger for her always. When one loves her, that is what one fears."

He said nothing. He stood there, leaning back against the window. Never in her life had she so spoken to anybody. For no one but this young Englishman, so lately a stranger, could she have found such words. They rose up from her heart unbidden, and the impulse beneath them was the deepest impulse of her life. More than the child's love for its mother. There was in it a maternal love, watchful and succouring, for a creature cherished and in peril.

She had not looked back at Giles, and he came presently to her table and stood above her, moving the objects upon it here and there, as if he could not find the words to use. And at last he said: "You are right to love your mother. Never think I don't understand that."

"Perhaps we both love in the same way, Giles," said Alix, still not looking at him. "You think of Toppie—and I think of Maman—perhaps in the same way."

Giles stood very still. Then he said gently: "Perhaps we do. I feel Toppie in danger; in dreadful danger of being hurt; if that's what you mean."

"Yes, that is what I mean. And I can help you with Toppie. I can help you to keep the things that would hurt her from her. And perhaps, some day, if the time came, you would help me with Maman."

Giles had ceased to move the inkstand and candle-sticks. He put his hands in his pockets. "What do you think of as her danger, Alix?" he brought out.

Alix had to think; it was not a new wonder; but she seemed to feel it newly, now that Giles was there to help her with it. "Perhaps you see it, Giles," she suggested. "Is it something in her nature? Is it because she left my father? Perhaps you see the danger I can only fear. You give me that feeling sometimes. I am so much younger than you. There are things I do not understand."

"Yes. I see. Yes." Giles stood there. "You trust me with it all, then."

"I trust you with everything, Giles."

"You help me, and I'll help you if ever I get the chance. I'll not forget, Alix." He put out his hand as he said these words and Alix felt that their clasp was on a pact. Yet, as he turned from her and went back to his chair, she had still the feeling that it was of her, not of Maman, that he was thinking. It was as if he saw her in danger.

CHAPTER IX

It was evident to Alix, thinking and thinking of it in the day and night that followed her talk with Giles, that the best way of helping him was not to be there at all. The greater the distance between her and Maman's life and Toppie's life, the safer would Toppie be. She should never, oh, never, have come at all, and Maman would never have let her could she have known that Captain Owen had kept that inculpating silence. But she could not tell Maman of that now. If Toppie must not be hurt, neither must Maman. It would hurt her, terribly, even if she, like Giles, saw at once the reason for it. But she wrote to Maman the next morning, sitting there behind Giles, and begged that she might come home.

She had been long enough in England, she said. It was not that she was unhappy; they were all too kind for that. But it was not her life. She was a sea-fish—Alix found the simile, feeling that it would be helpful with Maman—and they were river-fishes, and she was not comfortable in their water. Je vous supplie, Maman chérie, laissez-moi revenir.

Eight days passed before Maman's answer arrived. It was decisive. She could not think of having Alix back till Spring. It was everything to her to know that her darling was benefiting by all the advantages of Heathside. Even had there not been the wretched question of money, she would have chosen to have her there and Alix must not fret; how far less trying it was for her to be at Heathside with such good friends than if, like so many jeunes filles de son âge, she had been in a convent. As for herself, she was starting in a few days with friends for a little trip to Italy and would not be back in Paris till April or May. Maman was evidently preoccupied, yet determined. There was nothing for it but to submit.

A few days after this, Alix and Giles and Mrs. Bradley motored to Oxford. She did not enjoy the drive. It was sad to be losing Giles. She did not know how she would find Heathside without him. The cold, grey day matched her mood, and as they entered the mean, modern streets of Oxford, at dusk, she thought that she had never seen so triste a town and wondered that it could harbour beauty and antiquity.

Giles's rooms, however, were amusing. They belonged to another world. One went through old courtyards where the stone was peeling in great flakes from the walls, up narrow stone staircases, winding and winding, with names on the doors one passed, and found oneself at last, high up, overlooking a quadrangle of green, in a solid, pleasant room which might have been waiting for Giles during the years of his absence, so expressive of his personality were the blazing fire, the deep chairs, even the blue-and-white tea-cups that waited on the central table.

The books and pictures were to go up next day; but even so the room was cheerful, and a wise, middle-aged man, whom Alix at first, in some bewilderment, took to be a professor lending himself to friendly offices, perhaps in some English ritual of self-effacement, brought in an excellent tea.

"He's what we call a scout," Giles, smiling, explained to her.

"Not a Boy Scout!" Alix exclaimed. It was very confusing, and Giles had to explain it further.

She and Mrs. Bradley slept that night at lodgings in the town and Alix made her first acquaintance with the English lodging-house bed. There was no sommier and the mattress seemed to be filled with potatoes. One wound oneself among the lumps and contrived at last to sleep.

They helped Giles with his books and pictures next morning, and in the afternoon he said he must show her Oxford while his mother shopped. It was raining. Giles had on a raincoat turned up about his ears, and so had she. She had never seen so many bicycles, and from under a dripping umbrella, after one had dodged them, she found the Gothic quadrangles and deep emerald gardens, the meditative swans gliding, at Worcester, on the water, and the mist-washed vistas of the High, all triste. She was depressed at the thought of leaving Giles behind in such a damp, crumbling place where it was, indeed, natural to think of philosophers drinking hemlock, and where only in the refuge of one's own room with the wise scout to take care of one, might one find a sense of warmth and cheerfulness.

"You can't very well imagine how jolly all this is on a fine day," said Giles: "when the sun comes out, you know, and the distances are blue, and the stone golden, and the gardens full of flowers."

He was sad, too, Alix felt, though he tried to speak cheerfully and the day was unbecoming to him as to everything else. He looked a gaunt, uncouth student, his nose projecting under his cap and his eyes making Alix think, in their meditative melancholy, of the swans. He would, of course, be missing Toppie.

"All the women wear velour hats of the same shape," she observed as they made their way along the High. "All turn up behind and down in front. Now I would turn mine down behind and up in front—with a very slight curve to the side; the line is better. And for costumes tailleurs it is so needful that the skirt should hang evenly."

"Is it?" said Giles with a gloomy grin. "I'm showing you the architecture, not the clothes of Oxford."

"Are they all the wives of philosophers?" Alix inquired, and the question indubitably interested her more than the architecture.

"A good many of them are, no doubt," laughed Giles. "Do you wonder if my wife will look like that?"

Alix had a sudden vision of Toppie in the rainy High Street. Yes, even dear Toppie would sink, she felt, into the fatal sameness, embody the type. She could see her, slender, in her wet grey tweed, speeding on a bicycle in just such a velour hat. They, too, were perhaps Toppies if one could have a careful look at them.

"Do you intend to live in Oxford, Giles?" she inquired.

"I'd like to.—Here is Magdalen and the tower. Let's cross the bridge so that you can see the tower.—It's where I want to live."

They crossed the bridge and he told her about the tower and the May morning ceremony.

"It must be very charming, very gay," said Alix. "And would you care to marry soon?" The question, she knew, was academic, merely. There could be no hope of marriage for Giles as long as Toppie thought only of Captain Owen. But they could both pretend.

"I couldn't marry soon." Giles was still laughing, though evidently a little disconcerted by her lack of appreciation. "I've no money." He led her off to Christ Church meadows.

"None at all, Giles?"

"Well, only enough to have a very dowdy wife. To buy her a better hat and a smarter costume tailleur I'd need a great deal more."

"But Captain Owen was to marry." Alix ventured it. It was all so remote.

Giles felt it so. He elucidated the financial differences of the family. "We've all got a little. He went into the city, into stock-broking, and was making a very good thing of it. He could very well afford to marry."

"And do you not care for stock-broking?"

"No; I care for philosophy. Unlucky for my wife, isn't it, Alix?"

"I do not know. Perhaps not if she had taste. One can do so much with very little money if one has taste. But would they know—the others—if she had to live in Oxford, that her hats and dresses were different?"

"Oh—I expect women always know that—even the wives of philosophers!" laughed Giles.

In spite of her æsthetic deficiencies, she felt that she kept up his spirits.

For tea they went to a professor friend—a real professor this time—who had known Mrs. Bradley's father. Everybody seemed to have known Mrs. Bradley's father. He lived in the Banbury Road with two unmarried daughters, and was old but robust and bearded and jovial, and he kept a hand on Giles's shoulder for a long time and promised Mrs. Bradley good things of him.

Giles stood and smiled and promised nothing. She had an impression of his strength and self-knowledge.

Monsieur le professeur's daughters were middle-aged ladies with lean red faces and grey hair strained tightly back above their ears and clothes of which all that could be said was that they were warm and clean. So tall, so spare they were, the pair of them, so rigid and with such ingenuous eyes, that they made Alix think of the elongated figures on the western portals of Chartres; only the Misses Cockburn were not beautiful in their strangeness and had none of the exquisite chinoiserie of aspect upon which Maman and monsieur Villanelle had discoursed on that summer afternoon when they had visited the great cathedral. How it all rushed over her as she sat at the little table Miss Jennifer had placed for her near the window! She saw them all three, Maman in white under her white sunshade, in the hot French sunlight before the sublime object. Up into the blue it went, august, almost terrifying, so beautiful that it made one want to cry. And as they had wandered in and out, into the vast, illuminated darkness where the rose windows hung like apparitions, out into the fretted portals with the sunlight washing up their steps, Maman had told her of a Queen Alix who had borne a part in its history. Her heart contracted as she remembered it all. Maman might have been one of those queens. She so belonged to Chartres. When Chartres was in one's blood, what could one feel for Oxford?

She had time for these comparisons. The Misses Cockburn were kind, but they paid no attention to her beyond carefully feeding her; as if, she reflected, she had been a pet dog led in by Mrs. Bradley. People in England, she had already surmised, did not feel an obligation to entertain, further than by feeding, other people's friends.

She sat and ate her scone and drank her tea and looked out at a laburnum-tree and a hawthorn-tree, all leafless and dripping on the background of ornamental red brick opposite. All the houses were of red brick and all so singularly alike in spite of their adventurous excrescences. "Plus ça change, plus c'est la même chose," thought Alix, as she watched the tea-time lights come out in the bow-windows with Gothic points over them, and felt that they held learned, innocent people who would not be disconcerted by anything that happened in the universe. She had never seen a place that seemed to her quite so safe as the Banbury Road. And yet such safety made part of the tristesse. Dieu! how triste it was! How dreadful it would be to be caught and imprisoned there.

Miss Grace came to draw the curtain and asked Alix if she were warm and Alix said she was. Giles seemed quite at home, seemed, indeed, part of it, lifting the scones from the little brass stand before the fire, talking about municipal elections to Miss Jennifer and about the Bach Choir to Miss Grace. With Giles as the link of identity between them, she saw that Heathside was part of the Banbury Road, too. Even Giles seemed far away as the sense of alienation grew within her.

Then as she sat there, alone, apart, the throb of a big motor came up to the gate, and a moment afterwards a lady was among them who, by her presence, dispelled the sense of loneliness. It might have been into Maman's salon that she came, so vivid was Alix's sense of knowing what she would do and say and of liking both beforehand. All furs and pearls and softness, and such sweet smiles, she was one of the people who could see and blow and catch the soap-bubbles, the beautiful, impalpable things of human intercourse, and while she talked to monsieur le professeur, she cast mild, bright glances at Giles, at Mrs. Bradley, at herself. Alix saw that it was at herself that she looked most, and presently, when the lady and Mrs. Bradley talked, Mrs. Bradley called her to them, and holding her hand, scanning her face, the lady said she knew her name. "It's there behind me; where I don't quite know;—in an old letter; a volume of mémoires; an ancestor of mine, I feel it must have been, who knew a Mouveray in Paris before the Revolution. Yes, that was it. It comes back to me. A comte Henri de Mouveray."

Alix remembered, too. "He was guillotined at Lyon. He was a great-uncle of Grand-père's."

"And where is Grand-père?" asked Lady Mary Hamble, for such was her name. "Do you live with him?"

Alix told her that she had lived with him; but that he was dead. "I live with my mother in Paris," she said.

When Lady Mary was gone, Alix felt herself scanned by Miss Grace and Miss Jennifer as if from a spaniel she had altered to a monkey; not more interesting, but more curious. Monsieur le professeur still didn't see her at all. He brushed aside Lady Mary and went on talking about Relativity to Giles.

"Yes; was it not strange?" said Alix, as, in Giles's rooms again, Mrs. Bradley commented on the romantic encounter. "There was his portrait at Montarel, that Henri de Mouveray. So grave yet so gay a face, blue-eyed, and with dark hair."

"Like you, Alix," said Mrs. Bradley, and Alix remembered that he was like her; very.

"And to think that someone so near you was guillotined at Lyon," Mrs. Bradley mused. "He could have known your grandfather."

"Yes. If he had not been guillotined, if he had lived long enough, he could have."

"Don't you think Lady Mary very lovely, Giles?" said Mrs. Bradley. "She must be as old as I am, I suppose; yet how lovely."

"She's not nearly as lovely as you are," said Giles, poking the fire.

Mrs. Bradley laughed at the absurdity. "That's loyal—but not accurate, my dear."

"She's very pretty, and she's never had a doubt. She's always felt that she was lovely and that everyone thought her lovely, and I suppose that preserves the complexion," said Giles.

"But if everyone thinks one so, is it not likely that one is lovely?" Alix inquired. "And if one is so, why should one not think so oneself?" She considered that Giles was captious.

"No one is as right in every way as she thinks herself," said Giles. "No one can be so smooth without being artificial. She's awfully nice, I'm sure; but for beauty, give me Mummy."

It would not be polite to contradict him, but Alix, too, thought Giles absurd.

CHAPTER X

She and Mrs. Bradley motored home together next day. It had stopped raining and the air had the unexpected softness that mid-winter in England can mitigatingly display. Alix had never yet seen so much of Mrs. Bradley as on this drive. She was the most occupied person; she was always immersed in occupations; and to have her beside one, with nothing to occupy her except driving the car, was to see her with a new completeness. Mrs. Bradley was only not intimate because absorbed in affairs remote from her own interests. She was not even intimate with her own children, for Alix could not remember ever having heard her talk with them about herself. She tenderly took them for granted and took for granted—too much, Alix considered—their capacity for directing their own lives once the main lines were laid out for them. But to-day, with its sense of interlude, no papers to read, no committees to attend, it was as if without becoming intimate she became confiding. It touched Alix to hear her. It touched her because she felt that Mrs. Bradley must so often need to confide and would not know it. She talked to her about Giles. "I know he'll do well. I know he will be useful. Giles will always pull his weight wherever he is," she said, and the conception of life as a boat where one's meaning consisted in pulling one's weight was a very new one to Alix. When his mother so spoke, she saw Giles sitting, half stripped, in the chilly English air, grey water beneath, grey sky above, bent to the oars among comrades and ready for the word of command. That was what his mother desired for him; that strenuous, rigorous life. Maman did not think of life like that. She wanted no rigours for her child. She didn't care a bit about her being useful. Other people were to be of use to her and she was to enjoy herself. That was Maman's idea.

"You've seen, I'm sure," said Mrs. Bradley, her gentle eyes fixed before her as she drove, "how fond he is of Toppie. It's always been so. He's never thought of anybody else. Even before she and Owen fell in love with each other. I've sometimes wondered—I've sometimes wished—" Mrs. Bradley's voice dropped to a musing uncertainty.

"Giles was much younger than Captain Owen, was he not?" said Alix.

"Not so much younger. He is a year older than Toppie. Twenty-five. But it wasn't that. She would, I'm afraid, never have thought of him, with Owen there. Perhaps she had always been too sure of him and taken him too much for granted, while with Owen, until he did, at last, fall in love with her, she was never sure. He was fond of several people, you see, before he was fond of Toppie. I'm afraid she suffered, poor darling. And that's what one feels," Mrs. Bradley mused on, while Alix knew a growing discomfort in hearing her. "Owen could have been happy with so many girls; it wasn't, with him, the one great thing only; whereas with Giles it was."

"And perhaps if she had married him," said Alix, her thoughts held by that sense of something painful, twisted, difficult to see plainly, "she would have suffered even more. If he continued to be fond of other people."

"Oh, but that couldn't have been after they were married!" Mrs. Bradley exclaimed, and with a shock of surprise in her voice, while her eyes, almost scared by the suggestion, turned to scan the meditative face of the little French girl beside her. "That couldn't have been after he loved her at last; after they were engaged. Oh, no; Owen would have been faithful, always."

"But all men are not faithful, are they?" Alix commented, keeping her eyes before her and her voice quiet and impersonal. She felt that she would like to know what Mrs. Bradley thought on this subject. Had not Giles's horror been somewhat misplaced? "So many wives, I mean, from what one hears, have unfaithful husbands."

Mrs. Bradley continued to scan her and with even more alarm.

"But I hope you don't hear of such dreadful things, dear child. No good husband is unfaithful."

"Is it so very dreadful? Can one govern one's heart? I see that it is different for a wife," said Alix. "She is at home and has the children. But a man—out in the world—May he not form many attachments without so much blame?—I do not understand these things, but I cannot see why it is so dreadful."

"You are too young, dear, to understand them. Yet even you, I am sure, can imagine how terrible it would be to know that your husband, whom you loved and trusted, loved other people."

"It might be very sad." Alix considered the remote contingency. "I see that it might make me sad—if I loved him very much. But I should have the children, the foyer. And then he might still love me most, while loving others, too. Do you not find that possible, here in England? In France, I am sure, we do not feel it so strange a thought."

"We feel it strange; very strange and dreadful," said Mrs. Bradley with as much vehemence as she ever displayed on any subject. "And you will, too, I am sure, darling, when you are older and understand what it means to trust someone with your life.—No, no; such a thing would have been impossible with Owen and Toppie. All that I meant was that his love was different in quality from Giles's. Giles's nature, in some ways, is deeper than dear Owen's was."

"Oh, yes. Deeper. One feels that at once," Alix murmured, while the thought, seen at last clearly, pierced her through that Giles was held from his happiness by an illusion since Toppie might not have cared for Captain Owen had she known how much he cared for Maman. "Perhaps in time she will come to see what Giles is and love him. Do you not think so?"

"It's what I hope for more than anything, Alix," said Mrs. Bradley. "Giles has had such a sad life. You wouldn't think it, perhaps. He doesn't show it, unless one knows him very well. Even as a little boy I always felt him rather frustrated and sad. He adored Owen, who didn't pay much attention to him; and he adored Toppie who never gave him a hope. And then the war came and ended his youth and he saw worse things than Owen saw. He saw the worst things. His best friends were killed beside him. He went through everything. They all had to face the problem of it, the boys like Giles. It was never such a problem to men like Owen. They accepted it and didn't try to understand. Giles hasn't been embittered, as some of our young men have; but there is such a weight of grief on his heart. I feel it always. I so long for some happiness to come to him."

It was all true. Alix had seen it in Giles's face. Under his vehemence, his gaiety, he carried dark memories in his heart; and there were darknesses his mother did not know of. Perhaps it helped him to be less lonely that she should know of them and that they should be her darknesses, too. It gave Alix courage to bear the weight of perplexity and fear, during the winter, to feel that she shared the weight with Giles. She missed him so much at Heathside; yet he was there, too, in her sense that she was helping him with Toppie, that she, too, was shielding Toppie from hurt.

He wrote to her, and though he did not ask her for news of Toppie, she knew that was what he wanted and gave him every detail when she answered. Toppie went away to Bath at the end of February, but until then Alix sent Giles her bulletins. She and Toppie often walked together; they read together, too; and she often made Toppie laugh with her stories about the people at Montarel, the funny things they did and said. Giles was told of all this, and about the Greater Spotted Woodpecker that she and Toppie saw in the birch-woods, tapping with stealthy fierceness at a tree-trunk, beautiful in his Chinese white and black and vermilion; and about Jock who always came with them on their walks and had really adopted her as his most authentic mistress. She had not much to say about the High School and Ruth and Rosemary. But then it was Toppie Giles wanted to hear of.

Spring came at last, the early flowers, the returning birds, Toppie back from Bath and the Easter holidays hovering on a near horizon. And one day at tea-time Mrs. Bradley handed her a letter she had just received from Lady Mary Hamble, a letter in its unexpectedness and sweetness that was like the Spring. Could Mrs. Bradley lend Alix to them for a week-end, Lady Mary asked. There were to be young people in the house and a little dance and they would all enjoy having her.

At first, in her pleasure, strangely compounded of a sense of relief, escape, and the soft breath of a familiar balm wafted towards her, Alix did not notice the dates. Then, after Mrs. Bradley had said, "How delightful; of course you must go, dear," she saw that the Monday of Lady Mary's dance was the Monday of Mrs. Bradley's; the dance to which Toppie had promised to come; the dance for which Giles would be back; the dance to show her white taffeta dress; her dance; the invitations all out and all accepted. "But our dance is on that Monday," she said.

"It can't be helped," said Mrs. Bradley. "We'll have to give another smaller one some day later on. I don't think you ought to miss the much prettier dance at Lady Mary's. You have us always, you see, dear."

"But Giles."

"Giles doesn't really count at a dance," smiled Mrs. Bradley. "And he will be at home all the holidays. You won't be missing Giles."

Toppie was with them, and she smiled, too, looking at Alix and said: "You're right not to go. Giles will be coming home that very Saturday. You couldn't miss his coming home even if you did miss the dance."

"But she really mustn't miss the week-end at Cresswell Abbey," said Mrs. Bradley. "It's such a lovely place, I've always heard. And she'll be back on Tuesday."

"They'll ask her another time," said Toppie. "People would ask Alix another time," and she smiled on at her young friend, well pleased with her, Alix saw.

"Of course they'll ask her, Mummy!" cried Ruth who, with Rosemary, had sat transfixed with indignation while the invitation was thus discussed. "And it makes no difference if they don't. Who are the Hambles, anyway! What does Alix care about them? She doesn't know them and doesn't want to. I've seen your Lady Mary's picture in the 'Daily Mirror'—drooping around with bare shoulders and a plume and pretending not to know she's being snapped. I hate such empty-headed creatures, and Alix would be bored stiff by them. Of course she can't go! Of course she must be here for our dance!"

Alix was quite sure that she would not be bored by Lady Mary; but she was also sure that she could not go. No one at Heathside would appreciate the white taffeta as Lady Mary would. There would be no one at the Heathside dance she would like as much, she felt sure of it, as those young people at Cresswell Abbey—no one, that is, except Giles; and he, as his mother had said, truly she felt sure, did not count at dances; but all the same she could not go, and Ruth and Rosemary might think, if they pleased, that it was for their reasons.

She did not tell Giles in her next letter about the visit to Cresswell Abbey; but when he came home, Ruth told him, the first thing, at tea-time, all assembled as they were in the drawing-room, Toppie and herself in their accustomed places on the sofa beside Mrs. Bradley, and Ruth sitting on the arm of her brother's chair.

"Only think of it, Giles! Mummy actually thought she ought to go, because Cresswell Abbey is such a lovely place! The day of our dance, mind you! Toppie's cousins here and all!"

Giles seemed taken aback. "The week-end? She'd have been going to-day," he said.

"And missed your coming home, Giles! As if she could!" cried Rosemary.

"And Amy expecting her puppies any day now," said Jack. "I thought they'd have come this morning. She'd want to see them as soon as they were born, wouldn't you, Alix?—only we must be very careful not to look at them too often. Amy's awfully nervous when she has her pups."

"Mummy," said Giles, eyeing his contented sisters, "you ought to have made her go. Alix is over here to see England, all she can of it. And she really doesn't see so very much of it with us, you know."

"I did my best, dear," said Mrs. Bradley, pouring out her tea. "She quite refused. And Toppie aided and abetted her."

"Yes. I aided and abetted her, Giles," said Toppie, and she smiled now at him with more sweetness than Alix had ever yet seen on her face for Giles. "She can go another time to Lady Mary's."

"Oh, one never knows about that," Giles murmured. But now he was thinking more about Toppie's smile than about Alix's frustrated visit.

"Didn't you want to go to Cresswell Abbey?" he asked Alix next morning in the study, and with the question the time of their separation collapsed and, his eyes on hers, she felt him near and familiar once more, concerned, as always, for her welfare.

That was it. He understood that it might have given her so much pleasure and Ruth and Rosemary didn't understand that at all. And he wanted her to have gone because he wanted her to have pleasure. He was like Maman in that.

She confessed. "Yes, I did. But not so much that I could miss you and our dance. The dance was planned for me, Giles."

Giles rubbed his hand through his hair.—His mother should have corrected him of that trick, though Alix rather liked to see him do it; it left his hair very much on end.

"It's decent of you; awfully decent of you. But you wanted to go, of course, you dear little kid. And I'd like to think you were to get a wider look at England than you get with us."

"I think she will ask me again, Giles. Your mother wrote and explained it to her and she wrote back and said it must be for another time. I think she likes me," said Alix. "And I like her, too. Though Ruth and Rosemary find her empty-headed. Perhaps it is empty-headed people that I do like," Alix smiled. "Perhaps I am empty-headed myself."

"I saw you took to each other. I saw you belonged with each other," Giles mused. "I'm awfully sorry you didn't go."

"Would you rather I were staying with her than here with you, Giles?"

"No; I'd rather you were staying here. But I'd like you to have a slice of cake now and then after all the thick bread-and-butter. Now you, of course, would like to have the cake all the time," and Giles smiled at her, summoning her to confess to her frivolity. But when he asked her like that, there in the study, with the gas-fire and the untidy heaped books and the Greek temples and the foolish animals on the mantelpiece, Alix did not feel so sure. She liked Lady Mary. She loved the balm she wafted. She felt sure that no one here would appreciate her white taffeta; they would think Ruth's pink silk ninon with the embroidered edges just as pretty. But there would not, she felt even surer, be any one at Cresswell Abbey who would understand as Giles did.

PART II

CHAPTER I

"C'est la France," said Alix. She leaned beside him on the railing of the Channel steamer and looked through the blue of the July day to where the town thinly shaped itself, like a line of grey-white shells floating between sea and sky. Her phrase was spoken in a tone of quiet statement, unstressed by any emotion, yet Giles, while they watched the shore together, felt its echoes stretching back revealingly into the past and out towards the future.

That was really what had been at the bottom of her heart during all her time with them; France. And if she had talked about it so little that must merely have been, he reflected, because she cared about it so much. Of course she loved her own country; he could not expect or wish anything else; but had she, he wondered, any more love for England now than when she had first come among them? And he felt, when he asked himself the question, a little rueful and a little vexed. She was not a shallow child; that he knew; it was because she was not shallow that he minded her imperviousness to all that meant so much to them. With the imperviousness went an oddly mature security, as of a creature formed and fixed and not to be altered by circumstance; and it was when he thought of this security that Giles felt a little angry; for, after all, what had France given her, poor kid?

Giles did not think of his family, in particular, as benefactors to the little French girl. That side of her indebtedness was not one to engage his attention. It was England as a whole that he had hoped would by this time have crept about her heart; England with its gentle days of Spring, its balmy days of Summer; all the happy family life they had just come from; tennis, dogs, strawberries on the lawn, and long bicycle rides over the hills; England's sweetness and fidelity embodied in his mother; its holiness in Toppie.

The starlike image of Toppie rose before the young man's mind and with it his deepest doubt of the little French girl beside him. He had come from pity for the child's unconscious plight, pity for the cruelty of her position there among them—a little creature so proud that it would have been to her a burning humiliation could she have guessed how her mother had dealt with her and them in foisting her upon them—he had come, from this initial pity, to feel affection, then an odd, perplexed respect, and finally a profound, a tender solicitude. It was upon her future in France, with her mother, that it centred; but that was the outward aspect of the inner fear; for when he thought of Toppie and of holiness the question he had also to ask himself was whether Alix was impervious to holiness, too?

Giles felt that he would be better able to face that question, and with it the whole problem of the child's future, when he had seen "Maman." That was why he was here. That was why he had said "yes," on the morning, a fortnight ago, when Maman's letter at last had come summoning Alix home. Since their interview, long ago in the Winter, he and Alix had never spoken of their mutual secret, that dreadful one-sided secret that Giles visualized as an unexploded bomb lying there between them and liable at a touch to go off and scatter the family happiness to fragments. The interview had ended in a pact. She was to help him; she had, poor little creature, helped him; he still felt stung with shame to think how much; to think how he had profited, how they all had profited, by her falsehoods. And he was bound to help her. He knew, when Maman's letter came, all that lay behind the appeal as she said: "Oh, Giles, could you not come with me? and stay if only for a little while; so that at last you and Maman may meet?"

She felt that it would help if he were to know Maman. And it might well be that he could only effectually help Alix if he faced at last the baleful woman who had brought the hidden disaster to their lives. It was better that he should know, in regard to Alix's future, what they were "up against." It had not been of Maman he was thinking when he assented; it had been, as on that day last Winter, of Alix herself. And that was why he was here, on his way to Normandy and the village on the cliff, and it was Dieppe that was showing now, along its wharves, façades of sunlit houses.

"Don't you think, Giles," said Alix, "that the air in France is very different? Like golden wine?—There was a wine made at a little mountain village near Montarel—Vernay-les-Vouvières it is called—and the wine after it. I wish you could see that village. So high and steep it is, the road climbs for miles before you reach it; and higher still, above the village, is an old, old statue of la Sainte Vierge, looking down over the vineyards and blessing them. When one stands beside her one sees over all the crests of the mountain-ranges; like blue rolling waves. We used to drink Vernay-les-Vouvières at Grand-père's. It was very cheap, for it could not travel; it lost its bouquet at once if it travelled. And it was a delicious wine; so pale, so light, so delicate. One felt like singing when one drank it. I think the air of France makes one feel like that."

Mrs. Bradley's household, though not pledged to teetotal principles, eschewed all alcoholic drink, and Giles, as he listened, seeing the Virgin, the vineyards, the ingenuous piety, the pagan gaiety that Alix's words conjured up, wondered what her impressions of their unenlivened meals must have been.

"I wish I could see Vernay-les-Vouvières," he said. "A beautiful country yours must be, so near the Alps.—We have sunny days in England, you know. It's a French superstition to think that English people go staggering about in a fog all the year round. You ought to have got over that," he added. "Our weather is as good as the weather in Northern France; every bit."

"But different, Giles. As good; but not so happy. Never like wine, I think. Always there is something soft and sleepy in the air. After the air of France it is like milk."

"Milk is a very excellent thing."

"Yes. Excellent. As a food. But it does not make one want to sing."

To this Giles said nothing.

"For a French town Dieppe is not so specially beautiful," Alix took up presently; for she and Giles knew each other so well that a disagreement could be allowed to fall between them disregarded. "I do not think that for a French town it has special beauty; yet, seen like this, with the harbours, and the wharves, and houses—all so golden, do you not think it is very lovely?"

Giles had just been thinking so. "Yes. Quite lovely," he admitted. "For a French town it's rather rambling and shambling, too, and I like that."

"Ah, but it keeps its dignity all the same," said Alix. "It has gone where it meant to go and when it got there it stood up well."

"We have dignified towns," said Giles. "Edinburgh; you must see Edinburgh one day, Alix; and Bath; and Ludlow. Of course, as to ramble, London is a bad offender; but London is beautiful all the same."

"Beautiful, do you think, Giles? Beautiful you mean, then, as one might find the face of a dear, funny old great-grandmother beautiful, for what it means; but not for what it looks; I think it a very ugly town," said Alix in her tone of happy statement—for Alix was very happy to-day. "It is like an old great-grand-mother over a tea-pot; and Paris is like a goddess with a wreath."

"I like old great-grandmothers much better than goddesses," said Giles.

All the same he understood. She was initiating these comparisons—and it was so uncharacteristic of her to make comparisons—not from any desire to disparage, but from the deep, joyous excitement, the love and pride that could not be repressed and that she could not overtly have expressed without expressing emotion as well. She thrilled with it, he knew, leaning beside him, her profile, forcible, intent, golden against the sea. It looked golden like that because the sun fell on it and the sea was blue; but he had always thought Alix's skin a queer colour and never knew whether he liked or disliked it. Sometimes it was grey, like pussy-willows: and sometimes it was green, making one think of olive-trees or the patina on an old bronze; and sometimes, as to-day, it was pure gold; and always it seemed to be the final expression of significant structure rather than a decorative bloom, and to go with her blue eyes and black hair whichever tint it took. But, as he told himself, he was a sentimental Englishman and liked girls to be the colour of apple-blossoms.

Alix had fallen to silence now, and he was keeping his mind rather consciously on their friendly altercation, and even on Alix's profile, because he did not wish to reflect on what lay before him. He had not an idea of what he was to say to Alix's mother, or to do with her; and it was no good thinking about it until he saw her; saw her again.

Saw her again! How the phrase brought back the unforgettable pang and misery. How the unforgettable image floated in his memory, vivid yet unseizable; irrelevant as it were and not to be woven to any secure conclusion. It had been the stillest day, that Spring day in the Bois. The purpling grey of branches, above, behind the wandering pair, had melted to shroud-like distances and they had emerged before his astonished eyes like the spectral creatures of a clairvoyant vision; silent, and with linked arms. He had gazed at them, and as he gazed his impulse to go forward and greet his brother was checked ere it was formed. Owen here in Paris: Owen with madame Vervier—he had known at once that it was she; Owen to look like that. Rooted among the thinly scattered saplings of the wood he had remained, gazing until they passed away and the white distance received them into its folds as it had given them up—ominous disappearance of the brother he was never to see again. Rooted he stood, and heard the wild, monotonous phrase of a missel-thrush ring forth suddenly from overhead and felt his mind slowly take possession of the icy grief that crept upon it. Owen's face had given him all the truth; its rapture; its terrible stilled restlessness. And though she was so quiet, walking there, her head bent down a little, her eyes fixed before her, Giles had felt, for all the innocence of his chaste boyhood, that she was so quiet because she possessed him so completely.

How clearly he could see her still, with her brooding brightness, her soft gloom. He could not see her as baleful; he could not see her as guilty; he only saw her walking there secure in power and loveliness. And this was the irrelevance, the tormenting discrepancy; for she was the woman who had taken Owen from Toppie; she was the woman who, after her lover's death, had placidly made use of what assets he had left her; his family; and its trust in him and her. And she was the more baleful to him from the fact that, though he remembered her so vividly and knew such portentous things about her, herself he did not know at all.

There was one thing about her, however, that he could and ought to know at once, and the thought of it worked its way up into his mind while he and Alix leaned there. They had never again spoken of their secret, but, before he met her mother he ought to know whether Alix had told her what he knew of Owen's stays with them in Paris. Before he saw madame Vervier he ought to know what she knew about him; and suddenly, his eyes fixed upon the wharves and houses of Dieppe, he said: "You think she'll feel it all right that I'm come?"

"I wrote to her that you were coming," said Alix. Her mind had perhaps been following some train of thought not far removed from his, for she spoke as if they were continuing a theme rather than taking it up. "She will be delighted."

"Will she? Look here, Alix"—Giles gazed down over the railing at the sea—"she couldn't be delighted, I take it, if she knew that I had a grievance about my brother on her account."

He had spoken very abruptly, yet he had, he felt, put it well. In the little pause that followed his words, he was pleased with himself for having found any so colourless and unprovocative.

"What we know of your brother," said Alix after her pause, "would not give her a grievance against you; only against him."

"Against him?"

"Did he not deceive her, too?"

"Deceive her? Oh, I see. You think he didn't tell her that he'd kept us in the dark?"

"He could not have told her, Giles; if that is really what you are asking me."

Giles, a little confused, retraced his steps. "What I'm really asking you is whether you've told her. I want to know where I stand with her. Haven't you felt that she ought to be told?"

Again Alix was silent, and for a longer time. Then she said: "It has been my great perplexity. She does not know. Of course she does not know. But I wrote to her at once, that time last Winter, and begged that I might come home; and when I found she could not have me, I thought it best to say nothing then. Perhaps I was wrong. Perhaps you will blame me, Giles. But I thought it best to wait. It will give her such pain when she knows."

It would never have given her so much pain Giles, with a sudden glow of indignation, felt, as it had already given her daughter. What Alix had suffered in wrestling with her problem was in her voice. "Blame you? I? You poor kid!" he exclaimed. And he added: "After all, his silence meant devotion to herself."

"Do you think so?" said Alix. "I am afraid she will not feel it so. I am afraid she will feel that it meant cowardice and lack of loyalty;—as it does to me."

Giles was now aware of an uncomfortable astonishment. He had to remember that Alix was nearly seventeen. A woman could not have spoken with a more secure assurance of putting him in his place; and if, by the same token, she put Owen in his place, was she not, from her own point of view, her woman's dignity veiled only by her child's ignorance, justified in doing so? For if Owen had really kept madame Vervier in the dark she might have a right to resentment. The two culprits should have had no secrets from one another.

"I see," he repeated, lamely, as he felt. "And you would not like to spoil her memory of him?"

"We kept it from your mother and from Toppie because it would spoil their memory of him," said Alix.

"I know; but you'll own, won't you, that it would be a far worse spoiling for them?"

"Yes. For them it would be worse. But why should anyone feel pain now, when it is all over? Why should anything be spoiled?"

"It's only," said Giles, going carefully, "that it seems unfair to your mother to let me come and keep her in ignorance of what I know. It's for you to judge, Alix; but since you love your mother so much, I rather wonder that you can bear to keep such a secret from her. And, quite apart from me, oughtn't she to know just what she does send you back to?"

"Send me back to?" Alix echoed, and her eyes met his strangely.

"Yes. Before you come back in the Autumn, don't you think she ought to know?"

"Do you really imagine, Giles, that if Maman knew, she would send me back?"

"Well"—he felt that he flushed. He had not foreseen this emergency—"since I know, and since I want you back;—why not she?"

"Do you count Maman's pride for nothing, Giles?"

Madame Vervier's pride had never for a moment engaged his attention, and did not now. His attention was fully engaged by Alix's pride, facing him with a look of granite.

"I don't really see why she should take it so hardly," he said after a moment; but he was horribly uncomfortable, for he was not speaking with frankness to his young friend. "Your relation to us has, really, nothing to do with her relation to Owen. It's a new thing; and that's an old one; and as you say, it's all over."

"But she could not have me there on false pretences, Giles," said Alix. The pride had dropped now. It was as if with sudden sadness she saw too well the reasons for his misunderstanding. "I could not be there on false pretences. You have a right to think it of me since I have never told her. But it is all over now; the new as well as the old. I need never tell her. For I am at home again and I shall never go back to Heathside."

"Never come back to Heathside!" Actually for the moment Maman, Owen, Toppie, all the grief and perplexity that hung about these figures, were swept from Giles's mind by his deep discomfiture. "But this is only your holiday. Your mother's letter said so."

"She thinks it is only my holiday. But I am older now. I shall see to it that I do not return to England."

Ass that he had been not to realize the impasse to which their talk was leading them! Too obviously, from Alix's side, this was an inevitable decision. And Giles saw that from his side it should have been so, too. With Alix safely back in France, there would be no more danger of pain for his mother and wreckage for Toppie; Owen's memory might sleep in untarnished peace.

But Alix herself had come to count for far too much. It was as if he saw her walking away into a dark forest where dreadful creatures prowled. Ever since that day in his study, she had counted for too much. She was too fine, too brave, too loyal a little creature to be given up to her fate. He had felt that day that he would fight her fate for her, and he felt now that the moment had come for the first grapple. But the worst of the problem was that in fighting Alix's fate he must fight her. He could not tell her the fact that would have turned her pride to dust and ashes. He could not tell her that her mother had sent her to them on pretences so false that the minor falsity she repudiated paled beside them. Horribly handicapped as he was for the contest, he seized his bull by the horns: "Look here, my dear child," he declared, speaking with all the elder brother authority he could summon up, "you said to me that day when we talked that you were going to trust me. Well, I ask you to trust me now. I want you back. We all want you back. Let that suffice. No; wait a moment. I know what you are going to say;—if Toppie knew would she want you? I'll take the responsibility of answering for Toppie. She is so fond of you that I know she would. Isn't that enough, really? Can't we leave it at that? And you're quite right not to tell your mother. Let the whole thing rest for ever."

Her eyes were on his while he spoke to her and she listened to him gently; but her face still kept the invulnerable look strange in one so young. "You are kind, dear Giles," she said. "I do trust you. But you can't answer for Toppie. You can't answer for anybody. And I have not only myself to think of. I have Maman. I can answer for Maman in this matter. She would not let me come."

"Are you so sure of that?" broke from Giles. And now, pushed to it, he ventured far; he ventured very far, indeed. "After all she must have known that he kept a great deal from us. After all she must have known that he cared more for her than he did for Toppie; that he had been faithless to Toppie because of her."

Poor little Alix. It was not fair. She paled in hearing him. And for a long moment she stood silent beside him, looking down at the sea. "May he not have kept that from her, too?" was what she found at last to say.

"Do you think that possible?" Giles asked; but he was sorry now, seeing the deep trouble on her face, that he had spoken.

"Perhaps it would not have been possible," she said slowly. "But things may be known and yet remain unspoken, Giles."

He could not question her further. He could not ask madame Vervier's young daughter if she really believed that those things had been unspoken between his brother and her mother. There had been an element of desecration in going even so far as he had gone. And he had gained nothing by it, for after the little pause that fell between them, Alix added, in no spirit of retaliation as he saw, but as though she put up a final barrier against his persistence.

"And even if they were not there, Giles; even if all the difficult things we know of were not there, I should still not come back to Heathside. I do not care, ever, to leave France again. I could not, again, leave Maman."

CHAPTER II

The train moved slowly, almost ruminatingly, along the golden landscape, a little local train stopping at every station. The crops were still uncut and their vast undulations were broken only by lines of lonely, poplared road, or marshalled woods venturing out, here and there, upon the plains. Empty and rather sad, for all the splendour of the gold beneath, the blue above, it looked to Giles; but that might have been, he knew, because of its associations for him with scenes of the war; and he was feeling a little sick, too, apprehensions of the approaching future seizing him as he and Alix sat silent in the second-class carriage, where both the windows were tightly shut. Alix had widely opened hers on entering, but at the first station a lady had got in—little shopping people of the local bourgeoisie the passengers were, more estranged from fashion, Giles thought, than their equivalent English types—and, wrapping a scarf at once about her neck, she had complained of the effect of the courant d'air upon her névralgie. Without comment, Alix at once closed her window. No doubt she knew her compatriots and recognized the futility of discussion on this theme; but Giles reflected that Ruth and Rosemary would not so have submitted. They would have entered into altercation with the lady in the scarf and found pleasure in demonstrating her folly to her even if they did not succeed in keeping the window open. But to Alix altercation had no charms. Even when the lady, still mysteriously aggrieved in her furthest corner, murmured resentfully on about les anglais qui viennent nous déranger, Alix glanced meditatively at her for a moment and then resumed her survey of the landscape, indifferent to the misapprehension; and since Giles could not repress a smile, the lady, who still held up her scarf in retrospective protest, kept indignant eyes upon him.

"Now, you know, you are a worse-tempered people than we are. She's still nursing her wrongs," Giles murmured, and Alix, glancing at the lady of the névralgie, answered, "She is negligible."

Two men sat further on; one young, with high, ardent, excited eyes, like a collie's, in a thin head; the other obese and red with white hair en brosse and a purple nip of ribbon in his button-hole. They leaned across the carriage towards each other and talked without cessation, rapping each other on the chest to a constant refrain of: "Puis—il me dit;—Et—je lui dis." Passionately swift and even vindictive in utterance as they were, their personal geniality remained unimpaired.

A little boy on his mother's lap ate chocolates, smearing his cheeks and palms. Clambering down, he was permitted, unchecked, to lurch towards Alix, staying himself on the knees he passed, and when he reached her he stretched forth his hand with assurance for the box of apricots she held. "Est-il mignon!" exclaimed the fond mother. But Alix did not even turn her eyes from the landscape. The disconcerted child stood gazing at her, too much astonished even to weep, and Giles, taking pity on him, offered the tick of his watch and jingled his bunch of keys in an attempt to distract his attention. But the little boy gave him no heed, and after a prolonged stare at Alix he made his way back to his mother; his first encounter, Giles imagined, with an unresponsive universe.

"I say, you are really rather hard-hearted," he remarked. Here was another difference, for neither Ruth nor Rosemary could have remained so impervious to even such a repulsive little boy.

But Alix said: "I cannot look at a dirty face like that. If his mother had cleaned his face, I would have given him one."

"Well, since he's gone back to her, and you needn't look at him, may I give him one?" said Giles; and, as Alix smiling, assented, Giles handed an apricot to the little boy, who took it without thanks and ate it, staring solemnly at Alix the while.

A thin blue crescent of sea cut into the fields on the right. In the distance, on a rise of country, a pale pink château stood with wings of sculptured woodland on either side, a long green lawn in front.

"It cannot be far now," said Alix. The lady with the scarf, the mother with the little boy, the stout marketing lady, had all left them by now and she could open her window and stand by it to look out. "Vaudettes is four miles from the station. Maman will come to meet us, with monsieur de Maubert."

"Who is monsieur de Maubert?" asked Giles. He had never heard the name before. But then he had never heard any names connected with Maman. How could he, since he never spoke of her?

"He is an old friend of ours; a very old friend," said Alix. "I do not remember the time when we did not know monsieur de Maubert."

"You like him?"

"Oh, very much. C'est un homme fort distingué," said Alix, relapsing into French, with the effect, to Giles, of not sparing more than convention for their conversation. Her thoughts were fixed in anticipation. He could almost see her palpitate in her stillness with it. She might have been kinder to the little boy had she not been so unaware of everything but the approaching figure of Maman.

"How distinguished?" Giles, however, persisted.

"Oh, I am so ignorant, Giles. Wise things do not interest me, you know." Alix smiled slightly down at him over her shoulder. "He has excavated cities; Persian; Mongolian;—que sais-je. He writes on antiquities. He has a beautiful appartement in Paris with collections of gems and bronzes. He is at once savant and homme du monde."

"And will he be the only guest except me?"

"Ah, that I do not know. There are three chambres d'invités at Les Chardonnerets. But I have not heard that there is, as yet, anyone else."

"Chardonnerets? That means?"

"It means goldfinches. That was a bird we always knew, even"—Alix paused—"even before your brother told us more of birds. Flocks come in Autumn to the thistles on the cliffs outside our gate. When they all fly together one sees the squares of gold on their wings—it makes a pattern on the sky, like a chain of golden coins; monsieur de Maubert's strange old square coins. And their little twitter is like the chink of thin gold. We love them, Maman and I, and there is a tall ash-tree in the garden where they often perch in summer. You will see them, Giles. You will like Les Chardonnerets, I think.—Oh, now—I recognize now—I know those woods. We find daffodils in them, in Spring, among the faggots. You have not in England, have you, Giles, our great woods with all the ranged faggots that the woodmen pile so carefully in winter. And in Spring, at the edge of the wood, one sees around one the great plain, champagne-coloured. The next station will be ours," said Alix.

CHAPTER III

He could hardly find again the face of the February day in the Bois. It was her form, her poise that gave her to one now, and Giles's first impression of the white, sunlit figure waiting on the platform was of a Greek Victory, splendid, strong, exultant. Her face, under the falling lines of a white hat, was almost dissolved in a transparent shadow; only its grave, fixed smile, like a pearl in golden wine, remained, as it were, shaped and palpable.

He had seen her as the Parisienne; the creature of elegance and artifice; but he found her almost primitive, set here in the sea-breezes, and so much more robust than he had remembered; if anything so delicate could so be called. Freshness and force breathed from her, and the classic analogies she brought to his mind were emphasized by her straightly falling dress— a tennis-dress, perhaps, for her arms were bare—tying at the breast with tassels and at the waist with a loosely knotted sash.

"Ma chérie! Ma petite chérie!" she said.

The train had come to a standstill and it was as if Alix had flown into her arms. She had been as silent as a spectre on that spectral day when he had first seen her. Her voice now startled him, as the missel-thrush's voice had done. Tears were in it and tears were in her eyes as she clasped her child. And then, again, as they stood embraced, it was of something Greek they made Giles think; some beautiful relief on the pediment of a sunlit temple; garlands above them and happy maidens in procession on either side carrying baskets of fruit and chanting the reunion of mother and child. Ceres and Persephone it might be. Happy little Persephone, escaped at last from the kingdom of Dis.

Giles stood by, holding Alix's dressing-case, and felt himself a modern tourist gazing at the masterpiece. Just as little difference, he saw it suddenly and clearly, any knowledge of his would make to madame Vervier. She was lifted, how or why he did not know, far above the dusty impressions of the throng, impervious to their comments, whether of blame or admiration. Even when in another moment her lovely eyes turned on him and, holding Alix against her with one arm, she stretched out a welcoming hand to him and said "Soyez le bien-venu, monsieur Giles. My little girl has had only good things to tell me of you"—even then he could not feel that he had gained in significance. So a queen might have received the young equerry who had safely restored to her the princess royal. They had been good to her child, the dusty throng. That was the importance they had in madame Vervier's eyes; that, and no more.

Struggling with many thoughts Giles followed mother and daughter. The ghost of Owen walked beside him, and did it whisper: "You see: how could I have helped myself?"

Two other young men were also following madame Vervier and Alix. "Vous jouez le tennis, monsieur?" said one of them, the elegant one, in a gentle voice. He was a charming white-clad person, tall and slender, with eyes intensely blue, black hair brushed back from a starry forehead; and a face like a fox for finesse and flair and like a seraph's for sweetness. Perhaps he had perceived the something gagged and struggling in Giles's demeanour and had wanted at once to make him feel that, unimportant as any young man must be to a goddess, he might count on having significance for a new friend. Giles said that he did play, and he and the charming person exchanged smiles. They might, somehow, have fought in the same trenches, side by side, Giles felt. There was at once a link between them. The other young man, who must, Giles thought, be an artist, was dressed in brown velveteen and blue linen and had a dark, square, suffering head.

The place outside the station was white and glaring, and the noises that came from the café across it were glaring, too. Giles reflected, with a certain satisfaction, that Alix need, at all events, feel no pride in this typical scene, and it was disconcerting to have his companion, as they made their way to the little waiting car, indicate with a wave of the hand the dusty green trees, the dusty white houses, the untidy green shutters, and the brittle lights on glasses and brasses in the restaurant and say: "This is the subject that our friend here has just been painting. You shall see it. A little masterpiece of light and colour."

Of course, Giles growled inwardly as he doubled himself up on the strapontin at right angles to Alix and her mother—the two young men in front—of course, the fact that a beautiful picture might be elicited from the stimuli of the place did not make the place itself more beautiful. And yet the memory of it, framed in this new conception of its uses, grew vexatiously in his mind as they left it far behind, eliminating the weary traveller's impressions of noise, dust, and disorder, and growing to a pattern of white and green and grey wreathed harmoniously about a tawny ellipse. Yes, one could make something æsthetic out of it, ugly though it was for practical purposes; even inartistic he could see that—hang it!

The road counted off its sections in tall poplars. They passed behind madame Vervier's head, and, though Giles was so aware of her, he looked at the poplars and the fields beyond them rather than at her. She and Alix talked in French together and Alix's voice was revealed to him as like her mother's when she spoke her native tongue; musical; rhythmical; dipping; poising, and then rising to a final lift, like a swallow's flight. Their hands were clasped. Their eyes were on each other.

He could look at Alix after all, and from the poplars he shifted his eyes to her. He had never seen the child with that face before. Tender, radiant, and with something of pride so deep that it hovered on the brink of tears. Her glance met his and was tender for him, too, as though with Owen's ghost it said: "You see: how is it possible not to love her?"

But was she as beautiful as all that? Giles gathered himself away from the admission. Was she even beautiful at all? He would have to look at her carefully if he were to say, and he stayed himself on the conviction that if it came to structure and line she could not be compared to Alix.

It was not what she looked like; it was what she meant that he was so aware of now. He had never before found himself in the company of a woman who seemed so to typify the femme du monde, and if she were no longer of it, that fact was merely accidental. With every glance, gesture, rise and fall of voice, it was there that she belonged. He did not think that he liked the femme du monde, so apt, he felt, at showing you no more than what she intended to show you of her real purpose, so sure that for every occasion she would know what to do far better than you could even understand. And yet, more than the femme du monde she made him think of the mountain torrent—Alix had been right—in its strength, its splendour, and its danger, too. And he knew that he did not like dangerous women.

He had expected to find her gay, and, in spite of the memory, brooding, almost sombre, of the spectral spring day, to feel in her something of artifice and allurement. But if artifice there were, it was nothing added or adventitious; and of allurement there was none. She stood in her place, a goddess, and watched her worshippers, and when her human smile came, modelling her cheek to a sudden childlike candour, it had the oddity of an unexpected weakness.

It was to Alix alone that she talked; she had no word for him. Yet once or twice, as they drove, Giles was aware of being observed. All unimportant as he was, he felt her dark eyes turned on him, resting upon him, in meditation rather than in surmise. It was—he had noted this already—a curiously widely opened eye. Its rounded darkness gave to her contemplative gaze a fixed, abstracted quality. When you found her observing you, she did not look away; so that presently you wondered whether she was seeing you at all; whether the soft, wide gaze had not travelled to spaces far beyond you, including but forgetting you.

They had left the poplared road behind them and were among great fields, stretching on one hand to the horizon and on the other to the cliff-edge. A line of docile cows, tethered side by side, ate their way into a strip of wine-coloured clover; meadow pipits mounted from the turf and filled the salt, sweet air with myriads of falling silver bells; in the distance the tall palisades of a wood rose against the sky and it looked like an island floating on the level sunlight of the plain. The glimmer of white houses among the grey boles revealed, as they approached, an embowered village on the cliff and Giles needed to make no mental reconstruction of beauty here. He felt the authentic essence fill his breath as he gazed at the picture, never to be forgotten, he knew, of the vast blue sky, the vast sunlit plain, the tall trees green and silver, threaded with white cottages. His eyes were full of his delight.

"You know our villages?" said madame Vervier. It was the first phrase she had addressed him since they started.

"Only a few. Further north; and usually ruined ones," said Giles.

"Only the tragic ones," said madame Vervier. "Here we were untouched by the war, and our villages, too, are more beautiful than further north. In this part of Normandy they are often surrounded by these great ramparts of trees. It gives much character, much charm, does it not?"—and she smiled at him. She had noted his delight, and Alix was smiling at him, too.

"I've seen French pictures like it," said Giles.

"Yes; some of the early Corots give one the grey and green and white."

"Ah—it is too stately for a Corot." The young man in white flashed a smile round at her as he drove. "Corot would see its intimacy, its charm, rather than its gravity. That great design against the sky;—no; we must find somebody else."

Madame Vervier smiled back, sure of her point. "He would not look at the sky, my early Corot; he would look at the little white houses nestling in the trees; he would look at the curve of the white road with the whitewashed wall. That girl in the faded blue, with the brown hoop of bread upon her arm, he would put her in. Oh, yes; it is a Corot; an early Corot, André. I see the happy gentle touches of his brush."

"Elle a raison," said the young man with the dark square head, and André, driving with his easy skill, waved a hand of contented concession.

When they had passed within the precincts, the little town opened clearly to the sunlight and they were at once in the place that circled round a large pond where patient men in large straw hats sat fishing. Houses, stately in their modesty, looked over rows of pollarded fruit-trees and high walls tiled in red. Built of pale old brick and flint, with high-pitched roofs above dormer windows, they seemed to speak of a delicious leisure that was, in itself, an occupation. People who lived in such houses, Giles thought, would never be idle; yet all their industry would have the savour of an art. How darkly lustrous the windows shone; how unremittingly were those bright gardens tended. He saw, as they passed an open gate, a stout old man in a white linen coat tying muslin bags over the pears that ripened on the wall. Under a charmille a woman sat stemming currants. A family group in front of a shop were already taking the afternoon repose, the father with his newspaper, the wife and daughters with their sewing. Along the broad white street a peasant girl, her bare head as neat as a nut, clattered in sabots, carrying a great earthenware jar, and a small white woolly dog, of a breed unknown to Giles, barked languidly from his doorstep as they passed.

From the place the little town rayed out into leafy lanes and, as they entered one of them, a sunny round of sky and cliff-edge at the other end, framed in foliage, showed Giles that they were at their journey's end. High hedges and thickets of wind-swept trees protected the little house, brick, flint, and tiles, from the gales that must, in stormy seasons, beat upon it from the sea. Flowers grew gaily, though untidily, beside the narrow flagged path that led from the wicket-gate to the back door. They crossed a band of cobblestones where oleanders grew in tubs, and, as they entered, passed a kitchen gleaming with ranged coppers. Giles as he followed madame Vervier and Alix, had the sensation of stepping into a fairy-tale. The Three Bears and Goldilocks might have welcomed one to such a bright, dark little house among its sunny thickets; its very smell was a fairy-tale smell; beeswax, seashells, and coarse clean linen. Such a smell as a child, once meeting it, would never in a long life forget. A tall clock tick-tocked on the stair; there was a great Normandy armoire, softly gleaming, old and worn, at a turning of a passage; madame Vervier's white figure went on before, and as she bent her head to lift a latch he saw her russet hair twisted up from the nape of her neck; and that, again, was like a picture he had seen. And then they were suddenly out upon a broad verandah, broad and wide, washed with sunlight and opening only on the blue. Sea-gulls floated by, high above the sea, at the cliff's edge, on a level with the eyes. Vines fluttered, translucent, against the sunlight; the scent of the honeysuckle came balmily; the sea was sprinkled with white and russet sails.

A stately personage was reading in the shade. He was dressed in white; he had thick hair and a grey divided beard. Lifting his tortoiseshell eye-glasses from the bridge of his nose, he rose to greet them, and Giles found himself penetrated by the deep gaze of Jovian grey eyes set under a Jovian forehead; penetrated by the gaze and appraised, for the first time in his life, by standards mysteriously remote. This must be monsieur de Maubert, and Giles had never seen anyone like him, except once, perhaps, at Oxford, when a distinguished Frenchman had received a degree. Only the distinguished Frenchman, black, shrill, and restless, had so much less looked the part than did monsieur de Maubert. It was not exactly sustaining to say to himself that, hang it, monsieur de Maubert, after all, had probably never seen anyone like him; the advantage, he felt, must seem only to be his. But, under all his boyish perturbation, Giles knew that he was appraising monsieur de Maubert, too. Monsieur de Maubert was a magnificent person—magnificent, although his legs were short;—and he was a pagan. It was rather magnificent to be a pagan and Giles knew just how well he thought of the creed; but there were all sorts of things that monsieur de Maubert—he felt sure of it—could never see, and the difference between them was that, while Giles knew that he often groped in mystery, monsieur de Maubert would remain unaware that there could be anything significant unknown to him. Life, to him, was bathed in la lumière antique, and anything not so bathed was inessential. All sorts of things that Giles had only wondered about or surmised were suddenly made clear to him as he looked at madame Vervier's other guest.

Monsieur de Maubert turned from Giles to put his hand on Alix's shoulder. He observed her in silence for a moment with a most benignant smile, and then remarked: "Te voilà presque une grande personne, ma chère enfant," and, stooping his head, he kissed her hand.

"Now you will want to see your room," said Madame Vervier.

She had taken off her hat, and Giles for the first time saw her bareheaded. She stood there, looking at them, a little preoccupied, her hat hanging against her dress as she held it, and the sun flickered in upon her high-wreathed russet hair. Cut across her forehead and half tossed back, it seemed as simply, as cursorily done as that of a little girl who, for the first time, sweeps up her tresses. She was looking at them all; at monsieur de Maubert, at Alix, as he kissed her hand, and at Giles; but Giles felt, as he turned to her, that it was upon himself that the wide, abstracted gaze was dwelling. Monsieur de Maubert had appraised him; it was probable that madame Vervier had appraised him, too.

"After you have had your tea," she said, "you will perhaps like to rest. Or would you care to come with us to Allongeville, where we are to play tennis?"

Giles said that he would write some letters after tea. He did not see his friend in white, who had apparently gone away with the car. And the dark young artist, too, had disappeared.

With Alix's arm passed in hers, madame Vervier led him up a narrow staircase where the smell of beeswax, seashells, and linen seemed to cluster yet more thickly, and along a passage carpeted in matting where the sea-breeze, blowing in from windows at each end, made a singing noise. "Is Giles to have the chambre rose, Maman?" said Alix, and she exclaimed, as her mother, smiling, said, "Yes," "Oh, I am so glad! I hoped for that!"

It was at the end of the passage, and when one entered one had before one in the windows nothing but sea and sky. Grey woodwork framed panels of voile de Gênes, rose, white, russet, and sepia. The little Louis Quinze bed was of grey painted wood, stately under its pink and russet embroideries. A bowl of rose-coloured carnations filled the air with spicy fragrance, and there was a tiny cabinet de toilette with an ancient set of rose-and-white china. Giles had never found himself installed in such a lovely room.

"Yes; this is your room," said madame Vervier, as if she replied to a question. "You will be happy here, I think."

Giles could only murmur that he would.

"We are very primitive," said madame Vervier. "There are no bells. If you want Albertine, you must go to the stair and call down for her. She will hear and come."

"Ah, she will not always come," Alix demurred; whereat madame Vervier smiled and said that in that case he must call Alix.

Then they left him, and he could go to the window, turning away instinctively from the room and all it meant of madame Vervier, and stare at the sea, and, with a rising sense of dismay and fierceness in his heart, ask himself what he did there in the Circe sweetness. He was there because of Alix, of course; but how far away Alix had become. The process of removal seemed to have begun as they had leaned on the railing of the deck and seen Dieppe emerge over the water. In her declaration to him, when their talk so disastrously ended, she had drawn still further away; and now he saw her almost as a stranger, in a strange land. A foreigner; French; the daughter, only, of madame Vervier; no longer his little Alix.

When she knocked at his door, twenty minutes later, and told him that tea was ready, he felt that it was with a dull gaze that he met her. She had asked him to come because of something he could do to help her, but now her radiant demeanour seemed to demonstrate that she had brought him so that he might be enchanted. Madame Vervier was not a person in any need of help. There was nothing she asked less of you. Circe, Circe; that was the word in his mind. Only Circe, he supposed, allured; enticed; while madame Vervier only gazed at you with those wide, intent, indifferent eyes.

"Do you like Les Chardonnerets?" said Alix, standing in the door and smiling at him. She had changed her travelling dress for a white one, a straight white one made of a thin woollen stuff, like her mother's; and her mother must have had it in readiness for her, for he had never seen her wear it before. Nor had he ever seen her look so happy.

"I suppose," he said, with his hands in his pockets, standing in the middle of the lovely room, "you feel England has ceased to exist; and a good job, too."

"But not at all, Giles," said Alix, and there was a touch of gay malice in her smile. "How could I feel that when you are here?"

"Will cease to exist, as far as you are concerned, once I'm gone," Giles amended.

"France has never existed for you at all," Alix remarked, though her smile did not become less kind.

"I beg your pardon, young woman, it existed for me from the moment I set eyes on you," said Giles gloomily, "to say nothing of the year I fought over here."

Alix then did a very unexpected thing. She advanced into the centre of the room and clasped her hands around his arm and looked into his face. "Do not be heavy with me, Giles," she said, "when I am so happy."

He looked down at her fondly and sadly. "I suppose it's because I see you happy, for the first time, that I feel heavy."

"But why, Giles? Why? Must not a child be happy at finding herself again with her mother; in her own country? Would you not be happy in such a case? Were you not happy when you returned to your home and to your mother after the war?"

"That's not quite the same," Giles objected. "After all, you've not been in daily peril of your life. Of course you're happy. But try not to show me, too plainly, how little we all mean to you. Try not to show me how quickly you'll forget all about us when I'm gone."

"But I should never forget you, Giles, even if I never saw you again!" said Alix, holding his arm and looking into his face.

Madame Vervier, as they stood thus, passed along the corridor and paused and looked in at them; looked, Giles felt, with surprise. Alix smiled round at her. "He thinks I do not care for England any longer, Maman, or for him, because I am so happy to be back in France with you," she said.

Madame Vervier, after her pause, advanced slowly into the room, and her smile did not conceal from Giles her covert examination of himself. It was a smile deep and soft; superficially acquiescent; but concealing much. Vigilance was in it, and the sense, perhaps, of a special need for vigilance; the recognition, too, perhaps, of something unforeseen that England had already done to her child. Such untroubled intimacy between young man and maiden was not, Giles divined, in the traditions to which madame Vervier was accustomed. Yet her smile suggested no reproof and seemed to acquiesce serenely in Alix's demonstration of alien habits.

She moved to them, and passed her arm in Alix's, so that they stood, all three, linked together, and, smiling on, she remarked: "You must not give your good friend cause for such fancies, darling."

She spoke in English and her English was almost as perfect as Alix's. The r of "darling," just rolled, like the almost imperceptible ripple on the smooth surface of a shell, made the word at once more playful and more caressing. And she went on, looking from one to the other: "You must not seem to forget him in finding me. Our kind allies must have no cause, at any time, for suspecting that we French have not faithful hearts."

"But I have just told him, Maman, that I should never forget him," said Alix as they moved towards the door. "And there can be no question of that, Giles, for you will come often and often to Les Chardonnerets, will you not?"

Giles did not answer this question. It was unexpected, and its sweetness was unexpected. His mind, however, was occupied with the discomfort that came to him at seeing himself made to appear so personally involved in regrets for Alix's removal. It was not himself, first and foremost, he had been thinking of at all when he felt those regrets; it was of England; of his mother and Toppie; of the noisy, untidy, but devoted family life; of the birch-wood at evening where he had taught Alix the song of the willow-warbler; of his beautiful Oxford and "The Messiah" on Winter evenings. These were the things he wanted Alix to remember, and it could not console him to know that she expected to see him again when he felt sure that she would see his England disappear from her life without one pang.

CHAPTER IV

A table had been laid in a corner of the verandah, and a stout woman, bareheaded and in savates, was carrying out tea and coffee.

Madame Vervier rearranged the tray, setting the tongs on the sugar, the strainer on a cup, placing the plate of madeleines here, the brioches there; all mildly, with no savour of criticism for Albertine's haphazard methods. In England such a ministrant at the tea-table would have been felt as a flaw on the prevailing perfection; yet Albertine, Giles divined, was also the cook; and a bevy of trim, capped English maids could hardly have evolved the lustre of cleanliness that reigned throughout the lovely little house. It was difficult to think of madame Vervier as poor; and more difficult to think of her doing things for herself. Yet all the loveliness had, he felt, been gathered together with something of the same mild dexterity that now brought order and comeliness to the tea-table. Madame Vervier was the sort of person who would pick up lovely things for a song; the Louis Quinze bedstead, the voile de Gênes, the tall cream-white cafetière, like one he had seen in a picture by—Chardin, wasn't it?—and the teapot with a delicate spray of grey flowers, just touched with gilt, on its side—had all, he could imagine, been brought to her nest by the unerring instinct that leads the bird to select the white feather or the lichen. Alix had said, he remembered, that part of their revenue was derived from the rent of the fairy-tale house; he was sure that it was an investment that paid well. And she had probably herself made the dresses she and Alix wore. She could be extravagant if the money were there; if it were not, she was careful. One felt in her the essential freedom from material bondage.

Monsieur de Maubert was still in his shady corner with the Nouvelle Revue Française on his knee. The young artist had reappeared and was sitting on the steps, his chin on his hands, looking out at the sea. Madame Vervier took her place at the tea-table, monsieur de Maubert drew his chair beside her, and Giles's friend strolled up from the cliff-path accompanied by yet another noticeable personage.

This was a youngish woman, though younger in form than in face, bareheaded and wearing a very short white skirt and a flame-coloured silk jacket. It was almost like seeing a tongue of electric fire, brilliant, supple, cold, run in among them, so different was she from the sunlight which seemed so completely madame Vervier's element. It did not surprise Giles to gather, presently, that mademoiselle Blanche Fontaine was an actress, and a distinguished one. She was charming; he had seen that at once; but he had seen as soon that it was a charm with which he had nothing at all to do; the sort of charm one expected to pay ten-and-six for the sight and sound of and to feel, while it operated upon you, safely barred away from by a row of footlights. A presence so brilliant could not be said to cast a chill, but for Giles it certainly cast a discomfort. Who was she? What did she mean? Where had she come from, this young woman so lean, so white, so sickly-looking, yet so tough? Her smile, as she bit into her madeleine, brought a long dimple that was almost a wrinkle into her cheek and her long, pale eyes scintillated under darkened lashes. He realized how noticeably independent of artificial aids to significance was madame Vervier from noting how frankly mademoiselle Fontaine had made use of them. She might even, by nature, he surmised, be a swarthy woman; but art had transformed her to a dazzling whiteness and her crinkled hair, that might be really black, repeated the lustrous flame of her jacket. Something in the fervour of her thin, gay lip, in the vigour of her thin, questing nose, even suggested to Giles a Semitic strain; but upon the racial edifice she had laid a pattern of strange, chiming colour that seemed in its vehemence and oddity to alter the very contour of her face. She had made of herself what she would; what she was, was unfathomable by any plummet in Giles's possession.

They were all talking and laughing, all except Alix, who sat silent beside her mother, and the young artist with the dark, suffering head. He drank coffee; three cups of it, and black. Monsieur de Maubert's sonorous tones were lifted by a note of drollery.

"He has lost himself in the clouds of mysticism." They were talking of the book of a friend. "To stumble among rocks is less disconcerting than to stumble among clouds. Il erre—il erre— One sees him wandering away into the fog of his own imaginations."

"Did you enjoy yourself in England, mademoiselle Alix?" mademoiselle Fontaine asked. "Did you make good studies there?"

"Yes. I went to a Lycée with the sisters of monsieur Bradley," said Alix.

She looked more of a child, seen in this setting, than Giles had ever seen her look. Her silence was childlike; and her attitude, leaning slightly against her mother, her chair placed a little behind her. Yet, at the same time, Giles had never felt her manner more mature. She was familiar with mademoiselle Fontaine. She knew her of old. Yet what a sense of distance there was between them. Giles could not tell whether it was kept there, so unerringly, more by her manner or by mademoiselle Fontaine's. They knew their place; both of them. Giles suddenly perceived that people in England did not know their places with anything like the same accuracy as people in France. Mademoiselle Fontaine was the distinguished actress. Alix was the toute jeune fille; under her mother's wing. They might meet for years and never advance by a hair's-breadth to greater intimacy.

"Ah. Yes. You were with the family of monsieur." The dimple came for Giles. The brilliant eyes circled round him; pierced him; cogitated; deduced; summed him up probably, Giles felt—(so much more shrewd was he than mademoiselle Fontaine could guess, for all her brilliancy)— as "Jeune homme respectable et tant soit peu lourd."

"You must bring monsieur to tea with Grand'mère, Maman, and me, one day mademoiselle Alix," she said. It was surprising to find that mademoiselle Fontaine was so immersed in family ties. "I have un petit 'foaks'." So she pronounced the French term for fox terrier. "Tout-à-fait charmant. He will delight you."

"There is a charming 'fox' in the family of monsieur," said Alix.

"Some admirable work is being done in England," said Giles's friend, whose name, he now gathered, was monsieur le vicomte de Valenbois. "Your school of Bloomsbury. They are remarkable writers. They have invented a new method; oh, deep, crafty; though it seems to blow as easily as a flower. But then a flower has always its roots; its soil.—Tchekov, do you think? Dostoievsky?—They are much inspired, one feels, for all their sincerity, by the Russians. Or is it truly indigenous? Do the pavements of Bloomsbury really grow it quite spontaneously? That delicious Bloomsbury," monsieur de Valenbois mused, his happy eyes on Giles, "of the Museum, the squares where Thackeray walks, the smell of fogs and jam."

Giles was much bewildered. He did not remember ever having heard of a school of Bloomsbury.

Monsieur de Valenbois enlightened him and went on, putting Giles's best foot forward for him, since it was evident that he did not know how to put it forward for himself. "And then your extraordinary Joyce. Ireland is his soil, indubitably, and no alien pollen has visited him. What a talent! Solitary; morose; erudite. He will found a school here among nos jeunes. That is already evident. You have writers to be proud of. It is true we have our Proust to put beside them. You admire our Proust?"

"I'm sorry to say I don't know him; or the morose Irishman either," said Giles, with a genial grin for his own discomfiture.

"Monsieur Giles is a philosopher," Alix now suddenly and surprisingly contributed. Though so withdrawn she had been listening, watching, and it was evident that she had a different conception of Giles's best foot. "He is going to found a school, too. At Oxford."

"I say! Draw it mild!" cried Giles, casting a glance of delighted amusement at his young friend.

"But is it not true, Giles, that the old philosopher, with the beard, thinks that you will found a school?" said Alix.

"I'm afraid he only hopes I'll follow his," said Giles.

"Philosophy is, indeed, a magnificent subject," smiled monsieur de Valenbois, all gentle respect. "To follow a school adequately is often to find that one has founded a new one.—Does our Bergson interest you?"

Giles said that he did, very much, and found that Alix had succeeded in putting his best foot forward, for they now all talked about philosophy. Monsieur de Maubert, he gathered, was a disciple of Croce's; monsieur de Valenbois had read William James and the Pragmatists; and madame Vervier had attended Bergson's pre-war lectures at the Sorbonne. She found the élan vital in too much of a hurry.

"We gallop, we gallop," she remarked;—"but if I may not see my goal, let me linger by the way."

"As for me," cried mademoiselle Fontaine, "give me le bon vieux Papa de bon Dieu of my childhood! With him, at all events, one knows what to expect and where one is."

The young artist had made no attempt to join the conversation and, now that he had finished his coffee, he got up, taking an easel, a camp-stool, and a box of paints, and went away out on to the cliffs. His morose profile passed along against the frieze of floating sea-gulls and madame Vervier, sadly shaking her head, said that Jules was in one of his humeurs noires.

"Pauvre cher!" sighed monsieur de Valenbois.

It seemed that the young artist had an adored wife who was in a madhouse.

"I saw her before leaving Paris," said madame Vervier. "She is quite gentle. She allowed me to hold her hand.—But lost; altogether lost; she was like a tame bird that has strayed from its cage and cannot find its way in the forest. There it sits, on a branch, and stares into the darkness. It is pitiful."

A silence fell for a while after that, and Giles heard in it the echoes of the compassionate voice beating softly against each heart.

"He will do great things," said monsieur de Maubert presently. It was as if he turned away from the gloomy fact and displayed for their comfort the golden coin it had minted. "It is an authentic genius."

"Yes. If we can keep him alive to give it to us," said madame Vervier.

"If anyone can keep him alive it is you, Hélène," said monsieur de Maubert.

Charming people they were, and compassionate and wise, thought Giles, sitting there among them in the pellucid shadow while the gulls floated past in the golden light. Strains of Gluck's "Orpheus" floated with the gulls through his mind. The thought of the young painter's wife, lost in the shades, suggested that music, perhaps. But it was an Elysian scene.

When they were dispersed, all driving in monsieur de Valenbois' car to Allongeville for tennis, all except monsieur de Maubert who withdrew to his room—to sleep, Giles imagined—Giles himself did not write letters. He wandered along the cliff-path and saw the lovely shore curving, far away, in azure bays beneath the gold-white cliffs. He looked at the scene and was not consciously absorbed in thought; but a process of testing, of reëstablishing, went on within him as if he felt about his roots to see that they were firm. He would have need of firmness, and the figure of Toppie went with him as an exorcising presence.

It was late when the party returned and assembled for a supper of consommé, chicken salad and a cream for which Albertine, saturnine yet complacent, was warmly praised. Alix looked drugged with happiness and fatigue and madame Vervier soon sent her to bed. Mademoiselle Blanche Fontaine, in the drawing-room with madame Vervier and monsieur de Maubert, read aloud the manuscript of a new play; the young artist went away to his hotel on the place, and monsieur de Valenbois sat for a little while with Giles on the steps of the verandah to look at the fading dyes of the sunset and to talk of Scriabin, Stravinsky, and the Russian ballet. Giles had to own that he did not care much about the Russian ballet. He was always having to own things to monsieur de Valenbois who showed the happiest interest in his lapses, giving utterance, now and then, to a gentle long-drawn "Tiens!" Giles himself was very tired, however, and felt that he could not adequately defend his theories which rested upon an objection to the use of the body as a means of primitive expressionism. He soon said good-night and went up to his wonderful little room.

After he had gone to bed he lay for a long time awake, a fold of the coarse cool linen that smelt of orris root against his cheek. He heard mademoiselle Fontaine go away to her own villa, escorted by the other three. Then, when they returned, the Sacre du Printemps came softly humming up the stairs, showing him that monsieur de Valenbois was also going to bed. After that the only voices left below were those of monsieur de Maubert and his hostess, sitting in quiet converse on the verandah.

They talked meditatively with pauses of appreciation for the beauty of the night, and madame Vervier must once have risen to advance and look out into the starry vastness, for Giles heard her say "Tiens;—qu'elle est grande, notre étoile, ce soir!"

It was late before the final words were vaguely wafted up to him: "Bonsoir, mon ami." "Bonne nuit, ma chère Hélène."

CHAPTER V

He had not imagined madame Vervier coming down to breakfast; but she was up long before it. Giles, looking from his window at seven, was astonished to see her form, wrapped in a white bath-robe, advancing leisurely from the cliff that she had, evidently, just ascended after a morning swim. She was alone. It was so early that she had awakened no one to share with her the delicate sting of the morning waves. Giles indeed imagined, watching her, that these early hours were set apart by her for solitude; that no one ever shared them with her. She walked, her russet head bent down, a little as she had walked in the Bois; meditating, it seemed. He heard her afterwards on the verandah, in the salon below, moving quietly to and fro. Her calm voice directed Albertine. "Ne réveillez pas mademoiselle. Elle est si fatiguée," he heard.

A little while later, Albertine's voice broke out far away, at the garden gate, in vehement yet not unfriendly altercation with the baker's lady; and then, stealing deliciously into his sleepy senses, mingling with the fragrance of the carnations by his bedside, the aroma of roasting coffee-beans delicately tinctured the air. Albertine came in with a jug of steaming water and it was time to get up.

When he went down at half-past eight, monsieur de Valenbois was singing in the drawing-room with madame Vervier at the piano; the song was "D'Une Prison," and he sang well.

Albertine was laying breakfast on the verandah, and Giles stood leaning against a pillar listening to the song. At its end madame Vervier soberly commended the singer, yet turned a leaf, here and there, to suggest an alteration. "Qu'as-tu fait de ta jeunesse?" monsieur de Valenbois sang again, with a new poignancy; and yet again. "Bien; très bien," said madame Vervier's quiet voice.

Then monsieur de Maubert appeared, and they came out to greet him and Giles. Monsieur de Maubert wore a small white woollen shawl over his shoulders and madame Vervier asked him with solicitude whether he would rather have breakfasted in the salle-à-manger, as usual. It had seemed so deliciously mild a morning that she had told Albertine to lay the table here.

Monsieur de Maubert said he delighted in the plan. He would merely take precautions against a courant d'air; and to ensure him further from this calamity his chair was placed in a corner behind the table, Giles aiding in his disposal and amused by the idea of Jove sheltering from a courant d'air.

"Oh, breakfast here! Quel bonheur!" cried Alix, emerging. She made Giles think of a swallow as she skimmed out, her feet in their heelless espadrilles hardly seeming to touch the ground. André de Valenbois also, he saw, noted her swiftness, her light, direct movement; noted, too, no doubt, her clear face, stern in its carven structure, yet sweet in smile and glance. Alix was really growing up; she was already a person to be noted by a young man with an eye for beauty in all its manifestations, and Giles, while monsieur de Valenbois' eyes rested almost musingly upon her, knew a fraternal, nay, almost a paternal, stir of anxious surmise. Would that be a solution? He did not feel the need of a solution for Alix's problem to be so pressing as he had on the steamer yesterday. It was difficult in this radiant milieu to believe her so in need of rescue. However heinous madame Vervier's fault, she could not, without manifest priggishness, be seen as a mother unfit to care for a daughter. But problem or no problem, it would be a comfort to know Alix settled, and during coffee and rolls he began to see, very plainly, that this settlement must almost certainly have presented itself to madame Vervier. If André de Valenbois were here on these terms of happy intimacy, when her child arrived, had she not seen to it that he was here? Could she have chosen better? If Alix was charming, so was he; he was, indeed, Giles considered, having not thought much of Alix as in the category, more obviously charming than she was; a veritable prince of the fairy-tale in face, form, and demeanour, and if Alix was not already affected by his presence that could only be because she was still so much a child. He was not a young man to leave a maiden's fancy unaffected.

"A penny for your thoughts, monsieur Giles," monsieur de Valenbois' voice broke in, disconcertingly, upon his meditations. That he had allowed them to become absorbing was evident to him from the smiles that met his eyes as he raised them. He felt himself foolishly blushing.

"Giles never talks much at breakfast," Alix commented.

"I don't get much chance to, at home, do I?" said Giles, grateful for her intervention.

"You shall have every chance here," said madame Vervier. "We rarely have a young English philosopher among us. We must profit by the occasion." Her smile was very kind.

"I know what monsieur Giles was thinking of," said monsieur de Valenbois.

"Oh, no, you don't," Giles laughed.

"I wager you!" monsieur de Valenbois challenged him, tilting back his chair, his brilliantly blue eyes on his friend. "Do you defy me?"

"Absolutely," said Giles.

"Well, own to my perspicacity when I tell you, then, that you were thinking about mademoiselle Alix. You were reassembling your arguments against the Russian ballet and reflecting that the best of them would be that it is idle to go to art for something we can find more perfectly displayed in nature."

Giles stared at him. It was near enough to cause him to stare.

"Well?" smiled monsieur de Valenbois.

"How did you know I was thinking about Alix?" Giles demanded.

"How did I know?—Because I was!" laughed monsieur de Valenbois. "And the same thoughts."

Madame Vervier was looking at them both, and again, Giles imagined, with her veiled vigilance. "The Russian ballet?" she questioned. "What has Alix to do with the Russian ballet?"

"Forgive my execrable taste, chère madame!" exclaimed monsieur de Valenbois, "in making mademoiselle Alix the subject of these divinations! But did you remark the way in which she bounded out of the house just now? It was a remarkable bound," smiled monsieur de Valenbois. "It started the same strain of thought in me and in monsieur Giles, you see. We were discussing the Russian ballet last night."

"But I wasn't thinking about the Russian ballet," Giles rather helplessly protested, and he felt madame Vervier not quite pleased. "That's what I should have thought, no doubt, if it had come to my mind. But it didn't."

"Ah; but the essential you will not deny," said monsieur de Valenbois, and Giles, feeling his blushes mount again, wondered just how far the essential had indeed been divined.

Alix was gazing first at him, then at monsieur de Valenbois and then at her mother; and her mother's eyes, while they caressed and approved her silence, put her aside into the retirement suitable to a jeune fille.

"Monsieur Giles has disowned the essential," she remarked.

"Do you like him, Giles?" Alix questioned when, after breakfast, she moved off with her friend to the cliff-path.

Giles really felt a little abashed before her calm; felt that he deserved, rather than monsieur de Valenbois, madame Vervier's implicit reproof.

"Monsieur de Valenbois?" he questioned. "Very much. Don't you? I think him charming."

"Charming," Alix reflected.

"Have you known him for a long time?" Giles inquired.

"A long time? I?" Alix's eyes came back to him surprised. "I never saw him before."

"Really. He's a new friend of your mother's, then."

"Yes. They met at Cannes last winter," said Alix. "Charming. He is that, I suppose; but I think it a little agaçant for anyone to look so sure of happiness."

"Sure of happiness? You think he looks that?"

"Yes. As if, always, he had had everything he wanted. That is a little agaçant, I think. Though of course it is not his fault."

"It may be only a part of his intelligence, his general tact and taste, to look it," Giles suggested. "He would always be thinking about his responsibilities towards his surroundings. If he wasn't happy, nobody would know it."

"But would that not be for his own sake rather than for theirs? He would feel it a disadvantage to look unhappy," said Alix.

"But he's so kind," said Giles. "He seems to me, now that I come to think of it, even more kind than he is charming. He's been most awfully kind to me already."

"And why should he not be?" Alix inquired. She took off her hat and the morning breeze blew back her hair.

"Well, I'm a rather unprepossessing young foreigner. I shouldn't have known how to be kind to him."

"He is quicker on the surface than you are, Giles; but you are quite as quick beneath it, and deeper far, I feel sure," said Alix.

"Hang it!" said Giles, laughing, "how do you manage to think these things at your age?"

"I am of an age, it appears, to have monsieur de Valenbois discuss my appearance in my presence," said Alix.

"Oh—but just because you are so young," Giles, already alarmed for the good fortune of his romance, protested.

"Ah, but if I were as young as you mean, I should not be worth discussing," Alix returned.

Giles glanced at her from the tail of his eye. How young, how old, indeed, was Alix. His sense of a suffering only biding its time to spring upon her came strongly to him as he scanned surreptitiously the high young face that seemed to soar beside him, the vast background lending an added haughtiness to its delicate projections. How French, how French she was; how much a foreigner with all her familiarity; so much so that he could not, even now, foresee what she would feel, what love, what suffer. "And monsieur Jules;—I've never heard anyone call him anything but Jules.—And mademoiselle Fontaine? Give me your impressions of all these people," he said. "They are so strange and new to me."

"Poor Jules. I am fond of him. Very. I have known him for many years," said Alix. "Ever since Maman admired a picture of his and bought it and then found him, starving, with his little wife. Maman has been their good angel always. Success is coming to him now; now when it is too late. And mademoiselle Fontaine is an old habituée of Maman's salon. I have not seen her in the country before. She has taken this little villa for the summer to be near Maman. She does not seem to belong to the country. We will go one day to have tea with her and her mother and old grandmother and see the little 'fox,' " Alix added. "Her grandmother knew Chopin. She will tell you so at once; and George Sand. She was an actress, too. I do not think that I care much for actresses."

"And was mademoiselle Fontaine's mother an actress?"

"Oh, not at all. Her mother is quite different. Une bonne petite bourgeoise tout simplement; quite insignificant and creeping. They both adore the grandmother. You must see them," Alix repeated, a slight amusement on her lips, as if she spoke of quaint animals she had to display to her friend.

He and Alix and monsieur de Valenbois bathed before luncheon. Bathing at Les Chardonnerets was a rather arduous affair. One undressed in one's room and ran out over the cliff-top in espadrilles and bath-robe. The long iron staircase down the face of the cliff was almost as steep as a fire-escape in places, and at the bottom there was shingle to traverse and then, if the tide was low, as on this morning, a stretch of wet sand. Giles was an excellent swimmer and so was monsieur de Valenbois. Alix, not yet proficient, though her stroke was good, swam between them out to sea, and Giles, as he and the young Frenchman smiled at each other over her dark head, felt a growing assurance for his romance. André de Valenbois, he saw, found Alix a charming young creature, and what could be a better beginning than that? She rested, when they turned to come back, holding first Giles by the shoulders and then monsieur de Valenbois.

Madame Vervier was sitting on the grass, high against the sky. She watched them from under a white sunshade, monsieur de Maubert, under a green-lined one, extended beside her. "Now let me swim again and show her how much progress I have made," said Alix, and she bravely pointed her hands through the waves, Giles and André beside her, exhorting, directing, commending. Giles felt that madame Vervier, on her height, watched it all complacently. Complacently, yet with that vigilance, too. Alix was given the full liberty of the jeune fille moderne; but he had already noted that however far and free her roamings her mother was always aware of when, how, and with whom they took place.

It so befell that Giles made the acquaintance of mademoiselle Fontaine's family that very day. Madame Vervier and monsieur de Valenbois went off for a long motor drive and it was arranged with mademoiselle Fontaine, who appeared soon after the swim, that Giles and Alix were to drink tea with her and Maman and Grand'mère at their cottage. Monsieur de Maubert was spending the afternoon with friends in the country.

The smallest, most smiling little house it was, that of mademoiselle Fontaine's family. It stood behind a pink-and-grey wall in a tiny garden and when they entered the gate at four o'clock they were welcomed by the fox terrier, and found old madame Dumont, crumpled up in black draperies and under a black parasol all lace and fringes, sitting out in the sun on the flagged path with a row of white and purple petunias leading up to her. Mademoiselle Fontaine stood behind her chair and gently but forcibly shouted their names to her, and mademoiselle Fontaine's mother, who did not bear her name, but was plain madame Collet, emerged from the house with a tray of tea and coffee. She was a stout, pale little woman with a high, old-fashioned bosom and prominent, old-fashioned hips and an old-fashioned fringe across her faded forehead. Careful, cautious, grave and happy, she seemed as one who moved among precious objects to whose well-being and security she knew herself essential. "Is that as you wish it, Blanche?" Giles heard her whisper to her daughter; and to her mother, "You are warm enough, Maman?"

As for Grand'mère, Giles, in spite of Alix's intimations, was hardly prepared for such a fearsome old lady. Very fearsome he found her, peering shrewdly up at him through the fringes of her parasol with the beady eye of an old raven under a dark-blue beetling eyebrow. She was powdered and dyed, and an erection of black lace ornamented her ample indigo wig and fell in lappets on either side of her long Semitic cheeks. Her smile was histrionic and her voice hoarse as if with years of use for public purposes. Now and then she emitted a loud gong-like laugh, and Giles could somehow imagine her, so full of vitality did she still seem, standing in classic draperies on a vast stage and bellowing forth passages from Victor Hugo. She talked almost immediately of Chopin and mademoiselle

Fontaine stood leaning on the back of her chair listening to her as if she felt the rôle of listener, for herself as well as for them, a privilege. Giles could not but admire what, he supposed, was the effect of the French tradition of family life. It was difficult to associate an intelligence as versatile as mademoiselle Fontaine's with this derelict antiquity, and even more difficult to think of her as the daughter of the homespun little person who poured out their tea and coffee. But mademoiselle Fontaine showed no sign, apologetic or explanatory, of finding anything amiss with either of them, and if her manner towards madame Collet was often curt and authoritative, an affection that could show itself at moments in quite a pretty playfulness evidently underlay it.

"See what a naughty little mother I have, monsieur Bradley," she exclaimed. "She pretends always to forget that I do not like my afternoon coffee made with chicory. In the morning, yes; I admit it; later in the day, no. Ah, Maman! no excuses!! Je vous connais. Economy is the motive!— She has never escaped the fear that unless one saves all one's sous one may die in indigence."

"Chicory, Blanche? What do you say of chicory?" the old lady inquired, leaning an ear towards her grandchild. "Mais c'est très sain, la chicorée. Ca rafraichit le sang.—If you drink chicory every day in your coffee"—and now it was an eye she turned, half closed in sagacious admonition, on the startled Giles—"you will not need to purge yourself, my young man."

"Fi donc, Grand'mère! We do not talk of l'hygiène now!" laughed mademoiselle Fontaine.

"Ah, it is a thing never to forget," said madame Dumont. "If Chopin had not neglected his health, how many more works of genius he would have given to the world.—He was my master, did I tell you, monsieur Gillet?"—mademoiselle Fontaine had not succeeded in conveying Giles's name to her in a retainable form. "I had great talent for the piano. It was said to me, when I chose the theatre as a career, that it was one I chose and one I threw away.—You have heard of George Sand in England?"

Giles said that they heard of her.

"Femme exécrable!" madame Dumont exclaimed. "Femme sans cœur! How many lives did she not destroy!"

"Ah, but I am always on the side of the woman, when it comes to les affaires de cœur," said mademoiselle Fontaine, with a smile at Giles. "We are so often the losers that I feel a certain satisfaction when a woman, even if ruthlessly, redresses the balance. And with all its romanticism, what a great talent it was, that of the good George! Do not say too much ill of her."

"Good! You can call a woman good who tricks one lover under the nose of the other! Do you forget Pagello and Alfred de Musset!" cried madame Dumont. "As for Musset; let it pass; he was not one to be pitied.— But Chopin! A man as simple as a child. Non. C'était un monstre!" madame Dumont declared.

"And I will leave you to tell monsieur Giles what you think of George Sand while I ask mademoiselle Alix to come upstairs with me and see a new dress that has come from Paris," said mademoiselle Blanche, thus further demonstrating her intelligence to Giles, for indeed madame Dumont's reminiscences had begun to make him uneasy.

Alix had picked up the friendly "fox" and was giving scant attention; but once her impeding presence was removed, madame Dumont's recitals took on a disconcerting raciness and when, presently, madame Collet gathered together the tea-things and carried away the tray, the old lady, as if she had bided her time, lurched towards Giles, with a terrible leering smile, to whisper: "Elle est belle, n'est-ce pas, madame Vervier?"

"Très belle," said Giles, drawing away a little.

"Sa fille ne sera jamais aussi belle," whispered madame Dumont. "She need not fear her. What fate more pitiful for a beautiful woman than to find a rival in her daughter!"

"Nothing of that sort could ever happen between Alix and her mother," said Giles angrily.

"Nothing of that sort. Précisément. You, a young man, and I, an old woman, see eye to eye when it comes to such a comparison," madame Dumont disconcertingly concurred. "La petite Alix is not of a type to seduce. She has distinction; an air of race; mais elle n'est pas séduisante!— Tandis que la mère!"—and madame Dumont, with eye and hand uplifted, took Heaven to witness of her appreciation.

"That's not what I mean at all. You quite misunderstand me," said Giles, more angrily.

"Vous dites, monsieur?" said madame Dumont, fixing a very shrewd, sharp eye upon him as if she suddenly discerned new aspects of an obvious case. "It is the daughter you admire?"

Madame Collet reappeared and Giles maintained a hostile silence. To attempt to enlighten madame Dumont would be futile.

"It is time for your repos, Maman," said madame Collet. "She is so old, so very old, monsieur," she added, casting a glance of proud possessorship upon Giles. "Only by constant care do we keep her with us. And now it is time for the little afternoon nap."

The old lady, muttering something about chicory and hygiène, signified her readiness to withdraw and Giles assisted her daughter in hoisting her upon her feet. But for all her decrepitude she was still not lacking in female sensitiveness and had time, it was evident, to make her reflections upon something unflattering in the attitude of the young Englishman, for, before she disappeared into the house, she bade him farewell with an extreme and sudden haughtiness.

Alix soon came down after that and they went away.

"Well?" smiled Alix. "And did you appreciate the celebrated madame Dumont?"

Her smile hurt Giles. Its unconsciousness of what madame Dumont really meant; her ignorance of what such old harpies thought and said of her mother. "Horrible old creature!" he could not repress.

"Horrible?" Alix was evidently surprised. "That is very severe."

"I want to be severe. I think she is quite horrible."

"It is always horrible to be so old. But she is not stupid, Giles. She has been a great actress; at least, almost great. Monsieur de Maubert saw her act years ago, and says that it was good. And sometimes she will still repeat one of her famous scenes—as Phèdre or Athalie—to make one's blood run chill."

"She makes my blood run chill without any acting," said Giles.

CHAPTER VI

"C'est la belle madame Vervier," said a contemplative voice behind him, and Giles, glancing round, as he sat in the thatched chalet overlooking the tennis courts, saw that it was the lady in grey who spoke.

He had played tennis all the morning with Alix, André de Valenbois and another young man, a friend of André's, who had motored over from a neighboring château, and now that they had come back after tea, and, with madame Vervier added to their number, made a quartette without him, he watched them from the chalet, with a book. The small old houses and large new villas of Allongeville climbed a valley that rose in a wooded amphitheatre about the little watering-place and the tennis grounds lay just outside it, pleasantly disposed, the highroad with its poplars on one hand and on the other a hillside of tall grasses and wild flowers.

Giles that afternoon had strolled back into the town to look at the church and buy some tobacco. He liked the church, with its austere, benignant Gothic and whitewashed cool interior, clumsy wooden beams meeting in fishes' heads above his head and clumsy old wooden figures of saints standing against the pillars. Saint Martin was there with his cloak and the beggar; Saint Roch and his dog and a little round-faced Virgin Mary at the knee of Saint Anne. It was a homely, intimate church and a sense of peace fell upon the perplexed heart of Giles as he wandered about it. He wished, or almost wished, that he could kneel with as simple a faith as the washerwoman who set down her basket of snowy clothes in the aisle and said her rosary before the bright modern statue of the Virgin. The mere sense of haven expressed in the attitude of a sleeping old fisher-woman, with bare legs and hair like tangled seaweed, was enviable. Giles would have found comfort in placing a taper to burn on Toppie's behalf before the gold-crowned Virgin and he would have liked to doze beside the fisher-woman and feel that he had a right to do so. And although he did not belong there, the church seemed to accept his presence with a special placidity and kindliness as though it saw in him merely a strayed sheep. It was the true fold, it seemed to say, and it could afford to await, for centuries if need be, the return of all such wanderers.

From the church he crossed the place, paved with cobbles and bright with awninged shops, and entered a leafy path that led up to the cliff-top. A bench was placed in a grassy recess where one could sit and look out at the sea, and it was while he rested there that Giles saw the lady in grey emerge from a white house further up the cliff-side; a tall, sad, slender, beautifully dressed woman of middle-years, whose face, turned on him as she passed, made him think, with its inscrutable calm and mild dignity, of the face of a Japanese lady. As much as the Japanese lady, Giles felt, she belonged to an order, and the meaning of life for her would be in the fulfilling its requirements.

He was glad to see her reappear after he had established himself in the doorway of the chalet. A friend was with her, a stout, dark, sagacious person, and theirs were evidently the young people who played in a further court.

Giles rose when they entered and inquired whether his smoke incommoded them, and the lady in grey, seeing again the stranger of the cliff-seat, smiled kindly and said: "Mais pas du tout, monsieur." She was charming with her slanting eyes and delicate, faded face. She carried still further, though, as it were to a different conclusion, the impression that madame Vervier had so strongly made upon him, of always knowing what she meant to do and of saying what she meant to say. Even her manner of bowing her head and smiling as she replied to him had a technique. That was the only word for it. They had a technique for everything, these French people, Giles more and more clearly saw it, and not only the Samurai-like ladies, but the peasants, the shop-keepers, the maids and waiters. If you presented them with a new situation, they passed the novelty by and gave you the old answer.

The friends looked about them. The stout lady had a long piece of broderie anglaise, fastened, for more facility, to a strip of glazed green leather. The lady in grey had silk and a fine steel crochet needle. Giles could just see her long white hands from where he sat, with rings of black enamel set with pearls, and the long earrings on either side of her long white face were also of pearl and enamel.

They observed the play of the four courts. Madame Vervier and her party played in the nearest, and what more natural than that the lady in grey should make her quiet comment. But though there was no disparagement in her voice, Giles felt a slight discomfort in hearing her. Had she not noted him as a foreigner and seen him as unattached, she would not, he knew, so have alluded to his hostess.

"Tiens!" said the stout dark lady, and she laid down her embroidery to look at Alix's mother.

Madame Vervier playing tennis became an Artemis for speed, strength, lightness. She flashed there in the sunlight before them, her russet locks bound with white, her beautiful arms bare in the white tennis dress, her slender white-shod feet exquisite in their unerring improvisation. Her uplifted face, though so intent, had a curious look of indolent power.

"And the tall child, is she the daughter?" the dark lady inquired.

"I believe so. Yes. The daughter. She bears the name of Mouveray," said the lady in grey.

"Mouveray. Précisément. Her husband divorced her?"

"Or she him. I do not remember. I do not know where the fault lay."

"And this is the husband's child?"

"Ah, that, ma chère, is more than I can tell you," said the lady of the earrings with a touch of melancholy humour. "But she, also, is beautiful. I find her more beautiful than the mother."

"But with less charm," said the stout lady, evidently of madame Dumont's opinion, and she had even something of madame Dumont's expression in pronouncing it. "La mère est toute-à-fait séduisante. C'est une femme exquise."

"But the child has more distinction," said the lady of the earrings.

"It is a head that would tell well on the stage," the stout lady suggested. "And speaking of the theatre I saw mademoiselle Blanche Fontaine bathing here the other day. She is very well in the water."

"Yes. She is staying near madame Vervier at Les Vaudettes. She is a friend. The child is perhaps destined for the theatre.—I can hardly imagine mademoiselle Fontaine in the water," and the lady of the earrings smiled. "I can hardly see her off the stage."

"Ah, she is very well in the water," the stout lady again asserted. "Elle est fausse maigre. And she swims as well as she acts. What a talent it is?"

"A little shrill, a little metallic, perhaps," said the lady of the earrings; but the stout lady was quite secure of her admiration and said that she considered mademoiselle Fontaine the foremost of their young actresses.

A little silence followed, and Giles, who had contemplated withdrawal, settled himself again to his book when the talk, as the friends resumed it, turned on their families. The stout lady spoke of her Jacques at the Ecole Polytechnique; of le petit Charlot and his love for music. The lady of the earrings spoke of Andrée, who would soon be old enough to marry, and of Grand-père, left up at the white house on the cliff with Yvonne to entertain him. Ma tante arrived to-morrow to open Les Mouettes and was bringing a religieuse, an admirable woman, who was to take charge of Grand-père. "Quel homme surprenant," said the stout lady, and the lady in grey said that he was, indeed, wonderful. "Eighty-two, and interesting himself still in all our lives. I was discussing Andrée's marriage with him yesterday. We are fortunate, indeed, in having kept him so long with us."

Giles, as he half listened, gained a further impression, after his impression of the Dumont milieu, different, yet vividly the same in its one essential, of the solidly, complicatedly built structure of French family life; its dependencies; its responsibilities; its ramifications. They all meant each other. They all lived with and for each other, and the longer they lived the more important they became, thus inversing the natural course of family life in England. Andrée, old enough to marry, was a very insignificant person compared to Grand-père.

"And who is the young man with madame Vervier?" asked the stout lady, who had evidently just arrived at Allongeville, since she thus plied her friend with queries. "The little one is René Claussel, I know.—But the tall one? He is as handsome as madame Vervier herself."

"That is André de Valenbois. My uncle named him to me yesterday. Charmant garçon, n'est-ce pas?"

"André de Valenbois! But is he not to marry Babette de Cévrieux's daughter? Surely I have heard something of a marriage in contemplation there."

"Ah. That is a sad story. It was, indeed, arranged; the preliminaries, that is to say, in progress; the young people brought together; two very pretty little fortunes and a happily matched young pair. But it is owing, precisely, to madame Vervier that all has come to a standstill, as you can imagine from seeing him with her. He is the present lover. They were in Italy together last winter."

"But surely I heard of monsieur de Maubert as the present lover."

"Ah—no; that is ancient history. My uncle, who knows monsieur de Maubert, believes that the relation, for years, has been platonic. There have been many names since he was favoured. He is with her now, and it may, of course, be that he is an amant complaisant, though it does not seem probable. André de Valenbois, at all events, is the lover of the moment, and from what I see and hear poor Babette will have to be patient if she still thinks of him for Rose-Marie. A vulgar love would have been less devastating in a young man's life."

Giles now got up. Thrusting his book into his pocket he stood for a moment staring out at the tennis players. He could not pass them without speaking to them and thus reducing to painful confusion his unconscious informants. Yet he must get away. After a moment of hot uncertainty, he turned sharply round the chalet and began, behind it, to climb the hillside.

Well?—in what way was it a surprise? He almost challenged his sick dismay with the question as he went knee-deep through the daisies and scabious. Had not the horrible old woman's intimations of the day before prepared him for it? Had he really cherished the belief that madame Vervier, after her first disaster, might have known no other love than Owen? But the sickness answered for him. He had cherished just these beliefs, and if madame Dumont had left his illusions unimpaired while the ladies of the chalet destroyed them, that was because the first was an old harpy while the latter were women of madame Vervier's own world; of what had been her world. The truth, now, was not to be evaded. Alix's mother was a light woman; an immoral woman; only not of the demi-monde because, he might still believe it, she was not mercenary. His heart was cold with repudiation as he climbed. Owen was belittled by what he had learned; Toppie was more basely wronged; Alix's poor, proud little face sank beneath the waters. What spar of pride would be left for Alix to cling to when she knew? What would she feel?

But what did those women feel? Suddenly, the racial difference more sharply revealed to him than ever, he was aware that the cold repudiation was for them, too. It was the colder because of their kindness. They were safe in the citadel of their order. They were kind because they were safe. Because they were safe they accepted the jungle as having its own and its different code. They strolled peacefully along the city walls and looked down at the bright, prowling, supple creature without the city, and commented on its skill and beauty. One might almost say that the jungle itself was part of the order, since the demi-mondaine was taken as much for granted as the femme du monde. The bright creature was seen as dangerous, no doubt, to adventurers such as André de Valenbois; but Giles surmised that the danger was not great. Inconvenient was the apter word; inconvenient to the plans of the mères de famille. Young men who belonged to the citadel had, as it were, the freedom of the jungle; that was where it came into the order; for their pleasure. They issued forth to adventure; but they came back, they always came back—to Babette's daughter—in the end. Cruel; abominable, such tolerance, such connivance, combined with such repudiation. For it was there that Giles's austere young eyes saw the evil manifest, while the conception of a social structure more complicated and more rigid than any England could ever produce grew upon his vision. For nothing was worse than cruelty, and what was more cruel than to repudiate after you had connived?

And where did Alix, child of the citadel, but habitant of the jungle, come into the picture? His mind turned to her as he had left her, leaping in the sunlight, her head thrown back, her arm uplifted; straight, white, unaware.

He felt himself looking steadily at Alix, eliminating her companion from his field of vision. He could not look at André de Valenbois yet. He could never look at him and at Alix, together, again. The memory of his romance for them gave him almost a qualm of terror. André as an individual was hideously eliminated from any such romance; but, as a type, Giles could feel between him and madame Vervier's daughter no disparity or inappropriateness; none if he were a man with a spark of generosity or insight. But, as he looked at Alix and her future, Giles saw that for young men of the French citadel generosity and insight were sentiments strictly appointed and conditioned. They did not enter into the choice of a wife. How could they, since the choice was made as much by Grand-père at eighty-two, by all the family, as by the young man himself. There was in her own country no future for Alix at all; that was what he saw quite plainly as he turned down from the hillside a mile beyond Allongeville and marched across the road and made his way up the opposite rise of meadow towards Les Vaudettes.

He was striding along the upland now, among the fields of golden grain. The sea-breeze blowing on his face seemed to speak of Alix, and his thoughts, almost with a sense of tears, dwelt on her, on what he divined of the child's nature; so young, yet so mature; so sensitive, yet so hard; and above all so passionately loyal. What would she feel when she knew the truth?—He came back to the first question. They must all have an order, a code, these strange French people. They none of them stood alone. The individual was implicated through every fibre in the group to which he belonged. Would Alix, when she knew, accept the jungle and its code? What else was there for her to do? Giles was asking himself this fundamental question by the time he reached Les Chardonnerets and was finding the only answer to it. There was nothing that Alix could do. But he could do something. He and his mother and all of them. Keep her. Away from the jungle; and away from the citadel, too. "Damn it!" Giles heard himself remarking as he marched towards the verandah. "It thinks itself too good for her and she's too good for it. She shall belong to us. It's the only way out," said Giles.

CHAPTER VII

He had mounted the steps, head bent, hands thrust deeply into his pockets, and had actually cast himself into a garden-chair before he saw that he was not alone. Over there in the corner near the little table where the reviews and newspapers were laid, and the fluttering vines tempered the sunlight, sat monsieur de Maubert, a book upon his knee and his eyeglasses on his nose. He was looking above them, across at Giles, and the young man was terribly disconcerted in seeing him.

"I beg your pardon," he muttered; "I didn't know anybody was here."

"I have only just returned," said monsieur de Maubert in his Olympian tones, "and there is no occasion for apology. You were coming fast and you were thinking deep. You seem disturbed, Monsieur. Has anything occurred to incommode you?"

Giles had pulled his chair around a little so that he faced monsieur de Maubert and as he heard the suave question he suddenly determined to answer it. Whatever monsieur de Maubert's past relation to madame Vervier, he felt assured from what he had observed that his present one was based on a disinterested devotion. If he must try to persuade madame Vervier to give Alix up to them, it would assuredly be as well to gain monsieur de Maubert's sympathy.

"To tell you the truth, I am incommoded," he said. "I've had a very nasty shock. Is that right? Un mauvais coup?—Well, you understand, I'm sure. We're so fond of Alix, all of us, my mother and brothers and sisters; she almost seems to belong to us; and I've just been hearing two women talking at the tennis about her, and her mother; and about her future. Nice women. And they seemed to think there wasn't any future for her except the theatre."

"Well?" monsieur de Maubert removed his glasses as if for a more unimpeded observation of his companion. "And what is amiss with the theatre? You did not, evidently, suppose that they narrowed the opportunities of a young girl such as Alix to that career only; but it will suffice for the argument. What is amiss with it? It may be a great career for a woman of talent. Our friend mademoiselle Fontaine, for example, has made for herself a distinguished name."

Giles felt that his face was hot, but he went doggedly on: "I know. I'm not belittling it. But, from the way they spoke, I infer it's not what it is with us."

"A playground for pretty amateurs? A display of dressmakers' mannequins? No; it is not. We are a more serious people than you when it comes to art."

Giles was not to be abashed. "With us it is one honourable alternative among others. It's a career any young girl can follow, except among old-fashioned, prejudiced people. And I mean young girls of good character; of good standing."

"What you mean, I think," said monsieur de Maubert, "is that with us it is not seen as a suitable career for a jeune fille du monde. Alix is not a jeune fille du monde."

"No; I don't mean only that," said Giles.

"Or perhaps that it is not with us a career pour une vierge," monsieur de Maubert further defined. "There you are right. I do not easily imagine a great actress who is not also a woman of experience. That is all that it comes to, is it not?"

Giles wondered for a moment if this, indeed, was all that it came to for him. He had not thought of it in those terms, and it gave him an added chill to find that monsieur de Maubert did. "What it comes to for me," he said, "is that I don't think it a suitable career for Alix;—precisely because of what you say; and what's more, I don't believe her mother does, either."

At this monsieur de Maubert was silent for some moments, and in the silence Giles felt anew that, ambiguous, even sinister as he might be, his sympathy could be counted upon where any interest of madame Vervier's was in question. If he reflected thus carefully, it was, Giles felt, because from Alix they had passed to madame Vervier.

"You are right. Her mother is with you," he said at last, surprisingly. "It is because she is with you that she sent the child last winter. She sees the difficulties that you see. She would prefer, to any artistic career in France, that Alix should marry in England. Marriage is what she intends for her. She would, I am sure, be glad to talk of any possibilities for Alix with you."

"I hope she'll let me have a talk with her; I'm glad of what you tell me," Giles muttered, though bewildered by monsieur de Maubert's calm assumptions.

And he was going on as calmly: "For myself, I do not know that I am in agreement with her. Where her child is concerned, she shows, at times, for a woman so gifted and so sagacious, a certain conventionality of outlook. She who, for herself, has chosen the path of freedom, should have more courage for her child."

"Isn't it something of a criticism of the path of freedom that she doesn't choose it for her child?" Giles felt himself impelled to comment. "Aren't all mothers conventional when it comes to their daughters? Isn't convention, in that sense, only another name for safety?"

"Ah; you are a shrewd young man," said monsieur de Maubert with a smile. "Perhaps it is. Personally I feel that for our little friend the free life of the artist would be a happier one than the life of the English country lady. That life, for a vivid, vigorous nature such as hers, would be, I should imagine, bornée; fade."

"I don't see why it should," said Giles. "But I wasn't thinking of country ladies, or of marriage at all. We don't think of marriage like that. I thought of Alix making her living in England. I thought of a life where she would have love and respect about her and be useful and happy."

"I do not think that such a prospect would at all attract her mother," monsieur de Maubert remarked. "I do not see what more advantage it offers than a similar life in France. Do you consider, then, that madame Vervier has not love and respect about her and is not useful and happy?"

Giles at this, struck to silence, sat staring at monsieur de Maubert.

"You have doubtless," monsieur de Maubert continued—and Giles saw that it was not through any inadvertence that he had thus placed the situation of madame Vervier squarely between them; without any embarrassment, without any hesitation, he calmly selected the theme—"you have doubtless heard those women speaking of our hostess as if they did not respect her."

"Not quite that," Giles muttered. "They spoke merely as if she didn't count with them at all."

"And do you imagine," monsieur de Maubert inquired, "that they count with her?"

In spite of his confusion Giles could answer this question immediately. "They count with her for Alix," he said.

"For Alix?" monsieur de Maubert mildly, yet perhaps not quite ingenuously, questioned.

"You've owned to it yourself," said Giles. "It's their life she'd want for Alix. The safe life. The respected life. She'd rather that Alix should marry one of their sons than be the most wonderful of actresses."

"It may be so. Gifted and sagacious people have their weaknesses. You speak again of respect," said monsieur de Maubert. "All those who are honoured with her friendship respect madame Vervier. You speak of marriage. What wife can hope for adoration? Madame Vervier is adored as well as respected."

"I should have said that a wife could hope for adoration—and for fidelity as well," Giles returned.

"Very rarely," monsieur de Maubert smiled. "And I do not imagine that our hostess—of whom I speak thus openly because I see that between us there is nothing to conceal—has ever had to fear infidelity. She is in the fortunate position of a woman free to choose. She gives happiness when and to whom she wishes."

Giles sat battling with a confusion of thoughts. He had not meant to discuss madame Vervier with anybody. It was horrible to him that he and monsieur de Maubert should thus be discussing her. But without implying her present it was impossible to discuss Alix's future. "I don't call it fortunate," he said. "I don't call it happiness."

"You do not call it happiness to love and to be loved?" monsieur de Maubert inquired. "You have, perhaps, mystic consolations, monsieur Giles; but to the majority of our poor humanity this will always remain the one authentic happiness of life."

"We have different ideas," said Giles. "I don't see love like that. When you speak of her giving happiness, you mean, I suppose, that she has had a great many lovers. That is what those women said. I think that a tragic life, you see; and the more tragic, the more lovely the woman is who leads it."

"A great many?" monsieur de Maubert weighed it. "Hardly that. She is a serious, not a frivolous woman; and beauty accompanies her always."

"You see, we have different ideas," Giles heavily repeated, looking down and tugging at the wicker of his chair. "A love that can be repeated over and over, I don't call love."

"Bonté divine!" monsieur de Maubert laughed suddenly among the vines. "A fountain cannot throw itself into the air repeatedly and remain itself? Spring cannot return to us again and again? It is with our hearts as with nature; a renewal; a discovery of fresh beauty. And since we are all different, with each new love there is the discovery of new beauty."

"Love to me means nothing—worse than nothing—unless it means dedication; permanence; unity," said Giles.

"Ah, but then it ceases to be love," said monsieur de Maubert, "and becomes duty, affection, the joys and cares of the foyer; what the wives— if they are fortunate—may count on. A young man like you is surely aware of the difference between love the passion, and love the affection. We feel the latter for our wives and mothers; we feel something very different for our mistresses.—You will agree to that, I think."

"I've never had a mistress," said Giles.

"Tiens!" It was an exclamation of blended amusement, astonishment and most courteous respect for a strange idiosyncrasy, and Giles saw monsieur de Maubert in his dappled sunlight opening large eyes.

"What I'd like to ask you, if I may," said Giles, "is what you feel for mistress number one when mistress number two has deposed her; and what you feel for number two when you are devoting yourself to number three. You can't feel passion for them all, at the same time, I suppose. The present lady preoccupies you. What of the others, then? Have they ceased to arouse any solicitude or interest?"

"From the fact that they are gone, far less," monsieur de Maubert owned, shifting himself now in his chair the better to contemplate his companion. "One may think of them with gratitude or regret; with pain or indifference. One may have been abandoned, or one may have found oneself ceasing to desire. A man of honour will do all in his power for the woman who has been dear to him; who may still be dear. Affection and trust may still be there, though passion has burned itself away."

"That must fill your time," Giles muttered, "pretty considerably."

"Ah, it might"—if monsieur de Maubert felt the dryness of the young man's tone he did not stoop to any retaliation; he was all kindliness—"but charming women are rarely in need of consolation. Is not the fact you will not face, my idealistic young friend, the fact, simply, that passion, the flame, does burn out? That is a law of life. You will not alter it with all your ascetic moralities. And shall we turn from the flame, its ardour and beauty, because it cannot burn for ever? That would be an anchorite's error. Let us burn with it and rejoice, until it sinks. Unfortunately, the time of renewal passes," monsieur de Maubert sighed. "Spring goes, and Summer goes, and even of Autumn there is little left. Winter approaches and one grows old."

Giles sat silent looking out to sea. The things he held to be of infinite value were invisible to monsieur de Maubert. The things monsieur de Maubert held to be of value were clearly visible to him. He saw the beauty of flame and fountain and the old paganism in his human heart echoed to the thought of love the passion. But he saw something else, that underlay them all, not contradicting, as monsieur de Maubert imagined, but completing them. What that something was it would be useless to describe.

If one had come to life asking only of each moment what it gave and never what it meant, one became blinded to the meaning.

Sadness fell between them sitting there, and presently monsieur de Maubert said, showing that he felt it, "Well, the sun is setting; I will go in. You are sorry for me and I am sorry for you.—Do we terminate our discussion in a mutual sympathy?"

He had risen from his chair with a rather porpoise-like roll of his stout white body and stood, complete, assured, benevolent, looking down at Giles; and Giles wondered, looking up at him, whether the price one paid for such completeness was just that blindness.

"I suppose there is sympathy," he vaguely murmured. "I'm afraid it's true, though. I think you quite as wrong as you think me."

"Ah, when you are as old as I am," said monsieur de Maubert, unperturbed, "you will think differently. You will by then, assuredly, intelligent as you are, have learned to make a better use of your time. You will have learned to round out your life by a richer experience."

Giles, too, had risen, and he could almost have laughed as he listened; it struck him as so comic, with its sadness, that the traditional rôles of youth and age should be thus reversed. "You will have learned," monsieur de Maubert was going on, "to accept the full gamut of our human nature. There remains nothing, nothing, for the anchorite in his desert—let me assure you of it—but the handful of sand his dying hand clutches at. He has had, you will say, his mirage with which to console himself. That is a sorry consolation at the end. Accept reality, my young friend. Accept the full gamut. Neglect none of the strings of your violin. It is broken all too soon. And what more sad than to have stopped your ears against its sweetest melody?"

"What, indeed?" said Giles. There was hardly irony in his voice. It was contemplative rather. And smiling at monsieur de Maubert as they stood there in the sunset, he added: "We want different things." That simile of the unheard melody summed it up.

CHAPTER VIII

It was strange to meet them all again that evening, so unchanged to their own consciousness, so changed to his. Strange to find them still so charming and so to shrink from their charm. They came laughing up the steps of the verandah where he still sat, and he wondered if they felt in his voice and look, as he greeted them, any difference.

"Ah, it was an excellent set," André de Valenbois said, laying down his racquet and seating himself next to Giles. "Where did you disappear to, mon ami? We looked, and you were in the chalet, and when we looked again, you were gone."

"I felt I'd like a walk. I went up the hill behind the chalet," said Giles. "The country is lovely up there."

Madame Vervier's eyes were on him, hardly cogitative in their gaze, yet perhaps conjecturing something. She, doubtless, knew the names of the ladies of the chalet as well as they knew hers. She might infer the reasons for his flight. At all events, saying nothing, only maintaining her cool dim smile, she crossed the verandah and went into the house.

The evening meal at Les Chardonnerets was irregular in its hour and informal in its habit. Monsieur de Maubert and André de Valenbois only changed their flannels for light afternoon clothes, and Jules, when he came, did not change at all. Giles maintained his custom of evening dress, but he waited for some time alone in the drawing-room that evening, and even after André had joined him, exquisite in pale blues and greys, another five minutes passed before madame Vervier and Alix appeared.

Madame Vervier wore a dark silk dress, purple or red or russet—Giles in the waning light could not define the tint—fastening at the breast with a great old clasp of wrought gold. A fringed Empire scarf, purple, silver, and rose, fell about her beautiful bare arms; a high Empire comb was in her hair, and with her dark gaze she made Giles think of a lady drawn by Ingres.

She moved across to the window, her arm around Alix, and said, standing there and looking out: "La belle soirée!" It was a citron and ash sky above a golden sea.

"Maman, you will sing this evening," said Alix. "Giles has not heard you sing."

"Monsieur de Valenbois is the singer. I have no voice," said madame Vervier.

"One needs no voice to sing the songs I mean," said Alix. "Do you know our old songs of France, Giles?"

She looked round at him over her shoulder, palely shining in the white taffeta, and Giles, with a sinking and sickening as of an unimaginable yet palpable apprehension, saw that André de Valenbois' appreciative eyes were upon her; upon her, rather than upon her lovely mother.

"Do you know the one beginning, 'L'Amour de moi' " asked Alix.

Giles said he did not.

"Ah, it is the very dawn of loveliness, that song," said André, and in the words Giles felt the expression of a perhaps subconscious train of thought. "It is so young. It is all dew and candour. You must hear it, monsieur Giles." The young Frenchman wandered about the room, his hands in his pockets. "Of the time of your Chaucer," he went on. "Our countries then had much the same heart. It was the time when our great cathedrals rose and miracles were as plentiful as turtle-doves." He paused before the mantelpiece and took up one of the photographs set there. "This is of you, mademoiselle Alix?"

Madame Vervier had turned from the window, and, still holding Alix, she approached him.

"Yes; it is of me. It was taken in England," said Alix.

Giles had not noticed the photograph, but he noticed a change in Alix's voice. He, too, drew near, and saw the little snap-shot of Alix with the dogs at the edge of the birch-wood. But it was in a frame delicately embroidered in blue and silver, and he asked in all innocence, "Where did the pretty frame come from, Alix?"

"Toppie made it," said Alix. The alteration in her voice was now evident. He now knew why, and fell to instant silence.

"Toppie? What is Toppie?" André de Valenbois asked, laughing a little and looking at Alix over her photograph. "That is a name I have never heard before."

"It is le petit nom of mademoiselle Enid Westmacott," said madame Vervier, in tones sad and gentle. "She was the fiancée of monsieur Giles's brother, our friend, killed in battle, of whom you have often heard me speak. Mademoiselle Toppie"—how strangely the childish syllables fell from her untroubled lips—"made the little frame for me as a Christmas gift. Had you not seen it, monsieur Giles? It is exquisite. I was infinitely touched by her thought of me."

"Ah. It is, indeed, exquisite," André murmured, while Giles found no words. "One feels that only an exquisite person could have made it.—Yes, certainly I have heard you speak of monsieur Giles's brother, chère madame. But I did not know that he was betrothed."

He spoke in a respectful tone, holding the frame, but for all his resource and grace of bearing, filled, Giles suddenly felt, with a conflict of thoughts. Did he know of Owen? Did he accept his place, in the succession? Was he jealous in retrospect; or, like monsieur de Maubert, in retrospect complaisant? And that there was something to be kept up—or was it for him, Giles, that she kept it up?—was manifest to him from the deliberate adequacy with which madame Vervier advanced to meet the occasion, while Alix, her eyes turned away from them all, fixed her gaze upon the sky.

"She is, indeed, exquisite. I can say it, monsieur Giles, although I have never met her. It is not only from Alix's letters that I know her. Before that. Your brother talked of her always. She was always in his thoughts. One could not know him well, or care for him as we did, without coming to know and care for his beautiful Toppie. It was a great devotion," said madame Vervier, and her voice, in its sadness, sweetness, and decorum, seemed to lay a votive offering before Toppie and her bereavement. "I have never known a greater." But as she thus offered her wreath and bowed her head, Giles saw a deep colour rise slowly in Alix's averted face.

"And here is monsieur de Maubert," said madame Vervier, turning to greet the latest entry. "Jules evidently is belated in some distant village. We will wait no longer, I think. Albertine's soup will be spoiled."

"Have you not a picture of this lovely mademoiselle Toppie?" Giles heard André say to Alix as they moved to the dining-room, madame Vervier leading the way on monsieur de Maubert's arm.

"No, I have no picture of her," said Alix.

"You know her well?"

"Very well. She lives near Mr. Bradley's family."

If madame Vervier's voice showed full adequacy, so did her child's. Alix's adequacy, her grave courtesy, untinged by withdrawal, yet setting a barrier, filled Giles's thoughts during the meal. She, too, knew just what she wanted to say and just how to say it; yet how much deeper, he felt sure, was her perturbation than madame Vervier's. She had seen her mother, before the eyes of her English friend, involve herself in a web of implicit falsehood. How false was madame Vervier's web Alix could not know; but she had known enough to feel ashamed before him; not, Giles knew, because Maman lied; but because she had need of lies. She herself had also lied. Giles, on their journey, had seen Toppie's photograph in her dressing-case. She had lied because she wished to remove Toppie, as well as herself, from even an indirect intimacy with André de Valenbois. It was as though some deep instinct warned her against him. And though Giles again deplored her readiness, he could not feel that he regretted it.

She sat opposite him, all silvery in the soft candle-light, her young downcast face set in its narrow frame of hair, and he knew that grief and fear were in her heart. Madame Vervier talked much, for her, and her gaze, turned once or twice on her child, seemed, as was its wont, to include her and to carry her on to further depths of contemplation. But even madame Vervier could not guess what was in Alix's heart.

After supper they all went out on the verandah. The vines fluttered against a moonlit sky and moonlight washed in upon them like a silvery tide. Mademoiselle Blanche, wrapped in swansdown, came gliding in, and Jules, with a pipe, emerged from the shadows and sat in his accustomed place on the steps. Giles felt that it soothed the lacerated heart of the young artist to be with madame Vervier. Like a wounded wild animal, he drew near the hand he trusted. She was capable of compassion; of great gentleness; of most disinterested friendship. An enigma to Giles, there she sat, and her soft, meditative alto joined in the old songs they all sang together, while Alix, behind her in the shadow, leaned her head, as if weary, upon her shoulder and listened. But more than weariness was expressed in the child's attitude. Giles, listening to the dove-like tenderness of "L'Amour de moi," divined it all. Alix sought comfort from the pressure of new apprehensions, new intuitions, new complexities; and more than for herself, it was for Maman that she thus drew near. The very love, tender, devout, brooding, of the song, was in the gesture with which she laid her head beside her mother's and looked out across her breast into the unknown future.

CHAPTER IX

Madame Vervier did not come down to breakfast next morning. Giles had heard a murmur of voices in the room next his till late into the night and he saw from Alix's eyes that she had slept little. They breakfasted as usual in the little dining-room which overlooked the garden at the back of the house and might have been dark, with its old polished panelling, had not the sunlight at this hour so flooded it. A linen cloth of blue-and-white squares was on the table, and a bowl of marigolds, that seemed to bring the sunlight clotted and palpable among them, in the middle. Above the marigolds, Alix, in Maman's place, poured out their coffee, heavy-eyed but still adequate.

Monsieur de Maubert and André argued about politics with an impersonal vehemence that recalled to Giles, in its transposed key, the altercation of the friendly men in the train. He gathered, however, that they were both agreed on the necessity of a strong man for France and on many lopped heads. The French had not changed so much since the Revolution after all. Whatever the party, the solution seemed the same. Mademoiselle Fontaine, rushing in with a wonderful pink sunbonnet on her head, vividly contributed her own brand of violence, and then announced that it was the very morning for la pêche aux équilles. The tide was low; the sun shone; the breeze blew; and she had promised Maman and Grand'mère a marvellous friture for their déjeuner.

Giles had not yet seen this mildest sport. Armed with spades, bare-legged and shod in espadrilles, they made their way to the beach and, following the receding waves, dug vigorously for the evasive prey, half fish, half eel. He found himself laughing with them as they climbed rocks and raced to fresh stretches of wet, shining sand. He had never known anything more disquieting than the mingling of aversion and liking he felt for them. He and André and mademoiselle Blanche sat on a rock to rest while, at some distance, near the edge of the waves, Alix dug alone, and, as he listened to them and watched her, Giles realized that Alix had been with rather than of them. She had smiled, also, she had even laughed; but there was a disquiet in her deeper even than his own, and if she dug there so intently it was because she found relief in the childish toil.

"What a sky!" said André, looking up at the rippled blue and silver. "It is like music, is it not? Music of a celestial purity. Are you fond of César Franck, monsieur Giles?"

It filled Giles with gloom to hear André speak of celestial purity. It was not that he felt the charming young Frenchman to be impure. What separated them was their conception of life. André's, like monsieur de Maubert's, like madame Vervier's, was a pagan philosophy and his was a Christian. He did not believe that they could understand César Franck.

"Ah! He is not for me!" cried mademoiselle Blanche, appropriately, her chin in her hand as she looked out with brilliant, intelligent eyes at the far horizon. It was strange to see her sitting there, her face whetted by artificial emotion, dyed and touched and rearranged to suit a fashion, among things as primitive as rocks and cliffs and sky. "It is a music without breathing; without blood; the music of a trance. The waves do not break, the clouds do not sail, the birds are silent; one is fixed in an eternity. I do not like eternity."

"Ah, mademoiselle," said André, "monsieur Giles here, who is a Platonist, will tell you that only when we reach eternity do we find life."

André's fox-seraph face was artificial, too, though so differently. Everything he had experienced had been a selection. He had had, all his life through, only to stretch forth his beautiful hand and take from the heaped and splendid corbeille offered him by destiny what fruit, curious or lovely, most tempted him. And his grace, his gift, lay in the fact that he was tempted only by what was curious or lovely. There was nothing of sloth or sensuality in his being. Tempered like steel, he mastered every lesser taste by one finer, and Giles saw him like one of the gravely joyous youths of the Parthenon frieze riding life, as if it were a perfectly broken steed. How exquisite a being must madame Vervier be to have attached him! Such was the thought that passed through Giles's mind, revealing to him, as it did so, how far he had advanced in the understanding of pagandom. And a stranger thought followed it. Unwilling as he was to admit it, it was yet indisputable that Owen had gained a value in his eyes from having been chosen by such a being; from having been André de Valenbois's predecessor. Whatever Owen had lost—and Giles knew that the loss was beyond computation—that he had certainly gained. Meanwhile, on the subject of eternity and César Franck, he maintained a silence which, he hoped, might not seem too morose.

When they returned to Les Chardonnerets with their pêche, madame Vervier sat on the verandah embroidering. Monsieur de Maubert was beside her, and Giles felt sure, from the moment he set eyes upon them, that monsieur de Maubert had by now fully repeated to her the conversation of yesterday. Giles's impressions and discoveries and beliefs were known to her; and, no doubt, the fact that he had never had a mistress. She and monsieur de Maubert had talked him over and over and up and down, but what they had made of him he could not even imagine.

Her eyes met his with the bland serenity of a statue's. "Have you had a good pêche?" she asked Alix. She took her by the hand and drew her to her side and looked down into the bucket. "Admirable! Albertine will be overjoyed. Dieu, que tu as chaud, ma chèrie!"

"It is the climb up the cliff, Maman," Alix bent her head obediently while her mother passed a handkerchief over her neck and brows.

Monsieur de Maubert had got up and gone inside and mademoiselle Blanche had parted from them at the cliff-top.

"I will sit here in the shade with you and rest, chère madame," said André, casting himself into monsieur de Maubert's vacated garden chair.

"And you, ma petite," said madame Vervier, still holding her child by the hand, "may, if you wish, and if monsieur Giles will accompany you, bathe now. You will have time before lunch."

"I should like that very much. But I do not need anyone. It is quite safe," said Alix, with a curious lassitude in her tone.

"But, indeed, you may not go alone," smiled madame Vervier.

"And I should love a swim," said Giles.

So, presently, he and Alix were on the beach again.

But when they came to the rock where, with safety, the bathing-robes might be deposited, Alix, instead of doffing hers, sat down and said: "Shall we talk a little?"

"Do let us talk," said Giles, and a great wave of relief went through him. At all events, Alix would not keep things from him. He sat down beside her. Only the sea and sky were before them.

"I had to tell Maman last night, Giles," said Alix. She looked straight before her, wrapped to her chin in the white folds of her robe, and he felt that she had to keep herself by sheer self-mastery from reddening before him now, as she had last night when she had heard Maman talk of Toppie.

"Ah. Yes," said Giles as quietly as he was able. "I thought perhaps you'd feel it best."

Alix, her dark brows slightly knotted, looked before her. "And I think she sent me here with you so that I should tell you," she went on. "Tell you, I mean, that she believed what she said last night about Captain Owen and Toppie. That Toppie was first with him. Not until I told her of his silence to you all did she see—what you and I saw, Giles;—that he cared most for her."

Giles sat, struck to an icy caution. Yes; he saw it in a flash; that was how she would put it to Alix. He could find no word. But Alix expected none. Carefully she continued her tale. "It made her very sad when I told her of his silence. It made her cry. But she was not angry with me for having kept it from her. She understood."

"And was she angry with him?" Giles asked after a moment.

Alix at that turned her eyes upon him and he read in them a deep perplexity. "I do not know," she said. "She did not say. I do not think she was angry with him either. She is a person who understands everything. But I do not think she would have been so unhappy if it had not hurt her very much. Why else should she cry?"

Why, indeed? Was it for her unveiling before himself? How difficult to think it after the blank gaze of those dark eyes. Was it not, rather, in fear and grief at seeing her child entangled, at last, in her vicissitudes? However it might be, there was a new burden on her heart and, inevitably, Alix now must bear part of its weight with her.

"Well, I'm glad it's all out," Giles murmured. "It makes everything simpler, doesn't it?"

"Does it?" said Alix.

When she asked that, he was aware that part of his thought had been that it made it simpler in regard to Alix herself and what he hoped to do for her. But was he really so sure of this? Would madame Vervier be more willing to let them have Alix now that she saw all her vicissitudes disclosed to him?

"I hope she'll have a talk with me," he said. "One can't talk, really, if things aren't clear."

"She is going to talk with you, Giles," said Alix. She still spoke with her lassitude. It was as if Maman had stretched her too far. "I do not know when. She is occupied, as you see, with her other friends. But she will talk with you. You please her. Very much."

"Oh, do I?" Giles murmured. If it hadn't been his dear little Alix he could hardly have kept the irony from his voice. "I hope it will be soon," he said. "I hadn't intended my visit to last over the week, you know."

"I think it will be soon," said Alix. "But I cannot say for Maman. Shall we swim now, Giles?"

When they all met again at lunch, over the marigolds, it seemed to Giles that madame Vervier looked at him with a new kindliness. She seemed to take it for granted that from his little interview with Alix there must have come a gain for their relation. She asked him if he was coming this afternoon to tennis, and when he said no, that he had work to do, she went on, smiling at him: "You will be abandoned, then, for we all have our tea at Allongeville. But perhaps you will take refuge with madame Dumont and her daughter."

Alix had told tales. That was evident. Giles summoned an answering smile with which to own that nothing could be further from his wishes than to have tea with mesdames Dumont and Collet.

"You do not care for our ancient neighbor?"

"Not at all," said Giles.

"Ah, in her day, la pauvre vieille, she had her qualities," said monsieur de Maubert.

"Blanche told me that Grand'mère found you un jeune homme très sévère," said madame Vervier, her eyes still resting on him as if with a mild amusement. "She is not accustomed to young men such as you. I do not think she has ever met such a one. It is a heavy intelligence"—she now addressed monsieur de Maubert. "It must always, I imagine, have been a heavy talent. One wonders where Blanche found her delicious gift."

"A grandfather, a father, might account for that," said monsieur de Maubert.

"A father might. A grandfather has only madame Collet to his credit," smiled madame Vervier.

"Her talent is too sharp. Like herself," said André.

"But the parts she prefers need the keen edge," said madame Vervier.

"Every part needs a soul, and she has none; elle n'a pas d'âme," said André.

Madame Vervier defended her friend.

"With so much intelligence she needs less soul than other people."

"Pardon, chère madame. With so much intelligence one needs more. It is that one feels in her. The sheath is too thin. The blade comes through."

"Vous êtes méchant," said madame Vervier, and there was in her voice none of the inciting gaiety usual to the reproach; she spoke gravely, looking down at the cloth and slightly moving her spoon and fork upon it, and Giles suddenly divined that poor mademoiselle Blanche was in love with André.

"Mais non! Mais non! I think her charming," laughed André. "But I can understand that madame Dumont is her grandmother."

CHAPTER X

It was not until next day, after luncheon, that the time came, and Giles—as madame Vervier said to him, "I find it too hot for tennis to-day. Will you stay behind and talk with me, monsieur Giles?"—felt sure that it all had been planned, intended from the first. If she had thus delayed, it was in order that he should come to know her better and feel more at home with her. It was also in order that she should take his measure and see more surely what she was going to do with him.

Monsieur de Maubert, also, was going to Allongeville; André's motor waited at the gate. He and madame Vervier were to have the afternoon to themselves, and as they all parted on the verandah, Giles saw that Alix cast a long look at him.—Poor little Alix! How little she could guess at what he hoped for from this interview! If madame Vervier had her intentions, he had his. And though he believed they would not clash, his heart was beating quickly as he followed her to the drawing-room. So many things, lay between him and madame Vervier and her glance, her voice, seemed to tell him that none of them were to be evaded.

The drawing-room was fresh and pale; so pale in its citrons, whites, and dim jade-greens, that the sunlight outside, shining against the transparent reed blinds, looked tawny in its fierce, prowling splendour. The sea was there, sparkling in its immensity across the lower half of the long windows, and the sky of another blue was across the upper half and the vines and honeysuckle that garlanded the verandah outside hardly stirred in the brilliant air. There were bowls of sweet-smelling small white roses from the garden, and madame Vervier was in white, the thin woollen dress with the sash at her waist and tassels at her breast that left bare her lovely arms and neck. Her russet hair was all tossed back to-day and there was something ingenuous in the shape of her forehead thus uncovered; something candid and childlike. In her hand, as she sat before Giles, she held a stone, a flat, smooth stone, pinkish-grey, that she had perhaps picked up on the beach in one of her walks at dawn. She held it, weighing it slightly from time to time and from time to time putting it against her lips or cheek, as if to enjoy its coolness.

Giles had never in his life seen anything so beautiful. He knew that she was not beautiful if computed or examined by standards of exactitude; that her eyes were small, her nose a little flattened, her mouth clumsily drawn; but power so emanated from her gaze, magic so pervaded her lips and brows, sweetness lay with such a bloom of light upon her, that every imperfection was dissolved in the unity that made a sort of music in his mind. She was like an embodiment of music—and what was that urgent, searching rhythm, that evocation of flowers and dew and night? The melody of Brahms's "Sapphische Ode" surged into his mind and with it a deep, an almost overpowering sadness. With the song he remembered everything; everything was evoked. The Spring day in the Bois; Owen's face of love; and Toppie, far away, betrayed and forgotten, fixed in her trance of fidelity. To see madame Vervier, to remember Toppie, was almost to feel that he himself was Owen.

"You know, then," said madame Vervier. Her arm lay along the table beside her. She looked across at him and held the stone in her upturned palm.

That was the way she began; those the very first words she said after she had led him in, after their long silence, when they found themselves alone together. The throb of André's car had long since faded down the lane. The house was still; and Giles felt that his heart was trembling.

"Yes. I've known from the beginning," he said.

"Alix told me," said madame Vervier. "You saw us one day in the Bois."

"Yes," said Giles.

"And she tells me that you feel him to have been unfaithful to his betrothed."

"Yes," Giles repeated. He was amazed yet not overwhelmed by her direct approach. He kept his eyes upon her. "Unfaithful."

There was a weight in the word that madame Vervier would not feel, for André was now entangled with his thought of Owen. It was hardly eighteen months ago; and André had succeeded Owen. But all unaware, as she might well be, of his further knowledge, her next words answered, by implication, the charge. If she admitted contemporaneity in love, why not succession? "There," she said, "you were mistaken. We were lovers, it is true; but he knew that it was not to last. He knew that if not death, then life must part us. In his heart he was not unfaithful. He would have gone back to her."

"Do you mean with a lie?" asked Giles.

"With a lie? Yes; I imagine it would have been with a lie," madame Vervier did not hesitate. "But the essential would be there. He had not ceased to love her.—It was not his fault. He was swept away," she said.

Had she looked like that when she had swept Owen away? Was it an easy, an everyday thing to her, to see men swept away? He tried to beat down the visions that assailed him, but again and again, on the rising surge of the "Sapphische Ode," they returned. Owen sitting before her, as he now sat, in the pale, fresh, shaded room; Owen rising suddenly to take her in his arms.—There would be no surprise to her in that.—She would have seen it coming. "You mean that it was your fault, then?" Giles muttered.

"No. I do not mean that," madame Vervier answered, and as, in speaking, she weighed her stone lightly up and down, her eyes on his, he felt that it was his heart rather than her own guilt she weighed so in her hand.—How often she had weighed men's hearts! How conversant with their trembling must she be! "No; that is not what I meant.—He moored his boat at the edge of a torrent. That was all. He was swept away," madame Vervier repeated.

"That was what Alix said of you," Giles muttered again. He felt as if madame Vervier must see the throbbing of his heart.

"What Alix said of me?"

"That you were like a mountain-torrent. She wanted me to understand you. She thought I might be of help to you some day. She thought of you, poor child, as in some kind of danger; beautiful and in danger.—How can you say it wasn't your fault?" Giles demanded, and, with the thought of Alix and what she hoped from him, he felt that he struggled to keep his footing. "If you carried him away, it was your fault.—I believe that's what you live for; to carry men away," he heard himself unbelievably uttering, and it seemed to him, as the sombre magic of her eyes dwelt on him that it was for Owen he was speaking, and for all the others; since now he understood them all.

Madame Vervier, after he had said these last words, contemplated him in silence. For a long time she said nothing, and Giles, in the silence, felt that their confrontation was altered in its quality. When she spoke at last, it was not in anger. It was, rather, with a strange mildness. "I do not overflow my banks, ever," she said. "You must not launch your boat upon me; that is all."

If he had found himself understanding them all—all those others—was it possible that she saw him merely as one of them? Was she warning him? Had she seen his need of warning? Giles felt his face growing hot.

"You must not launch your boat upon me," madame Vervier repeated, observing him with grave but faintly ironic kindliness. "If I am a torrent, if I am dangerous, to myself and others, my nature is there as it was given to me. I may not alter it. The blame lies with those who are unwary."

"That may be true," Giles muttered. "I have nothing to do with you, of course. I don't understand you. But I do understand my brother. His weakness doesn't excuse him."

"You are severe. You have never felt a great passion, that is evident," madame Vervier observed. "The feeling he had for me was so different from the feeling he had for Toppie that infidelity was hardly in question."

"Hardly in question? Don't you see that it shut him away from her for ever?" Giles's voice was dark with grief. "Don't you see that a man who chooses one kind of love turns his back on the other?"

"Not if he is strong enough," madame Vervier, with her mildness, returned. "Your brother, I think, gained in strength from our friendship. We pay, it is true, for most things in life. It is painful to have a secret from the heart nearest ours; yet one need not regret one's secret. I believe that Owen would have been strong enough not to regret. Strong enough"—madame Vervier, while she dropped the quiet phrases kept her faint smile—"not to grow to hate me because he could not tell Toppie how much he had loved me."

Was it true? Giles wondered, sitting there before her, his head bent down while he stared up at her from under his brows, frowning and intent. Could Owen, ever, have been as strong as that? And would it have been strength? No; madame Vervier might have armed him against remorse; but she did not know Toppie. Toppie's radiance would have fallen back, dimmed, startled, from the presence of the thing hidden yet operative in her life and Owen's. A canker would have eaten; bitterness and darkness would have spread. Either her radiance would have withdrawn from him, or, beating too strongly at his defences, it would have discovered all. Dismay, devastation would have broken in upon them, and if Toppie could still have forgiven it would have been with a sick and altered heart. But he could not talk to madame Vervier about Toppie. The strange thing was, as he saw Toppie's radiance, that he felt himself safe from the torrent, and that he began to understand madame Vervier.

"You think of yourself as very strong," he said suddenly, and in their long silence he could see that something of her security left her; it was as if she felt the approach of an unexpected adversary. "You think you can do as you like with life. You're not afraid of life; and that's rather splendid of you—if I may say so. But it's never occurred to you to be afraid of yourself. And the time might come, you know, when you'd be carried away, too."

"Carried away?" madame Vervier repeated. Her voice was altered. She was unprepared. And in her momentary confusion it was with haughtiness that she spoke.

"Yes, carried away," Giles repeated, understanding madame Vervier more than ever and that the haughtiness was a shield. "And if you were, you'd be helpless, as he was; as all the others are;—and you'd find, I believe, that you couldn't go back quietly to the things you'd jeopardized.—I mean, they'd have changed; they'd have been spoiled. You made Owen suffer; I'm sure of it. You gave him more suffering than happiness. He lost Toppie through you, and he knew he'd lost her. He couldn't have lived with Toppie on a lie. The payment may be more than our own suffering; it may be other people's. That's what you don't seem to see.—And as for doing as you like, with yourself and other people, it doesn't work, the kind of life you lead. I'm sure it doesn't work. It will spoil you, too. More and more you'll be battered and bruised;—it's horrible to think of;—and at last wrecked. Or else so petrified and hardened that nothing can really come to you any more. That's the way it would happen with anyone like you." Giles had looked away from her in speaking, but now he lifted his eyes to hers again. "I feel sure of it."

Madame Vervier sat there, her arm lying on the table, her hand holding the stone, and looked fixedly upon him. He had thought of nothing definite, of nothing imminent in speaking. He had been able to speak only because the thought of Toppie had come to him so overmasteringly, arming him with such repudiation of madame Vervier's philosophy. But now, as she sat silent for so long, he saw suddenly what the fear was that, like a Medusa head, he had held up before her. She was older than André de Valenbois; she loved him passionately; and she was not sure of him. It was in her eyes, in her silence, as she faced him, that Giles read the fear; definite; imminent. And he was horribly sorry for her.

"You are a strange young man," she said at last. The haughtiness was gone. There was no resentment in her voice. She only spoke carefully, as though she felt her way in a world changed to ice. "How can you think you know me well enough to say these things?"

"I don't know you well enough. It's because we are so near. Through Alix. Through my brother. You've made such a difference in my life. Everything is changed for me because of you."

"It need not be as you say," said madame Vervier, and after her long pause it was as if the strength he had called in question came creeping back into her frozen veins. "Not as you say;—if one has wisdom. One may suffer;—do you imagine that I have not already suffered?—but one need not be wrecked. And I have great wisdom."

"I don't want you to be wrecked.—You know that," Giles muttered.

"Yes. I know it. I see it. You are not an avenging angel," said madame Vervier, and she was able once more to summon the faint, ironic smile. "You are really, under all the denunciation, so full of kindness. That is what makes you so unexpected.—So very strange.—But do not fear for me too much. I shall know when youth is over. I shall know when the laurels are cut and winter has come to the woods. I shall be able to furl my sails before the night comes on; and if one furls one's sails in time, monsieur Giles, one is never wrecked. And there will be, I trust, a little harbour for me somewhere. Alix's children to love. And my memories. I shall be in old age a much happier woman than most. Most old women"—madame Vervier smiled on, her eyes on his—"have only to remember how they were loved by nobody at all."

What was there to say to her? Giles, as he considered her, felt a dim smart of tears rising to his eyes. She had done with him as Alix had hoped she would. He saw her as lovely; as menaced. He wished that he could protect her. "I hope it will be with you like that," he said.

"Perhaps it will," said madame Vervier. "You have seen me and my life a little too logically, too rigidly, my kind monsieur Giles. I did not choose it so. It chose me, rather."

"Ah," Giles exclaimed, "that's what I feel in you. That's my excuse for what I've said to you. Why can't you turn back even now? You are so much too good for it. You're good enough," Giles declared, with a sense of further illumination, "for anything."

Madame Vervier, again arrested, considered him. Then, gently, sadly, with a compassionate sincerity, she shook her head. "One never turns back at my age. One's path has grown too closely about one. Other paths are all blocked out. And I was perhaps destined for it. For some women the life of home, the still, deep stream suffices. Children may fill their hearts and stifle the personal longings; but for others these compensations are not enough. They must have love. They must have a lover. And in France husbands are seldom lovers. So, if one is a mountain-torrent, one leaps over the precipice. Do you see? That is my history."

"It's different with us," Giles murmured. "We have different hopes for marriage. You didn't give yourself time. If you turn your back on a thing, you can't find out its reality."

"The mountain-torrent, at twenty-three," said madame Vervier, "is not a philosopher. No; I did not see what I was leaping to, but I saw plainly what I left. And I do not say that I regret. All that I do say is that I wish no leaps for Alix. Let us now speak of Alix. You have done your duty by me and read me my lesson, and it is all because you want to speak of Alix. I am well aware that you have not come to France in order to understand or grow fond of her mother—kind though you are."

"No; it was for you—only for you." Giles did not know how to put it. "Because of what I see in you. As to Alix, you want for her what I want."

"Safety. Yes," said madame Vervier. "The deep, quiet stream."

"She's that already," said Giles. "Alix isn't the mountain-torrent."

"Ah, we none of us know what we are till we come to the precipice," said madame Vervier. "But I am glad you feel that of my Alix. I trust your reading. I could almost believe, at moments, watching you with her, that you understand her better than I do. There is in Alix an austerity that sometimes disconcerts me. Yours is a nature nearer hers than mine. I have thought of it deeply in these last days, monsieur Giles, and I have made up my mind. Will you marry her?" said madame Vervier, laying down the stone.

CHAPTER XI

"There are many things to consider," madame Vervier pursued, simply and tranquilly, while Giles sat transfixed. "I should have to think of many things.—Your position; your prospects; they are not, I gather, brilliant. But one of the gravest disadvantages of a position like mine is that it narrows my field of choice; terribly narrows it. Family and position count for everything here in France. It is not one little individual choosing another little individual; we are more serious than you in that. It is one family choosing another. It is two foyers coming together to found a third. I have spoiled all this for Alix." Madame Vervier took up her stone again, again weighing it in her hand, and now it was as if she weighed the sense of her culpability towards her child. "I have spoiled it. Money would have helped me to atone; but not only was I not philosophe at twenty-three; I was also credulous; ignorant; reckless. The man for whom I left my husband was poor and had great schemes. I gave him all I had. He sucked me dry. C'était un bien méchant homme," madame Vervier remarked in a tone of surpassing detachment, "and what would have been my fate I cannot tell had not the admirable friend who rescued me from his clutches left me, on dying, a small annuity. That is all I dispose of. And with what I have been able to set aside for Alix year by year, I have amassed only the tiniest dot; hardly enough to clothe her.—I go into all this very summarily for the moment, though I owe you every detail. You shall have them later on. You shall hear of the old aunts who brought me up and who were, also, inveigled by monsieur Vervier. Even my family did not save me since I was so unfortunate as to marry him after the divorce. It is a long story. But for the present it is enough that you should see why, aside from my own position, there is for Alix no possibility of a suitable marriage in France. Whereas in England all is different."

"Yes, it's different in England," Giles muttered, since she paused as if for his assent. He was still too transfixed by the sudden theme to dispose of his own thoughts. He felt as if madame Vervier, with her calm, her deliberation, her fluency, were casting, loop by loop, a silken net about him. And he, the dismayed and astonished fish, looked here and there through the meshes for a means of escape that would not too violently tear the web.

"Quite different," said madame Vervier with confidence. "That is why I sent her to England. That is why I make you my proposal now. In blood Alix is much your superior; your fortune, I know is small; your position obscure. But I like you monsieur Giles;—I like you very much. Oh, I have studied you since you came among us! And," madame Vervier added, smiling with a kind of indulgence upon him, "you like Alix very much. I have seen that."

So she gathered up the last strand and considered her captive before drawing him definitely on shore.

"And poor little Alix? Where does she come in?" broke from Giles. After his long mute immobility these were the first words that came to him. "Is she to be considered in the matter?"

"Poor little Alix? Why poor?" madame Vervier questioned kindly. "It would not with you be brilliant; but it would be safe. You will be tender and faithful always. You have not to assure me of that. And you would, I am convinced, do all that is in your power to do in order that she may be well placed in the world."

"And aren't her feelings to count at all in this disposal of her? She'd never have me," Giles declared with a sort of indignant mirth. "I'm the last person in the world she'd ever think of."

"You underrate your attractions," said madame Vervier, still more indulgently. "Alix is very fond of you. And she is still a child; singularly still a child. We may for a year or two put the question of Alix's feelings aside. At her age one has no feelings. It lies with you, and with me, to see that when the time comes they are the right ones. She is devoted to you"— madame Vervier enlarged her assurance. "That is unquestionable."

"But I care for somebody else!" Giles heard himself almost shouting. It was unbelievable that he should have to say to madame Vervier what he had never explicitly said to himself; unbelievable that he must set the sacred figure of Toppie between them. But she was actually drawing him on shore and there was nothing for it but to break through.

"Somebody else?" madame Vervier repeated. Giles had grown pale with the shock of his own avowal, yet, all the same, he was aware of a side glance at the comedy of her discomfiture. It was as if all the strands dropped from her hands.

"Yes," he nodded; "I love somebody else."

She might be discomfited, but she retained her resourcefulness. "Somebody I know of?"

"Yes," Giles doggedly repeated. "Somebody you know of."

It was then madame Vervier, after their little pause, who supplied, with a strange softness, the evident name.—"Toppie."

"Yes, Toppie." Giles turned his head away and fixed his eyes on the blue outside.

And madame Vervier sat silent. Very gently she laid down her stone—Giles was never to forget the look of that smooth, pinkish-grey stone—and folded her hands in her lap. She rested her eyes upon the young man—though his head was turned away from her Giles knew that she was looking at him;—and the silence, in the pale room, with the brilliant day beating from without upon it, grew long. It grew so long that Giles had time to draw his mind from his own confusion and to wonder what was in hers.

Then, when she spoke, her voice was so new to him, so unexpected, that it was as if a new chapter in his knowledge of her opened gently before his eyes. Uncertainty, hesitation was in it; something almost shy; a lovely sweetness. It was revealed to him that for all her goddess-like invulnerability she might have known a qualm of pity for Toppie; it was revealed to him that a romantic girl still lived in her heart, rapt in the wonder of a love-story. "But then—does not that make it all right?" she said.

"How do you mean, right?" Giles asked.

"If you love Toppie?—Will you not marry her? Will you not both be happy?—In your beautiful English way of happiness—for ever after?"

She was smiling at him from her cloud of shyness, seeming to feel the secret disclosed to her too beautiful and delicate for her to venture near its nest; and the childlike quality he had seen in her forehead irradiated all her features, while in sincerest, most ingenuous joy she forgot her own hopes.

"You see," said Giles—and he spoke gently to that child—"Toppie would never have me. She'll never love anyone but Owen."

Owen's name did not for a moment stay her. "Never? Oh, no. You are young enough to believe in that word; and so is she. I am old and wise in that. You may trust me when I tell you that it is a word too large for our slight human nature. So many eternities"—madame Vervier smiled at him—"I have seen melt away."

"She'd never have me," Giles repeated.

"You think that no one will have you. It is not so.—Have you tried?"

"No." Giles shook his head. "I don't think I want to try, really—I don't think I want her different."

"Dieu!" madame Vervier now breathed. "You will embrace a celibate life?"

"I don't know. Perhaps I shall. I never thought about it," poor Giles muttered. "I've never thought about Toppie in that way. I've always loved her—ever since I was a boy—knowing that she could only be for somebody else."

"But then"—madame Vervier in a slight bewilderment groped her way among these unfamiliar shapes—"if you have never thought about her in that way—perhaps you will be able to think about Alix. She, too, cares so much for your Toppie. Toppie would become your patron-saint. Together you would worship at her shrine.—Does it interfere with what I had planned for you and Alix?"

"I'm afraid it does. I'm afraid it absolutely interferes." Giles, his face suffused with red, sat looking down, struggling with difficulty to master a sense of tears. "It's impossible, you know; quite impossible. Dear little Alix. All I ask, you must see that, is to take care of her."

"I have blundered," said madame Vervier. "Forgive me. We will speak of it no more."

"But you've spoken of it beautifully. I'm glad to have you know," said Giles, and the strange sense that this was so made part of his amazement.

"We will speak quite differently, then, of Alix," said madame Vervier. "We will talk of her, not as your future wife, but as your little friend. Even so she is fortunate. And I!—how fortunate I am—for I know that I can count upon you absolutely. You will help me as no one else can help me. If not you, then another English husband. Who is this Lady Mary of whom Alix has written to me? She has sons?"

It was like being borne on the wings of a great aeroplane from continent to continent;—one nearly as strange as the other. Giles really felt inclined to gasp and ask for mercy. He could not go so fast or rise so far without a sense of giddiness.

"Lady Mary Hamble? Sons? I'm sure I don't know," he said, staring at the pilot.

"You do not know her? You have no relations with her?"

"I've seen her only once in my life. Alix, as far as I remember, has seen her only once. Last winter. She's a nice woman. That's all I know about her."

"Yes. It was last winter. But she asked Alix to go to them. It was very foolish of her not to have gone. If I had been there it would not have happened so. Alix wrote of her with much liking. I gathered from the impression Alix had of her that it would be a good milieu."

"Oh, excellent I should say. Much better than ours, of course." Giles was able to recover something of his own broad smile, the farce of it, to his seeing, breaking through too strongly. "You're quite right about us. We're not brilliant at all."

"So I had inferred." Madame Vervier considered him with kind and lucid eyes. "She is a femme du monde."

"Very much so, I imagine. I don't know any femmes du monde, except you," said Giles.

"Ah, my claim to the rôle would be disputed," madame Vervier remarked. "She will, I think, have sons. Since it is a position, there will be a son to inherit it."

"Well, yes. There certainly might be," said the laughing Giles. He leaned back, clasping his ankle with his hands, and took open possession of his mirth.

Madame Vervier, all indulgence, showed her awareness of its grounds. "It is strange to you, almost horrifying, that I should have such computations; is it not?"

"Well, I don't know. Plenty of English mothers have them, of course. Only they're not so frank about them. All the same, you know, you mustn't count upon us. We couldn't do much in that line. My mother, for instance, would never think of such a thing, and if Alix came back to us she'd be like one of my sisters; trained, if you like, to a profession. Marriage would only be by chance; for her, as for them."

"Dieu! You are a strange people!" said madame Vervier. "To leave to chance what is of the most vital importance in a woman's life! No; you are not serious. You live dans le brouillard. Life must be less difficult a thing with you since it is possible to face it so lightly. I should not, it is evident, care to leave Alix among you unless it were in the hope of marriage. I could myself have her trained to a profession. If I gave her up again, it would be because I hoped for something better. I am not féministe. I think a professional life deplorable for a woman. A necessity in many cases, no doubt; but a deplorable necessity. An artist's life is happier; but I hope that my Alix may find the happiest life; the life of a woman married well. So, if she returns to England, it is for the sake of the chances, and you, I believe, will help to make them for her. To begin with, you will see that she accepts Lady Mary Hamble's next invitation."

"Confound her impudence!" Giles was saying to himself, but he was saying it tenderly. He was enjoying her impudence; it was part of the comedy that, for all her pitiful, her tragic aspects, she offered him. "I see that I am to be counted upon as a sort of père de famille for Alix," he observed, and though genial his tone was certainly ironic.

"Précisément," smiled madame Vervier. "You will not, I know, be a dog in the manger and grudge to others what you do not want for yourself."

"Ah, but that's a very different thing from asking Old Dog Tray to go trotting about to find her a husband," Giles objected. "I don't see myself as a matchmaker, you know; I can't promise to do anything at all in that line for Alix."

"You were not asked to be Old Dog Tray. You were asked to be le Prince Charmant," madame Vervier returned, a hint of the caustic in her kindness. "And I do not now ask you to trot. I ask you only, if an occasion offers, to see that she does not miss it. She has not the heredity of the English girl. She will not know how to make, or take, occasions for herself."

"I think you are being rather nasty about the English girl," Giles now commented. He and madame Vervier were on strangely intimate terms and could deal out friendly irony to one another. "The English young man counts for something after all. What we hope for, we romantic English, is that he will make the occasion."

"Oh, no. Not nasty; not at all nasty. I admire them, your English girls; I admire their enterprise," smiled madame Vervier. "Young men do not know how to make occasions, and since the English mother feels it beneath her dignity to make them, it is left for the girl to combine the rôle of mother and daughter. It is a difference of mœurs, that is all, and I wish Alix to have the advantage of your mœurs while keeping the immunities of her own. The question that now remains is: Does she return to you? She does not expect to. You will have gathered that she feels very keenly your brother's silence in regard to his visits to us in Paris."

Again it was a case of her surpassing detachment. She went to the heart of the matter as if it had been, merely, a question of his brother. Yet the strange thing was that, though so detached, she did not affect one as callous.

"Yes. She feels it very keenly," said Giles. "She can't, of course, understand the grounds of his shrinking. She was sure that when you knew you would feel as she did and would not think of letting her come back."

For madame Vervier had not known. He was sure of that now. She might be detached, and even callous; but she was not brazen.

"La pauvre chérie!" the mother ejaculated and it was on a sudden note of profound tenderness. "She is sensitive to such a point, and it is obvious that, had I imagined such a predicament for her, I could not have sent her among you. We must not blame him. He could not have foreseen what was to come." She mused now, compassionately, upon the grounds of Owen's shrinking. "But how much wiser had he written quite openly and naturally of his leaves to Paris. The tone should have been kept to the tone of Cannes. Ah, it is indeed a pity that he showed so little resource!"

"I don't suppose Owen was in a state of mind to feel resourceful," said Giles sombrely. When madame Vervier spoke like this, chasms opened between them. But were there not just such chasms between him and Alix? "I think I like him the better for it," said Giles.

"Ah—and I do not love him the less!" madame Vervier returned with an effect of quickness, though she spoke quietly. "I do not love him the less. I do not even blame him. And it is this leniency of mine that has given Alix her first perplexity in regard to my conduct.—Or is it her first? Who knows what goes on in those innocent but astute young hearts!—Ah, monsieur Giles, that, you would like to tell me, will be the worst punishment of all;—when Alix knows."

"I don't want you to be punished," said Giles sombrely. "I don't want to tell you anything."

"It is so sure to come that it needs no telling. That is perhaps what is in your mind.—Or, no; it is only that you are kind, strangely kind to me," said madame Vervier, rising as she spoke and moving, with her light, majestic step to the window. She pulled up the blind, for the sun no longer beat into the room, and stood looking out for a moment without speaking, her back turned to him; then she said: "Alix, too, is kind. I do not fear for our relation, hers and mine. When she is of an age to hear the truth, she shall hear it."

"She loves you very deeply," said Giles.

"She loves me very deeply," madame Vervier repeated. "I have no fear."

Giles, too, had risen, and moved to the mantelpiece where the picture of Alix in its blue-and-silver frame stood. He looked at it in silence for some moments.

"And how will you persuade her to come back?" he said at last.

"You want her back?" madame Vervier asked from the window.

"Of course I want her back," said Giles. He spoke quietly, almost casually; yet it was strange to feel the weight of his own decision. He pledged himself to something with his words. They implicated him in the situation from which he removed Alix. It was only for himself that he had a right to speak and in accepting Alix he accepted the cloud that hung about her; he brought it back among them; and he knew that the responsibility was heavy.

"Then she shall go to you," said madame Vervier. "I shall not be able to persuade her. I shall attempt no persuasion. She will obey me. That is all. She will wonder at me for sending her. She will feel that it should too much offend my pride to send her back on false pretences"—how they understood each other, mother and child—"but she will go. Our French children learn to obey. It is the first article in their creed.—And since the pretences are not too false for your taste, monsieur Giles, they are not too false for mine."

"They are too false for my taste," said Giles. He was implicated, but madame Vervier must see just how and where. "It's Alix I'm thinking of. I sacrifice my taste to her."

"And I," said madame Vervier, "sacrifice my pride."

She stood there looking out, white against the blue, and her voice, for all its calm, was sombre. "I am not ungrateful," she added. "Do not think me ungrateful. I see what you do for my child."

"I see what you do for her," said Giles.

"Yes;—but I am a mother!"

"It must be all the harder," said Giles. "You consent to see yourself belittled in her eyes. And you consent to live without her."

Madame Vervier stood silent at that for a long moment. Something of the grave ardour in the young Englishman's voice may well have touched her to a deeper vision of herself, and of him. It was as if arrested that she stood contemplating the novel homage laid at her feet. For, after her pause, she turned suddenly, and fixed her dark gaze upon him. He was never to forget her as she stood there, against the great sea and sky; never to forget, as the last of all the varying impressions of the afternoon, his sense of a greatness, a magnanimity, like the sky's, arching above her earthly errors. It remained with him even though the last words she spoke were so sad, as if, instead of the splendour he divined in her, she held out to him a handful of dust. "Do not think too well of me," she said. "I like you too much. With you there can be no pretence. Do not think too well. It is best for Alix; but it is best for me, too, that she should not be near my life."

CHAPTER XII

The tennis-players returned at tea-time, bringing monsieur Claussel with them. He was a young man with shy, soft, prominent dark eyes and the smallest dot of a dark moustache on either side of a nervous upper lip, and, when tennis was not in progress to absorb his attention, it was excessively directed to the social exigencies of the occasion. Giles imagined, as he watched him spring from his chair to offer it, stand back to let a lady pass, bow with heels together, and tentatively resume his seat only again to leave it, that he was perhaps less at home in the jungle than André, and felt, in his introduction to it, a doubled need for every amenity. It was his first appearance at the Chardonnerets tea-table, and in his presence, the presence of mademoiselle Fontaine, her mother and grandmother, madame Vervier may have felt a convenience. If she found it at all difficult to face Alix and André and Giles after the interview from which she had just come, her guests, and monsieur Claussel in particular, gave her an excuse for looking at them rather than at her intimates. And Giles felt sure that she avoided her daughter's eyes.

They were on her, those remote blue eyes of Alix's, with no insistence, no appeal. They dwelt in a wide contemplativeness that recalled to him madame Vervier's own, were it not that proud patience rather than security lay behind it; and Giles had the fancy, as he looked at her, that, in the gaze of Alix, the Mouverays, beneath the threshold of the child's consciousness, were judging Hélène Vervier. Whatever the verdict, Alix's tenderness for her mother would not waver; but he watched the Mouverays imparting to her need a further reënforcement of pride and courage.

Tea was prolonged. Madame Dumont, in a great crested bonnet, sat enthroned, receiving cakes and homage. She was rather silent, rather, in her black draperies, the sunken old raven, its feathers ruffled high. Yet Giles caught more than once the piercing glint of an avid eye, turning in conjectures that he could too well imagine upon madame Vervier and André; upon himself and Alix; and once, in the glance of mademoiselle Blanche, he seemed to see a stealthy hereditary surmise, and Alix rather than madame Vervier was its object.

Monsieur Jules was persuaded to bring out his canvases and range them for monsieur Claussel's admiration. The painful, vivid patterns and colours still distressed Giles, but, his eyes already acclimatized to their strangeness, began to exercise a charm. "Quel horreur!" madame Dumont cried, but was fondly checked by mademoiselle Blanche, who murmured to her, smiling over her head at Giles: "We are no longer in the days of Bouguereau and Meissonnier, Grand'mère!"

She confided to him, as they stood side by side, that monsieur Claussel was a devout admirer of modern art and that his admiration, since he was the heir to a fortune princière—faite dans les pâtes—might be of much significance to poor Jules. "She arranged it all, you may be sure," said mademoiselle Blanche, casting a fond glance upon their hostess. "It is always she who thinks of such opportunities for her friends.—What a heart, what a mind it is!—Whatever her own perplexities and anxieties— and I can assure you that her life does not lack them—she never fails in resource and kindness when it is a question of her friends' interests.—She is looking pale—very weary, is it not so?—You take mademoiselle Alix back to England with you?" And since Giles, disconcerted, remained silent, mademoiselle Blanche added: "She is ready always to sacrifice herself."

"Mais oui, c'est très bizarre," little madame Collet murmured, craning her neck to see the pictures, while Giles wondered over mademoiselle Blanche.

André, meanwhile, smiling in a happy confidence, pointed out planes and stresses to the heir of les pâtes, who stood with his little shoulders screwed up, his elbows in his hands, rapt away from shyness and self-consciousness by his sincere delight. Monsieur Jules remained morose; but it was evident that he had found a munificent patron.

And when they were all gone and an evening of dusky rose began, after the hot day, to drop softly from the sky, madame Vervier said to André that she must take the air. She would go with him for a little turn in his car.

She was not yet ready for a meeting with her child. If she was to think things over and decide how she should put them to Alix, she must get away to do it. Giles understood; but how could Alix understand such necessities? He guessed at the grief and perplexity that must strive within her.

"And now, indefatigable as you are, ma chère enfant," said monsieur de Maubert when he and Giles and Alix were left alone, "framed of steel and india-rubber as I sometimes feel you to be when I watch your day, you will doubtless wish to go for a walk with monsieur Giles. Do not hesitate to leave me. I shall, I think, have a siesta here with my head in the shade and my feet in the sunset; even in the details of life, monsieur Giles, I am, you see, the Epicurean."

Giles knew, then, that madame Vervier's intentions, in regard to himself and Alix, had been imparted to monsieur de Maubert who thus took occasion for furthering them.

But Alix said: "No; the walk is not to be with Giles. I have promised Annette Laboulie to catch shrimps with her on the beach till supper-time."

"And who," monsieur de Maubert, kindly, yet with a certain austerity inquired, "is Annette Laboulie?"

"She came with my shoes her father had mended, the other afternoon. Do you remember? A dark, thin girl. She has not enough to eat."

"You mean the sad young ragamuffin with the untidy hair? Not enough to eat? That must be seen to."

"She is a ragamuffin; and untidy; I reproach her for that. But she is clean. And she is a clever girl in all sorts of ways. There are eight children, and Annette is a mother to them all. We are great friends. I used to play with her when I was little and Maman and I first came here."

"Monsieur Giles, you are not flattered by this preference!" smiled monsieur de Maubert.

"And they don't even invite me to join them!" laughed Giles.

But he understood. After the longing to know what Maman had said to Giles must come the longing to know what Giles now felt about Maman; but Alix wanted none of his impressions until those of Maman had been vouchsafed to her. As if by some deep instinct she knew that her destiny had been in question that afternoon.

"But do come with us, Giles," she now said, and he replied that he really had letters he ought to write. "Letters home. You see my time here is up."

"Up? Indeed? Why up?" monsieur de Maubert inquired very kindly.

"Well, I've stayed already longer than I intended and they all expect me back in time to start next Monday on a walking tour around the coast of Cornwall."

"Next Monday? But that means that you will leave us the day after to-morrow. You will miss our Sunday excursion to Caudebec."

"I'm afraid I must."

Alix was looking at him; wondering, he knew, whether his resolve was sudden.

After he had written his letter to his mother, he went out into the village to post it, and coming back by the cliff he was able to see that even if Annette had been an improvisation the drama of the shrimping was being carried out. The two girls were pushing their nets before them on the sands, bare-legged, in the shallow water. Their voices, bell-like, came to him through the evening air. Alix laughed.

Her faculty for fraternizing with the people seemed to him a charming gift. Neither Ruth nor Rosemary would have known what to do with Annette in tête-à-tête. They could have dealt with her coöperatively; in the Girl Guides or one of Aunt Bella's clubs; but not as an individual. And Toppie, full of still solicitude, would have dealt with her as a soul. The difference was that Alix was not dealing with her at all. She was enjoying Annette as much as Annette was enjoying her. They were simply two girls engaged in a pastime delightful to them both; and Giles surmised that such easy intercourse was perhaps only possible in a country where caste was a thing so impassable that intimacy lent itself to no misinterpretation. Caste in France, he was coming more and more to see, centred itself on the question of marriage. In a country where the romance of the mésalliance, so dear to English hearts, was nearly unknown, there was little likelihood of its disintegration. How little do those know France, thought Giles, who imagine her republican at heart!

Madame Vervier did not return from her drive till supper time, and after supper, during which she talked cheerfully, if with a certain languor, she established herself in the drawing-room with monsieur de Maubert. There was no moon to-night and the light streamed out over the verandah from the drawing-room window. Giles, from his place on the steps, could see that madame Vervier, beside the lamp, had her embroidery and that she spoke to monsieur de Maubert in low tones.

Alix brought out a saucer of milk for a stray kitten that she and Annette had found. "I shall take it to Paris with me," she said, stroking the back of the little creature, while it drank, half choked with purrs and lapping.

"It is not a pretty kitten, mademoiselle Alix," said André, who sat beside Giles smoking.

"No; it is not pretty; except as all kittens are pretty—the delicate little paws; the beautiful movements. In time it will look better; with brushing and good food," said Alix. "And it has a charming little coral nose to match the coral beads under its feet.—Only hear it purr, Giles! Have you ever noticed the softness of a kitten's feet?—they are like raspberries to hold in one's hand."

André watched her meditatively.

"It is time for your bed, mon enfant." Madame Vervier's voice came from the drawing-room. "I will visit you before you sleep.—Ah, mais non!

You must not have the kitten with you. You would be devoured by fleas. It will be quite happy shut into the kitchen."

"But it is so young, Maman; so lonely. It must so miss its mother." Alix stood supplicating, the kitten held to her cheek. "I do not mind the fleas."

Madame Vervier was melted; or it was, perhaps, an evening on which she was inclined to indulgence. "Very well. If you do not mind the fleas! While it misses its mother, then. Too soon, alas, it will be a mother itself!"

"No; for it is a male cat, Maman," said Alix with austere realism. "You need fear nothing on that score. There will be no more kittens to trouble you."

"A la bonne heure!" laughed madame Vervier.

"But she returns to you, after her holiday with us here, the charming young creature," André, when Alix had carried away her kitten, observed to Giles. It was remarkable, the sense they all gave Giles, that Alix was permanently his responsibility, and André's voice had almost the geniality of family affection. If not he, then another English husband. Alix's future had been, by those most concerned with it—by himself and by her mother—definitely agreed upon; that was the fact to which André's voice and smile bore witness; and madame Vervier was certainly imparting the same news to monsieur de Maubert as she now sat embroidering beside him in her Ingres dress and scarf.

Alix herself, meanwhile, remained in ignorance of her destiny.

"Rather a shame she shouldn't know it yet," said Giles. "She thinks she's going back to Paris, you see."

"Shame? Oh, no," said André in gentle surprise. "It is much better that she should have her holiday unspoiled. We are to say nothing of it to her—as madame Vervier will tell you.—It would grieve her too much to hear it now. By degrees, as the time draws near, her mother will prepare her mind and bring her to see the wisdom of the decision."

That, of course, would be André's point of view. He took it for granted that jeunes filles should be kept in ignorance of their destiny until such time as their elders thought fit to enlighten them.

Giles was aware of a confused anger that seemed to involve himself as well as André and madame Vervier. "Since she and her mother are so devoted, it's a pity, I think, to hoodwink her," he said. "I hope her mother will tell her what she's decided on at once. I shall advise her to tell her."

At this point, suddenly, a voice dropped to them through the darkness. "I am sorry. My room is above you. I can hear all that you say." Alix's voice. Thrilling with bitterness.

The young men sat mute, eyeing each other.

"Dieu! Quelle gaffe ai-je commise!" whispered André, and—"How much has she heard?"

"As little as she could, you may be sure," Giles muttered.

André found his resource. "Très bien! Très bien, mademoiselle Alix," he called. "But this is a case where une écouteuse would hear only good of herself."

Alix made no reply. The windows of her room, Giles now remembered, opened beside his, on the roof of the verandah. She must have heard all if she had stood near them.

"This is very unfortunate," André murmured. "I have been stupid; very stupid. I must at once make my confession."

"Yes. You'd better," said Giles grimly. "It wouldn't do for her mother to go up now and pretend she'd made no plans at all."

"Oh—our hostess would be able to meet even that contingency," said André with, perhaps, the slightest flavour of irony. "A daughter, with us, knows too well that she may trust her mother to do the best for her happiness."

But, as Giles remained sitting on, hearing in the drawing-room the low murmur of consultation and André's repeated "Je suis désolé," it became disastrously clear to him that, more than Maman's intended accommodations of the truth, Alix would resent André's admission to Maman's confidence. How, indeed, could she interpret that?

The murmur in the drawing-room ceased, madame Vervier rose and went upstairs, and, before André could rejoin him, Giles had taken refuge in his own room. He could not face André; he could not face monsieur de Maubert, or madame Vervier herself, again that evening. None of them, not even madame Vervier, could see as he saw the disaster that had befallen his poor little friend. He leaned at his window feeling hot and sick, but even here, though the windows of Alix's room had been closed, the voices of mother and daughter came to him through the flimsy barrier of the wall. He could not hear the words, but in their sharp passionate rhythm he discerned what the words must be. "Why to him, Maman! What are his rights! He was a stranger to us when I left you!"

But madame Vervier would, indeed, never lack resource. Unready as she must feel herself to face this further predicament, Giles heard the muffled murmur of her voice, rising, falling, expostulating; urgent, tender, invulnerable. She would find answers to everything. Or was it that there were some questions her child would not ask of her? When, at last, she ceased, there was no reply. He heard that Alix was crying.

CHAPTER XIII

Next day, his last at Les Chardonnerets, dawned high, blue, beautiful, and looking out at sunrise Giles saw his wonderful hostess, as he had seen her on his first morning, walking back to the house across the grassy cliffs, wrapped in her bathing-robe. She came slowly. Her tread had not the buoyancy of the first day. Her head was bent; she meditated gravely. But she made him think of a goddess who had sought inspiration and sustainment from immersion in her own elements of sunlight and sea-water. Power breathed from her as she moved, and Giles, looking out at her, was filled with a deep yet beautiful sadness. It was like looking at a goddess. Madame Vervier seemed separated from him by thousands of years. She might have been a figure of myth and legend walking there, the outlines of her ruffled hair all haloed by the sunlight, her white arm crossed upon her breast.

When breakfast brought them all again face to face, Giles marvelled at Alix. If madame Vervier was ready, she was not less so. Pale, with darkened eyelids, there were certain appearances that she need not be expected to keep up. Monsieur de Maubert and André de Valenbois would understand that it had been a shock to her to learn that her mother was again to send her from her. But beyond the evidences of this shock they were to see nothing. Of the greater shock she had received, not a shadow showed itself in her glance or voice. She was grave and quiet only; she showed the calm resignation of the jeune fille sérieuse who bows to the decisions of her elders. She smiled at her mother; she held her kitten to lap milk. And Giles was sorry for his invulnerable goddess, for, if it was hard that she should have to shoulder the burden of André under Alix's eyes, when she already had more than enough to carry in Owen, it must be for her the bitterest of alleviations that Alix should do all in her power to make the burden light. Madame Vervier must feel, as he felt, that such resource, such understanding in Alix could only rise from the child's intuition of how sharp was her mother's need. She stood beside her mother. She helped her.

"Maman is going to take charge of my kitten while I am away," she said calmly to André.

If Alix could help her mother, Giles could help her. This was an opportunity. "But why shouldn't you bring your kitten to England, Alix?" he said. "There's no quarantine for cats. You could carry it easily in a basket."

From the quick, upward glance that Alix cast at him above the kitten's lapping head, he saw that its fate, in spite of Maman's assurances, had indeed preoccupied her. "Oh, may I, Giles?"

"Of course you may. Rather!"

"Your mother will not mind?"

"Can you imagine Mummy minding another animal at Heathside? Why, she's lived and breathed and had her being, always, in a swarm of dogs, cats, and guinea-pigs. You don't forget, I'm sure, those white rats all over the place last winter. She never said a word even when she found them in her bed."

"I remember. Yes. She is so kind. I should be very glad to have my kitten." Alix stroked the kitten's back. She looked down at it, and for a moment Giles was afraid that she might be on the verge of tears.

"And if mademoiselle Alix will permit me," said André, wishing to do his bit, but, for once, blundering sadly, "I will present her, in place of this very ugly little cat, with the most beautiful chat Angora that can be found in Paris. A superb white Angora, mademoiselle Alix; with blue eyes like those of a saint in a missal.—Cela vous sourit?" André's own eyes were as blue and as bright as those of any saint in any missal.

"Not at all, thank you," said Alix. "This ugly little cat is the only one I want."

Giles wondered, as the day went on, whether Alix was going to let him see nothing more than she showed the others. There must be for her a sense of bitter humiliation in Maman's failure to fulfill her proud assurances. And it would be like Alix to keep silent if she were humiliated. But how near him she felt herself to be was shown to him when, after tea, following the others along the cliff-path, she said: "So I am to go back to you, Giles."

She ignored the morning interlude. She dismissed it as the piece of acting it had been. She faced the whole subject for the first time, with him, her friend.

"Yes. So your mother told me. I hope you're not too sorry; for I'm so awfully glad," said Giles.

Madame Vervier, with monsieur de Maubert beside her, and André de Valenbois with mademoiselle Fontaine, went on before them. They were taking Giles, on his last evening, to see a little château that lay in its woods near the coast, in the opposite direction from Allongeville. Giles knew that madame Vervier had arranged that he and Alix should go together and that she trusted him to uphold her cause as best he could. "It was what I wanted, you know," he added.

Alix, as she heard him, fixed her eyes upon her mother's form, rounding a green projection of the path, her white sunshade upon her shoulder. "It was most of all what Maman wanted, was it not, Giles?" she observed, with a faint, curious smile.

"Not at all," said Giles. "You know how much I wanted it."

"You will hardly make me believe," said Alix, her lips keeping their smile, "that it was you who persuaded Maman rather than she you."

"There was no question of persuasion. How could there have been? When we were both agreed from the first."

"I wish I could understand what it was that made you agree so strongly," said Alix after a slight silence. "Maman says that it is for my good to finish my studies in England, among such friends. That does not seem to me a sufficient reason. I could finish my studies in my own country; and I have good friends here."

"She thinks, and so do I," said Giles, "that we are the best friends you have. Isn't that a sufficient reason?"

"It seems to me a reason for not taking advantage of such friends," said Alix, startling him.

"But that is what good friends ask," he said. "To be taken advantage of."

"You speak for yourself, Giles. There are others besides you. You have no right to speak for them."

She had his back against the wall, and Giles knew it. The worst of it was that she knew it, too.

"I can answer for them. I told you I could. I told you that Toppie was so fond of you that she'd feel as I do."

To this, after a moment's silence, Alix only said in a voice suddenly grown sombre, "I do not blame you, Giles."

"I hope you don't blame your mother," said Giles.

There before them went madame Vervier, her white, heelless feet hardly seeming, in their beautiful tread, to touch the grass she passed over. They had no glimpse of her face. She left them in their privacy, feeling so secure that their privacy, since it was in his hands, could only be for her benefit. How deeply madame Vervier had read his heart yesterday! How clearly she had seen that all that he asked was to show her beauty to her child and to help her, always, in hiding from Alix the pitiful handful of dust that, in her truth to him, she had displayed! "I hope you don't blame her," he repeated, for Alix had made no reply, and, glancing at her now, and seeing her eyes bent down, he guessed that at his question they had filled with tears.

"It would be strange, wouldn't it, Alix," he said gently, "if it were I who had to defend your mother to you."

"Very strange, Giles," said Alix in a low voice.

"It's all for love of you," said Giles; and in spite of the handful of dust he knew that this was the fundamental truth about madame Vervier— "because of what she thinks best for you."

"But may one never be a judge of that oneself?" said Alix.

"Not if you are a young French girl; no; you may not," said Giles, after a moment's reflection. "Isn't that just the great difference between you and us? We think for ourselves; but you, if you are a girl, may only think for yourself when you are married."

"I like England better in that," said Alix. "One should have a voice."

"Perhaps your mother feels that you'll learn to have a right to a voice by being in England."

"I do not think so," said Alix. "I do not think she believes in having a voice. That is another great difference. You believe that one learns to have a voice by being given freedom."

"You can't be free here, Alix; I see that for myself," Giles said, looking at her and wondering how far her thought could follow. Already in such unexpected places it ran ahead of his own.

She raised her eyes to his. "You mean it is not safe, in France, for a girl to be free?"

"I'm afraid not. Not yet."

"And what is our danger? Can you tell me that?"

Giles found an answer that he had only recently seen for himself: "The danger of growing up; in the wrong way; and too soon."

"And Maman thinks that I run that danger by remaining with her? Why am I, then, different from other French girls whose mothers keep them with them? Why is she different from other French mothers? You need not tell me that she loves me. I see how it breaks her heart." Alix's voice trembled suddenly. "It breaks her heart to have to send me away. And why should it be so?"

She mastered the tears that had risen while she spoke, and her eyes held his. It was the strangest thing in his experience of Alix to feel himself seeking the right word in which to justify her mother to her.

"She has special difficulties," he said slowly. "You see some of them already. You remember what you said to me long ago about her beauty and bravery, and her danger. It was all true. I've seen it now myself. And you wanted me to help her. You felt sure that if I knew her I'd want to help her. Well, I do. You must trust us both. For what I have to tell you now is that I can best help her by showing you how you can."

Alix's eyes, widened by the unshed tears, gazed at him. "I help her by not being with her?"

"Yes, by not being another difficulty, and the greatest of all."

"And for how long must I be removed?"

"Until you are old enough to be free."

"Until I marry?"

"Marry, or get the freedom of the English girl; the right to choose whether you'll marry or not."

"But how can I marry if I am in England. Is it to have me marry there that Maman removes me? Because," said Alix—and her voice, tearless now, dropped to an iron note—"that will never be."

Poor madame Vervier and her hopes! Giles continued to play her hand as best he could. "You wouldn't be made to marry in England against your will. You might meet someone you cared for enough. How can you tell?"

"Cared for enough! To leave Maman! To leave France!" Alix held her head high and stared before her, facing this confirmation of her fears. And suddenly, her last words echoing too unbearably in her heart, he saw her lips tremble; part; and the tears, at last, helplessly ran down her cheeks.

"Oh—my dear little Alix—don't grieve like that," Giles implored. "Of course you won't leave them;—unless you come to feel that you care so much for someone that you can.—And it would never be really to leave. And while you're over there, can't we count a little for you? Can't I count? You know how much I care for you. I'll do my best to make you happy."

Alix shook her head. "It is not that," she uttered brokenly.

"What is it, then? You shan't be married against your will." Giles tried to smile at her.

"It is not that," Alix repeated. "Already you are too good to me. You are unbelievably good to me.—It is Maman." Alix put her hand up to her eyes and hid her tears from him as she walked. "It is Maman.—How can she bear to let me go?—How can I bear to be parted from her; far away; hardly seeing her; until I am old?"

CHAPTER XIV

"Then she is coming back. I am so glad. I was afraid, from things she said, once or twice, about herself, about her life in France with her mother, that she might not be coming," said Toppie.

She and Giles sat up on the ridge where the junipers grew. The pine-woods were behind them; below were the birches in their autumnal dress of bronze and gold; and brooding over all a sky of dusty rose. It was the evening of the hottest September day and the breeze hardly stirred the spices of the pines.

Giles was only just back from his Cornish trip and Toppie and her father had been in Bournemouth when he had returned from France, so that this was their first meeting. Mr. Westmacott was not well and the sea had done him no good. Toppie was worn with nursing him. Giles had never seen her look so white.

From something deep and watchful in her eyes the feeling came to him that her father was even more ill than they had guessed and that she was schooling herself to the thought of losing him. With her father gone, Toppie's last close link with earth would be severed.

But she had not spoken of herself or of her anxieties this afternoon. They had climbed the hill slowly, stopping to look back at the sky, and Toppie had found this favourite spot among the junipers and had sunk down, taking off her Panama hat, battered like a boy's, and holding it with both hands clasped around her knees as she sat in the deep heather. She wore her usual grey, again an almost boyish formula; the thin silk jumper rolled back from the throat, the thin pleated skirt falling to her ankle. Her pale hair was ruffled up over the black silk ribbon that bound it. As she sat there while he lay beside her on his arm, Giles had never felt Toppie so near him. It was more sad than sweet to feel her so. It gave him the feeling he would have had if she were going away on a long journey and could be so near because she was to be so far. And she talked to him of his time in France and of Alix.

"Yes. She's coming back all right," Giles said. "I am glad you are glad; for I am. It's as if the child belonged to us, isn't it?"

"It is quite strange, Giles, how much I feel that," said Toppie, turning her eyes upon him.

They were such lovely eyes, those of Toppie's. Giles had always felt them, since he had first, a boy of fifteen, seen her, the loveliest eyes in the world. Not large; not vividly marked; her brows and lashes only a shade darker than her hair; they conveyed the impression of light rather than colour and of radiance rather than of warmth. It was as if they looked at you from the zenith on a cloudless, cold Spring day. And the words that had always gone with them, in Giles's mind, from the time that he had first seen Toppie, in church, in Advent, with pale, wintry sunlight streaming in over her, had been: "Dayspring from on high."

She had stood there, in the Rectory pew, all alone, tall and slender in her grey, with a little high tight fur collar up to her chin and a little round fur cap coming over her golden hair and down to her ears, and she had, while the Psalms were being sung, turned her eyes on the Bradley family in the pew across the nave; looking at Owen; at Owen first—Giles felt it even then; Owen, his nut-brown head held high while he happily chanted out the responses in his sweet, accurate tenor. And then her eyes had met Giles's solemn gaze. And those had been the words that had come to him; full of the Christmas beauty; full almost to tears, for the boy standing there, of radiant promise and of heavenly love.—"Whereby the dayspring from on high hath visited us."

So he had seen her first. So he had always thought of Toppie's eyes. They showered light and loveliness upon you; and it came from far away.

"Quite strange," she was saying now, thinking of him because she was thinking of Alix, just as she had always, in the past, thought of him because she was thinking of Owen. "From the first moment I saw her I felt that she belonged. Perhaps it was because of what Owen had written. He was so fond of her. She was the dearest little girl he had ever seen. Even then I used to think that some day, if the war left us to each other, we would have Alix come and stay with us often. And then the moment I saw her I felt that I loved her.—Giles, you were very bad about letters while you were in France. Never one to me; and hardly anything to your mother about madame Vervier. Only that she was charming and had a charming house. You told us more about monsieur de Maubert—was that the name?—and the young man who ought to have worn a ruff and fought with Henry of Navarre. I liked so much what you said about him. I felt as if he ought to have known Owen. As if they would have been friends. But of course what we most wanted to hear was about Alix's mother. Tell me everything now; everything you thought."

"Everything. Well, that's rather difficult, you know." Giles turned over on his elbow and looked down at the heather, pulling his hat over his eyes. "She's very different from Alix."

"Is she? I'd always imagined her so much the same."

"Almost as different as it is possible for a mother to be from her child," said Giles, while he thought intently. How it had pleased, how it had lightened his heart to hear what Toppie had just been saying of Alix and her return to them; and how dismayed he knew himself to be by this further stretch of her interest.

"As different as that?" Toppie questioned, and with the faintest flavour of distress in the question. "Owen always wrote as if she were lovely, too."

"Oh, as far as that goes she's lovelier, I suppose. Where Alix is like a crystal she is like a flower. And they both have that dignity and security, you know. Alix is such a dignified little creature, isn't she?"

"Yes. Beautifully dignified; beautifully secure. I always feel of Alix that she would be safe, always and everywhere. Yes; those are just the words for Alix."

"And it's not exactly righteousness, is it?" Giles went on, finding more words since Toppie liked these ones. "It's integrity. Like a little noble Roman girl."

"Integrity. Yes." Toppie mused on Alix. But then, alas, she came back to Alix's mother. "The same in loveliness; the same in dignity and security.—In what ways different, then, Giles?"

He knew that there was hardly anything he could say of madame Vervier that it would not be unwise to say. He watched an ant, disturbed by his change of posture, thread its anxious way amongst the tufts of heather and felt that he was like the ant. He, too, must go forward and find the path that promised most safety. "Well, she's more impulsive, I feel; more selfish; less fastidious."

Toppie, for a moment, reflected in silence. He saw her dimly, sitting there beside him, a grey silhouette against the sky. "Less fastidious?" she then said, and it was as if he had presented her with an object that she turned reluctantly, and with surprise, in her hands: "How strange. Owen gave me no impression of that. He gave me the impression of someone quite finished, quite exquisite; in every way. How do you mean less fastidious?"

"Oh, I don't exactly know," said Giles, and he feared it was uneasily. "Merely in the sense, perhaps, that she'd put up with all sorts of queer people, for the sake of not being bored, that Alix wouldn't care to have. She is exquisite; very exquisite."

"You did like her, didn't you, Giles? Very, very much?"

"Well, hardly very, very," he qualified, pausing with wary antennæ, as it were. "She's not my sort, really. That's all that it comes to."

He could not see Toppie's features, but he felt her more intent, and in her next words he saw that he had seemed to call Owen's taste in question—as well as madame Vervier's. "Wasn't that only because you didn't see enough of her? She was so much Owen's sort."

"It doesn't follow she'd be mine, would it? Owen and I were really very different, weren't we, Toppie, dear?"

"Yes; very different. But you always liked the same people. It surprises me—so much—that you shouldn't like Alix's mother."

"But I didn't say that, Toppie! 'Liking' isn't the word. She is charming. She is too charming; that's what it comes to." Giles felt himself go forward to a new outlet. "Too much the woman of fashion; too sophisticated and highly flavoured for anyone so simple as I am. You know I am much simpler than Owen. He was a man of the world, and I, however long I live, will never be a man of the world. If one's just the shambling, shabby, scholastic type one will never feel at home with brilliant, resourceful people. It's as if'—Giles found the simile with satisfaction—"I liked rice pudding while Owen could appreciate caviare. Madame Vervier is caviare, as far as I am concerned."

He glanced up at Toppie to see how she accepted the metaphor; but if she smiled it was with reserve. "You like me, Giles. I'm not caviare; but I'm not, I hope, rice pudding either."

"No, you don't come into such categories," Giles smiled back. "If one could find a fruit that tasted of frost and sunlight, a fruit one could pick only at daybreak—golden, and chill and sweet—that would be you, Toppie. A sort of apple of the Hesperides—that one must sail and sail for ever and a day to find."

Something that came into his voice made him stop suddenly. And Toppie, too, was silent for a moment. When she spoke it was carefully, as if guiding their steps away from a menace to their quiet.

"That's a charming compliment, Giles," she said. "I sometimes think, shambling and shabby though you call yourself, that you are a poet as well as a philosopher. But I'm sorry, you know, to feel madame Vervier lose by what I gain. Owen always wrote of her as someone he so wanted me to know. I can't believe he'd have wanted me to know anyone who was worldly and luxurious and meretricious. I can't help feeling that you must be unjust."

Meretricious, luxurious, worldly? Was that the picture he had, all unwittingly, drawn for Toppie? The blood came to Giles's face. It was to be displayed to his own eyes as disloyal. He saw madame Vervier's figure standing against the great arch of the sky; he saw her rising up from the sea at dawn; he smelt the beeswax and seashells and cool, clean linen.

"But I don't mean that at all," he stammered. "I don't think of her as any of those things. Nothing could be further from my mind."

"If she's like the things rich people eat in restaurants; if she's selfish; if she's unfastidious and resourceful—" Toppie's voice built up before him the shape of madame Vervier as she had seen him draw it.

"You mustn't press mere metaphor so far, Toppie. I said she was like a flower, too. She is as out-of-door a creature as Alix herself. She belongs more to the cliffs and the country than to restaurants.—That's really the most vivid impression I have of her"—he was striving to atone to madame Vervier for the false picture he had put before Toppie; yet trying at the same time for truth to Toppie. "As I used to see her at sunrise; coming up from the sea after a morning swim. Like poetry and music personified, she used to look, walking against the dawn."

Toppie's eyes were on him. It was curious how cold her eyes could be. It was as if, though Toppie herself were not judging you, the height, the light that her eyes conveyed revealed you to her as creeping and dingy.

"I don't understand you," she said. She spoke gently, as if to mitigate the coldness that fell from her gaze.

"But what is it you don't understand, Toppie!" Giles exclaimed, and he heard that it was with irrepressible fretfulness. He felt it so unfair that he should be displayed to Toppie as creeping and dingy when all that he was trying for was to shield her from any hurt. Yet that there was another reason for his fretfulness, he knew. His loyalty to madame Vervier had betrayed him to too much ardour. Ardour had been in his voice. And Toppie must have heard it.

"That you should say such different things of Owen's friend," Toppie replied at once. "You contradict yourself. It's as if you were hiding something from me."

Poor Giles. His hat-brim was drawn down, but that could not conceal from Toppie the helpless red that surged up over his face and neck as he heard these words. He felt it rise, the burning, dark confusion, while, with sudden fear and sickness of heart, he groped for an answer. And her blow had been so sudden and unlooked for that the only answer that came was as helpless as his blush, "I'm sure I don't know what you mean. What could there be to hide?"

But there was no escape for him in Toppie's gaze. Giles, his eyes fixed on the heather, felt it dwell upon him, and when, at last, she looked away, it was as if she had seen the falsity between them. And all that she said, in accents of snow, was: "I'm sure I don't know. Perhaps you will tell me."

"Toppie, this is absurd, you know," Giles muttered, staring down. "You put me in a ridiculous position. It upsets one, naturally, to be cross-questioned as if one were a shifty witness in the witness-box. People are complicated and contradictory creatures. One can't draw a consistent picture of them. On one side of her nature madame Vervier may be weak and erring and on the other she may be like a goddess. How do I know? I've hardly seen her."

And then Toppie made an astonishing statement. Turning her eyes from him, looking before her at the dull rose sky, coldly, though gently, and with a poise of tone that showed how deeply she was feeling, she said: "If you have fallen in love with her, Giles, why should you not say so? Why should you try to hide it as though you were ashamed? She is a widow, is she not? There is no reason, is there, why you should not love her?—It hurts me that you should speak like that—keeping things back; twisting your real feelings lest I should see them.—You speak of her as though you were ashamed of loving her."

CHAPTER XV

Giles, while Toppie spoke, had started up, resting on his hand and staring at her with eyes aghast and stupefied. What folly, what madness was this? How could Toppie find it in her heart to speak like this; to him—to him of all people?

Yet, in another moment, while he stared at her, memory had answered him. A vein of piercing intuition underlay Toppie's blunder. It was only a half blunder. His misery of confusion had been for Owen, because of Owen's secret that he had to hide. And she had seen it as for himself. But it was true that he had, if only for a moment, been in love with madame Vervier. He had, for a moment, partaken of the experience that swept men away. The figure of madame Vervier was haloed for him by fiery, dewy associations, and the pang of his sense of disloyalty to her would not have been so deep had he not known in her presence that poignant, perilous revelation of beauty. He saw all this while, silently, he stared at Toppie, and he saw that she could never, never understand or admit his half truth. It was a weakness even to think of its avowal.

"How can you say anything so monstrous to me, Toppie," he questioned, and it was sternly, "when you know I've never loved anyone but you?" This, indeed, was a whole truth that it behoved Toppie not to traduce.

But his sternness did not deflect her. "There are different kinds of love. I know you love me. I know you've had, always, a boyish, idealizing devotion for me. I will always be grateful to you for your devotion. But you are not in love with me. You've never known what it was to be in love till you met madame Vervier. Oh! Giles—you must see what I see so plainly! Perhaps you really think that I could be hurt and jealous in feeling myself no longer first. That is so wrong of you. It would lift a burden from me if I could see you married. I should be so glad, so glad of your happiness."

"Good Heavens, Toppie!" Giles had started to his feet and stood above her, crimson with grief and dismay. "This is the most extraordinary nonsense! Happiness! With another woman! With Alix's mother! She's old enough to be mine if it comes to that; and as to marrying me—she'd as soon think of marrying a Chinaman. People haven't these romantic ideas about marrying in France, I can assure you. Marry me!" Giles suddenly found himself forced by the thought to a loud laugh. "Besides," he added, "why should you think that monsieur Vervier is dead? Why should you think that madame Vervier is a widow?"

He felt in the silence that followed these last unguarded words that Toppie looked at him strangely and, as he heard them echo—what, indeed, did he know about monsieur Vervier, damn him! He had, actually, never considered monsieur Vervier except as a discarded, dangling phantom of the past—as he heard the words that disinterred monsieur Vervier and set him there between him and Toppie, he felt that the bewildered ant had, indeed, stumbled on a luckless path.

"Owen always wrote of her as though she were a widow," said Toppie, going slowly. She was not bewildered. She looked carefully, if with shrinking, at the figure he had placed before her in his foolish haste. "But you know so much more about her than Owen ever knew.—In those few days you saw and learned things he never saw. Perhaps you do know about monsieur Vervier. Perhaps you know that he isn't dead; that she isn't free. If that is so—doesn't it explain even more?—Oh, Giles—I am afraid"— She stopped. She looked away. He saw the blood rising in her cheek as she checked the speech that must give him too much offence.

"I suppose what you mean," said Giles gloomily, thrusting his hands into his pockets as he looked down at her, "is that I do know she isn't free, and that, therefore, being in love with her, my love is a guilty passion. Something of that sort, what? Well, if you won't take my word for it, there's no more for me to say, is there?" Resentment had come into his voice. "We'd better be going."

"I accuse you of nothing, Giles," said Toppie, still dyed with her blush; "only I am sure that I am right in feeling that something has happened. I am sorry, but I can't help feeling it. From the moment you spoke of madame Vervier I heard that your voice was changed;—so strained and strange; so full of reluctance. You wanted to say all against her that you could find to say. You wanted to guard yourself against your own feeling. But what came through, from the beginning, was that you found her— beautiful; mysterious; compelling." Toppie found the words, a strange tremor in her voice. "What came through was that she was a goddess."

Giles stood motionless, gazing down at her. He was seeing, suddenly, straight into Toppie's heart; straight into the heart of their situation. How futile were his denials, when he could deny only for himself—and not for the other. The vein of piercing intuition in Toppie had led her to the portals of the truth. The name she saw inscribed there was the wrong name; that was all. Change Giles to Owen, and the truth was in her grasp. She knew that madame Vervier was beautiful, mysterious, compelling. She knew that both he and Owen had felt her a goddess. A chill of fear crept about Giles's heart.

"Come; we'd better be going," he repeated. He heard that his voice was harsh. He would discuss no further and he held out his hand to her. Toppie took it and rose to her feet.

She meant to be kind to him. She meant to be his friend;—Giles said it to himself as, silently, they went down the hill together. But in spite of all his compassionate understanding of her, his fear for her, what came over him, in wave after wave of grief and resentment, was that she was cold and hard. He had made her suffer because of what she had felt as false in him; but it was now, as it had always been, of Owen that she was thinking. He had cast, thank Heaven, no shadow on Owen; but perplexity, mystery, pain had come into her vision of Owen's friend.

"Owen never said she was a widow; but I'm sure he believed her to be one.—Forgive me, Giles, but have you heard what makes you think she may not be? What do you know of monsieur Vervier? Alix has never spoken of him. It is so strange; for if he were alive he would be with them, would he not?"

"C'était un bien méchant homme." These words, in madame Vervier's tones of surpassing detachment, came back to Giles. "Alix probably never saw him. Her mother spoke of him. She said he was a bad man."

"She spoke of him to you?"

"Yes, to me."

"And she didn't say whether he were alive or dead?"

"No. We weren't talking about him. We were talking about Alix and her future. Alix will have hardly any dot, it seems, because monsieur Vervier made away with all her mother's money. They are parted."

"Did she leave him, or did he leave her?"

"She left him," said Giles after a moment and he felt his voice harden towards Toppie. "Continue your cross-examination, pray."

"But you know so much, so surprisingly much, Giles. How can I help asking? How can I help feeling interest in Alix's mother, in Owen's friend? It isn't cross-examination. It is unkind of you to say that. Horribly unkind."

"I don't mean to be unkind. It's you who are unkind, I think. Ask any questions you like."

"How long after her first husband's death did she marry monsieur Vervier? May I ask that?"

"Certainly you may," said Giles. His bitterness carried him so far. Then he paused, aghast. He had known that to Toppie Alix could never have spoken of her mother's misfortune as frankly as she had to him. He had forgotten the first misfortune. He was aghast; but while he made his pause he determined that there should be no half-measure here. Toppie should not again accuse him of double-dealing. "Didn't Alix ever tell you that her mother was divorced?" he demanded, and he heard how hard and dry was his voice.

For a moment Toppie said nothing. Then she spoke, softly, as if in all sincerity she could not believe what she heard. Disastrous, indeed, was the time for such a hearing. "What did you say, Giles?"

"Alix told me, the day I brought her here last winter, that her father and mother had been divorced. If she didn't tell you, that was, no doubt, because she took it for granted that I would."

And again came Toppie's dire silence. "And why didn't you?"

"Why should I? It was none of our affair."

"Isn't Alix our affair?"

"Certainly she is. And she has nothing to do with monsieur Vervier."

"She has something to do with her mother."

"Yes." Giles' voice grew harder, dryer. "What she has to do with her mother we see. She is the product of her mother. Do you find fault with it?"

They had reached the road that wound among the birch-woods and dusk had fallen in it. The sky, paled to a faint apricot tint, shone dimly between the trees. Toppie stood still on the wayside grass and looked at him. Ineffaceably, in this instant of strange, unbelievable alienation (for had he not, in his last words, challenged Toppie with madame Vervier's standards as set against her own?), Toppie's image was stamped upon his mind; as ineffaceably as on that first time he had seen her. And now all her light was withdrawn. It was the end, as that had been the beginning. Pale, wraith-like in the dusk, she fixed her eyes upon him and they were dark with their repudiation. "Alix is not the product of her mother. Alix is good and her mother may be bad. You know better than I do what you think of her mother. It's you I find fault with, Giles. Your words don't tell me what you think."

"I've kept nothing from you," said Giles. It was a lie. He knew it, and he saw that Toppie knew it. He attempted an amendation of his statement. "Everything you've asked I've answered."

"Have you? I will ask this, then. Did she leave her husband with monsieur Vervier? Did her husband divorce her because of monsieur Vervier? Was she unfaithful to her husband?"

"There were faults on both sides, I believe. Alix wouldn't have been given for half the time to her mother if there hadn't been faults on both sides." Giles forced himself to speak steadily. "She was very young. People don't judge these things so hardly nowadays."

Toppie, her eyes on his, put aside the palliation. "Did she leave monsieur Vervier with another man? Was she unfaithful to monsieur Vervier, too? Is she a woman who has had lovers?" said Toppie, and the word was strange on her lips.

Giles stood there, stricken. He was so aware of horrible danger, pressing in upon him and Toppie from every side, that he could hardly command his thoughts to an order. All that came was a helpless literalness. There was no refuge from Toppie's eyes; for her, or for himself. "Yes," he said, "I'm afraid she is. That's the trouble, you see."

Toppie then looked away from him. She looked round her, standing so still, with no gesture of amazement or distress. But there was a sudden wildness in her eyes.

"Toppie, dear Toppie," Giles pleaded. "She is not a bad woman. Wrong; but not bad. You can't judge of these things. I'm not defending her.—It's only that, seeing her, seeing all the beauty she has made in her life, I cannot feel about her mistakes as I should have thought I would. That's why you felt me strained in speaking of her. It was a shock to me. And I didn't want you to know. Put it away now, Toppie, I do beg of you. It has nothing, nothing to do with us. She's a very beautiful, a very unfortunate woman, and it's only by chance that we've stumbled upon these unhappy things in her past."

Oh, the fatal background to his words! He knew how false they were, spoken to Toppie, for all that there was of truth in them for himself. "Let's go home," he urged, "and not talk about it any more."

Toppie stood, her eyes fixed as if in careful scrutiny upon the distance. She had raised her hand, as he spoke, and pressed her fingers, bent, against her lips. He saw that she kept herself with a great effort from breaking into tears.

"It's not that," she uttered with difficulty. "It's you." And now she moved away. "I'm going home from here. I would rather be alone, please."

The road led over the common to Heathside; there was a short cut through the woods to the Rectory.

"But, Toppie—I do implore you." Poor Giles with his rough head and great round eyes stood and pleaded. "What have I done? What have you against me?"

"It's everything, everything," Toppie murmured. "It's all I've felt in you this afternoon. I've stumbled—from one hidden thing to another.—It gives me dreadful thoughts. It's as if"—she stopped again, her eyes still fixed on the distance—"as if there might be anything. She's changed you so much." And, her eyes coming to him at last, she spoke on, helpless in the urgency of her half-seen fear:—"It's as if she might have changed Owen;—if he had ever come to know her as well as you have."

Suddenly, at this climax, Giles found himself prepared. "What if she had?" he demanded, and it was like riding, with a great thrust, to the top of the breaker that threatened to engulf them. "What if she had made him judge things more kindly? No doubt she would have changed him. He would have felt her beauty, too. But she wouldn't have changed him towards you, Toppie; any more than she has me."

Then Toppie drew back. Seeing suddenly where she stood, seeing her fear as a disloyalty, she drew away. She looked at Giles and he saw the door, as it were, mercifully or terribly close against him and Toppie, demanding no further lies, shut herself away. "Perhaps you are right," she said slowly, and each word came with an effort, for they were, doubtless, the only false words Toppie had ever uttered. "Perhaps I am too ignorant of the world. I do not judge your friend. But if I knew her, I could not think her beautiful. I could not think a wicked woman beautiful. We must be different in that.—I'll go home now. I'd rather be alone. Good-bye."

She moved away into the wood.

Giles, standing where she left him, had the sensation of feeling his heart break. "Toppie," he said in a choking voice.

She stopped and looked round at him. Her grey form among the birches was almost invisible, but he saw the thin oval of her face.

"Toppie."—Only this—He could hardly speak. He was not thinking. Only that stifling pressure in his heart seemed to break its way out into words—"I do so love you."

He saw that he touched her. If not his words, then his face of anguish. For the first time that day, if only for a moment, her thought was given to him alone and he felt rather than saw pity in her eyes.

"Giles—I'm so sorry," she murmured.

"I do so love you," he repeated, gazing at her. But, even as he gazed, the worst of the anguish was to know that something in his love was changed for ever.

"Dear Giles," Toppie murmured again. "Forgive me." And again she repeated, and the phrase was like a fall of snow: "I'm so sorry."

PART III

CHAPTER I

What had happened to Giles?

He was waiting for her on the Victoria platform and his patient gaze and poise told her that her train was late;—but fatigue did not account for what Alix saw at once as she stood at the door of her carriage and found his face. Her dear Giles. Her good Giles. What had happened to him?

Alix was aware that a great deal had happened to herself since she had last seen Giles, only two months ago. It was not only her lengthened skirts and her turned-in locks that gave her her new sense of maturity. Perhaps one only began really to be grown up when one began to know why one was unhappy. A child suffers in ignorance of the cause of its suffering and it can forget more easily because of that merciful vagueness. Unhappiness is only a cloud to put away or pass out of. But grown-up unhappiness was four solid walls of fact enclosing one.

Groping round and round her prison and finding always that solid facts were there resisting all attempts at forgetfulness, Alix, though she still could not see just what they were, sometimes asked herself if that was because she was still too young to understand, or because Maman, so deftly, so tenderly, with as much compassion as compunction, passed a bandage round her eyes and kept her blindfolded? She could not tell; but she knew that another mark of her own maturity was her understanding of Maman, her new capacity for helping her; and more than in any other way she helped her by never lifting a hand to push away the bandage and by never asking a question that Maman might find it difficult to answer.

She had known intuitively, in the past, that some questions must not be asked; questions about her father; about monsieur Vervier; about divorce. But now there were more pressing questions, and the first and foremost of them was the question of André de Valenbois.

He was there; in their lives. She had left him behind her in Paris; no longer their guest, but as much as at Les Chardonnerets the presiding presence. He was a great friend. So Maman had said to her, strangely pale, on that night when at Les Chardonnerets she had heard Giles and André de Valenbois talk of her return to England. Maman had great friends. And great friends made one suffer—Maman had not said that but Alix had seen it—and many things in life must be sacrificed to them. It was not that they were more loved than a child—oh, she was sure not!—though that was a surmise that had pierced her through; it was simply that one could not be sure of keeping them always; as one was sure of keeping one's child; and because one was not sure, one suffered. It was something from which one could not free oneself. It was something that made one helpless.

So Alix knew herself changed; a grave, meditative person; garnering in her silence and her submissiveness a power to meet all the emergencies that must lie in her path since, so obviously, they lay in Maman's.

"Hello, Alix," said Giles. His eyes had found her and he was there below her, taking from her the basket she had lifted off the seat; and she said, "Hello, Giles," though it seemed to her always such an odd phrase to meet upon.

"Is this the kitten?" said Giles.

"Yes. This is Blaise. You expected him? I wrote to Mrs. Bradley."

"Expected him! Rather! They're wanting to see him almost as much as to see you."

"That is well, then," Alix smiled. "You haven't been ill, Giles?"

"Ill! Rather not! I'm as right as rain," said Giles; and he added, hastily she felt: "But I say, you're quite different. What is it? Your clothes? Your hair?"

"Maman thought I was getting too old for short hair. It is taken back from my forehead, too. It makes me very digne, I assure you. And my skirts are nearly as long, you see, as anybody's skirts."

Alix wore a dark blue dress and a dark blue cape, buttoned with little buttons on her breast and showing a satin lining of striped grey and blue. Her shoes and stockings were grey, and her loose, long gloves, and her soft little hat curving down over her brows with the big bow knotted at the side. Maman had made her, though so sober, very chic, and Giles was taking it all in; as far as he could; and that, she feared, with tender irony, was not very far.

Giles, as they moved along the platform, pursued the topic of her appearance, feeling it evidently opportune. He did not wish to speak about his own. "It's that you look so tremendously foreign;—the way you walk; the way your things are put on; the way your hat comes down like that. Even the way you speak English is as French as possible, for anyone who speaks it perfectly; and I'd never noticed that before."

"When you first met me," said Alix, putting the obvious explanation with mild competence before him, "what chiefly engaged your attention was that I spoke English at all. Now you notice that though I speak it so well I speak with my French accent. I am French, Giles." She slightly smiled round at him, for she need not emphasize it. He as well as she would remember their last talk on the cliff-path. "I am a foreigner."

"I suppose you are," said Giles, and it was gravely, almost gloomily that he said so.

"Was the walking tour a success?" Alix asked him, while they waited at the customs, Alix's box, this time, being larger than the last and subjected to the vicissitudes of a separate transit. "You did not overtire yourself? You look a little tired, you know."

"Do I really? I haven't been sleeping very well; it's been so hot. Cornwall was a great success. I want you to see Cornwall some day."

"It has been hot in Paris, too. But I always love Paris at this season, the stones all baked with sun, the trees all bronze. We have been dining in the Bois almost every night, at a little restaurant under the trees. It has been delicious. And the drive back down the avenue du Bois.—Calme-toi, mon chéri," she addressed the kitten who was wailing.

"Poor little chap. He hasn't liked the journey. Is he prettier?" asked Giles.

"He is uglier," said Alix. "It is l'âge ingrat, you know. No longer kitten, and yet not cat. Like me. It is only the basket that troubles him. I had him out for most of the day, in my arms, and he was quiet and good."

"It reassures me to see you still so fond of kittens," Giles smiled at her. "It makes me feel you are still something of one yourself."

"But I shall always be fond of kittens," said Alix.

They were again to spend the night with Aunt Bella and in the taxi Alix opened the basket and displayed her pet. Very ugly indeed; gaunt in structure, though fully fed, of a most undistinguished white and brindle, with a nose already over-long and ears over-large; but as it nestled into Alix's neck with loud choking purrs Giles owned that it was a nice little beast.

"And so full of love; and so intelligent, Giles," said Alix, pleased by his commendation. "More loving, more intelligent, these common little cats are, than chats de race, I always think."

London, dusty and drowsy on this Autumn evening, seemed to yawn and smile and had, Alix thought, a welcoming air. It was a kind city. She even saw beauty in it, and commented on the Royal Hospital as they drove through Chelsea. "How well it goes in the thick, soft air—that period, that colour." She had never liked London so much, although she came to it with an unwillingness so much greater than the unwillingness of last year, and it seemed to her, leaning back in the taxi beside Giles, her kitten against her cheek, that the dropped aitches, the little green-grocer's shops, the strolling lovers, and the river gliding silvery-grey behind its trees, all went together in the impression of ease and kindliness.

In Aunt Bella's flat all the windows were widely opened to the freshness, and Aunt Bella received not only her, but Blaise, quite as a matter of course. This matter-of-courseness, Alix had begun to feel, was a distinctive English trait. Once they knew you, they accepted you; you and your kittens. They had no surmises about you. You were simply there. Was it, Alix wondered, while she changed her dress in her little pink room— Blaise cautiously reconnoitring from piece to piece of the furniture—was it that Aunt Bella saw her benevolently as an œuvre de guerre, or sentimentally as a legacy from the dead nephew? As she reflected on her own presence, so intimately among them, Alix felt that if Maman's motives were mysterious to her from their complexity, Aunt Bella's would be mysterious from their simplicity. And it was all like London again; like the cosy little shops with the carrots and cabbages heaped before their windows, the muffling air and unadventurous river. There was peace in such simplicity, peace in being among people who had nothing to hide and who would hardly be able to imagine that you might have.

She felt at dinner that Aunt Bella looked at her, in her altered way of dressing, a little as Miss Grace and Jennifer had looked when Lady Mary talked to her about Henri de Mouveray. Aunt Bella, no doubt, found the little dress that Maman had so cleverly contrived out of two Empire scarves, curious rather than interesting. Charming in colour, dull blue shot with silver, it was a marvel of convenience as well as so pretty. One turn and it fell into place, leaving arms and shoulders bare, knotting low about the hips and falling in long silvery fringes to the ankle. Seen in Aunt Bella's flat it had undoubtedly a very Parisian air, and perhaps Aunt Bella felt it too Parisian, for she began to question Alix about France's foreign policy with some severity. Alix gathered that in Aunt Bella's eyes her country was behaving badly.

"But we want the Germans to suffer," she said. "If they are not made to suffer sufficiently, they will make us suffer again and perhaps destroy us."

"But that is being revengeful, my dear child. And so short-sighted, too. You don't change people's hearts by making them suffer. You harm yourself as well as them."

"I do not think we want to change their hearts." Alix, all unversed in these large subjects as she was, felt herself impelled to make the answer so obvious to every French mind. "I do not think we care about their hearts. When a bad man is guillotined, it is sufficient that his head should be gone. His heart does not concern us."

Giles at this laughed loudly and Aunt Bella's eye-glassed gaze turned to glitter reprobation at him. "She doesn't know what she's saying, Giles. She is too young to have followed or understood the lamentable policy of her country. You really shouldn't encourage her."

"But it seems to me she has been following. She's made the only honest answer. Have you heard people talking about it a good deal, Alix?"

She did not mind his mirth or Aunt Bella's reprobation. She did not care at all what they thought about France. How could one expect even English friends really to understand? "I have heard people talk at Maman's," she said.

Blaise was on a chair beside her eating an excellent dinner, and Giles, still laughing, said: "Do you know what he looks like? A Boche baby. There was one born in a village we occupied after the Germans had been there for two years. It was the funniest, jolliest little fellow; but awfully ugly; with a face just like that."

"But it was half French, I imagine," said Alix dryly.

"Certainly half French, I regret to say. But he looked all German. And I'm sure that if you'd had to take care of him you'd have been as kind to him as you are to your kitten."

"I do not care for babies," Alix objected.

"You'd have been kind to him all the same. You wouldn't have wanted to see his head cut off."

"I do not want to see anyone's head cut off; but if it were a choice between a Boche and a French baby, I should choose the French one to live. That is all we ask of our allies," Alix added, looking over at Giles with kindly determination; "to help us to live;—as we have helped them;— even at the expense of the Germans."

Aunt Bella, now, changed the subject. "How is Mr. Westmacott, Giles?"

"No better, I'm afraid."

"Have they a trained nurse yet?"

"He won't have one. He won't admit he's so bad."

"It must be very taxing for Enid." (Aunt Bella always called Toppie by her real name.) "How does she bear it?"

"She looks very worn," said Giles.

"And I'm afraid she won't be at all well off when he dies," said Aunt Bella, as though she placed Toppie's approaching bereavement and subsequent impoverishment in the same category. "She won't be able to go on living in the way she does now. And she has been trained to no profession. I have always so blamed Mr. Westmacott for keeping her with him and giving her no education."

"Toppie is educated, I think," said Giles, dryly, but his dryness did not conceal from Alix the distress Aunt Bella's surmises caused him. How much more capable Aunt Bella was, Alix reflected, of sympathizing with large vague masses of humanity than with one human being.

"Not educated at all from the modern point of view," she returned decisively. "Quite incapable of making her own living. A very dear, good girl, but a useless girl, and there is no room in the world nowadays for useless people."

"There's room for Toppie," said Giles coldly; and then, perhaps, Aunt Bella remembered that he had a special feeling about Toppie, for she desisted.

"I didn't know Toppie's father was so ill," Alix said to Giles when he and she were for a little while alone in the drawing-room, Aunt Bella engaged on the telephone in the hall. "I had only one letter from her, from Bournemouth, and it did not lead me to think he was so seriously ill."

"I'm afraid he is. She didn't realize it then, perhaps. I'm afraid it's only a question of time now," said Giles, sunk in a deep chair and watching her while she pretended to play with Blaise. Was it grief, anxiety about Toppie, that had wrought the change in him? It had to do with Toppie she felt sure; but had it to do with her as well? Aunt Bella still issued directions on the telephone and Alix felt suddenly that she must ask him.

"Giles," she said, not looking up from Blaise, who made soft onslaughts at her hand, "does Toppie know?"

"Know?" His echo had the strangest reverberations.

"About Captain Owen is what I mean;—that he cared so much for Maman." She looked down at Blaise and moved her knotted handkerchief before his nose; and she felt the colour rising in her face.

Perhaps it was because he felt her confusion and shared it that he had to pause before replying. "Of course she doesn't know," he then said very gently.

"And you will not forget what you promised me?"

"What did I promise you?"

"That if she did know she would still want me back."

And again there was a silence. How carefully Giles was considering his answer was made apparent by the length of the silence; but what he said finally, more gently than ever, seemed clear. "I'm more sure of that than ever, Alix. You see, she's so fond of you."

CHAPTER II

If Toppie, too, was changed, she was not changed to her. That was the first thing that Alix felt when she saw her again; next day;—for a note had been waiting for her at Heathside asking her to come to the Rectory.

It was a hot, still day and a bee was droning lazily about the Rectory drawing-room, flying out into the sunlight and in again to the bowl of mignonette that stood on a table near the window; and the bee made the day more still. It had been strange to find herself thinking of Racine as she waited for Toppie. Nothing so trivial and intimate as a bee could be imagined in any play of Racine's; yet its soft drone had accompanied her sense of a pause, of an ominous interlude, like the pause before a scene where the heroine was to enter with some quiet, conclusive word. It was, perhaps, because of this association of ideas that Toppie, when she entered, had looked to her like the Racine heroine, like a creature delicate and austere, dimly conscious of an impending doom. There was fear in Toppie's face as it found her there. Alix saw its white gleam mastered, resolutely veiled, while, at the same moment, the full security of Giles's assurance was brought warmly home to her by Toppie's encircling arms, by a new note of emotion in her voice as she said, kissing her, "Dear, dear child."

Toppie was changed; but it could not be because of her. It was her father's illness that had changed her and Giles had spoken the whole truth; but all the same, involuntarily, she found herself saying, while Toppie's arms were still around her: "Are you glad to have me back?" And she heard that her voice trembled in speaking.

Whatever the fear had been, Toppie had mastered it. She held her by the shoulders and looked at her, smiling, and said: "So glad, dear little Alix, that I feel we ought to keep you always." Then she held her off and looked her up and down, still smiling, and added: "But it isn't a child any longer. It's an almost grown-up young person."

It was strange to feel herself, all reassured as she was, wanting dreadfully to cry; but Alix, too, was an adept at mastering emotion, and she said, taking off her hat so that Toppie should see all the changes: "Do you like my hair?"

"I like it very much." Toppie kept her hand, turning her round. "I like seeing your forehead, such a gentle, thoughtful forehead. I like that big black bow at your neck."

"That is a jeune fille bow—a bow of transition," smiled Alix. "It is to be there while the hair grows long enough to make a knot."

"I like it all," said Toppie.

They sat down on the sofa side by side, Toppie still holding her hand, and then she said: "Toppie, I had not realized from your letter that your father was so ill."

Toppie looked at her in silence for a moment and, slowly, her eyes filled with tears. "He is going to leave me, Alix," she said.

It was her father, then. Alix could not but feel the deep, selfish relief. "Oh, you must hope," she said.

"I do try to hope. I try to live on hope. But I am afraid he is going to leave me," Toppie repeated. "He is not much changed," she went on, for Alix found nothing to say. "You will not see much change in him, I am sure. I will take you up to him presently. He likes to follow what goes on. In a way he follows more than he has ever done. It is a sort of clinging, I think. And he is quite cut off from his own work. I read to him a great deal. Perhaps you will come sometimes and read to him in French. He likes that, you know."

"I like it, too. You must let me come often. It is curious, Toppie, but when Giles is away my English life is really here with you; not that I am not very fond of them all at Heathside."

"Is it?" Toppie looked at her very intently. "I am glad of that. Glad that I can mean home to you.—Dear little Alix.—But you are fond of them."

"Especially of Mrs. Bradley. Only she is there so little. One hardly sees her. I am fond of Ruth and Rosemary, too. But I would rather be with you." Alix smiled a little.

"And it will be Rosemary only this winter, since Ruth is going to Oxford. I am glad she is to be there. Giles will like having her near him." Toppie spoke calmly the name of Giles.

"Do you think so?" said Alix. "Do you think she means much to Giles?"

"He is devoted to all his family. It will certainly be a pleasure to him to have her," said Toppie, and Alix now thought she detected in her voice a strange detachment.

"He is fond of them to do things for them; not to be with them—I mean his sisters. He is so unlike his sisters; and most of all unlike Ruth. Ruth is so stupid beside Giles."

"She is a very good girl; very courageous and honest," said Toppie. "I think I see Ruth's good points more than I used to. I think, Alix, the older one grows, the more one cares for those sterling qualities. Black would always be black to Ruth, and white, white. That has value, the highest value, in a person's character, you know."

Something in Toppie's tone now dimly offended Alix. "But you could not really compare Ruth and Giles, Toppie. Giles is all that she is and so much more besides. He sees the greys and all the delicate in-between shades, too. Nothing is really black or white, and that is what is so stupid in Ruth; she sees things so."

"It sometimes seems to me that they are nothing else," said Toppie very calmly. "And Ruth has, I think, because of that downrightness in her, more strength of character than Giles. He would so much more easily be mistaken;—misled." Toppie paused before finding these words. "He has what would be called the artistic temperament, I suppose; and that is the penalty one pays for having it; a certain weakness; a certain yielding. I feel that Giles would yield where Ruth would stand up like granite;—and I like the granite thing in people."

Alix sat in indignant astonishment. "I have never known anyone so true as Giles," she said slowly.

"I did not say that he was not true," Toppie returned, with a touch of severity. "I said that he would be more easily misled than Ruth. I said that he was weaker than Ruth."

They sat for a few strange moments silent.

"But it is as if you were changed to Giles," Alix cried suddenly. She could not repress the cry. "What is it, Toppie? What has he done to displease you? You are unkind to him. You speak as if you did not care for him."

A deep blush rose in Toppie's face; but it was not the blush of surprise or confusion. Alix saw a competent sternness in the eyes bent upon her. "You must not say things like that," Toppie said slowly, considering every word. "There are things you do not understand. I shall always care for Giles. I have not changed to him. No," she repeated as if to herself, "I have not changed to Giles."

They sat there, still hand in hand. Alix felt that she wished to fling Toppie's hand aside. In answer to her sternness she had felt an instant anger rise within her. That Toppie should reprove, rebuff her, was itself an affront she bore with difficulty—and bore only because she feared to damage Giles's cause by rejoinder; but her anger passed the personal wrong by and fastened itself, strangely, inevitably, on the figure of Captain Owen.

It was Toppie herself, in the picture she had drawn of Giles, who had set him so vividly before her. Captain Owen, not Giles, was the person who would blur black into grey; Captain Owen was the person who, in comparison with honest Ruth, lacked something. Giles was everything that his brother had not been, and yet it was Captain Owen who had betrayed Toppie—she found the word and it sank with a cold weight on her heart;—it was Captain Owen, now, she felt sure of it, who parted Giles and Toppie. She sat, her eyes fixed proudly before her; her lips hard.

"Alix," Toppie said in a gentle voice, "if so much has changed in my life—you mustn't change."

"It feels to me as if it were you who were changed, Toppie," said Alix.

"You must forgive me, then," said Toppie with her firm gentleness. "I am not quite myself, perhaps. I am rather on edge. I know I seemed to speak harshly. You see, dear Alix, you are still, really, a child—one cares for you so much that one forgets it. But there are things you cannot understand."

"Perhaps I understand some things better than you do, Toppie," Alix returned, still not looking at her friend.

At that, for a moment, Toppie sat quite silent. "Perhaps you do," she then said. "Some things, perhaps you do. But I feel sure that you do not understand the things I am speaking of."

After that they tried to talk as if nothing had happened. Toppie's manner had an atoning sweetness. Once or twice, in the way she spoke, the way she looked at her, it was as if, Alix felt, one of Toppie's doves had spread its brooding wings over her, protectingly, tenderly. She knew that she had not forgiven Toppie; and yet she was the fonder of her because she had not forgiven her.

She was taken up to see Mr. Westmacott, who sat at an open window, a reading-table before him with books upon it. Sitting there, as formally courteous as ever, with his tall pale head and eyes still clearly blue, he did not look so ill. It was more in his voice as he questioned her about her journey that she felt change. His voice had become dry and brittle, like a glacial wind fluttering the leaves of an old abandoned volume that no one would ever read again. He would soon die; Alix felt sure of that as she heard him. He would die, and Toppie would leave the Rectory and wander forth desolate, among her doves. Why, oh, why, would she not see and understand Giles? Why would she not marry him? "Oh, if I could see her married to Giles," she thought, when she had said good-bye to Toppie and was out again upon the common. "If I could only help Giles so that he should marry her, it would have been worth while that I should have come to England!" And that there was mistake, misunderstanding between Giles and Toppie, she was now sure.

She had gone halfway across the dried heather, when, as on the evening of her first visit to the Rectory, she saw Giles approaching her, Jock at his heels, and she knew now, as she had then only felt instinctively, that he had been waiting for her and that he was afraid of something. Of the same thing; yet of more.

Jock saw her and raced ahead to jump against her knees. He was still her special pet among the dogs and had received Blaise kindly. Alix stooped to caress his head while she watched Giles approach her.

"Well, how did you find Toppie?" he asked simply, as they met.—Giles not true! Giles easily misled! Alix felt herself suddenly blushing with anger as the thought of Toppie's strange delusion returned to her. Giles drew her arm within his and they went across the common towards the birch-wood. It gave her a deep feeling of consolation that he should thus seek refuge with the one person who could understand him.

"I find her changed, Giles," she said.

"In what way changed?" said Giles quickly.

And as quickly Alix answered: "Not at all to me, Giles."

"You see how desperately ill her father is, don't you?" said Giles. "She's quite worn out with nursing him, you know. In what way do you feel her changed?" he repeated, looking down into her face.

Alix was pondering. She was not a person who believed in black and white. She believed in the greys and the in-between shades. She did not mean to tell Giles how she thought Toppie changed. What she found to say was: "If Toppie were happier she would not be so hard."

"Hard?" She was looking at the ground, but she heard in Giles's voice how the word startled him.

"Do you not think Toppie hard?" she asked.

"If she is," said Giles after a moment, "it's because of what you say— that she is unhappy."

"And because she is too sure," said Alix. They had entered the birch-wood and their footsteps rustled in the fallen golden leaves. They went forward, aimlessly, not thinking of where they went, Alix intent on her reading of Toppie, Giles listening. "Too sure of what she loves and believes in. She has had to be too sure, because she is so unhappy.—Is that it, Giles? And the things she loves and believes in are not the things she sees. Perhaps that makes us hard—if we can only think of the things we love and never see or touch them—makes us hard, I mean, to the things we have with us."

Giles was, she knew, keeping his eyes on her as she put together these suggestions, and as he meditated for a little pause, her thoughts, in the silence, while she watched the golden leaves, took a long flight to France and she found herself suddenly wondering if perhaps Maman and André de Valenbois were wandering under the autumnal trees in the Bois—as Giles had seen Maman and Captain Owen wander under the Spring trees. And with the thought came such a pang of fear and grief.

"You're right, I think," Giles said. "And I see no help for it. She'll grow more and more away from the things she has with her and shut herself more and more into her solitude—where she is safe with the things she can't see.—What can we do about it, Alix?" said Giles gently, a little as if he spoke to a child from whose ingenuous wisdom he sought an oracle.— "Who can help Toppie in any way in which she'd accept help?"

Suddenly it was very easy, there in the twilight woods, to be courageous. She was so near Giles. It was as if her heart beat in his side. "No one can do anything for her but you, Giles. You must marry her and make her happy."

"Oh, my dear little Alix," he said, smiling bitterly, not even pausing to assess her daring, just as she herself had not needed to pause. "There's no hope for me. No one can help her less than I."

"Do you mean there never was hope;—or is none now?"

"There never was, perhaps;—but there's less now. Her heart is full of Owen."

"Yet if he had not been there, it would have been you she would have loved."

"Who can tell? Perhaps."

"And is it because of him that there's less hope, even, now?"

"Put it like that if you choose," said Giles. "Yes. Because of him."

CHAPTER III

The old life flowed round her again, outwardly the same, inwardly so altered. She had been, she saw it, like nothing but a glass of eau sucrée when she had first come to Heathside;—or if that was a simile too insipid for even her youngest consciousness, like eau sucrée with a squeeze of lemon in it. Now the wine of new perceptions, new emotions, tinged her deeply, and because she was enriched she saw a richer world about her. English history, from being a mere flat picture, dull at best compared to the splendid pageantry of France, began to take on depth and distance in her eyes. It was English history she saw now when she went up to Oxford with Giles and Ruth, and English history was English character; whereas event, in French history, played so much more potent a part. Wandering in and out with Giles, the beauty of the town, with its significance, stole upon her mind and senses. Meditative, benign, and so humane, it seemed to smile at you like an old ecclesiastic with kindly eyes for youth. As one sat in a sun-steeped garden or dim, carved chapel, one felt its quiet like that of a tree, full of life and growth, so that, though it was old, it was also young; the sap moved on to fresh leaves while the calm old trunk endured. Time had been distilled and preserved in it without a break or cleavage and its very light, she felt, in this autumnal weather, had that colour of time, as though it came through ancient glass. The quadrangles were brimmed with time and it brooded on the lawns of Saint John's where the Michaelmas daisies growing against the grey stone walls made her think of the ring on the benignant hand of the bishop. "One would grow wise by being here even if one only sat still, like this, and looked at it," she said to Giles. "I only wish one did!" said Giles. But he felt what she felt and was pleased with her for, at last, understanding his Oxford.

She began to wish for wisdom. Back at Heathside she bicycled to the High School every morning with Rosemary, through the birch-wood, past the red-brick villas of the town—villas upon which time had laid no kindly hand—and all the ugliness that had so fretted her fell into an insignificant background, since, for the first time, the day had its object. Knowledge, of course, was quite different from wisdom. The happy life depended on eyes to see the hands that blessed and the smile on the face of time; but it was knowledge that opened one's eyes and she found in its acquisition a zest and an enfranchisement. It was in order that she might see that smile in France that she worked so hard. The sooner was she equipped, the sooner could she return to France and Maman. Already she outdistanced

Rosemary, and she had a touch of kindly malice at seeing her friend of the chaffing complacencies and cheerful bullying left behind.

Rosemary was not ungenerous. She showed her chagrin and her admiration, openly. "It's not even as if it were your own language," she grumbled. "And you don't seem to take half the trouble over it that I do."

"Perhaps it is because you are in your own country and I out of mine," Alix suggested.

"Now what on earth do you mean by that?" Rosemary inquired.

"I have nothing else to do but think about my studies," said Alix.

Rosemary stared. "You've got the same things to think about that I have. Surely you are at home by now. All the girls like you and you're never left out of anything."

"It is not anything like that. Everybody is as kind as possible," said Alix. She could not, she knew, make Rosemary understand. Rosemary, fundamentally, could not take foreign countries seriously—could not believe that anyone lucky enough to be in England should have all their energies bent on leaving it.

"And what do you girls intend to do with yourselves?" Mrs. Bradley asked them one day at the firelit tea-table. She had, as usual, a pile of papers beside her and laid down her fountain pen to pour out the tea. "Alix is doing so well that she can really begin to think of choosing a career and it's not too soon to turn things in that direction."

Even dear Mrs. Bradley took it for granted that she might be quite satisfied to make a career out of her own country.

"I hope I shall marry when I go back to Maman," said Alix.

"Now isn't she altogether too priceless, Mummy!" cried Rosemary. "One would have thought that with all the time you've been in England, Alix, you'd have got over those French ideas about marriage.—I suppose you'll actually say that you'd let your mother choose a husband for you."

"But who would choose one so well?" said Alix. Yet it was not true; it was not true that she still believed this of Maman. England had already changed her so much. But she did not intend that Rosemary should guess it.

"Who would? Why, you yourself!" cried Rosemary. "What can your mother know about it? Aren't you an individual with your own tastes and feelings? And do you seriously think marriage the only career for a woman?—Do you really think getting married the whole meaning of life?"

"It is a sad thing to be a vieille fille, I think," said Alix.

"Sad? Why sad? You don't call Aunt Bella sad, do you? And there're thousands and thousands more like her. All of 'em as jolly as possible; the unmarried people nowadays. Jollier than the married ones, I think;—and no wonder."

"In their hearts, you may be sure, they wish they did not have to be quite so jolly," Alix demurred. "They must feel it sad when they reflect that they have only other people's children to care for—and those not the most interesting. And it must be sad to be alone at one's foyer."

"One may have one's own children and yet have to take care of the others, too, you know, Alix," Mrs. Bradley smiled, finishing her tea and taking up a packet of case papers. "All these are other people's children."

"One needn't care for one's own, or for other people's unless one wants to," Rosemary commented. "People specialize nowadays and know that some women are maternal and some aren't. I'm sure I'm not. I couldn't be bothered with children, or with a husband either—It's as good as a play to hear you talk, you know, Alix—all your quaint French ideas. What can one hope of a nation that still has them!—Cradles, hearthstones, hubby's socks to mend;—that's what really appeals to you, I suppose."

"What appeals to me is to be established," said Alix. "I do not care for babies; but they are a part of marriage, and no doubt one would come to like them when one had them. As for the socks—I should hope to marry well enough to have a maid to do that."

Rosemary's eyes rounded. "You mean you'd marry for money?"

Alix smiled: "You are so réaliste in some ways, Rosemary, and so romantic in others."

"I hope, dear, you'd never think of marrying for money," Mrs. Bradley put in. "Money is a very minor consideration in marriage."

"Romantic! I romantic!—It's merely a question of one's own dignity!" cried Rosemary; while Alix said: "There would have to be character and taste and position as well;—but don't you think, chère Madame, that it is well to marry suitably?"

"Suitably? Yes, of course." Mrs. Bradley was gently bewildered. "But the most suitable thing of all is to marry someone one loves."

Alix, in silence, wondered.

Mr. Westmacott seemed a little better now. She went to the Rectory twice a week and read aloud in French to him and Toppie. He seemed to enjoy it and followed if she read very slowly and distinctly. Toppie sat, her fair head bent over her knitting. She was knitting endless little vests for the poor babies of one of Mrs. Bradley's charities. Alix wondered sometimes what was to become of all those babies. Were they passed on from Mrs. Bradley to more Mrs. Bradleys, until, at last, in one of the hospitals administered by the Aunt Bellas, they closed their eyes? Would some be good citizens and some mere beasts of burden, and some, perhaps, thieves and scoundrels? All were to begin with those little snowy woollen vests, and all were to end in coffins. It made her feel strange to think of it. But when she expressed something of these thoughts to Toppie one day, Toppie looked at her very gravely, and said: "They are all to end in heaven, Alix. We are all of us only that; souls setting out on our journey." But Alix found it so difficult to think of some people as souls.

The babies' vests were a strange accompaniment to Saint-Simon's "Mémoires." She found these on Giles's shelves and asked Toppie if they would do. She had so often heard André de Valenbois and monsieur de Maubert and Maman quote Saint-Simon. Neither Toppie nor her father had read him and were quite contented with her choice, and she skipped about and found the people who most interested her. The French was strange, but it seemed to say more than modern French. The strangeness, she saw, was not apparent to Toppie and her father, nor was the acid irony nor the often unconscious humour. Toppie and her father rarely found anything to laugh at. Mr. Westmacott's chief preoccupation was to follow the relationships of the characters and to place them correctly against the background of contemporaneous history, and for this purpose there were many interruptions while Toppie went to fetch the encyclopædia. Alix saw that Toppie sometimes listened with a vague distress. Saint-Simon and the people he wrote of were as alien to her understanding—to say nothing of her sympathies—as the Chinese. To Alix, for all the travesty of their tails and crests, they were clearly recognizable types. She saw the court of Louis Quatorze as a great golden aviary where splendid creatures, plumed, absurd, and beautiful, paced and preened and surreptitiously pecked at each other beneath the proud gaze of the monstrous bird of paradise on the throne. There was something sinister about them, there behind their bars; but something familiar and lovable too. Toppie only saw them as the denizens of a rather disagreeable fairy-tale, though at some moments of the recital, obscure to Alix, she saw that Toppie's eyes rested upon her in a cogitativeness that seemed aware of too much reality. "They are all odious people, Alix," she said to her one day. "Odious; vindictive; vulgar and wicked."

"Oh; but not all, Toppie. Some are very good, like Fénélon—though Saint-Simon is unfair to him; and some are charming, like the Duchess de Bourgogne. She was too fond of pleasure, perhaps; but she is so merry and amusing that one can forgive her that."

"Very much too fond, I am afraid," said Toppie, colouring above her knitting. "I do not like her, Alix."

"If you feel the book unsuitable for our young friend, Toppie," Mr. Westmacott observed, "why should we not read 'Corinne'? I remember finding madame de Staël very interesting and any young girl could read her."

"But there are wicked people in all history," cried Alix, aghast at this suggestion. "You all read Shakespeare, though he is full of wickedness. It is the point of view. The point of view of Saint-Simon is not wicked. He is ill-tempered, disagreeable, but upright; he means always to tell the truth. And then he was so devout, Monsieur; he was such a devout Christian."

This was wily of her, and Mr. Westmacott, easily reassured, agreed; "Yes, yes, I see that."

When Giles came home for the holidays, Toppie and her father had gone again to Bournemouth. "She might have waited a week longer, so that I could see her," said Giles sadly. It was still taken happily for granted that Alix should sit with Giles in the mornings. There were fires everywhere this Winter, but she was more than ever glad of the refuge. Ruth had become a rather overwhelming presence. She had made new friends at Somerville and spent the first fortnight of her holidays with them in London, going to art-student dances in Chelsea and medical-student dances in Bloomsbury, and returning to her home with what Alix felt to be many a foolish flourish added to her sensible signature. She addressed Alix as "dear old ass," and her favourite exclamation was "God!"

"It is so unlike our mon Dieu," Alix could not forbear writing to Maman. "It is as if one saw a hen suddenly lay an ostrich egg—and so proud of it. I think when English people like Ruth become emancipated, they are very like hens laying ostrich eggs. There is such a strain; and, when it is all over, it is not an interesting object."

Ruth had been meant by nature to be like Aunt Bella, though with much of beauty added. She was tall and large and brightly fair. She had little gaiety, but she gave an impression of massive cheerfulness; and it knocked you down if you impeded it, and strode, almost gravely, on its way. Alix was pleased to feel that Giles, too, found Ruth irritating. He could be very sharp with her, especially when she patronized her mother. But Ruth now, fortified by her new experience of life and in less awe of a brother, was not to be quelled by sharpness, so that if Giles had not withdrawn into gloomy silences there would often have been quarrels.

"There's no harm in her. She's as good as gold. She'd go to the stake for Mummy if it were necessary, cheerfully and as a matter of course; only she's so insufferably conceited," Giles grumbled to Alix in the study. "Why didn't you tell her she knew nothing about it, when she was chaffing you about French manners and customs just now? All she knows about French manners are those of the professor's family she stayed with in Paris. Why didn't you tell her to shut up?"

"That would have been rude," said Alix.

"Well, she was rude."

"But that is no reason for me," Alix slightly smiled, looking up at him.

"By Jove, no!" Giles, with a rueful laugh, rubbed his hand through his hair. "Ruth's manners could never be a reason for yours, could they! I say, you know, that's a nasty one, Alix!"

"I do not mean it to be nasty. And she did not mean to be rude," said Alix. "She meant only to be funny."

"That makes her stupid, then, as well as conceited," said Giles.

If she took refuge with Giles, it was curious and touching to Alix to note that before Ruth's assaults Mrs. Bradley more and more took refuge with her. When Ruth, with a shout of laughter, crowed "Victorian!" at her mother, Alix begged that the inferiority of this term should be explained to her. "For in Maman's salon," she observed, "clever people—I mean the ones your clever people quarrel over in the reviews as to who should claim to have first read them—admire even George Eliot and Ruskin, I assure you. Admire them greatly."

"Help! Help!" shrieked Ruth. She knew nothing of the clever people in Maman's salon. She had not advanced to the recognition of cleverness beyond her reach; she had advanced only as far as scorn for unfashionable tastes, and in herself, as Alix, musing on her, perceived, she had none of the stuff from which new valuations are made.

"And you know," Mrs. Bradley, for the sake of historical accuracy put forward—evading by the mere force of her impersonality any altercation— "it wasn't really so long ago when I was young, Ruth. I didn't live in the time of crinolines. I was reading my Dostoievsky in French and my Hardy in English when I was your age, and I don't seem to see that you young people have got beyond them."

"Oh, Mummy darling, it's not a question of what you read or don't read!" cried Ruth, affectionately ruffling her mother's head. "It's the colour of your mind! It's the pattern of your complexes!"

"There's some truth in that, you know," Mrs. Bradley observed to Alix when, after this sally, Ruth seized her hockey stick and strode away.

Mrs. Bradley always saw whatever of truth there was to be seen in other people's positions. She felt no impatience or grievance against her merciless daughter. She had not time for such reactions. Her own work occupied all her time. And she hoped for her children that they, too, would find work that would thus become the meaning of their lives. It was wonderful in her, this detachment, Alix thought, yet she found fault with it, and it was the only fault she found in Mrs. Bradley. She should have felt herself more responsible for the uncouthness of her daughter; she should have given less thought to the welfare of the London children, and more to the manners of her own. "It would have been better for them," thought Alix, "if she could have become very angry with them. How excellent for Ruth and Rosemary if they could have been well whipped from time to time. And it is too late now."

Mrs. Bradley would have thought whipping irrational and cruel. "She is too wise, too quiet," thought Alix. "But then the saints were like that; wise and quiet and incapable of anger."

Alix had never cared at all about the saints, and it was strange to feel that this heretic lady, creedless and uncloistered, made them more real and more lovable to her.

"Do you not think so, too, Giles?" she said to her friend in the study. "Do you not see what I mean? She is like a modern kind of saint; so selfless and dedicated and laborious. She never thinks about being happy."

"You make her happy, Alix. Did you know that?" said Giles.—"Yes, I see perfectly what you mean. Yet Mummy never seems to me sad. Does she to you?"

"I do not know," Alix reflected. "She did not begin so quiet, I am sure. Just as the saints did not. At the bottom of her heart she wanted to be loved more; much more;—isn't that what all people want most, Giles?—And then when she found that she was not to be she must have felt very sad."

"But, I say, you know!"—Giles stared at her from his chair. "You do say the most astonishing things! Not loved enough! Why don't we all love her!"

"Oh, but it would have to be more than that. She would want far more love than English children could ever give to their parents."

"English children! Surely you don't think that the French love their parents more than we do!"

"But of course we do, Giles," said Alix in candid surprise. "Our mothers we do; for perhaps fathers do not count for so much with us, either."

"Oh, come, I can't swallow that." Giles smiling, yet disturbed, was rubbing his hand over his hair. "You—even you—don't love your mother more than I do mine."

"I think I do, Giles. I think we are more a part of our mothers in France. You stand more alone in England, in everything."

Giles in his disturbance of mind had got up and was looking out of the window. "And what about my father, then?" he said. "What about his love for her? That's what we think of in England as counting most in a woman's life. He was devoted to her."

Alix felt a little shy of sharing with Giles her deepest intuition about Mrs. Bradley's selflessness.

"I am afraid not enough, Giles. Did he really see her as you see her? I am afraid he was not a part of herself, and that is what one expects in England and that is why she must have been sad. And I think she loved best always—if you do not mind my saying so—the ones who were most part of herself—you and Captain Owen and Francis. One cannot help loving most people who are most part of oneself."

And though she still kept her French scepticism about marriage, the half-unconscious climax of a long process of change within Alix was reached when she added in her own thought: "How sad to be married to someone who is not part of yourself."

CHAPTER IV

It was in the last fortnight of the holidays that a letter, once more, came from Lady Mary asking, as if only a few weeks had elapsed since the last time of asking, if Alix could not now come and stay with them at Cresswell Abbey.

The letter was again addressed to Mrs. Bradley and again arrived at breakfast-time so that she read it aloud to the assembled family.

"You'll have to go this time, Alix," said Giles, with an air of fatherly authority.

"Where's the 'have' about it, Giles?" Ruth inquired, helping herself to mustard with her kedgeree. "She'll go if she likes, I suppose; and not otherwise. For my part I don't see why she should be at the beck and call of Lady Hamble, or whatever her name is. She's forgotten Alix for long enough."

"What's to the point is that she's remembered her for long enough," said Giles, "and that Alix has remembered her. Of course, you're going, Alix."

"Alix will be bored stiff among all those swells," cried Rosemary; "and, besides, she'll miss the Eustaces' dance. Do refuse, Alix."

"But I do not think they will bore me," said Alix. "I should like to go."

It was arranged that Giles was to motor her to Hampshire; the cross-country journey was too difficult by train, and while the map was brought and spread out over the jam-pots and butter-dishes and they all made suggestions as to the best route, Alix had time to wonder why, despite her assertion, her old eagerness about Cresswell Abbey and Lady Mary was much faded. Was it that she had grown fonder of Heathside? Yes; undoubtedly; but that was not the reason. It was not to lose Heathside to pay Cresswell Abbey a visit. But, with a new, unwonted shyness, she shrank from the thought of the environment that had, in Lady Mary herself, so reminded her of Maman. Maman would want her to go. She would want it more than Giles did; and did he not want it because he knew that it would be Maman's desire for her? It was almost to suspect them of planning it for her and it affected her with almost a sense of grief to see his dark head bent above Ruth's golden one while, so earnestly, he scanned the road that was to lead her away from them. Did he—with Maman to help him—believe that it would lead to an English marriage for her? The blood rose faintly in her cheeks as she sat there, silent.

But her disquiet was even deeper than this. She had no longer her old sense of security. It was Giles's presence that lent her what security she had and he would not be at Cresswell Abbey.

She was very silent on the morning they set out for their long drive. It was nearly mid-day, yet the hoar frost still made the woods thick and white against the sky, and the twigs were like antlers in their mossy branching outlines. When they passed into the open country the buffs and cinnamons and mole-colours of the fields and uplands were all powdered to paleness. The beauty of the day was like a promise, but Alix felt it like a farewell.

"You'll be back in the fortnight at most, you know," said Giles. He saw that she was sad and said it to reassure her.

"But of course I shall not stay for a fortnight, Giles," she said.

"Lady Mary didn't fix any time; but I do hope you'll stay for as long as she asks you," Giles returned. She made no reply. That, of course, was what Maman would wish him to say to her.

They found the way longer than they had computed, and Alix was very hungry by the time they reached the little market-town where they were to lunch. It was disappointing to find the mutton so tough, and the untidy and decorated young person who waited on them brought the cabbage and potatoes with such a languid mien that they seemed to be almost a concession to special greed.

"I think the cooks in your provincial inns have no pride in their calling," Alix observed, refraining from a very yellow custard pudding while Giles doggedly attacked bread and cheese. "It is a pity; for pride in one's calling gives a zest to life, does it not?"

"Good Lord, Alix! Don't rub it in!" Giles exclaimed, for the mutton had been very tough.

It was already four o'clock when they entered the lodge gates of Cresswell Abbey. The road through the park wound upwards and one saw the ample, happy house with the dropping sun yellowing its windows as it looked out over a southern aspect. Built of pale grey stone and thickly lichened with rosettes of gold, it belonged to an England almost intimate still in its associations. A Gainsborough lady, when it was but newly built, might, Alix thought, have come strolling out on the terrace, the white fur of her little silk jacket turned up about her ears, and a white dog, half Spitz, half Pomeranian, trotting by her side. There was nothing of the splendour or romance of antiquity about it, and Alix, as she saw it, a vision of haughty Montarel hovering at the back of her mind, was a little disappointed. But it was impossible to think of English people living at Montarel. How different this kind-eyed butler from Mélanie in her savates; how different the firelit hall, filled with the scent of pot-pourri and burning logs, from the gaunt cobwebby spaces of Montarel! A wide staircase turned to an upper landing from the hall, and on the turn, with an ascending row of Chinese paintings behind him, a young man in hunting-dress was standing, looking down at them, as they were ushered in, with soft, bright, interested eyes. A group of people, half shut in by a high Chinese screen of red and gold, sat round the fire and from an open door came the sound of a piano playing a reckless jazz tune. Alix felt her sadness dispelled by a sweet stealing sense of excitement.

And now Lady Mary was again before her, looking older than she had remembered her—and that was perhaps because another woman, radiantly young, sat knitting by the fire—but showing the remembered bright softness, and she was drawing them both forward and saying to Giles: "Oh, but of course you must stay—oh, not only to tea; for the night. It's so far. It's so cold. It's so late. Indeed, you must.—Jerry will lend you everything."

Jerry came down the stairs. He had auburn hair and auburn eyes and thick upturned auburn lashes. He was, of course, Lady Mary's son, and Alix was aware that during this little interval it had been at herself that he had been looking. She saw herself standing there as he must see her. The soft little grey travelling-hat came down over her eyebrows; the big, soft collar of her coat went up about her ears; there was not much of her face to be seen; but, for perhaps the first time in her young life, she knew—and the knowledge, mingling with the warm scent of the pot-pourri, the lurching, imbecile gaiety of the music, deepened her sense of excitement— that she held herself beautifully, and that as far as clothes were concerned she had no cause for disquiet.

"I am dark and she is fair," this was the thought that passed through her mind as she felt herself observed not only by Jerry, but also by the radiant lady at the fireside; "but I am even younger than she is, and, I imagine, more unusual."

"Yes, do stay," said Jerry, looking now at Giles and smiling as if he were specially glad to see him.

Poor dear Giles! How gaunt and shabby and shy he looked among them all; rather, thought Alix, like a rook softly entreated by a flock of doves. They cooed about him; Lady Mary with her soft dark eyes, and Jerry, and a kind elderly gentleman who had advanced from the hearth, the "Times" held behind him, and who, apparently, was Lady Mary's husband. Even the butler seemed to be one of the flock, and he gently withdrew Giles's greatcoat and carried it away as if the question were settled before Giles had had time, as she knew, to gather his wits together.

"You will. That's splendid," said Jerry, though Giles had not said that he would. "Let's have tea at once, Mummy; they'll want it as much as I do, and I'll change after."

Lady Mary, taking Alix by the hand, as though she might feel, as a foreigner, strange in a strange country, led her upstairs to a bright sweet room where rose-clotted chintzes were drawn back from the bed and windows and flowers stood on the writing- and dressing-tables and enticing bottles with little labels round their necks on the wash-hand stand.

"Debenham will get you everything. Ask her for anything you want," said Lady Mary, introducing the elderly maid who entered with hot water. "You can find your way down? We're having tea in the drawing-room, just out of the hall. And then you must have a little rest. Some young people are coming over after dinner to dance. Are you fond of dancing?"

"Fonder than of anything, I think," said Alix; and Lady Mary, smiling, said "Good."

When she was left alone and had taken off her hat and washed, and combed her hair, Alix stood before the glass and looked at herself attentively. She looked well after the long drive. It had not been really cold, though her lips were a little pale. She bit them to make the colour come, and wondered, bending closer, whether she should powder her face. She had never yet used the box of powder, teinte Rachel, in her dressing-case, though Maman had told her that she might do so if she thought it advisable. The radiant lady used liquid powder; Alix had seen that at once, and her lips were reddened artificially. Alix decided that she would leave herself alone. "It goes better with my hair; one colour all over like that; and the right colour," she reflected, while the spicy elation ran still more warmly through her veins. Maman had chosen with her, at a specially favourite little shop in the rue du Faubourg Saint-Honoré, the jumper of palest blue and grey, patterned like a fritillary; and the string of dull brown beads and the blue skirt and the grey shoes and stockings all went perfectly with it. "I am bien; très bien," she thought; and as she went down the passage and crossed the landing and looked down into the firelit hall with its flowers and screens and great blazing logs, she felt herself so strangely Maman's child. It was as if she knew, for the first time in her life, an elation that Maman had often felt.

They were all in the drawing-room where tea was being laid, Jerry and Lady Mary and Mr. Hamble, and two young girls and a young man and an old-young man, who had evidently been dancing and who wished to seem much younger than he was.—"I will avoid dancing with him," thought Alix. "He is too stout and he brushes his hair up over his head from behind so that it shall not be seen how bald he is."—And the radiant lady was talking to Giles. Giles stood with her before the fire and looked dreadfully cross, and that was because he did not like her. But other people liked her; a great deal. Her soft locks, now smooth, now clustering, were of the purest gold and her eyes of a marvellous blue, and she, too, was undoubtedly bien, très bien, in her white silk jumper and her white woollen skirt and string of pearls. But Giles did not like her. And she did not like Giles, either, though she was pretending to carry on the kindest of conversations with a dull young man, and when Jerry came up to Alix herself the golden-haired lady, smiling more sweetly than ever upon Giles, saw everything that passed between them and was not pleased. She did not care a rap about Giles. What she cared about was Jerry.

It was characteristic of Alix that the more she saw and felt, the more silent and aloof did she become. It might have been a fundamental racial caution in her blood; the instinct for being sure, first, where you were, and, second, sure of where you wished to be seen as being before you made a movement; and as she felt the pressure of all these strange new realizations—strangest of all about herself—she knew that she possessed reserves of courteous convention more than adequate for any contingencies that might arise at Cresswell Abbey. Quietly smiling at Jerry, she took the place Lady Mary indicated to her beside her on the sofa and saw that the golden-haired lady still watched her while pretending not to.

The two young girls were guests. They had very sweet voices that did not mean much. One of them was pretty, and the stout gentleman with the hair brushed over his baldness jested with her in a low voice, but, though he tried so to please her, the pretty girl, while she ate a great many cakes, looked at him with eyes that did not find him amusing. Alix felt with her.

"From Jack," said the radiant lady, looking up from a letter; the butler had just brought in the letters.

"What news of Jack?" asked Mr. Hamble. The golden-haired lady was married to his nephew and her name was Marigold. Jack, it seemed, was rather enjoying his job at Singapore. He wrote a long letter, and Mrs. Hamble's marvellous eyes became very wistful while she read, but Alix felt sure that if she had been reading alone in her own room they would not have looked like that; hard and indifferent rather.

"My dear, don't be so silly," said the other girl to the young man who was short and robust with a tanned jolly face. He was a sailor, and Alix liked his face and felt that with him she would like to dance. They all knew each other very well and laughed and talked and she felt they saw her as a very young school-girl, for Jerry was now talking to Giles about Oxford, and no one paid any attention to her until Lady Mary began to ask her about Normandy and then about Beauvais and Rouen and so on to Chartres, on which the bald man, whose name was Mr. Fulham and who wrote books, as if observing her for the first time, asked her if she knew his friends the marquis and marquise de Tréville in Normandy and, when she said she did not, turned to the pretty girl again.

After tea she found herself alone for a little while with Giles. She felt as if they met after long separation, so completely had the morning's sadness dissolved in the pervading sense of excitement.

"I like it here very much, don't you?" she said.

"It's a jolly place," said Giles. "And they're all so nice. I'm glad you like it. I'm glad you'll be happy here."

Giles no longer looked cross, but he looked thoughtful, and his eyes turned on her once or twice in a way that made her wonder, with a vague discomfort, whether he guessed at her excitement.

"I wish you were staying here, too, Giles," she said. But this was not quite true. She would be sorry to see Giles go; even a little frightened; yet if that sense of excitement were to environ her more closely she would not care to have Giles observing it.

"Oh, but I don't belong here at all," said Giles, stretching up his arms and locking his hands behind his head, while his eyes still studied her. "And you do."

"Why don't you belong here?" she asked. But she knew. He was a rook among the doves.

"I haven't done any of the things they do;—or very few of them."

"Neither have I."

"Oh, yes, you have; far more. Anyway, you're fitted for them and I'm not."

"Do you mean you look down upon them?"

"Of course not. But one has only time for so much in one's life and my line is taken."

"Philosophy and the Banbury Road," said Alix, rather sadly musing.

"Yes; philosophy, though not necessarily the Banbury Road," said Giles. "And tutoring and being poor. You couldn't combine those with dances and hunting; even if you had the choice; which I haven't."

"Lady Mary cares for the things you do, Giles. Books and music, and the country. I believe they all care. I think you would be quite happy with her and Mr. Hamble and Jerry."

"Oh, we'd manage for a week-end now and then, no doubt. He's a nice boy that Jerry," Giles added, moving his arms now, putting his hands in his pockets and looking with detachment at the foot crossed on his knee. "Lucky we're the same size, isn't it? I shan't look too much of an ass in his evening things."

"He is very nice, I think," said Alix. "I do not care much for Joan and Patience Wagstaffe, they seem to me rather nulle. But the sailor is nice, too, and Mr. Hamble is so kind. He told me that he would teach me to play billiards. They seem to find that Mr. Fulham very clever, but I would not have him however clever he was. I do not like him. He has a sly face and eats too much. And is Mrs. Hamble nice, Giles?" Thus circuitously Alix approached her object. "She is exceedingly pretty. You had a long talk with her."

"Oh, no, I didn't." Giles laughed suddenly. "She wasn't talking with me—only at me; to see what she'd catch as a rebound."

After all, it was always delightful to get back to Giles. After all, no one understood quite as well as Giles.

"What was she trying to catch?" Alix asked.

"Oh, just who we were, and what we were doing here, and why in the dickens you weren't just the quiet little French girl she'd expected. The funny part of it was," said Giles, smiling broadly as he thought of it, "she didn't know a bit that I saw what she was after. Silly ass; thinking herself so gracefully concealed and all the time as gross and as glaring as possible. She's stupid all right," said Giles. "Though I daresay it makes one stupid to imagine one's dealing with a negligible noodle. You let her alone, Alix. She's a cat."

This was very pleasant to Alix.

"She has a false face," she observed. "I shall certainly let her alone; for she displeased me from the first."

Then Lady Mary came back and sat down and talked with them, of France again, and of Oxford, and Professor Cockburn, and then Jerry, having changed his hunting-clothes for homespun, came and carried Giles off to billiards, but Lady Mary said she would keep Alix with her, and, when the two young men were gone, said: "How dear he is, your Giles; such a delightful solid mind," so that Alix flushed with pleasure. She was glad to have Giles appreciated and it made her fonder of Lady Mary that she should appreciate him.

Lady Mary then questioned her about Giles and his family and how she had come to know them, and Alix, replying, felt herself move along the surfaces prepared for her by Giles and Maman. She told Lady Mary about Captain Owen and how great a friend he had been and of how he had wished her to know his family. There was nothing else to tell. Lady Mary knew just what Mrs. Bradley knew.

She was glad to rest for a little while before dinner, lying in her room on the sofa with a soft cushion under her head and the firelight softly glowing on her closed eyelids, until it was time to dress. Debenham had laid out on the bed the very dress she herself would have chosen; her prettiest dress, of white and crystal; and the sense of elation and excitement mounted in her with thick swift strokes, as of rising wings, while, before the mirror, Debenham fastened it for her. Debenham thought her beautiful. Her quiet, sagacious face, glancing at the reflected figure, told Alix that she thought so; and Debenham had seen many pretty young ladies.

When she was left alone, she stood and looked at herself. Yes; was it true. Beautiful that little head; beautiful the long, splendid throat, the breast and arms so white. In the tilted mirror she looked like a naiad hovering within the thin falling lines of a fountain. Tiny crystal drops fell along her arms and flowed from breast to hem. She moved, and liquid lines of crystal moved with her. Her shoes were of silver and a fillet of twisted silver and crystal bound her dark hair. "Dieu que je suis belle!" Alix murmured. She seemed to float on a sense of buoyant power. She had never known such happiness.

They all thought her beautiful. She saw that as she came among them. Jerry was there—he was the first she saw, looking at her; and the young sailor looked; and kind Mr. Hamble; Marigold Hamble in pink and diamonds looked, too, very hard.

"The lovely dress! Paris, of course," said Lady Mary, smiling at her as though she were grateful to her for placing an object so decorative in her drawing-room.

"Paris and Maman," Alix smiled, and the memory of Maman rushed over her almost with a smart of tears. She owed it all to Maman, this transfiguration. She was not really so beautiful, by daylight. It was

Maman's magic that enveloped her, and Maman was not here to see her in it. It was cruel that a stranger, Lady Mary, should garner Maman's sheaves.

She saw now that Giles's large eyes were dwelling upon her from a distance; but they were not like the other eyes. They kept their look of thoughtfulness. He was not seeing her in the magic. He was only seeing her as herself. It would always be only oneself that Giles would see. From within her fountain of happiness she glimmered a little smile over to him—for Jerry was beside her saying that he was to take her in to dinner—and in Giles's answering smile she read something touched and gentle. She was glad that it should be so, for Giles might have looked gloomily at her, seeing her so happy at being beautiful; but he was only touched; and those gentle eyes of Giles's seemed at once to quiet the excitement and to reassure her, as though he said: "But of course you must be happy, dear kid."

The long table in the dining-room, shining under the candles, was like a lake of bright water all drifted over with floating knots of flowers. Everything made her think of gliding, falling water to-night; everything was beautiful. Jerry was beside her and he was used to beautiful people. He saw them every day of his life. He was like André de Valenbois in that. Giles's very thoughts about André crossed her mind as she turned her eyes on the charming face beside her. He, too, was a person removed from the earthy, primitive aspects of life; he, too, had only had, always, to choose what he would have and never to have what he did not choose. And now— she felt it falling around her, cool and refreshing as the sense of crystal drops—it was herself he chose rather than Mrs. Hamble. He did not look at Mrs. Hamble. He talked and talked, trying to find out about her all the things that interested him; her tastes, her prejudices, the colour of her personality. He talked happily, eagerly, with something of the ardour of a little boy playing at gardening; that was the simile that came to Alix while she smiled quietly at him—a little boy who gathers up armfuls of flowers and thistles, the lovely and the commonplace together, and brings them for admiration:—"Beautiful, isn't it?" was what he said continually; and he did not see that there were thistles. He was younger than André; much younger. She was dimly glad of that, for something in the likeness she had felt disquieted her. She liked him better than André, though he had not André's fine discrimination. His admirations lay along the paths of fashion, and the fact that fashion prided itself on being a pioneer led him into ardours for the new and the strange soon discarded for the newer and the stranger. He had an air, Alix saw, of caring, immensely, that you should sympathize with him about the latest painter, the latest poet, the latest composer. He did not really care whether you sympathized or not; but if you didn't, you were negligible for his purposes. She saw that he had already found Giles negligible; and she wondered why he did not put her into the same category. Did he imagine that she possessed and withheld even fresher appraisals? It was not so and she did not pretend it, looking at him with her quiet smile and softly shaking her head now and then. She had never thought of herself as a person whose appraisals mattered; she had thought of herself as too much of a child. But perhaps it was because Jerry found her beautiful that he was indifferent to her indifference.

After dinner they danced. Many young people arrived and the tall red Chinese screens in the hall were put back. There was a piano and two violins and one of the young men who played had such a gloomy face, like a French or Italian face—like Jules' face—that Alix wished she could talk to him and ask him if he were a foreigner. But there was no time for talk. She and Jerry found that their steps went beautifully together. She danced with him; many times; and with other young men; and Jerry helped her to evade Mr. Fulham who, seeing how many partners she had, wished to be one of them. But with Jerry it was best of all, and how much more important it was to have steps that chimed than to care about the same books and pictures! It seemed to-night, among the flowers, and lights, and music, the most important of all things; though once or twice, when she found Giles's eyes again, she knew that the sense of ecstasy on which she floated must have the evanescence of a mirage. Dear Giles. She made him dance with her and they laughed together as they went slowly round the hall, for Giles did not dance well. Afterwards she saw that he talked with Lady Mary and with Mr. Hamble. He did not go into the mirage. He only looked on at it.

When Alix fell asleep that night in the firelight, she dreamed that a cool crystal stream flowed round her and that she floated on its silver surfaces. Golden lights lay like a chain of little suns along its margin and her hands, softly moving in the current, felt rosy petals pass between their fingers. The throb of dance-music, sweet, reckless, imbecile, beat in her blood, and in her ears the sound of Jerry's voice saying: "Beautiful, isn't it?" And Giles's eyes were there watching her. In her dream she wanted to tell Giles that she had nothing to conceal. She tried to tell him, but she felt the silver stream flowing over her lips and making them dumb, though they smiled. If Giles looked at her like that she might begin to blush. But even so she did not want him gone. While he was there she was so safe.

CHAPTER V

"And you will see that Blaise is happy until I come back, Giles?" said Alix, as she stood beside the car next morning to say good-bye. "And you will write to me?"

"We haven't time for many letters, you know," Giles smiled reassuringly. "I'll see to Blaise."

"Give my love to them all," said Alix. The car was beginning slowly to slide away and she went beside it. She was not unhappy; not sad; it was only that she was a little frightened to see Giles go. If one night had changed so much in herself, what changes might not one week bring? She almost felt she loved Ruth and Rosemary this morning. Whatever their deficiencies they had not false faces. It was true that they could not, even if they had wished to, have concealed themselves gracefully; but it would never occur to them to wish to be concealed; gracefully or otherwise. Neither were they insipid like the two Wagstaffe girls. If Ruth and Rosemary were like roast mutton, the Wagstaffes, Alix reflected, were like fondants. She stood gazing after Giles for a moment as he disappeared among the beeches.

Jerry and his mother stood on the step above her, having come out with her to say good-bye. Lady Mary was looking at her, a little, she felt, as Giles had looked at her last night; thoughtfully, with great kindness in the thoughtfulness; seeing her as herself.

"Now you're going to let me teach you how to ride," said Jerry. "Mummy has a habit for you."

"An old one of mine. I don't ride any longer," said Lady Mary, putting her hand on Alix's shoulder as they went into the warm sweet house. "I think it will fit you beautifully. You and I are rather of the same build, aren't we, Alix?"

"Alix's shoulders are broader than yours, Mummy," said Jerry, "and I'm afraid, darling, that her legs are a little longer. She's rather like a Jean Goujon nymph and you are just a lovely mortal size."

It was odd, Alix thought, to have a young man define the length of one's legs; but not mal élevé, as it would have been in France. Jerry discussed the physical attributes of his friends as he would have discussed their moral qualities.

"The habit may be a trifle too short, it's true," said Lady Mary; "but that makes no difference. The Jean Goujon nymph will be able to get into it. We must dress Alix in the Gainsborough Blue Boy clothes one day,

Jerry, to show off her long legs. We must have a little fancy-dress ball in the Easter holidays."

"Oh, but I'm afraid I cannot be here in the Easter holidays," said Alix. "You see, those are Giles's holidays, too. I should miss him."

"You'll be coming here off and on, I hope;—and Giles will, too, perhaps," smiled Lady Mary. "I can always send the car for you. Where's Marigold, Jerry? Not up yet?"

"You know, she looks rather like the Blue Boy, doesn't she?" said Jerry. "Only his eyes aren't blue, and he has a gentler face. Alix's face is rather farouche;—is that the word?—You frighten me a little, Alix, with those cold blue eyes of yours.—Marigold's still in bed. She sent for me to see her just now. Writing letters," said Jerry, "in a most adorable little cap; a Watteau little cap; most frightfully becoming. That was why she sent for me, of course, so that I should see her in it; though the alleged motive was the Fairlies' ball."

"Naughty Jerry," smiled his mother.

"Not a bit naughty. I told her I saw through her. I told her that the cap was a brilliant success. Nothing souterrain about me.—Eh, Alix? Is that right?" They all called her Alix;—as if she had been ten years old; or as if they had always known her.

"I think you must try to talk a little French with Alix," said Lady Mary. "His accent is good, isn't it? But his verbs and genders are dreadful, and souterrain isn't right, my dear boy."

"Don't you think Marigold quite extraordinarily beautiful?" Jerry inquired. "Isn't the colour of her hair and eyes a Hans Christian Andersen fairy-tale colour?"

"But she is much more like a Watteau than like a fairy-tale," said Alix.

"But Watteau people are fairy-tale people.—You mean she's an artificial fairy-tale.—Yes, I see what you mean.—And it's really more Fragonard than Watteau, too—'A dainty rogue in porcelain,' that's what she is. Do you read Meredith? I love him, though I know he is démodé just now."

But Alix had not read Meredith.

Half an hour later, when Jerry had lightly hoisted her to the saddle and the groom had released the chestnut's eager head, Alix felt as if, at last, she had discovered her true vocation. This—yes, even more than dancing— was what she had been made for.

She did not feel that she had anything to learn. She felt no fear. Her hands went easily where Jerry told her to put them; her knee and foot found their security. Nothing this delicious creature could do, moving with satin ease and steel strength beneath her, would take her unawares. She understood him, and he, his gentle ears quivering at the sound of her voice, understood her. "Yes; yes, I see," she said, as Jerry gave his explanations. "Yes, we will walk to the end so that I shall be quite used to it and then canter on the turf. Yes; I understand; holding with my knee."

It was not swimming, or dancing, or flying, but it combined the delights of all three. One floated, buoyantly sustained; one embodied the beauty of rhythmic movement; one glided at a height strange enough for a sense of slight, delicious trembling. The earth was new, seen from this height; one looked into the branches of the beeches at the level where the chaffinches were perching and flitting.

"You sit as if you were born to it," Jerry told her, and she replied that her father had been a great horseman.

Then came the canter. It surprised her a little. For one surging moment, cheeks hot, lips closed fast, she felt that she was coming off and then, suddenly, that nothing could bring her off. Between that fast-held knee and that supple foot, she was poised in safety. Her mind and body adjusted themselves to the sense of mastered peril.

"Splendid!" Jerry smiled at her when they drew rein at the end of the long upland.

Below them the country fell away in rippled planes of colour, like a tapestry, russet, silver and blue. Alix seemed to see it threaded with ladies riding unicorns and wearing high white hennins. Fragments of song rang in her mind; the joyous melancholy of Les Filles de la Rochelle, the blissful sadness of L'Amour de moi. Riding brought such memories crowding to one's mind. This was a better intoxication than the dancing mirage. It went deeper. It set the bells of all the buried Atlantises of the soul ringing.

"What are you thinking about now!" she heard Jerry ask. She had almost forgotten Jerry while she gazed and listened;—far away in France; in an old, old France. But it was part of the better happiness to find Jerry again and to feel herself again a child, with Jerry her comrade. Mrs. Hamble was as remote as a lady on a unicorn. The woman's happiness of the night before, made up of power and conquest, faded before the child's mere joyousness. Jerry made her think of the chestnut horse she rode, with his eager russet head.

"Oh, I do so like riding, Jerry!" she exclaimed.

"You'd soon be able to hunt, if you get on like this. How I wish I could take you out hunting!"

"I should not care to hunt," said Alix. "This is what I like. Riding in a beautiful country with everything happy around one."

"But everything is happy around you when you hunt," said Jerry. "Hounds and horses and people. One is part of an immense shaded joy. And one never sees how beautiful a country is until one has ridden right across it and known that at every wall one might break one's neck."

"I like this better," said Alix. "This is like riding with a flower in one's hand, and that would be to ride with a knife between one's teeth.—Though I understand the pleasure of the danger.—But the fox would spoil it all for me. He would not be part of the immense joy."

"Oh, I assure you—he enjoys it, too, in his own sharp way. Imagine his joy when he outwits us."

"A terrible joy," said Alix. "There must always be terror in his blood. No; I could not bear to feel that he was there, with his straining heart, before us. I could never hunt. But I should like to ride for ever."

When they got back they went to find Lady Mary in the morning-room.

"Alix is a marvel, Mummy!" Jerry exclaimed. "She's not afraid of anything, and rides as if she'd been born in the saddle."

"I was afraid once," said Alix. "When we started to canter."

Lady Mary sat at her writing-bureau, photographs and flowers ranged about her, and smiling at them both she said: "You must come and tell me all about it, Alix, when you've had your bath. Will you? I shall be here."

"And I must do some reading," said Jerry. "Au revoir, Alix. Billiards after lunch, you know."

Lady Mary had finished her morning tasks when Alix returned and was sitting near the fire with a little table before her on which she was laying out tiny patience cards. Alix again thought of a lady in a hennin as she saw her there in her long, grey, fur-bordered robe; a hennin would have been so becoming to her.

"Curl up in the big chair," she said. "You must be tired, and you'll find yourself very stiff by to-morrow. Do you smoke? Not yet? Good. I'm glad not. Joan and Patience both do already, and I'm sure it's bad for them. That's all their life it seems to me; smoking and dancing. Have you many girls in France like that? I haven't stayed in France for so many years."

"I should not be allowed to smoke; not until I married, I think," said Alix, leaning her head on the side of the big chair and watching her hostess's white hands place the little cards. "I don't know about other girls. But I do not think that they have as much liberty as in England. I like liberty; but not for so many cigarettes."

She felt very much at home with Lady Mary, who continued to make her think of Maman.

"Liberty for the right things and not for the foolish things," smiled Lady Mary. "And it's a pity to have liberty for foolish things even when one marries. Tell me where you and Jerry went. Across the ridge and down to Minching's Pond? A wonderful place that is for birds in Spring—Three Oaks Corner; yes; only the oaks went during the war. Did Jerry tell you? Dreadful to see the empty places. And as far as the Mill. That was a splendid round. Ah, I felt sure you'd like Darcy. Isn't he a lamb of a horse! Jerry wanted you to have Darcy.—I'm so glad you are here to play with Jerry," Lady Mary went on. "Marigold is such a flirt. She can't help it." Lady Mary smiled at Alix and shuffled her cards. "She is a born siren. And Jerry is too young for sirens."

Alix had again the sensation of being confided in despite her youth. It was curious how quickly, if they liked you, they confided in you, these strange English people.

"You didn't answer Jerry this morning about her looks," Lady Mary was going on. "It's a thin little face, I feel, don't you? And too pink-and-white; too blue-and-gold. But perhaps that's because I'm dark. I suppose dark people, like you and me, Alix, usually suspect the white-and-gold ones of being cats."

"I do not like her face," said Alix.

"Whereas Jerry admires her immensely; and he's only a boy, only just twenty, you know, and it's rather tiresome. You will take his mind off her.—Not that it has ever really worried me," said Lady Mary; and Alix knew that it really had.

But Jerry and his flirtation was not Lady Mary's object. Alix began to see that her interest in herself was more disinterested than that. She was making her way, through smoking, and riding, and Marigold, to other topics. The topic she was really coming to was Giles, and she wanted to find out just how fond Alix was of him, and just how far went her commitments to him and to his family.

Alix fancied, watching her, that she had a habit of playing patience when she wanted to say special things to you and to keep them from seeming special.

"I don't wonder at their taking you in as you say they have," she remarked, when Alix expressed her sense of gratitude to the Bradleys. "Their brother, you know; what you and your mother had done for him.

Giles told me about that last night.—And then you are a nice young person in yourself, Alix. One might like having you about."

"But it is not because I am nice that they have me," Alix demurred. "And even if they did not like me so much they would take me in."

"Because of him?"

"Yes. Because he was so fond of me. And not even quite that. It is more as if I had been a fox terrier he had left behind him. I mean it was like that at the beginning. They would have taken it in and cared for it always, even if it had not been a very nice one."

Lady Mary laughed. "Well, you are a very nice one. I liked Giles's mother that day in Oxford. She is very earnest, isn't she?"

"Yes. And very good."

"But she hasn't much sense of humour?"

"She is so busy all the time," said Alix. "When one is so very busy taking care of people, there is not much time for humour. But she can be quite playful; like a young girl."

"I can't see her being playful," said Lady Mary. "Just as I can't see her with her hair waved or her nose powdered. I don't suppose she's ever powdered her nose, or rouged her lips, or had her hair waved, has she?"

"It would not go with her type," said Alix. "There is a natural ripple in her hair, and her nose is of that pale dull sort that does not need powder."

Lady Mary was laughing again. "She's a dear, of course. I saw that. And of course it isn't her type. It isn't his type either, is it; the pretty surfaces of life. Though he has humour," said Lady Mary, clipping down a card with soft deliberation and then shifting it. "Quite grim humour, too, I felt, once or twice. And I like that."

"I know no one who has a better sense of humour than Giles," said Alix.

"He is modest, too," said Lady Mary. "And most middle-class young men are so overweeningly proud of their brains. We must all be proud of something, I suppose. One rather wishes he was not going to be buried in Oxford; but one feels, too, that it is his métier. He would not care a scrap about getting on or making a name in the world, and it's such a happy life, that of the scholar. And if they don't intend to marry, there's no reason why they should strive and strain like worldly people."

"But then they do marry," Alix observed.

"Oh. Yes; perhaps so. But it depends to whom. It would be the unfortunate wife who would strive and strain in that case, wouldn't it? It must be a very dreary life. Marigold wouldn't like it, would she?" laughed Lady Mary.

"But they wouldn't like her," said Alix.

"It all depends on what you want, of course," said Lady Mary, holding up an undecided card. "If one wants earnestness and an unpowdered nose, that is one thing; and if one wants hunting and dancing and diamonds, like Marigold, that is another. I detest worldliness," said Lady Mary, "but I do like common-sense. Now your dear Giles, I could see that, has any amount of common-sense and not a scrap of worldliness."

Alix listening, while Lady Mary thus mused, finding his place for Giles rather as she found the place for the hovering card, recognized still further resemblances to Maman. Lady Mary, too, could be sweetly devious. She would feed you with spoonfuls of honey satisfied that you would never taste the alien powder that was being administered. She was talking to her now as to the clever child who could take no personal interest in the question of marriage. But the experience was to Alix a familiar one and the admonitory flavour at once detected. She was not to take an interest, but Lady Mary was taking an interest for her. Lady Mary was selecting her place for her very much as Maman would have done; and, as with Maman, Alix often found a malicious pleasure in seeing through her and pretending not to see, so now she pleased herself by saying nothing to Lady Mary of Giles's devotion to Toppie which would so have set her mind at rest. "Giles is my greatest friend," was all she vouchsafed presently, and Lady Mary could make of it what she chose.

There had been minor intimations gliding along beside the major one. If Giles, in his chosen career, was not to be thought of as a husband, Heathside and the Bradleys need not be thought of as essential to Alix's life in England. Not for a moment did Lady Mary intimate anything so gross as that Alix should abandon her friends; she only made it clear that, since she could now count on new ones, she was not dependent on Heathside. They were very strange, these English people, Alix meditated, her dark head leaning back in the chair, her blue eyes resting with their Alpine aloofness on her hostess. How much, if they once liked you, they took you for granted; and how very easily, so it seemed to Alix, they did like you. Lady Mary resembled Giles in that; and Toppie and Mrs. Bradley; and if they swallowed you down, asking no questions, was it because they were so extraordinarily kind, or because they were so sure of themselves and of their conditions that they could not conceive of your doing them any harm? The difference—how often Alix had meditated these differences—was that the French were so sure of themselves and of their conditions that they couldn't conceive of your doing them any good. The English, certainly, were more kind.

But were they kind enough to make themselves responsible for you? Giles would. Alix had seen Giles make himself responsible. She believed that Toppie would; and Mrs. Bradley. Even Ruth and Rosemary, if the test came, would, she believed, shoulder her. But strangely, painfully—for she, too, liked Lady Mary, though she did not at all take her for granted—Alix could imagine this new friend, if consequences proved troublesome or unpalatable, choosing, simply, as the easiest way out, to forget all about her. She was dove-like, but she was capricious. Her life was beautiful, and she enjoyed laying out other people's lives in harmony with its beauty, making a chiming pattern of you as she did with her patience cards, because she liked to make patterns and because she thought of herself as able to do what she liked. But it would be unwise to give oneself to the Lady Marys or trust them as they invited you to trust them. They, too, were far more implicated in the dust of human conditions than they knew themselves to be. They did not really know themselves, for they did not know the dust; and, where she herself was concerned, Alix deeply suspected that consequences might prove dusty; might prove troublesome and unpalatable. She felt herself to be older than Lady Mary as she watched her and listened to her; she felt herself wiser. Life required far more circumspection than Lady Mary imagined. If Lady Mary was circumspect it was subconsciously, for candour was her aim. But so one might mislead oneself and other people. And as all these thoughts went through Alix's mind, while Lady Mary laid out her pretty cards, there floated across it a memory of the shrewd old face of a priest to whom she had once gone for the yearly, the reluctant, confession. If one was more circumspect than any English person, was it because of the generations of Catholicism in one's blood? One's confessor always took so many disagreeable things for granted, about life and about human nature; and, on reflection, one usually found that he had been right.

CHAPTER VI

Under pressure from Giles, who wrote that of course she must stay on, Alix's visit to Cresswell Abbey lengthened itself over the whole remaining fortnight of the holidays. She went to the Fairlies' ball, where she wore her white and crystal dress, and to another, where she wore her pink with the wreath of rosebuds. She danced and danced. In the mornings she rode with Jerry.

How strange Heathside seemed to her when she at last returned to it, as strange as when she had first come to it from France. Life at Cresswell Abbey was so much more like life at Maman's than anything at Heathside. Always, at Maman's, there was that same sense of mental grace; always the people, the varying people, coming and going, who displayed it. The people at Cresswell were not so graceful or so interested in mental things; but, from the mere fact that there were so many of them and of so many varieties, they reminded her of the life in Paris with Maman. And besides the young men and the young girls who danced and played together, there were pleasant, sagacious women, all so beautifully dressed, and their political husbands. At Cresswell one had whom one chose to amuse or instruct one; at Heathside one had to take what the neighbourhood or the High School provided.

Oddly enough, however, she found herself, on her return, liking not only Rosemary, her daily companion, more than she had ever liked her, but the High School girls, too. It was, she knew, because she had seen so much of Marigold Hamble and because they were so different from Marigold. Marigold had not attempted to molest her in any way; she had, indeed, attempted to attach her; but Alix, in regard to Marigold, had never for a moment relaxed her circumspection, though, in regard to Lady Mary, it was impossible not often to relax it. She could match Marigold at empty affability, but she could not display Marigold's empty affectionateness, and the more it was displayed, the more she disliked her. If she disliked Marigold, Marigold hated her; she knew that unerringly with her growing power of womanly divination. Marigold hated her because Jerry liked her so much and because she never made an effort to attach him; while Marigold made every effort compatible with graceful concealment.

By the time she went away it was as if she had become almost as much a part of the life at Cresswell as she was part of the life at Heathside. Lady Mary was so fond of her and depended, strangely, Alix thought, on her taste and judgment about so many things;—and that was like Maman, too.

And Mr. Hamble was fond of her, teaching her billiards and cracking many cheerful jests with her at the expense of France. It was natural, it was inevitable, that she should come back again, and for almost all the winter week-ends she did come back. There was always a party for the week-ends, and sometimes Jerry motored down from Oxford for the day, and once he stayed the night for a dance, and Marigold, on this occasion, adopted a new and surprising attitude towards Alix, behaving as if she had never seen her before. She also gave scant attention to Jerry, and Alix remarked that though Jerry did not really like Marigold he was perturbed by her neglect; so perturbed that he even forgot to dance with Alix and stood watching Marigold fox-trotting with another man, his radiance all dimmed by resentful gloom.

"Poor darling; isn't he foolish?" Lady Mary commented to her young friend, and Alix, in no need of partners, said calmly that he was, telling herself that she did not in the least mind what Jerry did. But she did mind. Since the moment that she had seen his eyes fixed upon her from the stairs she had minded, not because she cared for Jerry, but because she cared, intensely, that he should care for her. Was she, then, another Marigold? She asked herself this question fiercely, lying awake in her firelit room, her immature young heart strained by the sense of contest between herself and the crafty woman. Why should she mind Jerry's gloom? What was Jerry to her? Nothing; nothing; the answer came to her irrefutably from the depths of her heart where anger and pride could not penetrate to blur the truth; Jerry was nothing more than the charming comrade, unless Marigold was there to take him from her. Her delight in Jerry, apart from their comradeship, was only her delight in his delight. She could not understand, she could not see what it was she wanted nor what was this fire that burned within her, but, feeling hot tears rising in her eyes, she remembered what the old priest had said about the wickedness of the human heart and knew again that he was right.

It was always a relief to get back to Rosemary. Rosemary had not a purr in her composition, and that was a defect; but she had not a scratch either. Even in the High School girls, whose virtues she had felt to be so negative, she appreciated now the positive quality of straightness.

When the Easter holidays came, Alix found that there was no reason why she should not go to Cresswell for the fancy-dress ball. Giles was to be away for a fortnight. She would not miss him in going. There were other reasons for accepting with a mind at ease. Marigold was safely in the Riviera and Jerry's letter, telling her of the fact, was very naughty, breathing as it did an evident relief. Jerry, too, was young and his heart, too, had been strained by the sense of pointless contest. Eager comradeship and an assurance of peace infused every line of his pretty dashing pages.

So Lady Mary's car came for her and she went off, Rosemary teasing her from the steps and declaring that they would all be on the lookout for her picture in the "Daily Mail" dressed as the Blue Boy. Rosemary was a dear, thought Alix, leaning out to smile and have a last glance at her.

Then came ten days at Cresswell; days that altered all her life.

She must at once tell Giles about it; that was the thought that filled her mind as she sat with him in the study, on the April morning after his return and hers. But there was so much to tell that she did not know how she should begin, and what made it more difficult was that Giles was very sad.

Toppie was in Bournemouth with her father and it was evident from her letters that Mr. Westmacott was dying. Although Giles had not seen her for such a long time, it was natural that he should be thinking of Toppie rather than of her, so that she said nothing, and it was Giles himself who introduced her theme.

"Why didn't you stay on at Cresswell?" he asked her. "I saw Jerry in Oxford just before I came down, and he evidently thought they were to keep you for a month."

"Oh, but I never intended that," said Alix. "I said I must be back here for your time at home."

"That was awfully sweet of you, my dear child," said Giles, who walked about, looking very tall in his new grey tweeds. "I'm awfully glad to find you here, of course; but you know what I feel about cake and bread-and-butter, and I should like you to eat the full slice. How was the Blue Boy costume? Jerry told me about that."

"It was very pretty. I looked well in it," said Alix. "Our photographs were all taken. You shall see how I looked, Giles."

"And you and Jerry rode a lot?"

"Yes. We rode almost every morning. I love riding, Giles. Even more than dancing."

"Yes. Of course you do," said Giles rather absently. "Why shouldn't you love it? You like Jerry as much as ever, don't you? You and he are great pals?"

Alix almost had to smile a little at this, it was so transparent of Giles, though, a fortnight ago, she would, perhaps, not have seen how transparent it was. It made it easier for her, however, and as she answered:—"Yes. Great pals. Yes; I like him as much as ever,"—she raised her eyes to his and saw that he continued to look at her as though aware of approaching confidences. It would not be at all difficult to make confidences to Giles. She felt him very, very much older than herself and, if that were possible, even kinder than before. How strange, the thought passed through her mind;—it was easier to tell Giles than it would have been to tell Maman. The moment had come and, keeping her eyes on her friend, she said: "He wants me to marry him."

She sat there on the sofa in her blue fritillary jumper and her dark beads, her hands lightly clasped around one of the old leather cushions, a little as she might have sat, in her early convent days, giving an account of herself in the parloir—where the lives of the saints, heavily gilded, lay symmetrically on the centre table—to the relative who had come to pay her a weekly visit. Decorum was in her voice and attitude; and though she knew a sense of trembling beneath her calm words she was sustained by her assurance of suitability. It was suitable that she should tell Giles of her offer of marriage.

And he did not seem at all surprised. He turned to get his pipe and filled and lighted it, first pressing down the tobacco with his finger in the way she liked to watch, and all this was done very deliberately before he spoke. Then he said—could anything be easier than to tell things to Giles—"And what do you want, Alix?"

He was very much older than she was, and very much older than Jerry. She almost wished that Jerry were there with her to take counsel of Giles. "You like him, too, Giles, do you not?" she said.

"Well, that hasn't much to do with it, has it?" Giles returned, looking down at her with his smile. "What's to the point is that you do."

"I should not care to like, very much, anyone you did not like," said Alix. "Jerry has faults. But we all have faults. I wish you knew him better. Then you could judge."

Giles was looking at her with a sort of astonishment, at once tender and amused. "But I'm not your father, Alix," he said.

"You are the only father I have ever known," Alix replied, and, looking down as she said this, she felt her eyes heavy with sudden tears.

"Well, then, dear little Alix,"—Giles must have seen the tears for he spoke very gently,—"since I'm to take a father's place, may I ask you what you said to this young man,—this young man, whatever his faults, whom I thought eligible in every way. Highly eligible and altogether suitable."

"I said I could not marry in England," said Alix, and it was with difficulty now that she restrained her tears, remembering her proud words to Giles about an English marriage on the cliff-path last summer; remembering Jerry, so bright and beautiful, and France, brighter and more beautiful and with claims far deeper than any Jerry could put forward. What meaning could life have for any Frenchwoman out of France? Did not all one's meaning come from her?

"And what did Jerry say to that?" Giles was inquiring.

"He said I was too young. He said he would wait. He said he could perhaps live in France for part of the time. He did not speak very reasonably."

"It seems to me that he spoke very reasonably, indeed. He can wait. And you are very young. How old is it you are now, Alix?"

"I shall be eighteen in July. Not young enough to change as much as he expects," said Alix. "No, he was not reasonable, for he contradicted himself a great deal. I am afraid he did not mean what he said. I don't think that he means to wait. I don't think that he really would live in France. Afterwards, when we had talked a little more and he had felt that I was not so young—he spoke very wildly."

"How wildly?"

A faint flush rose in Alix's cheeks. "He did not please me in the way he behaved. It could not have happened like that with us.—Our way, I think, is a better way."

"How did he behave?" Giles, after a moment, inquired.

Alix's flush was deepening. "He tried to embrace me. He tried to kiss me.—As if to be embraced and kissed would decide everything."

In Giles's gaze, bent upon her, she was aware of a growing wonder. "It does decide everything, sometimes, you know," he offered her, as if, for the moment, it was all that he could find to say.

"But not for people of character, Giles," Alix returned. She did not know from what deep tradition she spoke; but it was behind her, around her, in her very blood. She spoke for the order that was not there to protect her; for the sanctions that she lacked. Great events like marriage were approached with a certain austerity. So much more than oneself was involved. "It could only decide things for les gens sans mœurs," she said. "It displeased me very much that he should seem to think of me as one."

"But he didn't think of you as one. We're all like that, in England," said Giles, gazing at her with his wonder. "We're all sans mœurs when it comes to things like this. We think them so much more important than mœurs.— At least"—he stopped; he reddened:—"A man in love wants to find out, you see," he finished.

"To find out what?"

"Why, if you care for him. If you're in love with him."

"Can it not be found out without kissing?"

"Well—if you don't care enough for a man to kiss him—Oh, you're right, perfectly right, Alix, dear; for yourself you're perfectly right. I'm lost in admiration of your rightness. But didn't his love touch you at all?"

Alix at this contemplated her friend in silence for some moments. It was not the effort to be frank with Giles that held her thoughts; she found no difficulty in being frank with Giles; it was the effort to read herself. And, finding the truth slowly, she said: "Yes; it did touch me. That was my difficulty. That has been my difficulty ever since, Giles; for I cannot feel it right. He troubled me," said Alix, and she added to herself, in French, "Il m'a beaucoup troublée."

Giles then turned away from her, putting his hands in his pockets and going to stare out of the window, as he had done on that long ago winter day of their first great encounter when she had felt, without knowing why it was, that he was thinking of her and not of Maman. She could not see what it was this time, either, that so moved him. Perhaps to find himself so trusted. Yet he must have taken that for granted. If she were not to trust Giles, who on earth was there to trust?

She sat, her hands clasped on her cushion, and looked into the gas-fire which creaked and crackled softly. The little saucepan of water standing on it sent up a thin haze of vapour and from the open window came the loud singing of a chaffinch. Alix, as she listened to the chaffinch, felt herself mastering with difficulty that sense of tears. She was not happy. Not at all happy. There was something delicious in the thought of Jerry and his love; but something that twisted, dislocated all her life. How strange was life. How near it brought you to people; how far apart it could carry you, with the mere speaking of a word. If she spoke the word that Jerry had implored of her, would it not carry her far away from Giles. Oh, there was a darker surmise. Would it not carry her far away from Maman? Could Maman remain near if she were to marry Jerry? Jerry promised, promised everything. He did not know himself at all. He was very young. He was weak; and she, too, was young and weak, though to Jerry she had shown only her strength. Yet she knew herself. She could see her own weakness. "Il m'a beaucoup troublée." So much had Jerry troubled her that she had known for a moment, his ardent eyes upon her, the fear that she might forget Maman, France, Giles, what they might all demand, expect of her, for the mere joy of feeling his arms go round her.

Giles turned to her at last. "Well, then, Alix, how did it end?" he asked her, leaning against the window-sill and looking over at her with folded arms. "What was decided in your way, since you wouldn't let anything be decided in his?"

"What was decided," said Alix, glad to take up her tale, "was that he should tell his mother and father at once. He did not want that at all. He said his parents had nothing to do with it. He said that until he had my answer he would tell nobody. He said that they would think him too young, and that he would not bear interference. It was all so wild and foolish, Giles. Our way is so much better. But when I told him that unless they knew his feeling for me I could not return to Cresswell, he had to consent."

"Well. And what then? What did they say?" Giles inquired as she paused.

"Mr. Hamble said nothing; I do not think he ever has much to say in the conseils de famille. It was Lady Mary who came to me," said Alix.

"What did she say then? Had she expected it?"

Alix lifted her eyes to her friend. "That is what I find so strange, Giles. She had not expected it at all. Is that not a little naïf, do you not think? On the one hand to give perfect freedom, and on the other to imagine that nothing unforeseen shall happen. If one gives freedom, one must expect the unforeseen, must one not?—She was very kind. She said she had thought of me and Jerry as playmates, and that I was right to say to him that we were far, far too young. She was, I saw, much disturbed; but she was pleased with me, too, and kissed me and said I had been a good, wise child—much too good, she said, for her foolish Jerry. I saw that I surprised her. In all I had to say to her I surprised her. I do not know why."

"What did you have to say to her?"

"All my difficulties, Giles. The difficulties about France; how I could not leave my country; and about Maman, how I must be near her always; that it is like that with us; that we do not leave our mothers when we marry. And I said that since I am a Catholic, the children, if I married, would have to be Catholics, too. It all surprised her very much. It pleased her, too, and reassured her; for though she is so fond of me she would much rather her son did not marry a French girl and a Catholic. And she is right in that."

"I don't know that she's right," Giles muttered. "You must have surprised her very much, indeed, Alix. It's been left, then, as you intended to have it left?"

"Yes. For the present. I told Lady Mary that nothing could be done till she and Maman had met and I wrote to Maman and told her of the offer of marriage. I put only the difficulties before Maman. I am afraid Maman will see the advantages rather than the difficulties."

"The difficulties being that you cannot give up France and cannot give up your religion?"

"Yes. And Lady Mary may have others quite of her own. Maman will have to face them all. But I think she and Lady Mary will understand one another."

"And for yourself, which do you feel the greater difficulty, Alix;—your country or your religion? You never strike me as having any religion at all, you know. You always seem to me, as I told you long ago, just a little pagan."

"Ah, if it were for myself," said Alix, "I could give up my religion more easily than my country. Only my Church would not allow me to marry a heretic unless I promised about the children. It is simply not allowed with us, Giles.—Do you not know?"

"But why not turn heretic yourself, and settle the children like that?" Giles exclaimed, controlling, she saw, a strong inclination to laughter.

But Alix knew that though she was not dévote there were some things deeper even than France, or were they not the deepest things in France? They were there, to be taken or left, as one chose; but even if she left them they were still there, part of her heritage; like a great landscape on which one might not care to open one's windows. And it was a heritage of which one could not deprive others, whatever use one made of it oneself.

"That I could never do," she said, shaking her head. "I could not go against my Church. However much I cared, Giles, I could never be a Protestant."

CHAPTER VII

It was only a few days after this interview that the news of Mr. Westmacott's death reached them. Toppie spent ten days in Bath with friends before returning to the Rectory, and it was Mrs. Bradley who went to her first. She said, when she came back, that Toppie wanted to see Giles and hoped that he could come to her next morning. She wanted very much to see him. Giles, when he had been given this message, went away and shut himself into his study.

"Well, do you expect she's going to have him at last!" Ruth exclaimed. "For my part I believe she is, and a good job, too. Giles may be able to wake her up a bit. I find Toppie distinctly depressing myself."

"Poor old Giles," said Rosemary, "it made him look most awfully queer. It'll be a shame if she doesn't have him now, after the way he's waited.—If she doesn't have him, where do you suppose she'll live? There's that jolly cottage on the common empty. It would just do for her; with an old aunt to live with her."

"If she doesn't have him," said Ruth sagaciously, "my own feeling is that she'll go away as far as possible. None of us, except perhaps Mummy, have ever meant anything to her. She's not got much heart, if you ask my opinion. Or, at all events, only heart enough for one person."

"How did you find her?" Alix asked Mrs. Bradley when they were left alone. "She will be too unhappy now, so soon after her father's death, to think of Giles. But for the future, is there hope did you feel?"

"I really don't know what to think, dear," said Mrs. Bradley, taking off her hat and putting up her hand, with a gesture so like Giles, to push back her hair. "Toppie is rather strange. That is what I feel most. She doesn't seem unhappy. Not more unhappy than she's always been, I mean. She talked about Owen all the time. She said she had never felt him so near. That doesn't look very hopeful for Giles, does it?"

"She might say that just because she was really turning a little towards Giles. One might hope that it would work like that in her, perhaps," said Alix, though she had not indeed much hope.

"Perhaps," said Mrs. Bradley sadly. "But haven't you felt for a long time that something has come between Toppie and Giles? Since last Autumn I've felt it. I believe, when she came back from Bournemouth, he asked her, and that it displeased her and made her draw away."

"Yes, I believe, too, that it was like that," said Alix. "I have felt her changed."

"You know there's something in what Ruth says," Mrs. Bradley went on after a moment. "I've always loved and admired Toppie and thought her a lovely creature; but I confess to you, Alix—because you understand her so well—that she has always seemed to me a little heartless. Or is that too strong a word? I don't know. Something is lacking. She would spend herself for people and do everything for them; there is no selfishness in her at all; but it's as if she'd do the more because she felt the less, and had to make up for it. It's strange, Alix, selfish, warm-hearted people may give much less pain than lovely people like Toppie. Owen was selfish compared to Toppie; but I don't think he ever gave pain."

"He was like a pool, was he not?" said Alix, struggling with thoughts Mrs. Bradley could not guess at; "a pool rippling and perhaps shallow, but open to the sun; and Toppie is like a well, cold and deep and narrow. And Giles is like the sea; deep and broad, too. How happy she might still be if she could love Giles."

"Yes. Yes." The tears rose to Mrs. Bradley's eyes. "And all that he thinks of is to live for her and all that she thinks of is that Owen is near her. Isn't it cruel?—I can't believe that about darling Owen, you know. I haven't her faith, and that distresses her in me, too. She doesn't want to be with people who haven't her faith. I feel that. She doesn't want anything that seems to come in any way between her and him."

"And if she did not believe him so near, so specially near, she could think of Giles as near," said Alix, while a sense of unformulated fear, often felt, never seen, seemed to press more closely upon her than ever before. "It is Captain Owen who stands between them."

"I am afraid he will stand between them always, Alix," said Mrs. Bradley.

Giles went off to the Rectory next morning. Ruth, Rosemary, and the boys had planned a picnic with the Eustaces, but Alix said that she would remain behind with Mrs. Bradley. By luncheon-time Giles had not returned and, exchanging glances over the table, each knew that the other found hope in the prolonged absence, for would Toppie keep Giles with her like this unless all was going well?

"You will see him when he comes back, Alix," said Mrs. Bradley when, after luncheon, she stepped into the car to drive off to the station. She had an address to give in London that afternoon and would not be back till late.

"Ah, perhaps he will not want to see me," said Alix. "I shall be very discreet. I shall be there for him if he wants me; but not otherwise."

"I think Giles would always want to see you, whatever had happened to him," said Mrs. Bradley.

Left alone, Alix went out to her favourite walk, the little path under the garden wall, half obliterated by heather and grass, its bordering gorse bushes all broken into soft clusters of gold set in prickles and smelling of apricots. Bareheaded, her arms wrapped in her blue-and-grey scarf, she walked, smelling the gorse, feeling the sunshine, listening to a blackbird that fluted golden arabesques on the April air; while above her head the leaning fruit-boughs were full of thick grey-green buds.

The sense of excitement that had been with her since the day of Jerry's declaration was immeasurably deepened this afternoon by her imaginative sharing of Giles's ordeal. Jerry and Giles were mingled in her thoughts, and her mind recoiled from the striving of pain and hope and fear brought to it by their united images. Perhaps it was because she thus evaded her deep preoccupation, perhaps it was because she paced thus in the sunlight, as he had paced, that her memory, suddenly liberated, took a long flight backward to find Grand-père going along the terrace at Montarel with his dragging step and sombre eye.

It was so strange to think of Grand-père now. Since the day of her first arrival in England he had hardly visited her thoughts. And with what a new sadness she saw him again and felt once more his melancholy flow into her. Was it because she had for so long forgotten him and gone so far from him and Montarel that she felt thus suddenly the gloomy pressure of his eyes? It was as if he watched her, her life involved in lives so remote from his sympathy. It was not only the young yearning of her heart towards Jerry's yearning that seemed a betrayal of Grand-père; this sharper yearning, not towards but over Giles, showed her as even more removed and alien. Young love Grand-père might have understood; but hardly this identification with an Englishman's hopes and fears. She doubted whether Grand-père had ever in his life spoken to an English person. He had disliked the English. She recalled how, when she read her history to him, he would interrupt her to speak bitterly about them. "Un peuple pratique; sans idéal," he had said. And he had said that England had always schemed against France and made use of her grace and generosity. How strange that was to remember now as she waited for Giles and listened to the blackbird. They had not schemed against her; France's daughter; nor made use of her. Would it not be truer to say that France, through her helpless person, had schemed against and made use of them?

Maman schemed. Maman, with all her grace, her generosity, was oh! so practical. "And our people eat the blackbirds," thought Alix while the song, as she listened to it, brought Giles's face vividly before her. Jerry was like a goldfinch—golden flashes, summery sweetness, swift eagerness, and gay inconsequent song. Giles was the blackbird; its tenderness, its trust, its something of heaven and something of drollery too; and the way it brought long-past things back;—again; again; again;—brooding on the past with persistent fidelity. Faithful Giles; he would never forget. And why did the thought of goldfinches merge into this surreptitious aching? How strange it was that one should feel the anxious pressure of a new thought before one saw the thought itself! Goldfinches; Les Chardonnerets; André de Valenbois; she traced the sequence. Jerry made her think of André; only he was not so finely tempered; not so intelligent. But the thought of André was only a pain and a perplexity; whereas Giles believed her to be in love with Jerry; she had seen in his eyes that he believed her to be in love; and perhaps she was; only it was round the problem of worth that this new ache was centring. There must be so much worth on the one hand if, on the other, it was France that might have to be sacrificed. And Jerry was like the goldfinches. "Worth," she thought, listening to the blackbird's song. The word was such an English word. She loved the blackbird's song, best of all, she said to herself, trying to turn away from the still half-unseen trouble.

Suddenly, behind her, she heard Giles's voice speaking her name.

He had come up from the birch-woods; he had not come from the Rectory. He had been walking; his hair was ruffled with the wind; his shoes were muddy; he had not eaten; he was very tired. Alix saw all this in flashes as they approached each other, her mind catching at such straws. For it was shipwreck that his face revealed to her; so pallid, so haggard, with dark pinches in the eyelids under the eyes and strange, ageing furrows of suffering running down from his nostrils to the corners of his mouth. Could the shipwreck of all his hopes make Giles look like this? There had been no hope to lose.

He had spoken her name in a quite gentle voice, as if, indeed, he were glad to find her there; as if she were a haven for what he could drag of hull and spars up out of reach of the battering waves. He walked beside her, and said: "Can we get to the study without being seen?"

"They are all out," said Alix.

It was curious to feel, as she said it, as, silently, they made their way into the house, that it was as if they had left him to her. Even his mother had left Giles to her, and as they entered the study and she heard, through the open window, the blackbird, far away, still singing, she had the feeling of being in a dream. The past fell back into a strange, flat tapestry, russet, silver, blue, where the figures of Grand-père, Maman, and Jerry all went together. She and Giles stood against that background in the study.

He had walked in before her, to the window, and he stood looking out as if he, too, were listening to the blackbird, and when he turned at last and looked at her it was as if he asked her what he should do with himself. She saw him as a little boy who needed a mother to take him to her breast. And, like the little boy, he wanted his mother to ask him what was the matter before he could speak. So Alix asked him.

"What is the matter, Giles?"

Her voice trembled as she spoke. That was why, perhaps, Giles collapsed. He sank into the chair before the table and laid his head upon his arms and burst out crying.

Alix felt her heart stand still. "Captain Owen—Captain Owen has parted them," she thought. And the unseen fear that had that morning pressed so near was there beside her now. It was a compulsion laid upon her; a necessity that was not now to be escaped, though still she did not see it clearly. She stood by Giles, gazing down at him, and her young face was stern rather than pitiful. It was hardly of Giles that she was thinking; or it was of his suffering rather than of him. It was because of Giles's suffering that the necessity was laid upon her.

Even when, as if he felt her near in his darkness, he put out an arm and drew her to him, for the comfort of her closeness, even while she thought, "I am his mother now," her face kept its sternness.

He spoke at last. "She's going to leave us, Alix."

"Going to leave us?" Alix wondered if Toppie were dying.

"She's going into a convent. She's going to be a nun. It was all settled at Bath. But she's been meaning it for a long time."

"Yes. I knew," Alix murmured. "She told me that on the first day."

"You knew?" In his astonishment Giles relinquished his clasp and fixed his broken gaze upon her.

"On that first day. When I went to see her. She told me that she could understand the wish to be a nun. She told me that you had them in your Church. If one were alone, she said, it might be the best life."

Giles now got up and moved, stumbling, towards the sofa, and, Alix following him, they sat down.

"It's because of him," said Giles. He leaned his arm on the end of the sofa and kept his face covered.

"Because of him," Alix echoed, sitting straightly beside him and bending all her strength to thought.

"To be more near him. She says she feels she can be more near like that," Giles spoke dully.

"But that is not a vocation," said Alix after a moment. She was seeing the face of the old great-aunt at Lyons behind the grille. Pale old eyes; pale cold lips; a dead creature; yet—already the little child who stood there before her for her blessing felt it—living by a mysterious life unimaginable to those out in the great turmoil of the world. "You go into a convent to renounce the world," she said. "Not to keep it more near."

"Ah," said Giles, and he uttered a hard laugh, "she doesn't count Owen as the world. She counts him as heaven. He wasn't worth it, you know, Alix," said Giles, with the hardness in his voice. "Owen wasn't worth a devotion like Toppie's."

And, while the word "worth," laden with its thick cluster of associations, seemed to set a heavy bell ringing in her breast, Alix answered: "No; he was not worth it."

They sat then for a long time silent. Once or twice Alix thought that Giles was going to speak to her. She saw it all now; clearly at last; and must he, too, not see? Must he not, in another moment, tell her of the sudden resolve to which, at last, he found himself knit? But when she turned her eyes—appalled, yet ready, upon him, he was not looking at her; not thinking at all of what she thought; gazing merely at the fireless grate, his mind fixed on the one figure that filled it. Toppie a nun; Toppie blotted out from any life where he could see or hear her. And suddenly he said: "She was so kind to me. She was so awfully sorry for me. She's never been so kind—It was almost—I could see what it might have been—Oh, Alix, I'm so miserable!" groaned Giles, and again he put his head down on his arms and broke into sobs.

Alix looked over at him. No; it was her task; not his. Impossible for him; inevitable for her. It was a debt to be paid. A debt of honour. More than that. It was the crying out in her heart of intolerable grief. She could not bear that Giles should suffer so.

He hardly noticed it when she laid her hand on his head and said: "I will come back in a little while." He was broken. The waves were going over him.

She left him there. She left the house. At the garden-gate, looking through the sunlight across the common, she stood still for a moment, feeling that she paused, for the last time, in childhood, and that with the next step she left it for ever behind her. It was she, now, who took up life; who made it. Destiny went with her; she was no longer its instrument, but its creator. And in this last moment how strange it was to hear the blackbird still singing:—It would always remember; that was what it seemed to be saying:—It would always remember. Even when she had forgotten her childhood, the blackbird's song would remember, for her, how a child's heart felt.

Once outside upon the common she began to run. She was carrying Giles's heart in her hand and it was heavy to carry. From the tapestry she felt Grand-père's stern eyes following her; and Maman's eyes. Intently, intently Maman's eyes watched her as she ran. She could not read their look. And far away, as if he had forgotten her, Jerry rode into the blue distance with ladies in hennins mounted on unicorns; figures faded to the pattern of the background. Or was it she who had forgotten Jerry?

When she reached the Rectory, she did not ring. She entered softly, standing for a moment to regain her breath and listen. Footsteps were moving in the drawing-room. The drawing-room door was ajar. She pushed it open and entered.

CHAPTER VIII

Toppie stood in the middle of the room with open packing-cases around her. The sun came in and shone upon the walls and the room looked pale and high and vacant. There were no flowers anywhere; all the little intimate things were gone. Toppie stood alone among her doves. And upstairs, in Toppie's room, the doves brooded upon a little box where Captain Owen's letters lay.

She was packing the books, carrying them from the shelves that filled the spaces between the windows and laying them in the boxes; and as Alix entered so softly, closing the door behind her, she stood still, holding a book in her hand and looking up with what, for a moment, was only surprise.

A horrible blow of pity assailed Alix as she saw her. All in black; so white; so wasted, she was like the cierge unlighted. "But it is for her sake, too," Alix thought, seeing Toppie sinking, sinking away from the world of sun and friendship into the silence and solitude of the grave. "Better to suffer; better to suffer dreadfully, and come back to us," she thought. And the visions that had always accompanied her thoughts still moved before her so that it was pain like fire she saw lifted in her own hands towards the cold cierge; to light it into life once more.

Toppie stood holding her book and looking across at her, and, all unbidden and unwelcome as she must feel her guest to be, the deep fondness of her heart betrayed itself by a faint smile.

"I have come to speak with you, Toppie," said Alix. She could not smile back. She could not go towards Toppie with outstretched arms. The sofa where she and Toppie always sat together was on the other side of the room. She felt that she could not stand and tell Toppie; her strength might forsake her; she might find herself, when the moment came, turning away and escaping. If she and Toppie were on the sofa it would be safer. "I have seen Giles," she said. "It is because of what Giles has told me that I have come—May I sit down? Will you come beside me?"

Toppie said not a word. She stood there, her smile vanished, holding the book, and watched her as she crossed the room to the sofa and sank down upon it. Then, after a moment, she laid down the book and followed her.

"This is very wrong of you, Alix." These were the words she found. Her mind, Alix saw, fixed itself upon the time of her own former intercession for Giles. Coldness gathered in her eyes. "Giles did not send you, I am sure. You have no right to come."

Still, she had taken her place and was sitting there in her black, waiting for what Alix had to say to her.

"I know it must seem strange," said Alix. "When you have had so much to bear. But I had to come. No, Giles did not send me. He would not have let me come if he had known. He does not think of himself. He thinks of you—only—always. Giles would never lift a finger to save himself—although his heart might be breaking."

"Alix—this is impossible." Toppie was scanning her face with stern yet startled eyes. "No one knows as well as I do what Giles would do for me.—You are not yourself.—You seem to me to be hysterical."

"No; you do not know what he would do," said Alix. She felt that her heart had begun to knock with heavy thuds against her side and a shudder passed through her as she sat there straightly, her hands pressed together in her lap, her gaze fixed on Toppie; but she saw her way to the end of what she had to say and she could say it. "You cannot know it. No one knows but he and I—and my mother. He has spared you; and he has spared someone else. But I must tell. Toppie, your lover was not true to you. He did not love you as you love him. He did not understand love as Giles understands it, or love you with a tenth of the love that Giles has given.— Oh, Toppie—I am sorry"—Toppie had started to her feet and was drawing away with a look of horror—"But you must know. You must not shut yourself away from life because of someone who is not with you at all.— It was my mother that Captain Owen loved. He was with us three times in Paris and he kept it from you."

"You are mad! You do not know what you are saying. Go away. Go away at once." Toppie stood there as if she had been a snake—ghastly with disgust and repudiation.

"I am not mad. It is true. Giles knows. I lied to Mrs. Bradley when she asked me why we had never seen Captain Owen again. When I saw that he had hidden it, I lied. I did not understand why he had kept it from you all and it was Giles who told me—that it was because he had betrayed you by loving Maman most. Three times he was with us in Paris that Spring before he died."

"Do you know what you are saying?" Toppie stared at her with dilated eyes. "Do you understand what you are saying? Owen with you? Before he died?—Why not? Why not?—He was your mother's friend."

"It was friendship in Cannes. In Paris it was different. Giles made me see why it was different. He would not have kept it from you if it had been friendship."

"Giles? Giles made you see?" Toppie put her hands to her head as if her skull cracked with the dreadful blows Alix dealt her, and, while a deathly sickness crept over her, Alix went on relentlessly: "He had seen them together in Paris. They did not see him, but he saw them walking in the Bois. That was why, when I lied to his mother, he knew it was a lie. Last Winter, Toppie; when I first came. And I was to help him in keeping it from you always."

Toppie stood still, up there in the thin bright sunlight, her hands pressed now before her face; and, with the growing sickness, Alix suddenly seemed to see another figure beside her. It was as if Maman, too, was standing there, in the bright sunlight, with that intent look; dumb, like a figure in a nightmare; yet in her stillness conveying a terrible reproach. "It was not Maman's fault," Alix muttered. "She cannot help it if she is loved. She did not know that he had kept it from you."

From behind Toppie's hands now came a strange voice. It was as if it spoke from the pressure of some iron vice screwed down upon it.

"Your mother is a wicked woman. You do not know what you are saying; but I know that it is true. Your mother took my lover from me. She is a wicked woman and you are a miserable child."

Alix felt herself trembling now in every limb; but it was even more before Maman that she trembled than before Toppie. "Is it wicked to be loved? Is it wicked to be preferred?"

"Yes. It is wicked," said Toppie in the crushed and straining voice. "There is no greater sin for a woman than such stolen love. Your mother is an abandoned woman. She has lovers. No one is safe from her. I knew that already!—Oh, God, I knew it!" Was Toppie speaking on to her, or, in her agony, to herself? Alix, standing outside the torture-chamber, heard the cries of the victim. But she, too, was bound upon a wheel.

"You are not wicked. You had a lover. Captain Owen was your lover." She forced her trembling lips to speak. "Giles knows her. He knows that she is not wicked. It is false what you say. You must not say such false things of my mother."

"You do not understand," Toppie moaned. She had fallen down upon a chair, her face still hidden in her hands. "It is terrible to be so ignorant as you are. You are too old to be so ignorant.—Yes, it is true—all true. She took him from me. Oh, I know now—I know what Giles was hiding from me!—Go away, Alix.—You drive me mad!—Go away, poor unhappy child!"

Alix had risen to her feet, but still she could not go. To fly, to escape; to hide herself for ever; this was the cry of all her nature; but there was something else. It was not only upon herself, upon Maman, that she had brought this disaster. What had she done to Giles?

"I will not stay.—Do not think that I will stay.—You say things of my mother that are not to be forgiven.—It is only for Giles.—You will not blame him? He has done nothing wrong. You will see him? He will explain all that I have not understood.—It is for Giles.—Oh, Toppie—all is not so lost when Giles, who loves you, is still there."

"Yes. It is lost. All, all lost," Toppie murmured. Her voice had sunken to ashes now. Her head hung forward upon her hands. Looking at her, for the last time, Alix seemed, dizzily, to see her as a figure in a long-past epoch, a black figure, with bent fair head, sitting in the pale room with the doves about it. It was as if Toppie would sit on there for ever. "Oh, Owen!" Alix heard her moan, as she went, unsteadily, to the door.

CHAPTER IX

"Oh, Maman!—What have I done to you!" It was her own voice now that Alix heard. She was out again upon the common and she had been running. But suddenly she was walking very slowly among the gorse bushes in the bright sunlight, and she could hardly drag herself along. Her head ached as if it would break in two; her limbs were of lead; and now that she went so slowly she could no longer escape Maman. She saw her there, moving beside her, with the intent look; silent; without a word of blame.

"What have I done to you!" Alix muttered.

Maman went beside her, in her white dress, with the heelless shoes such as she wore at Vaudettes, and bare-headed. It was not blame. Maman's look had passed beyond all thought of blame; it had passed even beyond pity. Alix saw suddenly that what it meant was that she was waiting to see what Alix would now say to her.

"I must think. I must think," Alix muttered to herself. But she did not need to think. It was as if in a kaleidoscope, turned in her hands, memories, till now unrelated, fell suddenly into a pattern. "La belle madame Vervier. Divorcée, vous savez."—Grand-père's eyes. Giles's silence, when they had met. That strange, deep blush that had dyed Giles's face when, in the study, they had spoken of Captain Owen's leaves in Paris; André de Valenbois. Maman's lie to André about Toppie. All the things she had read in poetry, in novels, of beautiful guilty women who had lovers. And, creeping through her young heart like a slow surreptitious flame—falling into place, curving with darts of ardent colour into the pattern—most recent, most intimate intuitions of what a woman's love might mean. "Maman!" she moaned. She fell at Maman's feet in supplication. Yet, while she implored her forgiveness, she was sheltering her, too. She was putting her arms around her to protect her from the world's cruel scrutiny. She was promising her—oh, with what a passion of fidelity—that their love, the love of mother and child, was unharmed, set apart, firmly fixed and sacred for ever.

When she reached Heathside she heard that the little boys had returned. They were shouting in the garden with the dogs, and Alix retraced her steps, skirting the kitchen-garden wall, going softly in by the little gate, creeping along the back passages past kitchen and scullery unobserved. Here was Giles's study. She turned the handle and went in.

Giles was there, sitting at his desk and writing. He had a sick, dogged look; but he had recovered his composure. He even, as he turned his head and looked at her, tried to summon a smile of welcome and she knew that he felt ashamed for having broken down before her.

Alix shut the door and stood against it. "Giles, I have done a dreadful thing," she said. Only when she leaned against the door did she know that she was almost fainting. She felt that all that she desired was sleep. To tell Giles and then to fall into oblivion. Far away, in France, she saw where she and Maman, in a sunny garden, walked hand in hand. They both seemed very old. They were very sad. Yet they smiled at each other. But this vision was far away. The black ordeal was before her. "I have done a dreadful thing," she repeated. "Perhaps you will not forgive me."

Giles had risen to his feet and stood, over against the window, tall and dark with his ruffled head. He was looking at her and his eyes were frightened.

"I have been to Toppie," said Alix. "I have told her everything."

He did not find a word to say.

"It was for your sake I did it, Giles," said Alix in a dry, unappealing voice. "I told her so that she might know it was you who loved her; not he. Perhaps you will not forgive me."

Giles spoke. "You told her about Owen?"

"About Owen. That he was Maman's lover."

Giles put his hand up and pushed it through his hair. "You told her that for my sake?"

"Yes, Giles. So that she should not leave you to be nearer him."

"Did you know what you were saying, Alix?" said Giles, after another moment; and after yet another moment Alix answered him.

"Not when I told her. But afterwards. After what she said. She said that Maman was a wicked woman. She said that Maman was a woman who had lovers. She said that for a woman there is no greater sin. And now, I think, I understand. Giles—Is it true?"

"My darling little Alix," said Giles in a strange, stern voice, "it is true. But she's not wicked. She's wrong; but not wicked. She's lovely, and unfortunate, and wrong, and she needs your love more than ever."

As Giles spoke these words, Alix suddenly stumbled forward. She put out her hands blindly—for as she heard him her tears rushed down from under shut lids—and Giles's arms received her. She was sobbing against his breast. "Oh, Giles, thank you! Oh, Giles, do you forgive me?"

"My darling child—my darling little Alix—I understand it all," said
Giles.

PART IV

CHAPTER I

Two faces were with Giles that night as he turned, sleepless, again and again, on his pillow; Alix's face, and Toppie's face. Toppie was before him as he had seen her on the Autumn evening in the birch-woods when she had looked away from him with the wildness in her eyes and had said: "It's as if there might be anything. As if you might hide anything. She's changed you so much." She was before him as she said: "It's as if she might have changed Owen—if he had ever come to know her as well as you do."

It was he himself, in his stumbling confusion, his half truths and his half loyalties, who had that evening set the deadly surmise before her. She had not, he believed, since seeing it, drawn a breath at ease. She would have been ready for what Alix had come to tell her. She would have known, at the first word, that it was true. He saw her freeze to stillness before the Medusa head.

Yet, if Toppie's face brought the groan of helpless pity to his lips while he tossed and turned, an even deeper piercing came in the thought of Alix. She stood there, against the study door, facing him; facing the deed she had done; facing a truth worse than Toppie's. Toppie saw herself betrayed by what she had most loved. But Alix saw herself as a betrayer. Her look was that of a creature at bay, with wolves at its throat.

Again, with a suffocating compassion, he saw her blind, outstretched hands; he heard her gasping breath: "Giles—Is it true?" His arms received her and he felt her sobs against his breast.

She became, while his comprehension yearned over her, part of himself. Something fiercely tender, something trembling and awe-struck dawned in his heart as he held her. To understand Toppie was to see her sink away from him. To understand Alix was to see her enter his very flesh and blood. It was for him that she had dared the almost inconceivable act; and, as he thus saw her offered up in sacrifice for him, Giles knew, with all that had been destroyed, something beautiful had been given. It was his justification for the act that he had, from the beginning, dared for her. It was the answer to an old perplexity. He had seen the dear little French girl as so securely secular, so serenely pagan; so hard. His perplexity had centred round the word Holiness and he had feared that she might be impervious to its meaning. But as quietness descended slowly upon his troubled heart Giles saw, while a sense of radiance grew about him, that it was Alix herself who showed him further meanings in the word.

He found on waking next morning that, with all the sense of calamity that lay like a physical weight on his heart, the sense of beauty, of something gained, still shone round him. He needed light, for his path was dark with perplexity. Alix had left him yesterday to go to her room, and to bed. In the few words that passed between him and his mother on her return from London the child's shattered state was sufficiently explained by Toppie's decision. Toppie's decision, he felt, explained his state, too. Mrs. Bradley heard of it with consternation. "A nun, Giles! A convent!" she had gasped. Generations of candid Protestantism spoke in the exclamation. Nuns and convents were, to Mrs. Bradley, strange, alien, almost sinister anachronisms. Dim pictures from Fox's "Book of Martyrs" and the "Pilgrim's Progress" floated across her mind as she heard Giles. And tears rose to her eyes as she saw an end, not only to all his hopes, but to every link that bound them to Toppie. There was no need to explain anything further to his mother.

He had to face at breakfast the dismay of Ruth and Rosemary.

"Poor Alix! She's bowled out completely.—Says she doesn't want any breakfast; but I'm going to take her up a tray," said Rosemary. "No, not kidneys, Jack; if you're ill in bed you don't want kidneys;—a boiled egg's the thing, and toast, and tea. She looks rotten; perfectly rotten. She's awfully fond of Toppie, you see."

"I suppose there's no good whatever in my going over and seeing what I can say to Toppie," Ruth ventured to her brother when breakfast was over. "If she'd only let herself be psycho-analysed by Miriam Stott it would be sure to help. Miriam is extraordinary, you know. She's a friend of the Burnetts; she does it professionally. Toppie is just a case for her."

"My dear Ruth," said Giles, "I'm sure you mean well; but you are sometimes an arrant ass."

"It's all very well," said Ruth to her sister when Giles had gone to shut himself in his study; "ass or no ass, I've thought for some time now that Toppie was quite liable to go off her chump. It's sexual repression coming out in religious mania; plain as day."

"Sexual repression!" Rosemary stared. "What an extraordinary thing to say, Ruth! Toppie's no more repressed than you or I."

"Yes, she is. Sensible people like you and me work it off, sublimate it, in games and work and all sorts of healthy activities, whereas poor foolish

Toppie has always moped and brooded at home, never knowing what she was or what she wanted. You're old enough to read Freud now, Rosemary, and the sooner you do the better. He will explain it all to you." Ruth's universe was of the latest tabloid variety.

Giles, meanwhile, in his study, sat and wondered what he should do next. Until he had seen Alix again he did not know. How could he go to Toppie? What was there to say to Toppie? He had answered all her questions on the Autumn afternoon in the birch-woods. He had answered all her questions about Owen, and he had answered all her questions about himself. She had seen him on that afternoon place himself on the side of madame Vervier. "She is the product of her mother," he had said of Alix. "Do you find fault with it?" He had showed himself as understanding madame Vervier; as exculpating her. Toppie might come to forgive Owen, caught in the horrible siren's net; she would never, he believed, forgive him. Unless she sent for him, how could he go to her?

In the midst of these reflections he heard a motor drive up to the door and, going to look out, saw with astonishment Lady Mary Hamble descending from it. Lady Mary could only have come to see Alix and, after she had disappeared, he stood wondering what Alix would find to say to her. He had, while he had brooded on their disaster, almost forgotten Alix's love-story and it seemed now to have lost all its potency. Jerry was too light, too boyish to face the resolutions that would now be needed. "She's too good for him," Giles muttered to himself, as he had muttered of the French order on the summer day at Les Vaudettes, standing with bent head and hands in his pockets as if listening for what next was to happen. Too good for him. Yet perhaps Jerry would not fail.

What was next to happen did not long delay, and the sight of his mother's face in the doorway warned him that it was something quite unforeseen.

"Oh, Giles, dear!—Will you come?" Rarely had he heard his mother's voice so shaken, and if her face had shown consternation last night it was almost horror that it showed this morning. "Lady Mary is here," she said. "She came to see me. Oh, Giles—it is about poor little Alix. Lady Mary has heard—terrible things about her mother."

So it had fallen. Better so, perhaps, thought Giles, as for a moment he stared at his mother in a receptive silence before following her to the drawing-room.

Lady Mary was there, floating, to Giles's sense, in an indefiniteness, made up of lovely hesitancy, veils, and a touch of tears, that was yet more definite than a steely armour. She came towards him at once with outstretched hands, saying: "Dear Giles, perhaps you can help us."

"For it can't be true, can it, Giles?" Mrs. Bradley urged in her shaken voice. She was so much more worn than Lady Mary, yet she looked so much younger and Giles read on her face a resentment, all unconscious, against Lady Mary and her standards. "You know her, Giles, and can explain. She's unconventional, isn't she, and unworldly, and might do unusual things and be misjudged by worldly people;—but Alix's mother can't be a bad woman."

So he found himself face to face once more with the bad woman.

"I had to come and see if you could tell me more. I'm so fond of darling little Alix." Lady Mary had beautifully placed herself in a corner of the sofa, her furs unfolded, her long veil cast back from the framing velvet of her little hat. She was not thinking about looking beautiful;—Giles did her justice;—but she was thinking, very intently, about doing what she had to do as beautifully as possible, and that intention seemed to dispose her hands across the sables of her muff, to cross her silken ankles and tilt to a most appealing angle the pearls that glimmered in her ears. "You see— Jerry— It's all foolishness"—she found her way. "He's only a boy.—He falls in love with someone different every six months.—He fancies himself in love with Alix now—and I don't wonder at it. She's the most enchanting young girl I've seen for years.—But Marigold Hamble, my husband's niece, heard in Paris, just the other day, such deplorable things. Deplorable." Lady Mary's voice sank to the longest, saddest emphasis. "Marigold is a wretched gossip, and worse.—She's a mauvaise langue; I would not trust her story. But she gave chapter and verse to such an extent that I had to come to you—since you know madame Vervier."

"But gossip is always like that," Mrs. Bradley persisted, a spot of colour on each cheek. "Some people see evil in everything. And Giles liked her. And everything Alix has told me of her is so lovely. And my son, Owen, who is dead, was devotedly attached to her. It is because he was so fond of her mother that Alix is with us now."

For a moment, after that, Lady Mary's soft, bright eyes, from between the veils and the pearls, remained fixed on Mrs. Bradley's candid countenance and Giles knew that his mother had revealed more of the miserable truth to Lady Mary than she herself, he hoped, would ever know.

"You're quite right, Mummy, darling. I do like her," so he felt impelled to sustain her, though he knew that such sustainment might only be for her immediate bewilderment. "I do like her," he repeated, turning his eyes on

Lady Mary and bidding her make what use she liked of the information. And then he found the words he had used to Alix yesterday: "She's not bad. She's unfortunate and wrong. But, it's true:—I found out while I was with her, that she is a woman who—" poor Giles paused, while Lady Mary and his mother gazed at him—"who," he finished, "has lovers."

After this, it was Mrs. Bradley who first spoke. "Has lovers, Giles?"

He could almost have smiled—but he was nearer weeping at his mother's voice. Steeped to the lips in the woes of the world as she was, lovers—for anyone one knew—for anyone in one's own walk of life—was an idea almost as alien, and even more strange and sinister, than nuns and convents. Poor little shop-girls and housemaids had lovers, though usually known less romantically as the fathers of illegitimate babies; she had spent much time and strength in dealing with such sad cases and in pleading on committees that the man was most at fault. But even with Ruth flourishing Freudian theories before her and the latest novels of the newest young writers lying on her tables, Mrs. Bradley thought of unhallowed relations between men and women as of dark, mysterious deviations from the obvious standards of civilization. And now she heard Giles say that Alix's mother had lovers.

"Has had them for years and years, dear Mrs. Bradley," Lady Mary sadly but firmly defined for her. "Ever since she left Alix's father with, let us trust, the first of them. With the monsieur Vervier, who, Marigold heard, has never divorced her, and still lives. The last is an André de Valenbois and Marigold met his people. It was from them she heard the story, and from what Giles says I see it is all too true. She is a very distinguished, very dignified demi-mondaine. Quite, quite notorious. She's as well known in Paris," said Lady Mary with a sigh, relinquishing madame Vervier's corpse, as it were, to float down the tide of her destiny, "as the Mona Lisa. The masses may not know about her, but everybody else does."

"Not quite so bad as that, is it?" said Giles. He knew, while he listened to Lady Mary, that it would be difficult to say why it was not so bad; but the loyalty to madame Vervier that had so direfully betrayed him to Toppie rose up in grief and anger against these suave definitions. "Madame Vervier isn't mercenary," he said. "To be a demi-mondaine you must be mercenary. And I'm sure," he added, while his mother's eyes, aghast, and Lady Mary's eyes, imperturbably kind, dwelt on him, and he knew that to the one he appeared ominously mature, and to the other attractively boyish;—"I'm sure that Alix is legitimate; if that's any comfort to us."

"And why are you sure?" Lady Mary asked, Mrs. Bradley remaining helplessly silent.

"She confided in me," said Giles, and it was more difficult to face Lady Mary's kindness than his mother's dismay. "She was absolutely straight with me. It was when we talked about Alix that she told me everything. It was then I came to like her so much."

"But, Giles"—poor Mrs. Bradley now almost wept—"how can you say you like these dreadful people? You made friends with monsieur de Valenbois, too—how can you like them?"

"But, dear Mrs. Bradley," said Lady Mary with just the brush of a smile across her lips, "one does like them. Why not?"

"Dissolute people? People with no sense of conduct or duty? I've never met them. Giles has never, I am sure, met them before. I don't understand," said Mrs. Bradley, and her drawing-room seemed to be saying that it did not understand either;—the Watts's "Love and Life" and "Love and Death," the bowls of primroses picked by Jack and Francis, the crétonne covers, and the crayon drawing of Mrs. Bradley's grandmother, a dove-eyed lady with lace tied over her head and a cameo brooch.

"I've met them," said Lady Mary with sad equanimity. "I've cared very much for several women who were, alas, in that sense, dissolute. Only they were more fortunate than madame Vervier; or more discreet. They've not been dissolute openly. So one hasn't had to lose them."

"And one's sons can marry their daughters," said Giles. His mind was occupied by no anger against Lady Mary; only by that grief on madame Vervier's account; and on Alix's. Lady Mary he felt that he liked; much as he liked—it was the strangest feeling—madame Vervier. Lady Mary, too, was straight; she, too, was magnanimous; and, her eyes on his, she was liking him, liking him even while, not yielding an inch, she answered: "Exactly. One's sons can marry their daughters. The difference couldn't be put more clearly." And she went on, reminding him more and more of madame Vervier, "Some things fit in and some things don't. Women who have kept their place, fit; women who have lost it, don't. It's very harsh; it's very hypocritical, you will say, Giles; but it is the only way in which a civilized society can protect itself. It's impossible to judge each case on its own merits; so rules are made and the people who transgress them pay the penalty. It isn't really that they are put out; they put themselves out. One pretends about them as long as they allow one to go on pretending. And when it comes to the sons and daughters;—young people don't realize how horrid, how crippling, simple awkwardness can be. How awkward, for instance, to have a mother-in-law you couldn't possibly, ever, invite to the house; how awkward to have babies to whom you've given a demi-mondaine for a grandmother. It becomes too difficult. One wants to spare one's children such difficulty."

"And what does one want to spare Alix?" Giles asked. With all his liking, with all her grace, her frankness, her resolve not to hurt, he was feeling for Lady Mary the same repudiation that he had felt for the ladies of the chalet—the people who connived and had no right to reject.

Lady Mary thought for a moment before saying: "Alix can marry someone who doesn't mind."

"But anyone good enough to marry Alix would have to mind," said Giles. "Wouldn't you be the first to say that where she belongs is with the people who do mind? What you really mean"—and Giles heard that his voice became rather bitter as he went on—"is that the daughter of the demi-mondaine must stay in the demi-monde. I wouldn't blame you if you weren't so fond of Alix for herself. I wouldn't blame you if it were a moral objection; but it isn't. Those friends of yours are only in because they've escaped being divorced. Your objection to Alix is really, when you come to look at it, that her mother is unfortunate.—Isn't that so?"

Yes, Lady Mary reminded him, vividly now, of madame Vervier. Her soft gaze was fixed upon him with something of the same surprise, yet with all of the same security, that madame Vervier's had shown. Madame Vervier, in Lady Mary's place, would feel precisely as she did. And he could see madame Vervier, after the little pause, bow her head as Lady Mary bowed hers in saying: "I accept it all. That is my objection. Her mother is too unfortunate. That is exactly what it comes to."

Mrs. Bradley, shut out from her son's understanding and from Lady Mary's tolerance, looked from one to the other of them, a deepening flush on her girlish cheeks. "But it's worse, far worse than unfortunate," she said. "How could she have lived a life like that with a little daughter to care for? It isn't as if she had had only to leave a bad husband, Giles. One could have understood that; one could have felt her right. But to have lovers—Don't say only unfortunate when it's so much worse."

"I did say she was wrong, you know, Mummy." Poor Giles rubbed his hand through his hair. "She knows how wrong I think her. I told her. But the point for us is to make up to Alix for her mother's wrongness, isn't it?"

"We must keep her here," said Mrs. Bradley. "We must keep her away from her mother's life. It is too terrible to think of our darling little Alix exposed to such depravity."

"Well, that's what I felt, you see," said Giles.

Lady Mary was observing him. "You have been making up to Alix from the first, haven't you, Giles?" she said, and though the kindness of her voice was unaltered there was in it a touch of dryness, too. "You've been engaged from the first in rescuing her from the demi-monde. It must have been a wonderful scene that between you and madame Vervier, when you told her how wrong you thought her and promised her to do your best to place Alix in another world than hers."

Giles, his hand still clutched in his hair, now stared at Lady Mary, arrested. "It was you who sought Alix out, you know," he reminded her after a moment. "It wasn't I who asked for anything for her. You took your chances with Alix, just as we did. It was all on your own responsibility."

"Dear Giles—I don't blame you in the least for not telling me," Lady Mary assured him.

But Giles would have none of such assurances. "I didn't imagine you could. I hadn't told my own mother. If anyone can blame me, it's she."

"And I'm sure she forgives you," said Lady Mary.

"But, of course, darling," Mrs. Bradley, confused, murmured. "How could you have done differently?"

"And did you think, then," Lady Mary, all mildness, continued, "that it would never come out?"

"I knew it would have to come out if Alix ever got married," said Giles. "In your case, I knew that you and madame Vervier were to meet. Alix had seen to that."

"Yes," Lady Mary meditated, her eyes on his. "Alix saw to it. Yes; you knew you could count on Alix. We can all count on Alix. Alix was perfect." She had moved away from the theme of reproach, but it still smarted in Giles and it was with a heavy gaze that he listened as she went on, sweetly showing him that she, too, appreciated to the full their little French girl. "She made everything clear. I never met such clearness. It was wonderful to hear her on that day. Jerry had really, I believe, touched her heart a little—poor little dear—but the last thing she was thinking about was her own heart. She was thinking of all sorts of strange claims and duties. The children, if she married, would have to be Catholics, she told me! And she could not marry anyone who asked her to give up France."

"I hope you recognize," said Giles, his heavy gaze on her, "that she would have been just as perfect if, not being French and not being a Catholic, she'd accepted Jerry."

It was then as if, in the heavy eyes of the young man sitting there, Lady Mary found herself arrested by an unfamiliar image of herself. She had come to do exquisitely what had to be done; and to do it so exquisitely that the element of forbearance in her attitude should be barely, if at all, perceptible. She was, perhaps, doing it exquisitely; but the mirror of dispassionate contemplation presented to her in Giles's gaze showed her, for perhaps the first time in her life, an unbecoming distortion of her features. She might have been seen as poised there, regretting that she had exposed herself to the revelation. Then, feeling, no doubt, that no evasion was possible, she submitted to seeing that while she could retain the grace of candour she must lose the grace of disinterestedness, and answered: "She wouldn't have been nearly so perfect for my purposes."

Giles, at that, turned his eyes away.

"You see, the truth is, my dear Giles," said Lady Mary, and it was perhaps not the least part of her discomfort to know that he was uncomfortable for her, "dear little Alix needs someone better and braver to deal with her situation than I can afford to be. Someone quite, quite detached and devoted must fall in love with her; someone without a worldly mother to shackle his impulses.—I'm sure he will turn up,"—Lady Mary's smile dwelt on him, but Giles did not meet it. "And as far as I am concerned, my best security is Alix herself. I'm perfectly aware of that."

"What is your difficulty, then?" Giles inquired, still averting his eyes from Lady Mary.

"Why, Jerry, of course," she said, glad to escape to the wider theme. "He won't leave it where Alix made it so possible to leave it. He is indignant with me and furious with Marigold. He says he won't give up Alix if her mother is a Messalina. I'm afraid he's coming here to see her."

"Aren't you rather proud of him?" Giles inquired.

"No, my dear Giles, I am not proud of him!" Lady Mary now gave herself the relief of impatience, and Jerry was to bear the weight of her discomposure. "He isn't like Alix. He doesn't see other people's point of view. He is thinking only of himself. It was just the same last year when he wanted to marry a little dancer."

"He's thinking of Alix as well as of himself. And you must own that he's improved in taste since last year," said Giles.

He looked at Lady Mary now, and her eyes searched his. "Does that mean that you're going to help Jerry?"

Giles reflected. "It means, I suppose, that I'm going to help Alix. If he's really good enough for Alix—of course I'll do my best for them."

He and Lady Mary gazed deeply at each other. She was clever. She was as clever as madame Vervier. She saw that she had not concealed herself from him and that he had recognized her intimations; first that, again the old dog Tray, he should marry Alix himself, and then, that if he did not marry her, he should at all events secure Jerry from the unpropitious match by removing her. Yet, still, he liked Lady Mary. "Why don't you stand by them?" he suddenly suggested.

At that, Lady Mary rose; mournful, but showing no reprobation. "I would stand by them, of course, if it had to be. But I must try to prevent its being. I must stand by my darling, that's what it comes to, as you must stand by yours. Jerry is my only child. I don't want madame Vervier in my family."

"You could count on her, too, you know," said Giles. "She'd do everything to make it easy, for Alix's sake. You see, already she gives her up to us."

"Ah—but only because of what she hopes you can do for her!" Lady Mary exclaimed, and it was now, again, with the note of impatience. "No; the only person I count upon is Alix herself. I don't see Alix entering a family that doesn't want her. She will draw back when she feels that we can't come forward. She'll send Jerry away—whatever her mother, or you, or Jerry himself, may say—when she sees that he speaks for himself alone. And Jerry, when he's given a little time, will come to feel that it's all too difficult. After all, they're only children. Little by little he will forget her."

"And will you?" asked Giles.

Lady Mary, with sweetest, softest emphasis, had pressed Mrs. Bradley's hand in farewell and now moved beside him to the door. She was gracefully occupied in swathing and enfolding; she dropped her veil; she drew her furs together; she avoided meeting again the mirror of his eyes; and she said: "At my age one has learned to give up things. I must give up my dear little Alix."

She made Giles think of a soft white hand, withdrawing itself, while avoiding all danger of a rent, from a glove that has proved a misfit.

CHAPTER II

When Giles got back to his study, he found Alix there, looking out of the window. The sound of Lady Mary's motor had hardly died away. He saw that there was nothing now that could be concealed from Alix.

"She had come to speak about my mother," said Alix.

It was strange to hear her say, "my mother," and pitiful. Her voice was strange; yet he knew, in seeing her, that he, too, whatever her sufferings might be, must count upon Alix. It was Alix who would shield them.

"Yes. Marigold Hamble has just come back from Paris," he said. The gas-fire was alight this morning, burning rather low. He went to it and turned it up so that there should be a brighter glow; and then, since there was nothing he could say to Alix, he waited for what she would find to say. She watched him while he bent to the fire. He felt her eyes on him. Then, with a slow step, she came forward and sank down in her corner of the sofa.

Alix was very pale; her eyes were set in dark circles. Glancing at her, Giles wondered with how much of strength she thus, after the shipwreck of the day before, possessed herself before him. He guessed from her attitude as she sat there, straightly, yet leaning a little against the cushion, that it had only been by the determined exercise of her will that she had forced herself to rise on hearing the motor arrive, and to descend to meet whatever fresh disaster her presence among them might have given birth to. She had parted from him the day before, broken, speechless, disfigured with weeping; but now she showed him only calm. Sorrow had not softened or disintegrated her. It had knitted her to a new hardness, and what she found to say as she sat there looking into the fire was:

"So Mrs. Bradley knows now, too. Everybody knows about my mother."

"She doesn't conceal anything, Alix, dear," said Giles, dreadfully troubled. "Everybody who meets her must come to know that her life is— unconventional."

"Does Mrs. Bradley know that I know?" Alix asked.

"Not yet," said Giles. "I told her just now that I'd rather not talk about it for a little while. She's a good deal knocked up. But, if you agree, all I need say to her, Alix, dear, is that I myself have explained to you the grounds of Lady Mary's objection. Toppie, I am sure, will say nothing. Mummy need never know more than what she's learned from Lady Mary. She doesn't know what Toppie knows."

Alix sat silent, looking into the fire.

"We needn't talk about any of that, you see, any more," Giles took up presently, having walked to the window and back again while he raged at his helplessness. "Never forget what I said to you yesterday. That's all you need understand. I'll make Mummy understand it, too. And as for you, she only loves you the more because of your—your difficulties. What we must talk about, you know, is Jerry. I'd really forgotten all about him."

"Yes, I had, too." Alix did not raise her eyes. "What is there to say of him?"

Giles, his hands in his pockets, gazed down at her. "He hasn't forgotten you."

"I hope he soon may learn to," said Alix.

"But, Alix, Jerry is sticking to you," Giles protested. "Jerry is all right. I'm very pleased about him. I thought it probable he wasn't good enough for you and now I find he is."

"I am quite sure he is good enough. That is not the question," said Alix. She sat there, leaning slightly against her cushion, her hands folded in her lap, and looked into the fire. "I need not think of Jerry now. I have only one person to think about, and that is my mother. I must go back to her at once. To-morrow, Giles."

"But surely you're not going to chuck Jerry!" cried Giles.

For a moment, at this, Alix raised her eyes to his, and it was as if in their dim surprise he read a reproach; the reproach of a serious race who saw facts as they were. There was no humility or confusion in Alix. She would not say to him that it was she who was not good enough for Jerry; but certain facts were there and her glance told him that he did not help her by pretending not to see them.

"Dear Jerry," was what she said and she then looked back at the fire. "I am sorry if he is to be made sad. But it will not be for long. He will get over it," said Alix, and her voice was almost the voice of madame Vervier and of Lady Mary. "He is so young. And he must come to see that with objections on both sides what he hoped for is impossible."

Giles now came and sank down on the other end of the sofa. He had not been pretending. He saw the facts quite as clearly as Alix could ask him to do; but what it really came to was that his race, he believed with all his heart, saw further and more important facts than the French did.

"You know," he said, while Alix continued to gaze at the fire, "I don't believe you are looking at it in the right way. You're looking at it as—as his mother does, as your mother would, from the point of view of convention. Why impossible since you care for him?"

"Because it would not be happy," said Alix, who felt, evidently, no uncertainty. "It would have been an unsuitable marriage before, when mine were the only objections; it is much less suitable now. Such a marriage would make his mother very unhappy. I do not believe it could make my mother happy either. We do not think of marriage, we French people, as you do. What you think wrong, we think right; convention, suitability is right for us. We are not romantic in your English way."

"And can you really believe that your way is the right way, Alix?" Giles inquired. "Can you imagine anything more unhappy than having to spend your life with someone you don't love? That's what the mariage de convenance must often mean;—and, since one hasn't found love in marriage, looking for it afterwards outside."

Alix's eyes, as Giles thus indicated the tragic unveiled figure that stood between them, remained fixed upon the fire and she did not flush. She only seemed to meditate, and, after a further pause, she said: "Even marriages for love sometimes end like that. People's hearts may change. The heart is not always a guide. That is perhaps the great difference; we do not believe that the heart is the guide; and you do. We believe that since the heart can make such mistakes—both inside and outside of marriage—we must depend on other things as well."

"On the suitable things, you mean," said Giles. "But isn't it better to make mistakes for ourselves, and to abide by the consequences, than to have other people make them for us? As for suitability, in all the essentials you and Jerry are perfectly matched. It's absurd to wreck his happiness and yours because his mother finds disadvantages in your mother's position. Do look at it straight, Alix."

"But I do look at it straight, Giles," said Alix. "And all that I can see is that it would be impossible for me to marry Jerry."

After this a little silence fell between them. It was strange to feel, sitting there in the familiar room, with Alix beside him, that the grief that had brought them so near had also set them apart. Alix had never been so near him as yesterday; she had never been so far as now. A cold apprehension entered Giles's heart as he felt it. If with her first step into maturity she was so removed, how much might not the future remove her? What claim, what charm could England have for Alix now? And as if she answered his thoughts she said: "Will you help me to go back to Maman to-morrow, Giles?"

"But, my dear Alix," cried Giles, rising and walking up and down the room, "why go now? How would you explain your sudden return to her? Surely you're not going to deal her such a blow as to let her know what has happened?"

"I have thought of it all, Giles," said Alix, "and Jerry will be my explanation. She knows of Jerry's offer of marriage, and what is more natural than that I should return to her if his family object to me? I shall tell Maman nothing; but I hope that she soon will feel that she has nothing more to hide from me. When Maman knows that his family object, she will be able, very soon, to guess why."

Giles had turned at the end of the room. "You need never say anything, you mean?"

"I need never say anything"—Alix looked back at him—"except that Marigold Hamble went to Paris and that when she came back and had seen Lady Mary they objected. Maman will guess."

"Well; and after that? What then? When she's guessed," Giles asked, "what is gained?"

"What is gained is that I shall have my right to be with her. I shall have my right to help her. While she had things to hide I could not help her; she would not let me. Now, if other things should fail her," said Alix, "she will know that I am there to be depended upon." And with the words it was as if he saw her go forward and take the tragic unveiled figure by the hand.

She must have felt some strain in his wide gaze, for, meeting it, she turned away her eyes, adding: "It was Maman's mistake ever to have sent me here. I felt that long ago."

"And mine to have kept you, then." Giles turned to look out of the window, struggling with the sense of tears. His little Alix! To what did she return? What was the destiny there before her in the jungle? "Do I count for nothing in all this?" he asked. "I wanted you to stay in the first place for your own sake. I want you to stay now for mine. Put Jerry aside. Think of me for a moment. I've nobody but you. You're the only person in the world who knows what I've been through, and isn't it true that I'm the only person who understands your life? That's a bond, isn't it? What shall we do without each other?" said Giles, and, helplessly, his voice was a younger voice at that moment than Alix's. He was the lonely little boy begging not to be abandoned.

Behind him Alix was silent for a moment; then she said, very gently: "But even if I had not Maman to think of, Giles, we should not be together; you will be in Oxford."

"And my idea is that you should come to Oxford next year and study at Somerville. Even while you were here we'd see each other constantly. It would be everything to know that you were near by."

"But it is impossible, dear Giles," said Alix. It was the same word she always found.

He turned to her from the window. "Do you mean because of Toppie? My mother? Toppie will be leaving us. My mother's first thought was that we must keep you always."

"She wishes to keep me in order to keep me from Maman."

"She doesn't know your mother. I'll make her understand. She wants to keep you because she's so fond of you."

"But that's not enough now, Giles," said Alix, looking across at him. "You must see yourself that that cannot now be enough. Anyone who loves me now must take in Maman too. It is Maman I must think of. And my place is beside her. You will see it, too, dear Giles, when you have had time to think. I must go to-morrow, and you must help me. Will you, Giles, for I have no money?"

He saw that he must yield. Such resolution could not be opposed. And after all wasn't it best to let her go? He would have struggled against her longer had it not come to him that nothing would move further the cause he had at heart, Jerry's cause, and Alix's, than her withdrawal. Better, much better, were Lady Mary to see that Alix was removed; better for Jerry that he should find something to endure and wait for and win with difficulty.

And, more than all the rest, he was sustained by that sense of secure radiance that had come to him from Alix herself. Wherever she was, whatever befell her, Alix would be safe. He could not have given way, he could not have consented to see her go, if he had not felt sure of it. So it ended as she had meant it to end.

"Of course I'll help you, dear," he said.

CHAPTER III

He saw Alix off next day. Her departure cast consternation through the Bradley household. An unfortunate love affair, the fact that Alix did not wish to marry Jerry Hamble, could not be made to bear the weight of such a sudden mystery.

"I always knew those Hambles would do her no good!" cried Rosemary.

"The truth is, if you ask me," said Ruth, "that she wants to go back to France. She's never really cared about being here at all."

But against this Jack and Francis protested hotly, asserting that Alix liked nothing better than playing games with them.

Poor Mrs. Bradley was dismayed. Giles could do nothing to make her understand. "But she's been happy here; I know she's been happy," she said. "I see that you can't explain to her why she should stay with us. But, oh, Giles, she ought to stay till she is much, much older. We can take her away. I can take her to Edinburgh, to stay with the Raeburns, if she wants to avoid Mr. Hamble—I'll do anything to keep her."

Giles could only reiterate: "Alix is very wise, Mummy. You must trust her to know best. I think she suspects already that things aren't happy with her mother; and she wants to be near her."

His mother asked him not another question about madame Vervier. She made no surmises about Owen's friendship. Giles at moments wondered, with all her ingenuousness, whether some dim suspicion had not entered her mind, as it had entered Toppie's, and he blessed her for her gift of silence.

He thought for a moment that Alix was going to cry when she bade his mother good-bye; tears were in Mrs. Bradley's eyes.

"Darling, whenever you want to come back to us—you will know;— we'll always be waiting, Alix, dear."

"Good-bye, old thing," said Rosemary staunchly.

"We'll come to see you in France," Ruth assured her, "at your Vaudettes place; though I do hate shingle to bathe on."

"All of you must come, whenever you will," Alix murmured, pale in her little blue buttoned cape. Alix knew what they did not know, that they would never be allowed to come.

Then he saw the last of her. She stood leaning on the railing of the steamer deck, Blaise in his basket beside her, and waved to him until the blue mist of the April day dissolved her form, and as he saw her disappear

Giles felt a dreadful loneliness. Tame, flat, colourless did life become to him. The sense of Alix's presence had been in his mind like the sense of Alpine flowers brought within one's own garden precincts, sweet, strange, yet intimate; like the sense of mountain ranges on one's horizon, aloof, mysterious, yet visible. "Beautiful, darling creature," he heard himself murmuring as he drove home through a country that had lost all savour. The loss of Toppie from his life was like a pervading, half-stupefied aching; but from the sharpness that the loss of Alix brought he saw how little in comparison Toppie's going meant real loss. He had never possessed Toppie. The ache might now be deeper, but it was still the same ache that the thought of Toppie had always meant.

He had not seen her. None of them had seen her again. And on the morning of Alix's departure they heard that she had returned to Bath. Another three days passed before a letter came for him. It was short, yet it brought him more comfort than he could have believed possible.

"Dear Giles," she wrote, "I think I begin to understand all that you have tried to do for me. It was wrong of you; but I think I understand. I have been wrong, too. Perhaps this came to show me that one can love wrongly. I do not think I love him less now; only differently. I know that he suffered before he died. When I read his last letters now, I can see the suffering in them. I send my love to everybody.

"Always your friend, dear Giles,

"Toppie."

And a postscript, written hurriedly, ran: "Keep poor, brave little Alix with you."

Under the dry phrases he read the mastered anguish. But it was mastered. That was the comfort that Toppie's letter brought him. She had risen already above her own sense of personal wreckage and could contemplate its meaning. As her piercing intuition on the day among the birch-woods had led her to the portals of the truth, so now it had led her to its heart. She saw at last, truly, what Giles had done; she no longer misunderstood him. Even, perhaps, she had begun, dimly, to understand what manner of woman madame Vervier might be. Toppie was noble enough for that. It would appease rather than lacerate her heart to believe that the woman to whom Owen had given his heart was not ignoble.

It was on the morning of Toppie's letter that Jerry was ushered into Giles's study.

Giles, as he rose to greet the bright apparition in his doorway, did not know whether it was with more gloom or satisfaction that he saw it. He was glad that Jerry was holding on, yet his presence there seemed to add to his own sense of bereavement. He could do nothing more for Alix. She had shown him that he could do nothing more. But though she had disowned Jerry, it now remained to be seen if Jerry could do something.

"Is she gone!" Jerry exclaimed. Giles's face might have told it to him and his charming eyes, so like his mother's, went swiftly round the room, partly as if they might still discover the missing Alix, and partly in the unconscious appraisal of a new milieu. Like his mother, Jerry would always see everything, wherever he might be.

"Yes. She's gone," said Giles, giving a push to the sofa. Strange, indeed, to have Alix's suitor sitting in Alix's own corner; Giles was aware of a sense of relief as Jerry did not yet take it. "It seemed the simplest thing for her to do."

For a moment, then, he seemed to detect, or suspect, a flavour of relief in the discomfiture on Jerry's face, but it was in immediate self-exculpation that he said, as if Giles might call him to account: "I couldn't get here before; really I couldn't. I've been away. I didn't know till yesterday that Mummy had stolen a march on me. Mummy couldn't hide from me—she didn't try to—I'll do her that justice—how splendidly you've been standing up for us.—If she's gone, do you mean she knows?"

"She knows, or has guessed enough," said Giles. "I don't really think she'd have seen you if you'd got here before. It's three days now since she went. What she says, you see"—and Giles again indicated Alix's corner to Jerry—"is that there are now insuperable objections on both sides, and that her place is with her mother. Do sit down."

But Jerry stood for a moment longer, gazing. "Yes, I see," he then said. "Yes. That's just what she would say. But how disgusting that she should have to say anything about it—poor little darling. Isn't it a miserable business," he added, as he dropped on to the sofa and glanced with a sort of gentle alarm at the gas-fire, rather as though he might, unless he held himself in, shy at it. He was making Giles, too, think of a nervous, charming horse.

"Yes. It's very miserable in some ways," said Giles. He did not sit. He stood, his hands in his pockets and leaned against the mantelpiece looking down at his visitor. Very much like a charming horse was Jerry. Giles could almost see him nibbling reconnoitringly at the edge of the stained-oak mantelpiece or choosing suddenly to take a flying leap out of the window.

Jerry offered his cigarette-case as though it might help them.

"It's that confounded Marigold nosing out this story about Alix's mother," he said, striking his match. "And it's true, you say?"

"Not exactly as she put it, I gather; but true enough. Since it is true enough, it's better, I suppose, that it came out as soon as possible," said Giles.

"Oh—I'd rather it had never come out at all," Jerry objected. "It makes no difference to me. I don't care a hang about ancestors and all that sort of thing, and I expect we've plenty of rotters among our own. It's Mummy who takes it so hard. If only Alix had consented to marry me at once, when I asked her, we'd have been all right. People always put up with the fait accompli, don't they, and Mummy's so awfully fond of Alix. Marigold might have come trotting with her little tale of woe, but she'd have been too late. Well, she's too late now, and I'll show her so—horrid little cat. I shall go over to Paris at once, and I don't suppose I shall meet with much opposition from madame Vervier."

"I think you'll meet with a great deal from Alix," said Giles, aware of restlessness and inquiry beneath the brave parade of Jerry's words. "I don't think you've a chance of marrying her against your mother's wishes. Your only chance is to bring your mother round. That will take time. You'll have to show your mother that you mean it."

Jerry eyed him for a moment. "Well, Alix is a French girl. She's rubbing it in enough that she's French—and she'll obey her mother. If her mother tells her that she's to marry me, I expect she will; and I'm pretty sure I could get round madame Vervier. By the way, what sort of a woman is she, really?" Jerry added, and boyishly, touchingly in Giles's eyes, he suddenly flushed.

Giles was thinking how like wax in madame Vervier's hands would Jerry be. "She's a charming woman," he said.

"Well, of course she's that," Jerry assented. "But I mean, is she a lady, all that sort of thing?—Not that I care."

Giles reflected. "The only person I ever met who reminds me of her is your mother."

"Mummy?" Jerry stared, indeed.

"They're not alike at all in what they've done; but they are very much alike in what they are. You could count upon madame Vervier as you could count upon your own mother. She'd always know what to do. If you and Alix married, she'd never trouble you."

"You mean she'd give up Alix if it was for her happiness?"

"Absolutely. What she wants most is Alix's happiness. Your difficulty wouldn't be at any time with madame Vervier, but with Alix herself."

"She wouldn't give her mother up, you mean?"

"From what you know of her, do you think she would?"

Jerry turned his eyes upon the fire and contemplated it. "She's awfully young," he suggested.

"Yes, but she won't change, in that respect, in getting older. It would be difficult. Alix's feeling for her mother would make it all very difficult. You'd have to face that, Jerry."

Jerry had never had to face anything that was difficult. Everything about him seemed to be saying that as he sat there, his thoughtful cigarette in his hand, his russet head poised meditatively. He saw Alix as a bright object that he naturally wanted, and now it was shown to him that, bright as she might be, darkness lay about her. It was evident to Giles that he turned away from the thought of darkness as he said presently: "Isn't she absolutely the loveliest creature you ever beheld?"

"Do you know," Giles confessed, surprised by the change of theme, but willing to follow to the best of his ability, "I've never thought much about Alix's appearance. I don't suppose one does when one has known someone from a child. I suppose she is lovely. I like everything her face means; and the more I know Alix the more it goes on meaning."

"She's a Nike," said Jerry, gazing at the fire. "She's on the prow of a Greek ship flying over the wine-dark sea. You've seen her dance—in that white and crystal dress with the silver round her head—it's like the rhythm of Shelley's Hymn of Pan. When I look at her dancing, I long to dance with her; when I dance with her, I long to be looking at her. Odd, isn't it, how one never can get enough at once. She's got the most extraordinarily cold eyes, you know," said Jerry, fully launched upon his theme. "Even when one's dancing with her and looks down into them;—she's so happy, she smiles up at you—and yet they are as cold, as blue, as deep as mountain lakes."

"Yet she's not cold," said Giles. He was seeing Alix as Jerry spoke about her eyes, not dancing, not smiling, but looking as she had looked the other morning when she had said: "Now, if other things should fail her, she will know at least I am there to be depended upon." With the words he had seen her go forward to take her mother by the hand. A tenderness, passionate, enfolding, had thrilled beneath the quiet words. How right had madame Vervier been in believing that she could count always upon Alix.—And Jerry only saw her dancing.

But he himself wanted Alix to dance. He wanted her to marry Jerry. He believed that it might still be possible if Jerry could be good enough. "If you hold on, you know," he said—and Jerry could not think it irrelevant—"I feel sure your mother will stand by you, and if she stands by you, everything will fall into place and you and Alix can go on dancing. So hold on. Deserve her. I'm standing by you already, as you know." He smiled down at Jerry, so young, so slight, but so charming and so sound. If Jerry could get strength enough to hold on, he would waft Alix far away. Philosophers could have little to do with dancing white and silver Nikes. "Deserve her, you see," he repeated.

"Not go over to-morrow, you mean?" Jerry questioned, looking up at his host, docile to any suggestion. "I'd so much rather have it settled straight off. And I have a feeling that if I could get at Alix over there, with her mother to help me, I should get it settled."

"I'm sure you wouldn't. And nothing would unsettle your own mother so much. You'll gain everything with Alix, and with your mother, if you show them that you can wait. Write to Alix, of course; write constantly. Tell her all about it; your feelings, you know, and what you think about her eyes.—You both care for the same things: riding; out of doors; fancy-dress balls, and the 'Hymn of Pan.' What you've got to uphold, you see, Jerry, what you've got to justify, is our English conception of being in love. You must overbear convention; you must break down parental scruples. You must show yourself so much in love to Alix that you'll convince her that romance is common-sense. You see, I want you to win her, not only for yourself, but for England."

Jerry's eyes were on him while he spoke and they dwelt for some moments of bright contemplation as if for the first time he was looking at Giles more carefully than he had looked at the gas-fire and the mantelpiece. "You know, if I may say so, I do think you're a very remarkable person," he observed.

"Am I? Why?" Giles asked, smiling rather sadly.

"Well"—Jerry continued to look at him, but he blushed again—"to care so much about a girl you're not in love with yourself. Doing everything for her. I've heard a lot about you, you may be sure. Alix thinks more of you than of anybody in the world."

Giles, too, was blushing now. "Does she?" he said. They were suddenly two boys together, and as they spoke of love and of Alix their words, to Giles, seemed to lift her far away out of childhood and to set her, a woman, between them.

"I'm most awfully fond of Alix," he said.

"I know. That's what's so remarkable," said Jerry, shyly smiling. "To be so fond, yet not to be in love."

"You see," Giles found himself offering, really as if in a sort of exculpation, "one may be in love with someone else; that would prevent, wouldn't it? And you can care immensely about someone without being in love with them."

"Could one? When she's Alix? I can't imagine it," Jerry a little nervously smiled. "Unless, as you suggest, there's someone else, and then I shouldn't have time to care so much for another girl."

Jerry's ingenuous analysis certainly had its potency; Giles did not quite know what to say to him. "Even if I had been, it wouldn't have done me any good," he suggested. "Alix would never have thought of me."

"Well, you mustn't ask me to say that she would!" Jerry laughed out at this.

He got up as he spoke and went to the mantelpiece, picking up and examining one of the horrid little china animals thereon. But he was not seeing it.

"England will get her in a much more satisfactory way, for Alix, than it would if I were in the running," said Giles.

"And you really think it may get her; you really think I can manage it," Jerry murmured, still examining the china cow. Jerry, more than ever, because he saw him as so remarkable, was depending upon him for sustainment. It would have been a comparatively easy matter for him to leap over the barriers and make off to the beloved. To wait, to hold on, was a different matter, and Giles knew a little turn of fear as he saw it. It was no good Jerry's thinking that anyone else could hold on for him.

"You can't manage it unless you can count on yourself," he now informed him. "There's nobody else for you to count on. Alix is against you, and your mother is against you. It won't be an easy thing to marry Alix. It's not only as a dancing Nike you have to think of her. It's as madame Vervier's daughter, too."

"And as a Catholic. And as French," Jerry murmured, setting down the cow to take up the cat. "You know she said—funny little darling—that the children would have to be Catholics. Not that I'd care a rap.—Only, it does somehow make everything more difficult."

"It certainly does. Alix has all her objections. Nothing could be more difficult," Giles rather heavily assured him.

"And as the English lover it's up to me to overcome them; show her that I can carry her off in spite of them—in spite of herself—what? How would you like it if your children had to be Catholics?" Jerry very gloomily inquired.

Giles did not have to reflect for long. "I should not like it at all. It's one of the things I'd put up with if I were in love with Alix and she in love with me."

"Do you know, I almost wish you were," Jerry now said, and he spoke from a sudden cloud of darkness.

Giles paused. "Does that mean that you've given her up?" he inquired.

"No, I've not given her up." Jerry looked down at the china cat. "I'm going to try to live up to the part of the English lover. It's only," said Jerry, "that I see the difficulties."

CHAPTER IV

Before Giles went back to Oxford a short letter came to Mrs. Bradley from Toppie saying that she was going to stay on in Bath for the present and that her determination to become a nun was unaltered. After that, for many weeks, he heard nothing more of her, and it was not until the end of June that he received a letter telling him that she was at Headington, staying with an old friend of her mother's before entering her novitiate, and asking him to come and see her. The old friend lived in a little house sunken among the high walls and deep leafage of a garden, and the drawing-room, where Giles waited for Toppie, its long windows opening on a little lawn, seemed part of the garden, it was so full of flowers and sunlight.

Giles stood at a window and looked out and listened to a garden-warbler singing ceaselessly, like a running brook, among the branches. His heart was full of presage, for he had not seen Toppie since the dreadful day that had severed them from the past. Yet the song of the garden-warbler, rippling incessantly over his fear, seemed to dissolve it into a happy melancholy.—"The past is over, not forgotten, but over, over,"—the song seemed to be saying. "This sweetness, this sunlight, this tranquillity is the present. Believe in it, live in it, as I do. She is not angry with you any longer. You have not failed."

And when Toppie entered, he saw that she was not angry and that he had not failed. More than that; there was much more than that for him in Toppie's face; but he could not at first determine what it was.

She was changed. So changed that it was almost as if he had forgotten her and was seeing her for the first time again. Perhaps it was that since last seeing her all his thoughts of her had been changed. Personal hopes, personal longings, were gone, and seen without the aching glamour that they had cast about her Toppie was at once less and more beautiful. For never before had he recognized the defects and deficiencies of her face. She was a pale, thin, freckled girl, slightly featured, with dry lips and colourless eyes. Yet in this newly perceived earthliness there was revealed to him the fulfillment, as it were, of that celestial quality he had from the first divined in her.

This was what Toppie was; this was the material that had been given her to work upon; and it was as if he saw her, through the power of prayer, lifting from cold and arid soil flowers and fruit to heaven.

She looked at him sweetly and calmly giving him her hand, and saying: "Dear Giles."

"I'm so glad.—I've so hoped you would see me," Giles murmured.

"Of course I was to see you. It only wanted a little time—to settle things," said Toppie. "Let us go into the garden. Isn't it the dearest garden?—I used to come here sometimes when I was a child."

"Is it all settled?" Giles asked, as they went out and walked along a grass path to the shade of a lilac-tree. "I mean about the convent; about your leaving us?"

"It's all settled.—But we don't think of it like that, you know," said Toppie. "We think it's to be much nearer you, really.—And then, of course, I shall be able to see you all sometimes."

They sat down under the lilac-tree. It was in thick bloom and the fragrance fell about them.

Giles saw now what his greatest fear had been. And he knew that it was groundless. Toppie would never ask him a question. The past was over; not forgotten; but over. That was what her departure, her silence, had won for them. She could not, at that past time, have kept herself from pressing against the swords of every fullest realization. She could not have kept herself from seeing, as balefully as he had seen them, the figures of Owen and madame Vervier. She would never ask those questions now.

And presently it was of Owen himself that she was speaking.

"I wanted to tell you what peace it has given me, Giles, to feel that he did love me," she said. The soft sweet flowers of the lilac were behind her head, the shadowy green of its leaves. He seemed to see, as her eyes dwelt on him, what Toppie would look like as a very old nun. Not so different from now. Nuns had changeless faces.

"He loved me," she said. "But not as I loved him. When one accepts the truth, Giles, it gives peace. And now I see that we are not meant to ask for the same love back. It is enough to love; and I shall always love him."

"He always loved you, Toppie," Giles murmured. "He was swept away." After he had said these words he remembered that they were the words of madame Vervier.

"Yes," Toppie accepted quietly. "Swept away. And he was alone; in a strange country; in a time of dreadful strain. And she was so kind and so lovely.—And she does not believe the things we believe—I have seen it all, Giles. I have forgotten nothing of all that you tried to tell, to explain to me on that day. Wrong, you said, not wicked. And Alix is her child.—I have seen it all—and how he suffered. He has suffered, Giles," said

Toppie, looking deeply at him. "But now, with him, too, there is peace. I believe it. With all that has come between, we are not separated, he and I."

Looking into Toppie's eyes, Giles could not but believe it, too.

They were silent for a little while. Then Toppie said: "And you, dear Giles?"

"I? Oh, I'm getting on quite nicely, Toppie, dear," Giles smiled back at her. "I shall take my First, I think."

"Yes. But I didn't mean you only, you alone. I mean you and Alix. What are you going to do with our dear little Alix?"

"Ah, there's a long story there," said Giles. "Have you heard anything about Jerry Hamble?"

"Only what your mother wrote about some trouble that Alix felt it better to be away from.—I knew it could not be only that. I knew what other trouble there was.—Oh, Giles—I was so cruel to Alix.—I could not think of what I said.—But tell me about Jerry."

Giles found, when he began to tell her about Jerry and Alix, that it was not easy. There were still things that he must hide from Toppie. It was, he knew, everything to her to believe that Owen had given his heart to a woman not ignoble. But with all the celestial charity that had come to her vision of life, how could she believe madame Vervier anything but ignoble if she knew of Owen's successor? "Lady Mary heard things about her, you see," he said. "She heard the things we know, Toppie. Madame Vervier has made them easy to hear, and Lady Mary felt that since it was so Alix wasn't a possible person for her son to marry."

"But I thought she loved Alix," Toppie said. She was not thinking of madame Vervier and the things Lady Mary had heard. She was thinking of Alix.

Giles knew again the flavour of his old bitterness. "She doesn't love her enough. Perhaps one shouldn't expect it."

"But one does expect it. And does he love her enough?" asked Toppie.

Giles stopped to meditate. He had often to meditate over Jerry. "I see a lot of him, you know," he said presently. "He's always coming to me. I think he regards me as their tutelary deity. He shows me all her letters—I think he'd be quite willing to show me his.—Yes, they write to each other. Alix writes one letter to his four, Jerry complains, and her letters are models of deportment. They might be read aloud to anybody. Yes;—he loves her quite enough, if she'd have him now, against his parents' wishes. It's waiting that's so hard for Jerry. He needs to do things on the crest of the wave, and Alix keeps him in the trough. He gets absolutely no encouragement from Alix. Thus far and no farther, is what all her letters really say."

"I can't help feeling that he isn't good enough for Alix, Giles," said Toppie. "He's too young and light and gay."

Again Giles stopped to think. "I don't say he's good enough. But who is good enough for Alix? She's stuff in her for two, and lightness and gaiety are in her blood as well as the things Jerry lacks. Jerry could make her very happy. That's what I'm quite sure of, Toppie. I want him for her, and I shouldn't want him unless I believed he could make her happy.—For who is good enough, really, for our little Alix?" Giles repeated.

Toppie had listened to him, her eyes looking out over the garden. Now, turning them on him with a smile, she said quite suddenly: "You are good enough. You must marry Alix, Giles."

How strange it was. Madame Vervier had said almost those words only a year ago and they had wakened not an echo in him. Now, as he heard them spoken in Toppie's confident voice a great confusion of fear, pain, loneliness started up in Giles's heart. It was as if he had been waiting for Toppie to say them; as if he had felt that deep-toned bell hanging in some sanctuary of his nature and known that Toppie would thus strike upon it, sending the reverberations far into the past as well as into the future. For a moment he could hardly think, he was so deafened by the clamour, and then the first words that came were helpless words: "She wouldn't have me, Toppie, dear."

"Why not?" smiled Toppie. She had taken his avowal quite for granted.

"If she loves anyone, it's Jerry."

"They won't marry," said Toppie. "There are too many difficulties; and he doesn't love her enough."

"Yes, he does, if he's helped. It's someone like Jerry she needs; someone young and gay, with things to offer her. I've nothing to offer Alix."

"You have your love. No one will ever love Alix as you do." Toppie's loving eyes scanned his face while her confident voice thus assured him.

"But that's no reason, for her.—She'll have other people's love. It's true, dear Toppie; of course. I see it's true; and I suppose I've known it for a long time. But Alix would never think of me like that. She thinks of me as her brother. She thinks of me as her father, almost; as someone kind and gruff and paternal. Alix is the fairy princess, and I'm just the good old beast who carries her around on my back."

"Fairy princesses marry the good old beast and then he turns into a fairy prince," said Toppie. "You're so much more of a fairy prince already, Giles, than you imagine."

"But she has her full-fledged fairy prince waiting ready to fly off with her. He may have his defects; but, all the same, he is the real thing. He can give her the crystal dress and the prancing steed and the dancing to flutes and cymbals.—Oh, you know perfectly well, Toppie, darling, all the things I can never give her and that she loves with all her heart. It's queer, you know; I've wanted so to make Alix over into something more English, and what I see is that she's made me into something more French. I'd have been indignant at the idea of fairy princes two years ago; and at marriages with an object of advantage in them;—but now I've been inoculated with a drop of the French realism. Alix accepts the world and sees it as it is in a way that you and I, Toppie, and people of our sort, never could. And she's made me worldly for her. I see the advantages for her, and I want her to have them. She's not a romantic English girl. She'd never believe in all for love and the world well lost."

Toppie was considering him. "You say she's made you more French. It's true that you understand things you never could have understood before.—You know how horribly afraid your understanding made me once.—But as I listen to you it seems to me that you are the most English thing there is. What Frenchman would ever do what you have done, or feel what you feel about Alix? Isn't it an English way of feeling to love like that, without a thought of self?—And Alix has shown us, shown you and me, Giles, how she can love."

"I know, Toppie, dear, I know," Giles murmured. "But with her it's just because she loves me selflessly that she'll never love me differently."

"I believe she may. I believe she will. And what you must do," said Toppie, "is go over and see."

"With Jerry in the way? I couldn't do that."

"Let him have his chance, then, first. Let him go to France and ask her. I'm not afraid of Jerry. I feel as if I understood Alix better than you do. May I tell you something, Giles? You must not think me foolish, but things seem to come to me so strangely now.—I've always wanted this for you. From the first time I saw Alix, it was what I wanted. And now, when I shut my eyes and think of you and her, it is always together that I see you . . . with my doves around you. That would be my wedding-present to you, you know," Toppie smiled at him and her smile had the colour of light and came from far distances; "all my doves, to watch over you and Alix and keep you safe together always."

CHAPTER V

Giles did not believe in what his dear Toppie had told him; did not believe that the fairy princess could ever be for him; but the thought of her words hovered round him as if her very doves sought the nest she promised. It was impossible. He could not recall a glance or word of Alix's that made it seem possible; yet it hovered. The thought of Alix accompanied his days. He had said that he had nothing to give her and it was true that he had no fairy-prince gifts; but sculling quietly on the Cherwell at evening, Giles, resting on his oars and watching his beloved Oxford glide past, would remember how many things they had shared together, simple, happy things, the gifts of life that were there for everybody to share. She had liked Oxford, too, when she had last come. He treasured every discerning phrase that his memory could recover. She had said that it was kinder than anything in France; and the simile of the humane old bishop, with his ring and robes and benignant face, came back to him, and how one day, when they read "The Scholar Gipsy" together, she had said: "It seems to me that learning is happier with you than with us, Giles, and goes with happier things.—Some day you will take me for all those walks your gipsy took."

Yes, he could see himself and Alix in Oxford together and walking in Oxfordshire and Berkshire fields and lanes. More than that. There was another figure that Toppie had not brought into her picture; but she would have thought of it. It was the figure that stood between Alix and all those other dreams he had woven round her and Jerry. Who but himself could care for Alix's mother and accept her into his life? Madame Vervier, he knew, would never have come to Oxford. He need not, disconcertingly, try to see her there. But there were the long holidays when he and Alix might have gone to her. Who but he could have kept Alix's mother near her? "But it's only dear Toppie's dream," thought Giles, watching the towers glide by. "And there's Jerry."

It was late one evening, at the end of Commemoration Week, that Jerry burst into his rooms. Ruth and Rosemary and his mother had just left him. Ruth and Rosemary were now old enough to join in any of the Oxford festivities that he could offer them, and his mind was in a daze from the mid-Summer excitement. It bubbled at the bottom of the glass like froth after a long satisfying draught, for he knew that he had done well in his exams and now only his viva lay before him;—so that the wreathed, dancing heads of young girls, and the sun-browned heads of youths on the river, glided past on a queer background of metaphysics. He has seen Jerry dancing, and he had seen him on the river. Lady Mary had waved to him from a barge in mild, unallusive affectionateness, and for a moment they had spoken together in the crowd leaving the Sheldonian.—"I think you could tell me that I might be proud of Jerry," was what she had said, and it was a very odd thing for Lady Mary to say. It showed Giles that if to him Jerry showed his weakness, to his mother he was showing his strength.

It was neither strength nor weakness that Jerry showed him now. All that Giles could read in his headlong face was immense perplexity, and he cried at once on entering: "I've had a most amazing letter from Alix."

Giles pulled himself up in his chair and Jerry sat down on the edge of the table beside him. It was a painful perplexity; humiliation; bitterness; cogitation were mingled in it, and as Giles saw it fear rose in his heart, though he asked, "Well?" with the voice of the friend and counsellor.

"I was going over in a fortnight," said Jerry. "I wrote and told her so. And I told Mummy, and Mummy has behaved splendidly. She's in a frenzy underneath, no doubt; but she shows nothing. I expect she relies on Alix to back her up. Well, by Jove, she may! Alix does more than back her up. Here's her answer. Am I really dished, do you think?" cried Jerry, "or is it just to put me off?"

Giles read. Alix wrote in English as if to make herself more clear.

"Dear Jerry: You must not come. I have told you that I could not marry you, but I blame myself because I spoke that time in the Spring with some uncertainty. It is not only the objections now. There is another reason that did not then exist. Please do not question me; and please forgive me for any pain that I may cause you, but it is someone else that I love. I did not know what love was when you asked me. You must marry some girl of your own race, dear Jerry, and be happy. I shall never leave France now.

"Your friend,

"Alix."

Giles read, and his heart stood still while brightly, balefully the fox-seraph visage of André de Valenbois rose before him. Alix's letter was dated from Vaudettes-sur-Mer.

Jerry was watching him. "Now isn't that rather thick," he said.

But Giles, gazing at the letter, found no reply.

"It must, of course, be some Frenchman," said Jerry. "Can you imagine who it is? Have you heard anything at all?"

Giles shook his head.

"Does her mother know any decent men?" Jerry inquired.

Giles folding the letter tried to think. Were they decent men? Judged by the world's standards, André de Valenbois was as decent as Jerry himself. The difference was that he would not be decent for Alix. "Yes," he said, then, slowly. "I suppose they are quite decent. Only Frenchmen are different, you know."

He felt Jerry scanning his face. "You mean that no decent Frenchman would think of marrying her?"

At this Giles felt as if he clutched Alix back from a danger. She might have betrayed herself to him; he could not bear to see her betrayed to Jerry. "She may marry someone quite decent, you see, but not of her own class. Some nice young artist, for instance, some savant. Her mother knows all sorts of interesting people."

"But she doesn't say anything about marrying," Jerry persisted. "It doesn't somehow sound like getting married, does it? She'd tell his name if it was that."

"Well, I don't know. Not at once; not to you, so soon. It may be only coming on between them. Nothing definite may yet have been said."

"I didn't know French girls were allowed to have things come on," said Jerry. "I thought it was arranged for them."

"But we may have changed Alix about all that," said Giles.

Jerry at this was silent. He sat on the table and swung his leg. The letter lay beside him where Giles had put it, and after a little while he picked it up and read it over again. "Do you think she's telling the truth?" he then questioned. "Isn't it still possible that it's all her pride? If Mummy could have written to say I was coming and that she gave me her blessing— mightn't it have been different?"

Giles for a moment contemplated the hope. Then he rejected it. "It sounds to me like the truth," was all that he could find. It sounded to him too horribly like the truth. Something dry and cold breathed through Alix's few words, and to his apprehension it was the dryness, the coldness of her despair. For if Alix knew that she loved her mother's lover, what must not her despair be? Only one gleam of ugliest hope he suddenly saw and clung to;—in that case would she not have snatched at any refuge; would she not in that case have married Jerry on any terms, if only in order to escape her jeopardy?

Giles felt himself swinging in the void. How could one tell what was at the bottom of Alix's letter? Was it not even possible that, with all the revelations that had overpowered her, she had not yet thought of her mother as involved further than with Owen? Might she not think of the truth, to which he had helplessly assented when she had asked him for it, as applying only to the past? Might she not still have her ignorances? Madame Vervier would have done all in her power to preserve them.

He was not thinking of himself or of Jerry. He was thinking only of Alix, and his absorption was so deep and so bitter that he was not aware how long Jerry, sitting there beside him, had been observing him, until, looking up, he met his eyes.

"It's pretty sickening, isn't it?" said Jerry.

Giles did not quite know to which aspect of the disaster he referred, but he assented. "Yes, it's pretty sickening."

Then he saw that Jerry referred to his disaster. "I'm not an utterly blind and complacent young donkey," said Jerry, swinging his foot, while his voice trembled a little. "You mind as much as I do; and you mind more, because you really love her more. Whatever you may have been in the Spring, you're in love with Alix now, and I must say that I call it a rotten shame."

"My dear boy!" Giles ejaculated, faintly smiling.

"You'd have stood by and helped us. You'd have helped us to the end; I see that," said Jerry. "And you'd have been satisfied in feeling her safe, in feeling that England had got her, even if you hadn't. And now you've lost even that."

"It looks like it, doesn't it?" said Giles. There was really no use in denying anything to Jerry; but at the same time this was the final bitterness. He had never been so sure of wanting Jerry for Alix.

"Perhaps there's still some hope," he said suddenly. "I'll have to go over, of course, as soon as I've had my viva, and see whether there's any hope."

"Do you mean for me or for you?" Jerry inquired.

"I mean for you," said Giles.

"You'd make her happier than I should," said Jerry, swinging his foot and looking a little as if he might cry. "You're much more the ideal English lover than I am. Carry her off from him; for yourself.—It's only what I deserve."

"If there's anyone in England that Alix could have fallen in love with, it's you. And it's the person she can be in love with who can make her happiest. That's our English belief, isn't it?" said Giles. "I am in love with Alix, Jerry. It's perfectly true. But it's you I want her to marry. And I've never felt so sure of it as now."

"I'm living up to your ideal, what? Well, I'd like to do that, you know. I like you to think me worthy of her even if I'm not. I leave it in your hands, then," said Jerry, getting off the table and turning his head away while he stared before him. "I'm such a silly rotter that I want her a great deal more, now that I know she may really be in love with someone else."

"Unless"—Giles had got up, too, and was gazing intently at his young friend—"unless Jerry, after all, you went yourself."

"No; I leave it to you." Jerry shook his head, moving to the door. "I leave it to you and Alix."

"I don't know; I don't know," Giles pondered. "It might be better. I kept you back before. That may have been my grievous mistake. I don't believe in wooings by proxy."

"Well, I didn't make much headway when I wooed in person," Jerry remarked. "No. Clear away the other fellow if you can. And then we'll see. After all"—Jerry had actually got outside now, but he put his head around the door to utter these last words—"you've never asked her yourself yet. She's never seen you as a lover."

CHAPTER VI

Giles, as he leaned out of the train, almost expected to see the white form of madame Vervier awaiting him on the platform as she had awaited him and Alix last year. His heart then had been like a load in his side, and how much heavier was the clogging weight upon it now; but, from the fact that his sensations were so much the same, all the pageant of last year's arrival was summoned back into his memory with its climax in Hélène Vervier's uplifted gaze. But she was not there. On the sunny platform it was Alix and André de Valenbois who stood side by side looking towards the train, and Giles knew that it was sheer terror that he felt as he saw them there together. Something in their stillness, their silence, made part of it. Tall and white they stood, side by side, and in their demeanour he read, with the sharp intuition of a first impression, the curious quality of a constraint that expressed at once familiarity and withdrawal. They stood so still because they did not care to stroll up and down together, and they were silent because there was nothing that they could say. Was it already as bad as that? Giles asked himself, feeling the hot blood of the surmise beating up into his neck and mounting to his face as he turned to pick up his bag and gather his coat over his arm.

If it was as bad as that, André, at all events, could assume his old air of unclouded radiancy. His eyes knew no shadow; his voice no hesitancy. Delicate, sweet, sharp, able to do what he liked, with himself and others, he was ready for any encounter, and Giles even imagined, as he stepped down before them, a touch of sullen anger running a darker vein along the heat in his blood, that André looked upon his English friend as offering little complexity or difficulty. With people so simple, so guileless, so ridiculous—for would not André see him as rather ridiculous?—nothing more was really needed than a light hand on the rein and the easiest of eyes on the landscape. They would go just where one wished and see as much or as little as one intended them to see. "Not so simple as you think, perhaps, my friend," Giles was saying to himself. But to know that he might see things that André would not suspect him of seeing did not exercise the sickness in his blood. At the same time, underneath everything, he was astonished, in a side glance as it were, to see that he was not hating him; was still feeling him charming.

"Here we all are, then, again. What a triumph over destiny!" was what André was saying—and it was on him that Giles kept his eyes. He felt that he must pull himself well together before looking at Alix.—"I never expect happy things to repeat themselves."

"No more they do," thought Giles. But he could play up. "Is it all the same as last year?"

"Exactly the same; but for the absence of Jules. Even your old friend madame Dumont survives and is eagerly awaiting your arrival."

"Still there, is she?" said Giles. "I'm not surprised. Unhappy things, at all events, repeat themselves."

"Oh," laughed André, "your standard is too high.—I, more easily contented, should count the old lady a very amusing piece of bric-à-brac. We must have a furnished world, you know.—There is room for all sorts of oddities."

"No room at all, for that sort, in my world," Giles returned.

They were walking, Alix between them, to the car outside and he could glance at her. Rather than the constraint he had guessed at it was now the cold dignity of complete self-mastery her profile showed him. He knew that she had smiled at him—and had it not been with her old sweetness?— when he had greeted her; but he felt, as they went thus together, he, she, and André, that chasms lay between him and Alix. Seas lay between them; race and tongue. Her voice came back to him as she had said, last year when he had found her again, "But I am French." Only it was so much more now just that old difference. Her calm could not hide from him how much more it was that lay between them. And what did it hide from André? How was it possible, if deep instinct or the new knowledge of her mother's life had not armed her against him, that she should not love him? Jerry was a boy beside him; beside the power of André's beautifully possessed, beautifully balanced experience, Jerry would always seem a boy. He remembered, snatching still at hope, that Alix had found such completeness agaçant; but then she might not really like him even now. It might be some helpless hereditary strain that had brought her, her young heart proudly pruned of its first happy buddings, under the spell of the love that monsieur de Maubert had defined on the distant Summer day; the love that burns itself out and that may have nothing to do with liking.

She had said no word as yet, but as they emerged into the sunny place she remarked that she had to buy a baba-au-rhum for tea and asked André to drive them across to the pâtissier's.

"Alix is sad," André observed when she had disappeared into the little shop, where cakes blandly masked in chocolate, cakes touched with rosettes of pistachio, cakes crusted over their glitter with crisp nuts, were placed enticingly on crystal stands in the window. "Her cat was run over yesterday by a motor. The very ugly cat;—you know him well, of course. It was an instantaneous death, but her mother says that she takes it much to heart. Elle a un gros chagrin," said André.

"Poor Blaise dead.—Oh, I'm sorry," said Giles. But he drew a dim comfort from the news. There might be other and more childish reasons for Alix's aloofness. He knew how remote and stern she could look when controlling tears.

Now that Alix was grown up, now that she was so obviously a beautiful young girl, he noted that André made no comments on her appearance, though it was hardly likely that he would remark it less. It was courageous of madame Vervier to have them there together; though, in spite of the fear he had seen so plainly in her, it might well be that the special fear had never occurred to her. Sitting there in the French sunlight, Giles felt again his old sense of astonishment that such computations should, so inevitably, on this soil, occur to him; that he should feel himself, with whatever moral bitterness, accepting situations that could hardly, in England, present themselves to his imagination. He felt himself immersed in madame Vervier's milieu; he felt himself implicated, for was one not implicated when one still felt all its members charming? But one could not pretend to understand the French unless one recognized in such situations the workings of a drama to them commonplace. That special terrible roman-à-trois of mother, lover, and daughter, might not arise among the bien pensants of the nation; but the bien pensants themselves would accept it as a commonplace. They all accepted love as a devastating natural force, overriding, where no barriers of creed were there to withstand it, the scruples and inhibitions of taste and principle. They all saw love, unless it were the duly stamped and docketed love of the Church, as Vénus toute entière à sa proie attachée.

And with this moral difference there went the difference in everything;—the sunlight and the shadows, the streets, the houses, and the people. Sunlight and shadows were blue-and-gold, strong and deep, and the forms they defined revealed, under their spell, a classic harmony. The people passing, intent on business, or sitting in front of the cafés, at ease in idleness, saw idleness and work as two quite different things, not to be confused; each yielding its own savour, its own satisfaction. The sense of savour, of satisfaction everywhere; of life as its own justification. The very smell, warm, golden, balmy, wafted towards him from the pâtissier's was such as no pastry-cook's shop in England could ever yield; a dank surmise of suet and strong tea would there hang about it and none of the cakes would give one the same confidence of tasting as good as they looked. Why was it, Giles wondered, as Alix came out with her flat-bottomed, cone-shaped, snowy little parcel, saying as she stepped in beside him: "It is in honour of your arrival, Giles, the baba. Maman remembered that you liked them last summer."—For no girl in England would look like Alix.

It was not only that she spoke and moved as they did not and that her clothes were differently adjusted. These signs were only the expression of a deeper divergence. Her face, still almost the face of a child, had, notwithstanding, an almost alarming maturity. It was at once more primitive and more civilized than English faces, but the primitiveness was nothing shapeless or unpredictable; it was preserved and used; it was, perhaps, only a deeper layer of civilization. Druidess or Roman virgin, who could tell which underlay the something resistant, enduring, in the structure of her head, sweet in glance as an Alpine flower, remote and inaccessible as the mountain?—and, glancing at her as she sat beside him, Giles could gauge something of the change in his own feeling towards her by the fact that he was afraid of Alix. Not only that; France had already done more to him; for it was as if he were afraid of himself, too. As they sped out into the radiant landscape and he felt the breeze blow strong and sweet from the sea, he was aware of currents of strange feeling in the tide which bore him; bitter, dark, delicious, and tumultuous.

"I am dreadfully sorry about Blaise," he said—"André was telling me."

"Yes," said Alix, looking down at her parcel, "it is sad."

"The comfort is that he had a very happy life," said Giles, feeling foolish, for indeed he was not thinking of poor Blaise.

"I never feel that a comfort," said Alix. "I think it most sad of all; that happiness should end."

To this Giles found no answer.

"And have you taken your degree, Giles?" Alix inquired, with the air of leaving an untimely subject. "Are you now a distinguished philosopher?"

"Well, I've taken my First all right," said Giles. "I've done pretty well. Next term will see me settled in Oxford. But it will need a great many years, I am afraid, to make me distinguished."

"And where will you live?" Alix inquired. "Still in the same rooms, high up, looking at those rather sad grey stones?"

"Oh, I shall be a Fellow of my College and have rather beautiful rooms; quite a vast sitting-room looking on a beautiful garden. I'll be rather a swell. You'll be surprised when you see."

"Oh, I am glad of that," said Alix, smiling and passing by his allusion to her return. "And there, in the beautiful rooms, you'll teach philosophy for the rest of your life?"

"Well, I expect I shall. And write it, you know; and play cricket, and sing in the Bach choir. Sometimes I'll go up to London and see pictures and a play; in the Summers I'll walk round the Cornish coast or climb Welsh mountains. It's just the life that suits me."

"Yes. It will suit you admirably," said Alix.

André, white against the blue, drove in front of them and, turning his head, smiling, he now observed: "Alix has been reading philosophy of late. She must tell you. She has been reading Bergson."

"I find him interesting, but I'm afraid that I do not understand him," said Alix, and Giles saw that she slightly flushed as André thus addressed them.

"He's far too difficult to begin on," said Giles. "He's not for the beginning at all; he's for the very end."

"But I thought that was just his point, that he started at the very beginning," said Alix—"with germs, or atoms, or small things like that."

"Ah, those are the things one should end with," Giles assured her, "because, you see, they are the furthest away from us. The beginning is an idea, and the end is an atom. You can't understand an atom, that is, until you understand an idea. If you'll come to Oxford and let me teach you, I'll land you safely in Bergson after three years."

"No; I shall read no more philosophy," said Alix. "I shall not go as far as ideas or atoms in either direction. I shall stay in between. All the nicest things are in between, I believe."

"Bravo! Bravo!" André smiled round at her, and Giles could not interpret his smile. Alix did not reply. She turned her head and looked out over the plains.

Vaudettes-sur-Mer in its palisades of trees was before them now, painted in delicate washes of colour against the sky. "It looks like the beginning of a fairy-tale, doesn't it," said Giles and brought Alix's eyes to Vaudettes.

"Yes, like the place children find on the front page," she said. "And a happy fairy-tale, isn't it?"

"But it can't have the real fairy-tale pang and flavour to you," said Giles. "It's a place I find, but can never keep. You wake up to it and I wake up out of it. It's my dream and your reality."

"But you can keep it, Giles, as much as the Cornish coast, or the Welsh mountains," smiled Alix, "as much as we keep it, really;—for it is our fairy-tale, too.—You have only to come back and find us in it," said Alix, and, while she looked before her steadily, he almost thought he saw a hint of tears in her eyes, as though what he said of her loved Vaudettes touched her too deeply. Did she see in it the fairy-tale place of childhood never to be regained?

It was, as it had been last year at Les Chardonnerets, a blue and golden day. The gulls were floating past on a level with the cliff-top and on the verandah were monsieur de Maubert and madame Vervier.

They had passed through the wind-bent thickets and seen the sunny flags with their oleanders and smelt again the fairy-tale smell Giles so passionately remembered. But—he knew it as he came out on to the stage, as it were, of the drama—the fairy-tale was spoiled for ever. Madame Vervier had been its centre; the wine-like sweetness of her smile, her Circe security, had been its atmosphere. And now the magic was broken. He could see nothing else as she came forward to greet them, so lovely, lovelier than ever to his eyes, so kind and simple, welcoming back with her wide, enveloping gaze the friend who knew so much.

"We have watched your crossing," said monsieur de Maubert, as the greetings passed, "in imagination. It has been a sea of glass. A sea for the Venus of Botticelli on her shell.—You rise before us in a guise even more welcome than that of the amiable goddess."

Monsieur de Maubert also was changed, though Giles had no time just then for more than a passing glance at the recognition. He spoke with a certain heaviness; as though he came forward to lend a hand.

"A kind young Englishman in tweeds is, I can assure him, far more pleasing to me than any Venus ever painted by Botticelli," smiled madame Vervier.

"Giles has become a great philosopher, Maman," said Alix. She untied her baba at the table and placed it carefully on a plate in its little pasteboard dish.

"He always was a great philosopher," smiled madame Vervier. "He is the wisest young man, as well as the kindest, that I have ever known."

"Ah, but it is now a professional wisdom as well," said Alix.

Albertine, with a saturnine smile of welcome for Giles, brought out the tea and madame Vervier took her place at the table.

Everything in her loveliness was altered and, as he looked at her, with surreptitious glances, aware, so strangely, that André was looking at him, Giles suddenly felt that it made him think of the alteration in Toppie's face. She, like Toppie, had drunk tears night after night; she had seen the truth and been shattered by it; and she, like Toppie, was built up again. A drift of lilac went behind her head in his imagination while the link so marvellously bound them together. For had she, too, not relinquished? It was as Alix had said it would be. She had guessed everything. Yet, though so wan, so careful, so oppressed, she was serene. Her strength, her security, even, was still there, but disenchanted, turned to other uses.

"I feel it so strange that English people should be philosophers," she said. Giles saw that she intended them all to talk.

"Do you think it too reasonable a pursuit for such an irrational people as we are?" he asked.

"Yes. Just that. You are a people who improvise as you go. To philosophize would have been, I should imagine, against the genius of your race."

"Oh, we're not all of us, all the time, lurching along on mere instinct. We do, some of us," said Giles, "stop, now and then, and reflect."

"But lurching becomes you," André at this put in. "You lurch, as a rule, in the right direction—for yourselves. Look at your Empire," he smiled, taking a slice of baba, "all made up of lurches and success."

"We planned to have India, you will remember," Alix, at this, suddenly remarked. "We planned and even plotted it. It was only as they worked as best they could against our plots that the English won it, not intending to have an Indian Empire at all.—I always like that. That always seems to me just. And history is so seldom just."

Giles felt that the eyes of her mother and compatriots were turned upon her, as she made this statement, with a certain astonishment. "And I think it is rather noble of those who do reflect," Alix went on, calmly, knowing evidently what she thought of the question in its national and its personal applications; "for the others, those who lurch and make the Empire, can pay so little attention to you. It is very disinterested."

"We practise philosophy for our own satisfaction, what?" Giles laughed, though aware of ambiguous cross-currents. "I'm glad you find us noble."

"She is quite right, mon ami," André said cordially. "You are a race of adventurers. And it is as adventurous to reflect among a people indifferent to thought as it is to set forth with a bundle on your back and conquer a continent by chance. You are a people, in other words, who do not need to see your goal."

"But you prefer your own rationality," said Giles.

"I prefer it; yes. I distrust instinct; perhaps because in our history, as mademoiselle Alix has pointed out, we have so often been foiled by it. I don't see it as innocent, you know. I see it as crafty. As craftier far than our open-eyed planning. And, apart from large questions of national destiny, it is, I think, more comfortable to live among a people all of whom reflect, if only a little, and all of whom know where they want to get to. Our horizon is more restricted, but because we see the frame we can fit our picture into it. Life with you, over there across the Channel, for all your charm and force, is essentially confused and haphazard. It goes through everything; from your younger sons, flung out to swim or sink as best they can, to your towns and your Shakespeare. You may, in one sense, beat us; but in another we have, I think, the advantage. You take in more, but you don't know what to make of it. To make all that can be made of the time and space at our disposal, that is our wisdom, mon cher Giles, and can there be a better one?"

"And what is the time and space at our disposal?" Giles felt Alix's eyes upon them. He did not quite know what he was defending or against whom he was defending it; but it felt to him as if he were upholding England, and all he wanted Alix to gain from England, against all he feared for her in France.

"What we can make use of, what we can see and understand," said André promptly. "It's because of our sobriety that we French are capable of living a life beautiful in itself; a self-justifying life. We know how to use life; we know how to shape it. The very workman, sitting at midday in his café, makes a ritual of his meal of sheep's trotters and sour red wine. The frotteur enjoys the polish he puts on the parquet, and the bonne enjoys her bed-making and dusting. We don't do things because of something else; we do them because we find them in themselves enjoyable."

"Yes. It's true." Giles was thinking of the French sunlight; of monsieur de Maubert's philosophy; of the pâtissier's. The difference went down to the very roots of things. "We are discontented and clumsy and romantic, compared to you; it's our very religion to be discontented, with ourselves and what we can see. We are rebels; that's what it comes to. Rebels are the people who refuse the seen for the unseen."

"And yet who pick up the seen, in their stride, as it were, and then don't know what to make of it.—It is that with which we reproach you. You spoil one world in trying to reach the other."

"Ah, these are themes too profound for my tea-table," madame Vervier interposed, while Giles, meeting André's eye, felt, suddenly, something challenging, sword-like, beneath its blue smile. "We will not pass from history to metaphysics, if you please. Are you tired, Giles? Will you rest? I have some letters to write for the post. After that we might have a little walk if you felt so inclined."

Giles said there was nothing he would like better. He would unpack and rest a little and then join her.

She was in the salon with mademoiselle Fontaine when he came down half an hour later, and on the verandah monsieur de Maubert sat alone, heavily, Giles still felt, in his sunny corner; not reading; looking out at the sea. Giles was aware of feeling sorry for him; but he did not want to talk to monsieur de Maubert. He went out quietly at the back of the house, and wandered through the garden, finding himself suddenly, as he came to the gate, bareheaded, his hands in his pockets, face to face with old madame Dumont and madame Collet. They sat in a small wicker pony-chaise drawn by a ruminant stout pony, and Giles inferred, since there was only room for two that mademoiselle Fontaine had walked beside the pony's head, taking her parents out thus for a peaceful airing. They waited at the gate for her.

"Ah. C'est monsieur Gilles," madame Collet simpered. "You remember monsieur Gilles, Maman."

Madame Dumont was not much altered. The vulture-like poise of her head was perhaps more sunken, and her raven eye less piercing; but a light came to it as she saw him; an old resentment and a present glee. "Charmée, monsieur, charmée de vous revoir," she assured him, and as her eye measured the morsel thus presented to its greed Giles seemed to see the vulture roused and rustling its feathers. "You are just arrived?"

Giles told her that he was.

"You find your friends again," said madame Dumont, and there was a quaking note of hurry in the majesty of her tones. "You will, however, find them changed.—Ah, changes are sad; disastrous. She has had much to bear. It tells; it tells upon her. You find madame Vervier aged? Altered? Sadly altered?"

"I see no alteration at all," said Giles grimly, his eye turning on madame Collet, who murmured a low word of protest to her mother. But madame Dumont was not to be curbed. She leaned from the chaise and laid her lean hand in its black silk mitt on Giles's arm. "Il l'a lachée," she said in a harsh whisper. "Il va se marier."

"Maman; Maman," madame Collet urgently whispered, casting a helpless glance at Giles. "You must not thus repeat gossip about our friend. Monsieur Gilles will not know what to think of you. Do not heed her, Monsieur.—She is so very old."

"What are these manners! To whom are you speaking! Old! I am old, indeed, if I must thus accept impertinences from my daughter!" Madame Dumont thundered, turning a terrible glance upon her child.

"Mais Maman, Maman, je ne veux pas vous offenser!" Giles heard poor little madame Collet plead as he hastily muttered an adieu and fled from them.

In the door he nearly collided with mademoiselle Blanche. If madame Vervier was altered, mademoiselle Blanche was more so. Suddenly, looking at her chalk-white mask, glittering there in the sunlight, Giles saw the catastrophe that had befallen them all with a cruel sharpness that the side-issues of a situation may sometimes display more cuttingly than its centre. In mademoiselle Blanche's face he read that any reversionary hopes she might have cherished were withered. It was not to her that André had turned. He would never turn to her. He had been sorry for monsieur de Maubert, sitting in his patch of sunlight; and he was sorry now for mademoiselle Blanche. She had a brilliant smile for him. Her scarlet mouth made him feel sick. He promised her, did he not, to have tea with them one day. Giles said he was afraid he had only a very little time to spend at Les Chardonnerets this year.

"You have come to take mademoiselle Alix from us again?" smiled mademoiselle Blanche, the cold flame of her eye traversing him, so that he saw again, in a direful flash of prescience, that in old age her eye would be like her grandmother's. "You once more carry off our lovely little Persephone?"

How mademoiselle Blanche desired that he would! The fear that circled round Giles fastened a tentacle in his heart as he saw how mademoiselle Blanche, all hopeless as she must be, feared Alix's presence.

"I'm afraid not; I'm afraid I shall have to leave her where she wants to be—with her mother," he said, feeling a slow red mount to his face as he saw all the things in mademoiselle Blanche that she did not want him to see. For one strange shuffling moment the pretences between them fell, and mademoiselle Blanche looked hard at him, looked as one human being may look at another, with deep inquiry and surmise. Then, murmuring a hasty farewell, she fled, a white marionette, down the path between the nasturtiums.

CHAPTER VII

On the verandah Alix sat beside monsieur de Maubert reading "Bérénice," aloud to him. André was stretched near them in a deck-chair, his eyes following the smoke of his cigarette, and madame Vervier emerged from the salon, a little sheaf of letters in her hand. She laid them down on a table and André said that he would presently post them. "Yes. You and I would rather go by the cliff, Giles," said madame Vervier.

She wore a white dress, not the tennis dress; this was fashioned differently, with floating panels and long loose sleeves. She was bareheaded, a sunshade in her hand.

"Alix reads to him every afternoon," she said as they went towards the cliff. She spoke of monsieur de Maubert, but her heart, Giles knew, must be shaken by the interview with mademoiselle Blanche.—Mademoiselle Blanche could only have come to measure her pangs, surreptitiously, against madame Vervier's. "His eyes trouble him of late, le pauvre cher. He enjoys hearing Alix. He is very fond of her."

They walked along the little path beaten in the grass at the edge of the cliff. The sea was the Botticelli sea and against the sky went a flock of young goldfinches.

"Our birds," said madame Vervier, pointing to them, and he still heard the breathlessness in her voice. What had she succeeded in concealing from mademoiselle Blanche, and what had mademoiselle Blanche succeeded in concealing from her? "See the pattern made by the triangles of gold on their wings," she said.

"We call such a flock, a charm of goldfinches," said Giles. "Isn't it a pretty name?"

"A charm. A charm of goldfinches. And what a happy name. They look that." Madame Vervier's eyes followed the flight of the bright birds. "I wish one did not have to think of snares and cages when one sees them. Our people are so cruel for birds. I wish such happy things might escape the snare."

"A great many do. We shouldn't be seeing that charm now unless a great many escaped," Giles tried to smile at her.

"But it is the way of life, is it not, to snare and spoil happiness," said madame Vervier.

They left the woods of Les Chardonnerets behind them. Before them was the great curve of the cliff and the empty sky.

"So, you see me punished," said madame Vervier.

Giles walked beside her and found no word to say.

"Even you, stern moralist as you are," madame Vervier pursued, "could hardly have foreseen such a punishment.—To know that I have ruined my child's best chance of happiness; all that I could have hoped for her.—To know that she is suffering because of me."

"No, I didn't think it would come like that," Giles murmured.

"Ah, but it has come in the other way, too," she said, looking round at him in the pale shadow of her sunshade;—"though I have forestalled that calamity, and a calamity forestalled is always endurable. André and I are parted." Madame Vervier continued to look at him steadily. "I have told him that this Summer is the end. He still believes—or tries to believe—that he loves me; but he consents. I knew that he would consent."

Giles walked beside her filled with a confusion of pain and pity. Never before had madame Vervier openly admitted her relation to André; admitted it to Owen's brother. "He doesn't look like partings," was all he found, most helplessly, to say.

"Partings, at his age, are the preludes to beginnings; and André has the gift of looks. He is, perhaps, not quite at ease; but he has wisdom—our French wisdom, Giles. His mother, already, is arranging a marriage for him. As soon as our rupture is definitely known, he will be able to settle himself in life;—se ranger," said madame Vervier. "And he will be glad to be settled; he will be glad to be married to a charming young girl whom he has known since boyhood;—a young girl," madame Vervier continued in her steady voice, "whom your madame Marigold met when she came to France last Spring."

"You know all about that, then?" Giles muttered.

"How should I not know?" madame Vervier returned.

He saw her maimed for life. Yes; it had, with André, gone as deep as that. She had unflinchingly performed the surgical operation, severed the limb and bound the arteries. He saw her bandaged, spotted with blood, drained of joy; but tranquil; moving forward.

"It was time," she said as if to herself, looking before her. "When Alix returned to me, when I saw what I had done to her, I knew that it was time."

He could not think of one thing to say to her; not one word of comfort or approbation. He would have liked to say that she would be happier; but he did not believe that she would be. He would have liked to say that she had behaved worthily; but the note of moral appraisal was repellent to his imagination. And under everything went that bitter memory of who André was, and whose successor.

"But there were further reasons for André's acquiescence," said madame Vervier suddenly.

They had gone for a long way in silence. A light breeze met them, now that they had rounded a headland, and the thin panels of madame Vervier's dress were blown backward as she went. Goddess-like as he had always felt her, there was something disembodied, unearthly in her aspect now. It was as if, gliding through sad Elysian fields, beautiful, changeless, with gazing eyes, she contemplated the sorrows of the past. Yet her voice, as she spoke again, was not the voice of an Elysian spirit. He recognized as he heard it that a bitter humanity still beat at the heart of her confidences and that her tranquillity was not the shining of an inner peace, but a shield proudly worn. What she had to tell him was the thing most difficult to tell; the thing that throbbed and echoed in her, as the scar of the severed limb burns and remembers; and all her voice was altered as she spoke of it.

"There were further reasons," she repeated, turning her face away from him to the sea. "He knows that it is best to go, since to remain would be to love Alix."

And through all his fear, Giles saw it now; he had clung to the hope that it was an ugly dream. He measured, in a sense of physical sickness, the difference between an ugly dream and reality as in madame Vervier's words his dread was made close and palpable.

"But isn't that impossible?" It was his English voice that asked the question. His French understanding knew that it was possible.

"Why so?" madame Vervier's French voice returned. All the acquiescence of her race spoke in it. "Alix is exquisite."

Alix's face swam before Giles. "But she is your daughter."

"That would offend his taste. That does offend it. That is one of the reasons, as I have said, for his consent to our parting. It is not a reason, if he stayed, that could repress his heart."

"Couldn't Alix be trusted to do that?" Giles asked after a moment. He must ask it. He must approach, in order to know whether madame Vervier saw it, too, the deepest fear of all. And with what a complex thankfulness he heard in her reply that Alix's secret was safe with him. It did not exist for madame Vervier's imagination even. A deep, strange bitterness spoke in her voice as she said: "Her dislike of him is an added attraction."

"Her dislike of him? Does she dislike him?"

"Surely you have seen it. As if by instinct. Always. From the first. It is an added attraction," madame Vervier repeated; and with a little laugh, more bitter than her voice, she said: "It is the first time in his life that André has found himself disliked by a woman."

How strange, how tortuous, how self-contradictory was the human heart, Giles thought, walking beside his unhappy friend. With all her passionate maternal love he felt, thrilling in her tone, a resentment against her child that she should be indifferent to the charm that had so subjugated herself. Giles felt it cruel to ask the further question that came to him, yet he wondered if she had not, often, asked it of herself. "He consents to go, then, because he is hopeless?"

She had, indeed, often asked it. He heard that in her voice as she answered: "Oh—do not let us deprive him of all merit!"

They had reached by now a further promontory of the cliff and looked over a long stretch of the coast, pale blue sea, pale cliffs, a delicate distant finger of the land running out, against the horizon, with a tiny lighthouse upon it. A bench was set amidst the grass before this view and madame Vervier sank down upon it as if exhausted. Giles sat on the grass at her feet and for a little while they surveyed the azure scene in silence.

"And now," said madame Vervier, and he heard that she gathered her thoughts from dark broodings, "let us speak no more of me, but of Alix.— Of Alix and Jerry. For you like this Jerry. It is because of him that you have come."

"Yes. It's because of him. I like him very much." Giles looked down at the grass. "I saw him before I left. All that he asks is to marry her at once."

"Ah, he loves her, I know. He is an honourable young Englishman and he loves her. That is what I have gone upon from the beginning. It is not Jerry who is the difficulty. It is Alix."

"We must give her time, you see," Giles murmured. "Her pride had such a blow."

"Give her time! I would give her anything!" madame Vervier exclaimed. "But I can do nothing with Alix."—Rien! rien! rien! she said in French with a crescendo of grief and impatience almost comic to his ear for all its pathos. "You have altered my Alix for me, you English, Giles. You have given her a different heart. It is strange, strange to me—and bitter—to feel how changed she is. She loves me. More than ever. She has guessed everything, and she loves me more than ever; but with a love almost maternal; a love terribly mature. I could not have believed it possible in so short a time that a child should grow to womanhood. She is docile, still; obedient; but she does not deceive me;—it is only in the little things—the things that do not count. If, in the great things, she would obey, nothing need be lost. There is now only a rangée mother to explain, to efface, to avoid.—How easy I would make it for my Alix to avoid me if her happiness demanded it!—But, no; she will not hear me. She is a stone to my supplications. She denies that she has ever loved him. She takes her life into her own hands and says that she will never marry, that she will stay with me always and be happy so. I dash myself against a rock in Alix. More than that;—she watches me; she suspects me—as if I were the daughter—bon Dieu!—and she the mother!—I wrote to Jerry. I told him to come;—it was but the other day.—I told him that it was best that they should meet, and that I would help him. And Alix intercepted the letter. Yes;—you may well stare. She confronted me with it and tore it in two before my eyes. She told me she knew too well what I had said to Jerry and that she had herself written and that all was over between them. Cold! Stern!—I could hardly believe it was my little Alix.—She spoke as if I had done her a great wrong.—As if I were the child and she the mother," madame Vervier repeated, a note of bewilderment mingling with the grief of her tone; and, indeed, as she made him these ingenuous confidences, Giles saw her as the child, the tricking child; all the French rôles reversed and Alix sustained in hers by what England had given her. No wonder madame Vervier was bewildered.

"But that was very wrong of you," he said, as he might have said to the child. "You had no right to do that."

"No right! I, her mother, am to sit by with folded hands and watch her ruin herself! Those are your English ideas. Those are the ideas that Alix has made hers. She, too, said I had no right. As if a mother's right over her child's life were not supreme!"

"We don't think it is, you see. Not when the child has reached Alix's age. You don't want her to marry a man she does not love."

"Love! Why should she not love him, since she loves nobody else!" cried madame Vervier, a deep exasperation thrilling in her voice. "And even if she did not love him, she cares quite enough. He is an admirable parti, this Jerry; I could not have chosen better had I been free to choose; he is an admirable parti and can give her all that I cannot give; security, position, wealth. Such a marriage would atone for everything that my darling has lacked. And love would come; why should it not? It is, as you say, her pride only that stands in the way. Ah, if she would only trust me!" madame Vervier's voice for the first time trembled, and looking up at her he saw tears in her eyes—"If she would only trust me! I could arrange it all."

He could not put before her the old, romantic protests. They had ceased to have validity for himself. All that madame Vervier said was true; truer far than she could know.

Better, far better, that Alix should marry Jerry, not loving him, than be exposed to the perils of her life in France. She had loved him once; why not again? She was a child. She could not know her own heart. Her pride had had a dreadful blow; and she had come too near the fire; that was all. She must trust them; it was true. She must trust him and her mother. To this strange pass had France brought Giles.

"I've come over to try to help you, you know," he said. "I want it as much, I believe, as you want it. About her pride—Lady Mary, I'm sure, expects them to marry now.—She shall hear that."

"Ah, I felt that you had come to give me hope, Giles," madame Vervier breathed, and her hand, for a moment, rested on his shoulder. "You are wonderful. You are impayable.—No one would believe in you.—If anyone can help, it is you. Alix will listen to you when she will listen to no one else."

"I believe she will. I'll do my best," Giles muttered.

Yet, as he looked down at the grass, sitting there filially at madame Vervier's feet, he knew that his heart was torn in two and that he longed to put his head down on her knees and tell her that no one in the world would ever love Alix as he himself did.

CHAPTER VIII

When Giles came down to breakfast next morning, Alix was already there, setting a bowl of nasturtiums on the blue-and-white cloth. He had not had a word with her last night when a sudden fall of rain had kept them all in the drawing-room, and he seized his opportunity.

"Will you have a long walk with me this morning, Alix?" he said. "A really long one, you know. I want to go to Allongeville and see the church again; and then, oh, a long way further. Along the cliffs for ever so far."

She looked at her flowers, drawing a leaf forward here and there around the edge of the bowl, and he saw that she was troubled. But she said: "We will go to the church, at all events. Yes. I should like a walk very much."

André entered as she spoke the words and she went on quietly, giving Giles a suffocating sense of the imminence of peril from her very readiness, her very calm: "Do you not think nasturtiums very charming flowers, Giles? No one ever speaks of them;—yet they are charming. The leaves; the colour. I like them, and yet I do not love them. Why is it? There are no yellow flowers of Summer that one can love. The yellow of Spring is so different."

"One doesn't love any of the things of Summer as one does the things of Spring," André remarked, strolling to the window to look out, and, clearly this morning, Giles divined what he had only surmised yesterday, that his temper was not attuned to brightness; that there might even lurk beneath its graceful surface a vindictive watchfulness. And when he had spoken he turned, leaning against the window, and looked at Alix, poised in her whiteness above the bowl of glowing flowers, looked at her as Giles had never before seen him look; as if with resentment that she should be so beautiful; as if with a challenge to her to deny his right to find her so.

"Oh, but that is not so," said Alix. "One loves roses—especially white roses;—and carnations; and jasmine; nothing in Spring is more lovely than jasmine."

"I would give them all for a handful of primroses," said André, his eyes fixed on her.

"Would you?" said Alix.

It was nothing; it was everything. It revealed nothing, yet it might conceal anything.

"Yes: I would, mademoiselle Alix," said André, laughing a little as he stood, leaning, his arms folded, against the window. "Indeed, I would."

Giles, watching the confrontation, sick with dread and fury, knew himself as much baffled as André.

Alix showed nothing to him, too; or she showed everything. Just as one chose to take it. "Here is our coffee," she said. "And here is Maman."

Lovely in her white, the white rose, the jasmine, madame Vervier bent her forehead to Alix's kiss and something in the daughter's eyes made Giles think of a sword in the hand of an avenging, or protecting, angel.

André bowed over his hostess's hand.

"Giles and I are to have a long walk, Maman," said Alix, going to her place.

"You will be caught in the rain," said André. "Have you noticed the sky? It is threatening."

"But see the sunlight," said madame Vervier, pouring out the coffee. "It will be a beautiful morning of great clouds and sunlight. There is nothing I love better."

"Then you will perhaps have a long drive with me, chère madame," said André.

"If Robert may come, too. I do not like to leave him behind."

How easy she made it for André to pretend that the relinquishment of the tête-à-tête was a favour he granted her with difficulty!

"But certainly.—Since you ask it! Certainly he must come.—Does he still suffer this morning with his head, do you know?"

"I fear so. Albertine has taken him his breakfast to his room. That is a bad sign. A drive will do him good."

"He will not like being rained on, you know," André smiled.

He was so glad that he was not to be alone with madame Vervier that he dared thus embroider his feint of disappointment.

"We can shelter him," said madame Vervier.

"While Giles converts mademoiselle Alix to the methods of the British Empire," said André, sitting with his back to the window where the sunlight fell about him and buttering his roll with a curious light crispness of touch, as if he were painting a picture. There was something in the play of the long, fine hands with the bread that Giles was never to forget; something cruel, controlled. He read in the young Frenchman's face the signs of an exasperation mastered with difficulty.

"But the method of the British Empire is unconscious," said madame Vervier. "It seeks no converts."

"I am a little jealous of Giles, you know, mademoiselle Alix," smiled André, just raising his eyes to hers. "As a Frenchman, I am jealous of his unconscious proselytizing. Once or twice yesterday I was afraid for France. Do not forget, when you listen to him, that our French roots are the most tenacious in the world. Perhaps that is why we do not found empires. Sever us from our soil and we bleed to death—or else, a worse destiny, wither. Do not forget that the unconscious is crafty."

Alix, opposite her mother, sat silent. Whether, in her mother's presence, she had lost her readiness Giles could not divine. But she made no reply.

"Alix has learned in England to be dispassionate," said madame Vervier, her lovely russet head a little bent downward. "She has learned to combine love for another country with loyalty to her own. That is something England has given her."

"Ah—but that's impossible;—impossible, for our French hearts, you know!" laughed André. "We are not dispassionate. To be dispassionate is to be tepid, sleepy, indifferent;—to be withering, in fact. No, no, no, if mademoiselle Alix transferred her love, it would be to transfer her loyalty also. It is for that that I beg her to stand firm;—to remember that England can never give her what France can give."

"Encore du café, Maman, s'il vous plaît," said Alix. She passed her cup to her mother. She did not look at André at all. Her voice, for all its disconcerting matter-of-fact, conveyed no provocation. But, glancing over at André, Giles saw that he suddenly blushed hotly, and then, as she took Alix's cup and poured out the milk and coffee, that a deep colour mounted also to madame Vervier's brow.

Yes. It would probably rain, thought Giles. He waited for Alix on the cliff. It was a sunny, yet tumultuous and menacing day. Great clouds piled themselves along the horizon; the sails of the fishing boats were bent sideways as they went, on a ruffled sea, before the wind. "Yes. Rain is coming," he muttered to himself, though he was not thinking of the weather. They had all parted in silence at the breakfast-table. Even madame Vervier had found no words.

Suddenly André came down the steps of Les Chardonnerets. He had his cigarette and an odd bright smile was on his lips; yet as he approached he reminded Giles of the sails on the sea. André might still try to keep up appearances; but the wind was blowing him.

But he was not going to keep up appearances. "So," he said, "to-day is a day of destiny. You are not at all unconscious, are you, Giles? You have come to plead the cause of your laggard young friend the Englishman?"

Well, was the thought that went through Giles, let him have it, then. "Why do you call him laggard?" he inquired, and he knew that the anger that boiled up in his breast was so violent that he could have struck André as he stood there. "Would you be eager to take into your family a young girl placed as Alix is placed?"

André became very pale, but his eyes lighted. His sail scooped the sea.

"Will you plead my cause with her if I say that I would?" he asked.

Giles stood there, still; rooted to the ground. André had not meant to say that. Something in his own look had made him say it. It was the blow returned.

"You don't think of marrying Alix?" said Giles in a low voice.

"I do," André replied. "I think of it; now. It is my way out. Why should I retire when there is that way? Little as you could imagine it, I care for her enough."

"Care for her enough?"

"Yes, if you like to put it so. You see where I stand. Don't keep up pretences," said André. "It's come on slowly;—but it has me now and there is no escape.—Elle est dans mon sang.—My family would have to submit;—and her mother's consent I could gain;—to marriage.—Why do you look at me with that face? She does not love your Jerry. And in marrying me she would marry a man whose devotion to her mother would never waver. Don't imagine," said André, eyeing his friend, "that my devotion to Alix's mother has wavered. It is altered; yes; that is inevitable; we have no power over these changes. But she will always remain for me the most generous, most admirable of women."

"You don't see the hideousness of what you propose?" Giles felt his foundations tottering beneath him. André's aspect, bright and baleful, seemed to tower above him like one of the darkly radiant clouds in the sky. And it was a thunderbolt he had launched.

"I deplore a marked awkwardness," he said. "Especially since Alix, I fear, has become aware of it. Your English plan of destroying the innocence of young girls has grave disadvantages. You will own that. But, in any case, hideousness is not a word I could connect with any project of mine."

"She'll never take you! Never!" Giles cried. He felt himself trembling with the fury of his repudiation. "I can tell you that now. She would feel it as I do. She would see it as hideous."

"You don't know what she would see; nor do I," said André. "She thinks she hates me. You needn't tell me that. But I am not ignorant in women's hearts. Hate may be the best of beginnings. The struggle may be a little longer;—I like struggles, let me tell you; the longer they last the sweeter is the surrender at the end.—And I have every reason to believe that to begin with hate is often to end with a more complete surrender."

As André gave him this information Giles saw Alix emerge upon the verandah of Les Chardonnerets.

She could not hear their voices, but their confrontation she must remark.

Seeing Giles's eyes fixed, André turned his head and looked for a moment, also. Then he glanced back at Giles. "Plead your Jerry's cause," he said. "Je vous cède le pas." He turned on his heel. "If you fail, I shall plead mine."

Giles was aware, as Alix approached him, that he must seem to stare stupidly. "I could gain her mother's consent." Of all the brazen words that André had uttered, it was these that rang most brazenly in his ear. Was it true? Was it possible? If Alix already loved him? Could he be sure of his Alix were the hideous complicity of events thus to disclose itself? He could have fallen at her feet, in tears, clasping her and supplicating her not to be abased.

But, as she approached him, silent, he muttered a trivial word and they turned to walk along the cliff-path, while the clouds piled themselves higher in the blue sky and the wind blew yet more strongly from the sea.

Alix did not say a word. She held her soft hat at her side and the wind blew back her hair. Over her white dress a long white woollen cloak was knotted at her throat, and it, too, blew back from her as she walked. She looked before her with the high, majestic look he had already noted on her face in moments of great emotion.

"Alix," said Giles in a low voice.

They had gone for a long way in silence. The sea now was green beneath them. The sky was a wild grey and all the grass silver as the wind blew it towards their feet. He did not know what he was going to say. He did not look at her. But he saw that she turned her face towards him. A clue then came. "Alix, do you remember, long ago, you promised me that you would never tell me a lie?" he said.

Not unclosing her lips she nodded. He had glanced at her and met her eyes, but he could not read her look.

"Well"—he heard that his voice trembled and he was suddenly afraid that he should not get far without crying—"Jerry, before I left Oxford, showed me a letter he had from you. It troubled him; badly; but he couldn't know how it troubled me. You said you could never marry him because you now loved someone else. Was that true, Alix?"

She turned away her head and looked before her; and again she did not speak.

"Please tell me. Was it true? Do you love someone else, Alix?" Giles pleaded.

She was terribly pale. Did she expect him not to have heard? Not to ask, since he knew? "Please, Alix," he repeated; and then, once more, she bowed her head.

"Well"—Giles did not know how he forced his voice along—"One more question. Will you tell me this—Is it André de Valenbois?"

"Oh, Giles!" said Alix.

She stopped short there in the wind, turned to him. The wind blew her hair across her face and mechanically she put up her hand and pushed it back while she gazed at him. "Oh, Giles!" she repeated, putting back the short tresses that whipped across her eyes and lips. "Can you ask me that?"

Her face was like a beacon set against the storm, high in the sky. In its light he read all the monstrousness of what he had asked, and her hand, still holding back her hair, seemed to clear it for him so that he could receive the full illumination.

As he read her look and saw the tears that suddenly welled up into her eyes, Giles, with an overwhelming lift of the heart, felt himself sobbing. "Forgive me! Forgive me, darling.—It was all that I could think."

"Oh, poor Giles," she said brokenly.

They were walking on, quickly now. Somewhere, near by, Giles was conscious of a great brightness approaching him.

"I was horribly afraid. I could think of nobody else. And he loves you;—you see that."

"I see it.—Yes.—You have suffered."

"And though it seemed to me that you hated him;—it might not have prevented."

"Do not let us speak of it.—And she has suffered. You would think, would you not, that I would hate him more for what he has made her suffer." Alix spoke with difficulty, in short breaths; and though the wind blew her hair backward, now that they again were breasting it, she still kept her hand up against her face, looking before her as she tried to tell him her difficult thoughts.—"Yet it is not so. It is not so," she repeated. "I feel as if I understood it all.—It is so strange, Giles, all that I have had to understand in these last months. I seem to understand people like him and Maman.—They are helpless, Giles. They are like that."

"Oh, my darling!" said Giles.

They went on side by side. The rain had begun to fall in great drops. On their tip of promontory they seemed poised between sky and sea, the marshalled chaos—above, below. And the brightness was spreading in Giles's heart.

"There is Allongeville," said Alix. The town lay beneath them, half obliterated with the rain.

"Let us run," said Giles. "We can go into a shop."

"Or into the church," said Alix.

He put out his hand for hers and they started to run.

He could have sung with exultation. Not only André's sinister shadow was gone; but that tumult in himself. He was a boy again, and Alix, his child, his darling, was beside him. They ran, with deep breaths, smiling round at each other. The long wooded allées of the town stretched nearly to the cliff-top, and once beneath a steep, green tunnel there was no need to go so fast, for they hardly felt the rain, so dense was the roof of green; only heard it pattering heavily on the leaves above their heads. But, still running, they reached the emptied place, its cobblestones glistening with the wet, and as they passed Giles saw an astonished face at the toy-shop door, where stout madame Bonnefoix stood looking out between bunches of spades and buckets, string bags full of brightly coloured balls and festoons of dolls in stiff muslin chemises. The peaceful sculptured porch of the church was before them, and it seemed to Giles that it had been waiting for them—for centuries.

When they entered, they found the church, with its whitewashed walls and innocently bedizened saints, light and smiling after the darkened day outside. A smell of incense, flowers, and cobwebs was in the air.

Alix paused to cross herself with holy water from the bénitier carved into the stone of a pillar and bent her knee before the High Altar as they crossed the nave, while Giles held his Protestant head bashfully high.

They sat down on a bench far back in an aisle and smiled, tremulously, at each other. They were so much more alone than on the cliff with the rain and sea. No one was in the church; no one was in the place outside. It was very still, and the sound of the rain falling straightly and steadily outside made the stillness more manifest. The wind had already dropped. It was a summer rain, now, full of sweetness.

"May we talk in church?" Giles whispered. He looked away from Alix at the remembered statue of the Virgin, all white and blue, with pots of pink hydrangeas at her feet.

"I think we may," Alix said. "We disturb no one."

"Your saints won't mind, will they?" Giles could not keep the tremor from his voice. "Such a good Catholic as you are, Alix!"

"I think my saints are pleased," Alix's voice, too, trembled; though she was not as shy as he was.

"You know, Toppie has gone into her convent," Giles said, gazing at the Virgin, whose uplifted, blessing hands brought the image of Toppie so vividly before him. It was as if Toppie herself stood there, smiling down upon them.

"Your mother wrote of it," said Alix.

"We met again in Oxford, only a little while ago," said Giles. "She saw something that everybody has been seeing; even Jerry saw it.—You know, Alix, I love Toppie as much as ever; yet I'm so changed. It's all so different. Can you understand that?"

"I never dreamed you could be different about Toppie," Alix murmured after a moment.

"Was that why you thought I'd never guess, even if I saw your letter to Jerry?"

"I did not think you would ever guess."

"I didn't. I never dreamed there was a chance for me; never dreamed it.—That's what I told them all;—that there wasn't a chance."

Alix, too, had been gazing before her, sitting there beside him in her wet white cloak; but as he said this she leaned forward and put her hands up to her face.

"Oh, darling, are you crying?" Giles's arms were round her as he asked it. "Have I been so stupid?—Is it really me you love?"

"Ever since that day I came to you from Toppie."

She was crying; but it was in his arms and his cheek was against her dear wet head.

"Happy;—Happy;—Happy"—were the only words in Giles's mind and they went on and on like a song while he heard the rain falling sweetly and the brightness was all about them.

He listened to the rain for a long time, but when he spoke it was to answer her last words.—"It's been since then with me, too."

Alix's head lay against his shoulder and he held both her hands in his against his breast; and he was seeing the little French girl, the strange, ominous little French girl, sitting in the Victoria waiting-room with her straight black brows and her eyes calm over their fear. He was seeing the lovely dancing head bound with crystal, aware of him, looking for him even in her joy; he was seeing the Alix who had come from Toppie. "We've always been so near, from the first, haven't we?" he said.

"So near, Giles. That was what troubled me, though I did not understand, when Jerry asked me to marry him.—You were so much nearer than Jerry."

"And who did you think I should believe it to be, darling, when I saw the letter to Jerry?—Didn't you know I'd have to ask you some time? Did you really believe, when we were so near as that, you could hide it from me?"

"I thought I could. I had to stop Jerry from coming. I could have pretended that there was someone you didn't know.—Someone who might not love me, but whom I should always love."

"You who promised never to tell me a lie!"

"But for those things women must always lie, Giles."

She raised her head now to look at him. Her face was radiant yet grave. "There will never be anything to hide any more;—never—never.—There is nothing you do not understand. You understand all my life. You understand Maman.—Giles, how happy this will make her."

"I hope it will. But I came to plead Jerry's cause, you know. She thinks I'm pleading it now."

"How happy it will make her that you did not have to plead it."

"Will it? I can't help being afraid that she'll be disappointed. She'd have preferred the better match for you, darling little Alix."

"She will not think it better. It was all she had left to hope for, that was all. It has wounded her pride horribly to have to hope for it—after the bitter things it has meant for her and for me."

"But—if you could have cared.—Everything would have come right. Lady Mary is so fond of you and she would have stood by. Darling, it isn't only loving;—no one knows that better than you do;—it's living. Do you face it all? To live in Oxford? To be the wife of a humdrum scholar? To have no balls and no riding? To wear"—Giles found—"the wrong sort of clothes and think about ordering breakfast. Darling, Jerry loves you, you know, and the bitter things would all fade away. Such a different life is there for you to take. I can't help seeing, though we love each other, that it's the life you were meant for and that the life with me in Oxford isn't."

"Oh, no, Giles, you do not see that," said Alix. She put her hand on his shoulder, as if with its pressure to help him to think clearly. "You are English and believe that more than anything it is right to marry the person you love."

"But you are French, Alix. It's the other belief that's in your blood. The belief in what's suitable."

"Ah, but it is true what Maman says to me, when she reproaches me; I have in some things become English. I think the thing most suitable of all is to love one's husband. To marry Jerry, loving you;—no, Giles; you know that that would not be possible to me. And I do not love him at all. He is not near me at all; while you are like a part of my life.—No, listen to me, dear Giles.—This is not making love. It is being French; it is being reasonable. Even the clothes and the breakfasts;—oh, I know that they are important.—But I am used to being poor and to knowing how to be right with very little money.—In clothes and in breakfasts, Giles, I shall know how to be right."

Her eyes, resting on him, were the eyes of the English Alix, of the woman who chooses, for herself, her life and the man she will share it with; yet their look was a French look, too. The look of one who has no illusions; who sees an order and accepts it; an order to live for and to make one's own. "And there will be the ideas and the atoms to watch, and the Bach choir to sing in," she finished; "and walks in the country;—and then I shall be in France, for all the holidays, with Maman, Giles."

She rose as she spoke, for the storm had passed. Sunlight was flooding in through the high pale windows of the clerestory. The Virgin's crown glittered against her pillar. Slowly, hand in hand, Alix and Giles walked down the nave.

But there was something more he had to say to her, here, in her France, in her church, beneath her Virgin's blessing hands. This woman Alix had made none of the conditions that the child Alix, bewildered, charmed, afraid, had asked of her first lover. She asked no promises. She left everything to him. It was his order she accepted.

And before they turned aside to go, Giles paused and took both her hands in his. It was at the feet of the dear, silly Virgin in her white and blue and gold that he made his promise: "Darling, you shall lose nothing, nothing that I can help. It will never be alone that you'll come for those holidays. If you take England for me, you must give me all that you can of France.—Everything that is sacred to you, is sacred to me, too."

When they opened the door the world was dazzling with sunlight and a great white cloud towered up like an august and welcoming angel in the sky, while across the place the little Curé came hurrying, stout and active with his rosy, peasant face and thick grey hair. He looked at them kindly, if very shyly, murmuring a word of greeting to Alix as they all met in the porch, and Giles, in deference to convention, dropped the hand he held. But Alix, as she smiled at the Curé and smiled beyond him at all the sunlit world she was entering, took Giles's hand in hers again, and said: "Monsieur le Curé, may I present to you my fiancé?"

FINIS